RUDOLF BAHRO
Critical Responses

RUDOLF BAHRO
Critical Responses

EDITED BY ULF WOLTER

M. E. SHARPE, INC., WHITE PLAINS, NEW YORK

The essays in this collection were drawn from *Antworten auf Bahros Herausforderung des "realen Sozialismus,"* edited by Ulf Wolter, and from *kritik*,
vol. VI, no. 19, both © 1978 by Verlag Olle & Wolter, Berlin, and are
published by arrangement with Verlag Olle & Wolter.

Published simultaneously as vol. X, no. 2-3 of *International Journal of
Politics.*

Library of Congress Cataloging in Publication Data

International Congress for and About Rudolf Bahro,
     Berlin, 1978.
     Rudolf Bahro, critical responses.

     "The essays in this collection were drawn from Antworten auf Bahros
Herausforderung des 'realen Sozialismus' . . . and from Kritik, vol. VI,
no. 19."
     Includes bibliographical references.
     CONTENTS: Weber, H. The third way.—Fleischer, H. Bahro's
contribution to the philosophy of socialism.—Marcuse, H. Protosocialism
and late capitalism. [etc.]
     1. Bahro, Rudolf, 1935- —Congresses. 2. Communism—Congresses.
3. Socialism—Congresses.
I. Bahro, Rudolf, 1935-.   II. Wolter, Ulf.
III. Title.
HX280.5.A8B334 1978   335'.0092'4   80-15954
ISBN 0-87332-159-6

RUDOLF BAHRO
Critical Responses

Rudolf Bahro, then a functionary in the party-state apparatus of the German Democratic Republic, captured worldwide attention in 1977 when his book *The Alternative: A Contribution to the Critique of Actually Existing Socialism* was published in the West. Bahro was arrested by state security forces, charged with espionage, and sentenced to an eight-year term of imprisonment.

An "International Congress on and for Rudolf Bahro," organized by a broad spectrum of European leftists who called for Bahro's release, met in West Berlin in November 1978 to discuss the ideas put forth in *The Alternative*. The papers collected here in translation were written for the Congress. They reflect not only the lively critical discussion sparked by Bahro's book but also the perplexed and perplexing condition of the European left, both Old and New. Today Bahro—released in the amnesty that marked the GDR's thirtieth anniversary and now residing in the West—is himself a participant in the ongoing debate.

Contents

RUDOLF BAHRO
Critical Responses

HERMANN WEBER

The Third Way: Bahro's Place in the Tradition of Anti-Stalinist Opposition

In his critique of real socialism, Rudolf Bahro can be said to have emphasized political economy (to use the categories of Marxism-Leninism as is usual in Soviet communism), whereas Robert Havemann, for example, focused on philosophy. Certainly Bahro's critique is comprehensive; indeed, what is notable in his study is its universality. However, inasmuch as Bahro proceeds systematically, historical lines of development are not empirically examined, or only marginally so. Thus, in his methodological approach Bahro seems at first glance to take a position quite distinct from that of earlier members of the communist opposition. The latter sought to ascertain those factors that led to the transformation of Russia's revolutionary regime into Stalinism. It was Bahro's purpose to analyze "actually existing socialism as a unique kind of social formation,"[1] hence he takes as his focus the economic foundations of the system. However, Bahro also wants to create political instruments for altering real socialism (indeed, he proposes to spell out the programmatic positions of a new communist league, which in his opinion is necessary).[2] This is quite within the tradition of previous Marxist critiques in communist-governed systems.

And it is no accident that Bahro not only turns immediately to the historical dimension of his critique in his book *The Alternative*,[3] but also in his *Lectures* points up the problematic of earlier communist heresy. Here too he is within the tradition.

However, we must free ourselves from the old orthodox Marxist sectarianism. We cannot learn the way from that opposition, which at one time lost its struggle against the rise of the Stalinist despotism as its own irritation grew. In a certain phase of breaking away from the domination of the apparatus, every revolutionary communist after 1917 has felt himself to be Trotskyist. However, this position is actually historically futile. We do not wish to restore old norms, but create new ones. We need no longer confine ourselves to intra-Party constellations; rather we must consciously derive our support from broad social forces . . .[4]

While this self-evaluation shows a critical distance from the earlier intra-Party opposition, it cannot conceal the fact that Bahro too remains within the tradition of the intracommunist opposition. The core of this opposition has always rested with a criticism of, and struggle against, the existing communist-governed systems from Marxist positions; it has attempted to surmount the historical reality by making use of the theoretical conceptions and emancipatory demands of Marxism. Bahro proceeds from the position of democratic communism; he goes further in the conclusions he draws, but that is only a logical development.

Typically too, Bahro contrasts the goal of the 1917 revolution with its results. One of his initial theses states: "Since 1917, a quite different social order has emerged from the revolutionary process than that which its champions had expected."[5] Official communist historiography and conservative historiography alike reject this position, both postulating a linear development for the Russian Revolution. For the intracommunist opposition, however, that there was a break in Soviet development has always been the keystone of their attitude (although the precise time at which this break is said to have occurred has varied considerably depending on the particular position). In the following we shall outline some communist oppositionist tendencies that are relevant to the GDR, and will elucidate Bahro's position within the tradition.

Opposition in the German Democratic Republic

Twenty years ago an (anonymous) author called attention to the distinctions, the contradictions even, within the opposition in the GDR. Even at that time he felt that the opposition of the bourgeoisie should not be overestimated: "The remainder of the bourgeoisie and the independent farmers are indeed opponents of the regime, but they possess neither political organizational forms nor economic means of power." On the other hand, he saw "the most active forces of opposition among the intellectuals and the workers," but stressed that these "challenged the system from a left-wing platform," since this opposition "proposed to realize a de-Stalinized Marxism."[6]

Since then the significance of this opposition has been much discussed.[7] While the classification of a bourgeois, a social democratic, and a communist opposition in the history of the GDR may simplify reality, it is nonetheless usable for our context. It should be remarked that the notion that the bourgeois opposition is necessarily without any significance underestimates the influence of the example of the German Federal Republic (FRG); but what is at issue here is the ultimate objective of *any* opposition. Bourgeois opposition in the GDR embraces a general rejection of the social system, including its forms of property. The social-democratic position (with which broad circles seem to sympathize[8]) is opposed to the political system and the ideology; it too of course looks to the Federal Republic, but more especially to its welfare-state aspecs. In contrast, the communist opposition in the GDR, since its emergence from the groundsoil of the existing economic and social order, has aimed for a democratization, i.e., above all a change in the political system and the steering mechanisms of the society and the economy. This opposition saw itself as anti-Stalinist, not anti-communist, and thus continued the line of the anti-Stalinists in the world communist movement of the twenties and thirties.

We cannot here retrace the path taken by communist opponents of Stalin.[9] Let us but note that even during the period of Leninism there was a communist opposition (the Workers' Opposition and the Democratic Centralists in Russia, left radicalism in Germany, Holland, etc.).[10] And with the emergence of Stalinism came an opposition that saw itself as Leninist and for the first time put forth the thesis that Russian praxis was departing from the objectives of the October Revolution. Accordingly, this opposition contrasted the realities in Russia with the theory of Marxism and Leninism as a contrary conception. The reproach that the new bureaucracy had abandoned communist principles and betrayed the revolution was first voiced in 1923 by the Trotskyist and left opposition in international communism.[11] After Stalin's left turn in 1928 a right opposition developed as well, whose criticism was of course more moderate.

The anti-Stalinist opposition emerged from the political situation of the time and as a consequence was of course divided into several tendencies. Initially the points of difference were almost always only of a tactical nature. The struggle of the left communists against the right communists stood in the forefront of the disputes within communism, and for this reason the apparatus was able to split the anti-Stalinist forces, play them off against one another, and drive them out of the movement. Even after the anti-Stalinist opposition had assumed definite contours at the beginning of the 1930s, its evaluation of Stalinism varied considerably, extending from criticism of Russian hegemony in the Comintern, its methods of control, and Stalin's mistakes (right wing); through the thesis of a degenerated workers' state and the domination of the bureaucracy (Trotskyist); down finally to an objection to the "rule of the kulaks" and to "red imperialism" (the ultra-left, Karl Korsch, etc.).[12]

The Stalinist purges of 1936-38 and the extermination of the old Bolsheviks led to a radicalization of the old anti-Stalinist opposition, which at the same time, however, saw its importance in world communism waning steadily. Gone were views that Stalinism was capable of reform; political revolution was regarded as indispensable, especially in the eyes of the Trotskyist opposition.

The defeat of fascism and the formation of the people's democracies in Eastern Europe led to a new situation within world communism. In Germany many communists who had earlier been in opposition returned to the ranks of the Communist Party of Germany. When the Socialist Unity Party of Germany (SED) was founded in the Soviet occupation zone, many former members of anti-Stalinist groups found a political base. But the very first purges within the SED were directed not only against former Social Democrats, but also against former members of the communist opposition. In August 1949 there was a call for struggle against "Trotskyist views" since "Troskyism was nothing more than a camouflaged fascism"; and likewise the danger of "right opportunism," which showed up in "labor unionism and conciliationism with the Schumacher ideology, an offshoot of American imperialism."[13] After the Third Party Congress of the Socialist Unity Party in July 1950, it became apparent that the SED was repeating the process of Stalinization which the Communist Party of Germany (KPD) had already been through in 1924-29.[14]

After 1947, as today, the SED leadership carried on the struggle against the communist opposition with coercive state measures rather than ideological means. The earlier right-wing communist opposition (the KPO, active as the Workers' Politics Group after 1945[15]) had initially had functions within the SED. For example

Alfred Schmidt, a former Prussian parliamentary delegate who was Regional Director of the Foods, Luxuries, and Restaurants Union in Thüringen, was expelled from the SED for his criticism. In 1948 a Soviet court condemned him to death, but later the sentence was changed to 25 years in prison. Other right-wing communists were forced to flee to the Federal Republic.[16] Known former right-wing communists were attacked increasingly bitterly as enemies of the Party and the people.[17] The earlier KPO leader Walcher and the former Saxon MP Lieberasch were expelled from the SED in 1951 and not rehabilitated until the period of de-Stalinization.[18] Thus the repressive measures against the earlier oppositional communists[19] reached considerable dimensions.

After Tito's break the national-communist, Titoist opposition came under the fire of the leadership, alongside the Trotskyist and right-wing communist deviations.[20] As was customary with all Stalinist purges, many functionaries who had been faithful to the line found themselves tossed in together with actual oppositional elements; but again, we are unable to investigate these purges here.[21]

What is important is that the anti-Stalinist opposition of the twenties was resuscitated briefly in the SED but was quickly suppressed. The positions taken were themselves not original, not derived from the special situation of the GDR, but rather matched the earlier views of the anti-Stalinist communists. These left-wing or right-wing communist tendencies developed further in the West, and had only an indirect influence on the GDR.[22] Nonetheless, the SED continued to have difficulties with this traditional opposition far into the fifties. In the 1951 examination of the Party ranks alone, over 150,000 members and functionaries were expelled from the SED. It further became evident that the deviations extended into the top levels of leadership. As a Stalinist party the SED tolerated no opposition in its ranks, to say nothing of the formation of factions. However, since the Party had by that time assumed a position of political monopoly, and hence was the only political forum, the contradictions within the society were reflected in it. The dissatisfaction of broad circles of the Party (at that time there were about 600,000 workers in the SED) provided the basis for the oppositional currents. The three crises of leadership—in 1949, 1953, and 1957—reflected this situation within the Party.

On August 24, 1949, a member of the Politburo, Paul Merker, was dropped from its ranks; Leo Bauer, Lex Ende, Willi Kreikemeyer, and other functionaries were expelled. The wave of purges was a consequence of the Budapest trial against Rajk; all the functionaries were accused of contacts with Noel H. Field. The purge was aimed at old communists who had worked independently in Western emigration and were seen as potential opponents. Bauer and Kreikemeyer were immediately arrested (Kreikemeyer died), and most of the other accused were arrested in 1952. The purge was an attempt by the Ulbricht leadership to carry out a show trial in Germany and to intimidate and nip in the bud any opposition.

The GDR workers' rebellion of June 17, 1953, once again revealed the instability within the SED. Not a few members and even functionaries were on the side of the workers and against the regime on June 17, 1953. Once again conflicts emerged within the top-level leadership. At the Fifteenth Meeting of the Central Committee in July 1953, Wilhelm Zaisser and Rudolf Herrnstadt were expelled from the Politburo and the Central Committee, and in January 1954 from the SED as well, as an anti-Party faction. Anton Ackermann, Hans Jendretzky, and Elli Schmidt lost their functions in the Politburo and the Central Committee. In January 1954 Franz Dahlem, Ulbricht's strongest opponent, was removed from the ranks of Party officials. A thorough cleansing of the Party apparatus took place at the same time, and over 60 percent of the members of the SED regional leaderships were forced to resign their posts. The purges among the top-level leadership were not against former Social Democrats (who had long since been expelled), but against communist functionaries. The points of difference concerned the political line (Ulbricht's hard line was being attacked), or reflected differences within the Soviet leadership.

The last major purge of top-level leaders, in 1957-58, had the same basis. At that time the second man in the SED after Ulbricht, Karl Schirdewan, along with Ernst Wollweber, former head of the State Security Agency, and Fred Oelssner, former Party ideologue, were disciplined.

The leadership crises were not only the expression of the contradictions within the system at the time; they also aroused hopes of changes in policy. The hierarchical organization of the Party and state were such that changes in general could only take place if changes took place in the leadership as well (as later developments in Czechoslovakia showed). Thus reform notions of opposional members within the Party during the early fifties corresponded with the deviations within the top-level leadership.

The third way

Like the remaining vestiges of the left and right communist opposition, these oppositional currents, in accordance with their origin and historical development, saw themselves as a part of "the Party." They were all fundamentally opponents of capitalism, and wanted only to improve the policies of the SED on the basis of the existing order. These oppositional elements still saw the Stalinist dictatorship as a "deformed workers' state," and the "socialistic" basis of the property relations was for them the decisive criterion. As an independent communist opposition grew in the GDR (as in the other socialist countries), a more clear-cut and fundamental delimitation from Stalinism ensued: the notion of a third way was directed equally against Western capitalism and the Eastern Stalinist dictatorship.[23] The notion of a third way[24] was premised on the one hand on a spread of theoretical Marxism, and on the other hand on a dissatisfaction with the purportedly "Marxist" realities of the GDR.

The ideological influence had left traces in the fifties, and a relatively broad intracommunist opposition began to develop among Party and university intellectuals, and especially the youth. It was the working-class children above all who were promoted through the transformed educational system, and a strong ideological indoctrination had begun in the schools and the universities. Broad circles of youth began to think in Marxist categories. Like the Party leaders, the young generation too had been raised to think in categories that implied that the struggle against exploitation and repression, and activity for the liberation of the working class and for the revolutionary movement, were just as worthy goals as solidarity with the repressed peoples. The great revolutionaries were put up as examples worthy of imitation, beginning with Spartacus, leader of the historic slave revolt in Rome, through Thomas Münzer in the Peasant War, Babeuf in the French Revolution, down to Marx and Lenin. The leadership of the SED hoped to fortify its position by spreading the Marxist view of history, and wanted to demonstrate that the Party was the legitimate heir of all progressive tendencies in history and especially the labor movement. But with this view of history, the struggle of the labor

movement for social justice and for emancipation and freedom became the focus of ideological education, and this had some portentous consequences.

The realities of the GDR looked completely different from the
ideals of theory: exploitation and repression continued to exist,
as did lies and careerism; there were incentives enough for revolution. The fact that the reality of the GDR corresponded so little to
revolutionary theories could not but shake the idealism of many
supporters of the system. To be sure, this was presumably only the
reaction of a minority, for the majority was rather politically in-
different or responded to reality with conformism or cynicism.
Nonetheless the effects were considerable. Like their prototypes,
the communists who had come into opposition wanted to change
practice and adapt it to their (i.e., but also the official) ideals.
Thus in 1956 and 1957 among the younger generation the voices
multiplied demanding a democratic development on the basis of
an appeal to Marx. And indeed this was not least due to the fact
that many of them had come from working-class backgrounds,
where the contradictions were especially drastically in evidence.
Thus the opposition of the third way evolved as an ideological
conception, independently of (and presumably without any
precise knowledge of) the earlier internal communist opposition.
This new opposition, anti-Stalinist but not anticommunist, rejected
capitalism as well as the structures of domination of the GDR. They
wanted to create a humane socialism by reforms and democratization. Thus Marxist education in the GDR had created not only faithful supporters of the system but also Marxist rebels, who even
worked within the SED.

However, that this development did not remain limited to only
a few individuals, but grew into a political current, was due to a
sudden shock. This took place in the GDR as a result of the reve-
lations at the Twentieth Party Congress of the CPSU in 1956 about
Stalin's role.[25] The Twentieth Party Congress (as would the invasion of Czechoslovakia to a much greater degree in 1968) not only
released forces of criticism, but also shook up numerous faithful
and true supporters of the system. The renunciation of Stalin and
the revelation of his crimes came as a shock to many convinced
Stalinist intellectuals and youth, who then had to seek out new
pathways. For the majority of the intelligentsia, the beginnings of
de-Stalinization in 1956 provided an incentive for opposing the

primitive and dogmatic methods of the leadership of the Party apparatus. In the universities especially, the discussion in 1956-58 went far beyond the limits set for it by the SED, and was coming close to the conception of a third way. (We should point out in passing that Rudolf Bahro was studying philosophy at Berlin University in just these years, from 1954 through 1959.)

Although their critical opinions varied considerably, the intellectual supporters of the third way represented the following demands: 1) purging of Stalinist dogma and falsifications from Marxism and Leninism; 2) no interference of the Party apparatus in questions of science; 3) the right to free and creative discussion without having to fear coercive measures; and 4) abolition of the dogmatic leading role of dialectical materialism in the specialized sciences, and the institution of scientific objectivity.

Overall the idea of a third way was hardly concrete and tangible; it was reduced to a verbal criticism of the existing situation. This was due first and foremost to the fact that the discussion was primarily carried out in the individual disciplines, and hence focused on specialized problems. Nonetheless, for the SED leadership these discussions represented a warning signal; the basic conception of the communist oppositionists could ultimately be dangerous for the system, as for example the developments in Hungary and Poland, which had begun similarly, demonstrated.

In July 1956 Robert Havemann started off a discussion in philosophy when he called for an abolition of the Stalinist thesis that the dialectical approach was the measure of questions of natural science research. Martin Strauss even criticized Lenin's "Materialism and Empirio-criticism." The influence of Ernst Bloch, who at that time taught in Leipzig, was even greater. His students drew political conclusions from his teachings. Richard Lorenz, who later fled to avoid arrest,[26] demanded: "The cult of personality must be seen as a social phenomenon, and the alien structures to which it has given rise within socialism must be investigated concretely."[27]

The discussion soon extended from philosophy into other sciences, and economists, literary critics, jurists, and historians took up a more or less oppositional position.[28] Naturally, given the many different levels of the oppositional currents, no well-rounded conception emerged, and the consistency and logic of the scientific discussion varied considerably. Finally, the political climate and the measures of the state security agency induced many critics to retreat again quickly.

The Harich group

But there was a group that attempted to work out an overall concept of opposition for the third way: the Harich group.

Wolfgang Harich had a critical integrative significance for the anti-Stalinist opposition in 1956-57.[29] Born in 1921, Harich had been in the communist movement since 1945 and had an important function in the Party intelligentsia as a Professor of Philosophy, editor-in-chief of the *Deutsche Zeitschrift für Philosophie*, and reader for the Aufbau Publishing House; further, he was a leading SED ideologue. After extensive discussion in the Aufbau Publishing House, Harich worked out the basic features of an oppositional conception together with the secretary of the editorial board of the *Deutsche Zeitschrift für Philosophie*, Manfred Hertwig,[30] the director of the Aufbau Publishing House, Walter Janka (old communist and Spanish Civil War writer), the editor-in-chief of the cultural magazine *Sonntag*, Heinz Zöger,[31] and his representative Gustav Just. It later became the platform of the group. The economic analysis was provided by Bernhard Steinberger, member of the Academy of Sciences (who from 1949 to 1955 had been imprisoned in the USSR, presumably on suspicion of espionage; however he had been rehabilitated in July 1956 and fully admitted into the ranks of the SED). The group (with which Richard Wolf of Berlin Radio would also be convicted) attempted to make contact with prominent opponents of Ulbricht such as Franz Dahlem, and communist leaders such as Paul Wandel and Fred Oelssner; they also established connections with the former Politburo member Paul Merker.

To be sure, in its platform the group said that it did not have the intention of causing a rupture with the Communist Party,[32] but it did consider forming a league of communists or even an organized SED opposition.[33] Since there was no possibility in the GDR of conducting open propaganda for the ideas of a third way, the possibility of spreading the objectives of the group from bases within the Federal Republic or from Poland (where de-Stalinization at that time seemed to have proceeded apace) was discussed. Harich therefore journeyed to the Federal Republic and to Poland,

and even took up contacts with the Social Democratic Party (SPD) in West Berlin. But the group did have hopes of supporting their views themselves within the SED, given the situation of turmoil after the Twentieth Party Congress of the CPSU. Harich presented the basic features of his reform program to the Soviet Ambassador then in the GDR, and even had a talk with Ulbricht. The Party group in the Aufbau Publishing House encouraged Harich to bring together his ideas in an article, which the Party group wished to discuss. Later Manfred Hertwig reported on this:

> Thus Harich wrote down his reform proposals. Before he presented them in the Aufbau Publishing House, he wished to discuss them with me and the economist Bernhard Steinberger, whom he had met through me. On November 22 we three met in Harich's house. We had come together to discuss legally compiled reform proposals on the behest of a Party group. Later, in the accusations and in the sentence, this November 22 was transformed into a day of conspiracy. . . .
>
> What were the main thoughts we discussed? We felt the following problems were in need of immediate solution: dismissal of those members of the Party leadership and state apparatus who were mainly responsible for the consistent importation of the Stalinist line into the GDR; creation of internal Party democracy; transformation of the Volkskammer into a democratic parliament; the restoration of legal guarantees; abolition of the state security agency; democratization of cultural life; decentralization of the direction of the economy; abolition of superfluous ministries; a switch to general long-term planning; a reorientation of the middle-stratum policy; cessation of all forced collectivization.
>
> After Harich read off these principal ideas—with which Steinberger and I agreed—we discussed quite freely, in the form of a nonbinding conversation, the possible future political developments in the GDR and in Germany as a whole, as well as questions of our attitude toward these developments. Out of this the state security agency later constructed the various plans for insurrection that appeared in the statement of charges.
>
> Actually our estimate of the situation on November 22 was still that a legal opposition against Ulbricht was possible without coming into conflict with the state security agency. We only revised our appraisal a few days later when Molotov became the Minister of State Control.[34]

Under these circumstances the hurriedly prepared platform could only discuss the most important political ideas of the third way cursorily and in summary form, and hence was not without its contradictions (quite unlike Bahro's study, which was systematically worked out over the years). Of course, Harich's political and even philosophical positions (which he had already published and had later developed further[35]) played a role, but at this point we shall only discuss the platform which articulated the "revisionism" (as the SED leadership called it) that was already widespread among Party intellectuals, even if only as a general mood. The platform spelled out its own place within the intra-Party opposition in this way:

> We wish to discuss legally and to implement within the Party and the GDR our conception of a special German way to socialism and our platform for a Marxism-Leninism freed of Stalinism.
>
> However, this legality has its limits, and it ends where the present Party leadership itself leaves the field of legality. In our opinion, the Party leadership has already left this field of legality. The foundations of our oppositional work are the Party Statutes of the SED, the Twentieth Party Congress of the CPSU, and the resolutions of the Twenty-eighth Plenary Session of the Central Committee of the SED. We wish to carry out our oppositional work fully legally on these foundations; however, we shall also take up the methods of faction formation and conspiracy if the Stalinist apparatus forces us to do so.
>
> We shall establish ties with oppositional forces within the people's democracies in order to effect a mutual exchange of our experiences. The oppositional SED comrades must forge close contacts with the population of the GDR, criticize the policies of the Party leadership among the population, deepen the schism between the population and the present Party leadership, but at the same time prevent a popular rebellion in the GDR.

The theoretical and ideological views were described as follows:

> In Eastern Europe, economic structures have emerged that—if radical reforms are effected and their degenerate aspects are overcome—are capable of realizing socialism in the Eastern countries sooner than this will be possible in the Western European countries with their predominant capitalistic economic structures. A radically de-Stalinized Eastern economic structure in the USSR and in the people's democracies will gradually influence the capitalist West as it develops further. . . . At the same time the West will influence the East with democratic and libertarian ideas and views, and force the East to dismantle step by step its totalitarian and despotic political system. . . . We wish to reform the Party from within. We want to remain on the positions of Marxism-Leninism. However, we want to move away from Stalinism.

Elsewhere we read:

> We don't wish to break with Marxism-Leninism; but we want to free it

from Stalinism and dogmatism and restore it to its humanistic and un-
dogmatic ways of thinking.

The USSR was regarded as the first socialist nation of the world,
and in the statements of the platform even Stalinism could alter
nothing of this fact. Of course it was denied that Soviet socialism
represented a model, since in its present-day form it had become
even "an obstacle to further socialist development in the USSR."

The concrete reforms the Harich group platform demanded for
the GDR were the abolition of the hegemony of the bureaucratic
apparatus over Party members, expulsion of the Stalinists from the
SED, the restoration of absolute legal guarantees, the abolition of
the state security agency and the secret court, workers' shares in
the profits in factories, and an end to collectivization in agriculture. Further demands were that the parliament should be sovereign
and that there should be elections with several candidates as in the
Polish model, although "the reformed SED was to remain at the
top." On the question of Germany's reunification, the Harich group
envisioned free elections throughout all of Germany, the result of
which was expected to be a majority for the Social Democratic
Party, which the SED had to respect. The prospect was a unified
pan-German workers' movement.

We have dwelt so extensively on the Harich viewpoint because,
despite the many contradictions in its basic features, it shows the
main demands of the internal communist opposition in the GDR
in the fifties, and because even then the SED responded with the
same repressive methods as it did to Bahro's theory: Harich and his
friends were sentenced to between two and ten years in prison.[36]

The views of the Harich group corresponded to the wishes and
demands of many intellectuals in the SED, and showed a tendency
of a partly open, partly latent, oppositional current. They also,
however, reflected the dissatisfaction of broad layers, especially
the workers, with the system of domination in the GDR.[37] Now as
then the platform has been variously appraised: on the one hand it
has been called "typical and especially significant for the development of reform communism,"[38] while elsewhere the "programmatic contradictions" have been stressed, and the quest for theoretical foundations called a "total failure" because of the "motley
mixture"[39] of philosophical and historical arguments.[40]

A comparison of Bahro's theoretical views with those of Harich
does indeed bear out this critical conclusion. But a formal study

should take into account that the platform was an *ad hoc* outline of political ideas that developed under quite different temporal conditions. The basic questions and the problems taken up are in just as much agreement as the effect and function of the communist opposition in its time.

Havemann

For the 1960s Robert Havemann developed much further the theoretical formation of the anti-Stalinist opposition in the GDR. After speaking out in 1956 against dogmatism in philosophical discussion, in 1963 he carried his criticism further into the domain of political theory when he took up the problem of the freedom of the individual in communist-governed society.

Born in 1910, Robert Havemann entered the Communist Party of Germany in 1932.[41] As an active antifascist in 1943 (the year he received his doctoral diploma), he was condemned to death by the infamous People's Court. However, he survived the Third Reich in Brandenburg Prison, where of course Erich Honecker too was incarcerated, and in 1946 became Professor in the Berlin Humboldt University. In 1950 the esteemed scientist entered the Volkskammer as a delegate. Havemann's critical lectures on philosophical problems[42] in 1963 were before packed halls, especially because his philosophical critique took into account the concrete reality of the GDR. This accounted for its "unique impact."[43] Havemann took a position against deformations in the GDR regime and spoke out for a socialist democracy, which, as he said, could not exist without open criticism and relevant debate and discussion. He therefore demanded "more freedom in the GDR" than even the Western democracies could give to their citizens. The GDR leadership also took repressive measures against Havemann; these were at first restricted to denying him the right to practice his profession, but later he was isolated. Havemann's reply was a critique that shifted increasingly from philosophy to politics. In 1968 he wrote in a Prague magazine:

> Democratic control of the government from below is crucial for democracy. This means the right of opposition in public, in the press, on the radio, and on television, as well as in the parliament and in popular representative bodies whose members are determined by free and secret ballots. This also means that judges must be independent and that

administrative courts must be set up to which the citizen may turn in complaint against official arbitrariness. Democracy also means that to govern is made more difficult, and to be governed, easier. Both are very useful . . .[44]

The "Prague Spring" and more recently Eurocommunism show that the theses Havemann developed in the GDR and the problems he took up have a role to play in the whole of today's world communism. The further theoretical development of communist criticism of "real socialism" undertaken by Havemann is well known; we need not discuss it in detail here. His writings were eventually published in the West (and not in the GDR).[45]

Havemann continues to regard himself as a critical communist. For him capitalism is no alternative, since he feels that the capitalist economy has reached the limits of its "conditions of existence."[46] At the same time he is a democratic communist; he invokes Rosa Luxemburg and derives from her theses the demand for a free socialist society

> . . . with freedom of the press and freedom for divergent thinking, freedom of assembly, the right to strike, freedom of religion, philosophical views, artistic creativity, i.e., the abolition of any interference into culture and science by the state or patronage of these areas by the state. Socialism does not mean collective uniformity, it does not mean the abolition but rather the free development of the broadest diversity in human life and thoughts. Socialism is free pluralism in all areas of social life.[47]

For Havemann the "bringing of socialist democracy to perfection, i.e., the realization and implementation of all political human rights, has become No. 1 on the agenda of history."[48] Thus Havemann too is an example of how the opposition of the third way further developed, and how fundamental positions of democratic communism step by step began to be expanded theoretically. There should actually be no question but that Bahro must also be ranked in this tradition.

Democratic communism

The theoretical conceptions from Harich to Havemann and Bahro have all started out from the same premise: all check the reality of communist states against Marxist theory, and from the contradiction between theory and practice, between the claims and realities, they derive their demand for the elimination of the bureaucratic dictatorial rule. Freedom of information, and discussion, and finally organization for ensuring that the will of the majority prevails, as well as the protection of minorities (on the basis of the existing communist order) thus became the goals of democratic communism. Of course this line did not develop just in the GDR, but also in many other communist states and parties. Finally the demands for civil rights, freedom of opinion, freedom of press, legal guarantees, independence of the people's representative bodies, etc., were realized in part in Czechoslovakia in 1968. Thus the concrete content of democratic communism became discernible—the linking of the communist socioeconomic order with elements of democratic codetermination and institutionalized legal guarantees. Czechoslovakia showed that the ideas of democratic communism are by no means only the utopian ideas of political dreamers. The invasion by the Warsaw Pact troops was directed against the practical implementation of the everywhere latently existing ideas of democratic communism.

The possibility of implementing democratic communism was first and foremost a question of the ability of communism to change at all. It has been shown that communism had been flexible in the past.[49] Eurocommunism shows us that communist parties not in power (and perhaps, specifically for that reason) are moving in the direction of democratic communism. For the countries of the Warsaw Pact, and hence also the GDR, the example of Czechoslovakia 1968 shows the narrow limits that the Soviet hegemony in real socialism has set. On the basis of this experience, Bahro was able to develop his innovative analysis of the new, peculiar type of social formation.

The possibilities and limits of democratic communist ideas thus become evident. The importance of the theories from Harich to Bahro lies in the fact that they reflect the contradiction that exists between official ideology and practice, which time and time again has led to oppositional moods especially among the youth. As long as political and social tensions exist and are ideologically glossed over, political thought must give rise to an immanent criticism. Only if the gap between the ideal and the reality is reduced to a minimum or indoctrination is abolished can this process be prevented. Since both seem to be impossible for the SED, the democratic communist tendency may crop up again and again.

Since on the other hand the system in the GDR, as in all communist-governed states of the Moscow type, depends on the friction-free functioning of the apparatus, it is indispensable that the ruling elite maintain closed ranks and that the functionaries be incorporated into the hierarchical apparatus. Any opposition within the apparatus touches the very roots of the system, and the leadership must therefore prevent deviations within the apparatus and maintain democratic centralism as its instrument of control. How, ever, the apparatus is more susceptible to an immanent opposition of democratic communism than to any other deviations. To this extent democratic communism is indeed a danger, which explains why the SED leadership reacts so vehemently and is so quick to resort to repressive measures. Hence the significance of humanistic and democratic aspects of Marxist theory for the development of GDR communism should not be underestimated. If one looks only at the political realities, and disparages ideology as utopia, one overlooks the role and the possible impact of revolutionary ideas and their feedback effects on reality.

Of course, neither should the effect of the opposition on the political stability and power system of the GDR be overestimated. As long as bureaucratic dictatorial communism functions in the USSR, there is probably no real possibility for the GDR to develop in isolation and on its own in the direction of democratic communism. The previous history of the GDR does indeed show that oppositional currents of various convictions continually recur, but that the system of rule on the whole is more firmly entrenched (and often also more flexible) than is assumed by public opinion in the West. However great the theoretical significance of Bahro's work must be, we must warn against overestimating its effects on practical policy; indeed, that has been amply demonstrated by the tradition of democratic communism.

Our sketch of some of the problems of democratic communism has been limited to the question of identifying the tradition in which Bahro finds himself. The complex and complicated problem of democratic communism[50] is but suggested here. We have been able to present the tradition of the third way in barest outline, and have dealt in just as little detail with the diverse currents[51] as with the international dimension (as for example the Russian left opposition of today).[52] We have not described the current discussion, subsequent to Biermann's expulsion,[53] nor the fundamental discussions about Marxism in the GDR which now and in the past have moved in the direction of democratic communism.[54] Nor have we touched upon the problem of growth, of welfare communism,[55] which Bahro discussed, or the problem of the apparatus.[56] Finally, we have not gone into the influences of social development on ideology, the general structural development of the GDR,[57] the problem of intellect and power,[58] or the distinction between democratic communism and democratic socialism.[59]

Our purpose was only to provide a sketch of the relevant group within the democratic communist tradition on the basis of general statements reflecting the third way. We found that the goals as well as the critical method all stem from Marx,[60] and that in all cases the point of departure is the development of the Russian Revolution of 1917. Bahro's ideas of a "minimal program for a democratic revolution against the political bureaucracy" are just as much a part of this context as are his more original observations.[61] Bahro himself sees the weak points in the tradition, specifically the lack of a socioeconomic line:

> Since 1953, the progressive communist forces—even ignoring their objective weakness while the cold war was still in progress—have time and again proved insufficiently prepared. At bottom, they still stood on the same political and theoretical basis as their opponents, and could be ideologically blackmailed by them via their common interest in the autonomy of the noncapitalist road. Above all, they had a poor understanding of the ground on which they were fighting. Their various action programs were based more on temporary negations than on a socioeconomic analysis.[62]

Bahro did not mean that this was true only for the GDR (he was discussing the developments in Czechoslovakia). But with reference to the GDR one must also ask whether the revisionist economists' opposition in the context of that time did not provide the impulses which Bahro took up. After all, Behrens and Benary not only advocated the dismantling of centralism and the institution of elements of self-administration, but also criticized the role of the Party, the political bureaucracy.

With his fundamental questioning of the new, peculiar type of social formation, Bahro goes much further than the attempts of the former oppositional economists to correct the mistakes in the system.[63] But it remains an open question whether Bahro, with his considerable bias toward political economy, might not underestimate the problem of institutions and the power apparatus. Perhaps this is the reason why Bahro on at least one central point falls behind Trotskyism and Eurocommunism: he does not advocate a multiparty system. But in this too Bahro is quite (and one might say even too much) in the tradition of the third way. Indeed, in general Bahro has provided new and crucial impulses for democratic communism, for a turn away from the thesis of the Party as guardian—a theory which is in fact only a synonym for a Party dictatorship in ideology and practice.

Translated by Michel Vale

NOTES

1. Rudolf Bahro, "Zur Kritik des real existierenden Sozialismus: Sechs Vorträge über das Buch 'Die Alternative,'" in Rudolf Bahro, *Eine Dokumentation*. (Cologne-Frankfurt/M, 1977), p. 9.

2. Ibid.

3. Rudolf Bahro, *The Alternative in Eastern Europe* (London: New Left Books, 1978), pp. 19 ff.

4. Bahro. "Zur Kritik," p. 49.

5. Ibid., p. 9.

6. *Das Parlament*, No. 23/58, 1958, pp. 305, 308. On the diversity of the opposition in the GDR at a later time, see Karl Wilhelm Fricke and Peter Dittmar, *Gegen 99.8%: Opposition in der DDR* (Cologne: Deutschlandfunk, 1974): "They are members of the intelligentsia, the scientists, philosophers, and writers. Also some of the younger generation. They include both convinced socialists, who in their quest for a third way between East and West have come to take up a criticism of the system, as well as convinced Christians. A third group is constituted by the core of politically conscious workers, who are still under strong social democratic influences and traditions. Finally, the fourth group should not be underestimated: decision makers at all levels of the Party and state apparatus who in their own way, usually inconspicuously, seek to eliminate the contradiction between theory and practice in socialism, and in this way come into opposition with the politics of the SED."

7. See Martin Jänicke: *Der dritte Weg. Die antistalinistische Opposition gegen Ulbricht seit 1953* (Cologne, 1964). See also the later discussion, which, to be sure, also deals with reform communism in Czechoslovakia, but treats of the same problems; in particular: Peter Christian Ludz, "Der 'Neue Sozialismus,'" *Die neue Gesellschaft*, 17, No. 1, 1970, pp. 50 ff, and Ludz, "Dreispaltung des Marxismus?" *Die neue Gesellschaft*, 17, No. 6, 1970, pp. 810ff; and Wolfgang Leonhard, "Dreispaltung des Marxismus," *Die neue Gesellschaft*, 18, No. 1, 1971, pp. 45ff.

8. See the correct comment by Peter von Oertzen on the role of Willy Brandt in the GDR in Hannes Schwenger, ed., *Solidarität mit Rudolf Bahro. Briefe in die DDR* (Reinbek bei Hamburg, 1978), p. 60.

9. We shall merely refer to Robert Vincent Daniels, *The Conscience of the Revolution: Communist Opposition in Soviet Russia* (Cambridge, 1960). Also Ulf Wolter, ed., *Die linke Opposition in der Sowjetunion 1923-1928*, Vols. 1-5 (West Berlin: Verlag Olle und Wolter, 1976/77), and Wolter, ed., *Sozialismusdebatte* (West Berlin: Verlag Olle und Wolter, 1978).

10. See the two volumes of "Dokumente der Weltrevolution," *Arbeiterdemokratie oder Parteidiktatur* (Olten, 1967) and *Die Linke gegen die Parteiherrschaft* (Olten, 1970). See also Gottfried Mergner, ed., *Die russische Arbeiteropposition* (Reinbek bei Hamburg, 1972); Hans Manfred Bock, *Geschichte des "linken Radikalismus" in Deutschland* (Frankfurt/M., 1976).

11. The "classical description" is Leon Trotsky's *The Revolution Betrayed.* See also the later outlines of the former right-wing communist Paul Frölich, "Beiträge zur Analyse des Stalinismus," in *Arbeiterbewegung. Theorie und Geschichte*, Jahrbuch 4 (Frankfurt/M., 1976), pp. 141ff. On ideological development: Ulf Wolter, *Grundlagen des Stalinismus* (West Berlin, 1975).

12. See K. H. Tjaden, *Struktur und Funktion der "KPD-Opposition" (KPO)* (Meisenheim am Glan, 1964), pp. 162ff; Karl Korsch, *Politische Texte*, ed. Erich Gerlach and Jürgen Seifert (Frankfurt-Cologne, 1974), pp. 70ff.

13. *Dokumente der SED*, Vol. II (East Berlin, 1952), p. 310.

14. On this point see Herman Weber, *Die Wandlung des deutschen Kommunismus. Die Stalinisierung der KPD in der Weimarer Republik*, Vols. 1 and 2 (Frankfurt/M, 1969).

15. On this point see K. P. Wittemann, *Kommunistische Politik in Westdeutschland nach 1945. Der Ansatz der Gruppe Arbeiterpolitik* (Hannover, 1977).

16. See, for example, ibid., p. 374.

17. This was a term used by the former Saxon state chairman of the SED, Lohagen, in an article against Arthur Lieberasch, Paul Hempel, and other Party functionaries. Printed in Hermann Weber, ed., *Der deutsche Kommunismus. Dokumente* (Cologne-Berlin, 1963), pp. 587ff.

18. See the biographies in Weber, *Wandlung*, Vol. 2, pp. 207f, 334f.

19. The same was the case for left communists; thus the Trotskyists Oskar Hippe and Walter Haas were arrested at the end of 1948 and sentenced to 25 years by Soviet courts; in 1950 the former KAP functionary Alfred Weiland was abducted from West Berlin and imprisoned. In 1953 Hermann Möhring was seized and imprisoned for as many years. See *pro und contra* (West Berlin), No. 6, June 1950, p. 15; No. 12, December 1950, p. 3; No. 1, January 1953, p. 20.

20. At the Second Party Conference of the SED in 1952, Ulbricht spoke of the "abysmal betrayal of the Tito clique." *Protokoll der II. Parteikonferenz der SED, 9-12 July 1952.* (East Berlin, 1952), p. 58.

21. On the purges see Karl Wilhelm Fricke, *Warten auf Gerechtigkeit. Kommunistische Säuberungen und Rehabilitierungen* (Cologne, 1971), pp. 62ff.

22. The comprehensive discussions of the left-wing and right-wing communist groups in Western Europe and Stalinism cannot be taken into consideration in this context.

23. On this opposition see, above all, Jänicke, *Der dritte Weg.*

24. In GDR literature the social democracy is often ascribed the notion of a third way, but that can be left out of account here.

25. See also Reinhard Crusius and Manfred Wilke, *Entstalinisierung. Der XX. Parteitag und seine Folgen* (Frankfurt/M., 1977). On the effects, see the contributions by Ernst Bloch, Hans Mayer, Berni Kelb, Herbert Kuehl.

26. Gerhard Zwerenz was also able to flee, but Günter Zehm was arrested. On the details see Jänicke, *Der dritte Weg,* and Fricke, *Warten auf Gerechtigkeit.*

27. *Sonntag,* (East Berlin), November 4, 1956.

28. We need only point out the economists Fritz Behrens, Arne Benary, and Günter Kohlmey, literary experts such as Hans Mayer and Alfred Kantorowicz, jurists such as Karl Bönninger and Hermann Klenner. For details see Jänicke, *Der dritte Weg,* as well as Melvin Croan, "Die Intellektuellen in der SBZ während der fünfziger Jahre," in Leopold Labedz, ed., *Der Revisionismus* (Cologne-Berlin, 1965), pp. 357ff.

29. Jänicke, *Der dritte Weg,* p. 156 and also references to individual groups of students, trials, etc.

30. See Hertwig's article in Crusius and Wilke, *Entstalinisierung,* pp. 477ff.

31. See Zöger's article, "Die politischen Hintergünde des Harich-Prozesses," *SBZ-Archiv,* 11, No. 13, July 1960, pp. 198f.

32. The platform of the Harich group is printed in *SBZ-Archiv,* No. 5/6, March 25, 1957, pp. 72ff; Günther Hillmann, ed., *Selbstkritik des Kommunismus. Texte der Opposition* (Reinbek bei Hamburg, 1967), pp. 189ff; and Weber, *Der deutsche Kommunismus,* pp. 598ff. The following quotations are taken from these sources.

33. See excerpts from the judgments against the "enemy of the state Harich group" in Fricke, *Warten auf Gerechtigkeit,* p. 243.

34. Hertwig, op. cit. in Crusius and Wilke, *Entstalinisierung,* p. 482.

35. On this point see Peter Christian Ludz, "Freiheitsphilosophie oder aufgeklärter Dogmatismus?" in Labedz, *Der Revisionismus,* pp. 384ff; Wolfgang Harich, *Zur Kritik der revolutionären Ungeduld* (Basel, 1971); and Wolfgang Harich, *Kommunismus ohne Wachstum?* (Reinbek bei Hamburg, 1975).

36. In the first trial (March 7-9, 1957) Harich got 10 years, Steinberger 4 years, and Hertwig 2 years prison. In the second trial (July 23-26, 1957) Janka got 5 years, Just 4 years, Wolf 3 years, and Zöger 2 and a half years in prison.

37. On this point see Benno Sarel, *Arbeiter gegen den Kommunismus. Zur Geschichte des proletarischen Widerstandes in der DDR (1945-1958)* (Munich, 1975).

38. Wolfgang Leonhard, *Three Faces of Communism* (New York, 1974).

39. The platform states that Marxism-Leninism must be supplemented and expanded by the views of Trotsky and especially of Bukharin, the views of Rosa Luxemburg, Karl Kautsky, Fritz Sternberg, the Yugoslavian and Chinese experience, etc.

40. Croan, "Die Intellektuellen," p. 366.

41. On Havemann see Robert Havemann, *Ein deutscher Kommunist. Ein Interview mit Manfred Wilke* (Reinbek bei Hamburg, 1978).

42. Robert Havemann, *Dialektik ohne Dogma* (Reinbek bei Hamburg, 1964).

43. Cf. Ludz, *Freiheitsphilosophie*, p. 389. See also Dieter Knötzsch, *Innerkommunistische Opposition. Das Beispiel Robert Havemann* (Opladen, 1968).

44. "Robert Havemann meldet sich zu Wort," *Deutschland Archiv*, 1, No. 3, June 1968, pp. 328ff.

45. Robert Havemann, *Fragen—Antworten—Fragen* (Munich, 1970), *Rückantworten an die Hauptverwaltung "Ewige Wahrheiten"* (Munich, 1971), and *Berliner Schriften* (Munich, 1977).

46. Havemann, *Berliner Schriften*, p. 185.

47. Ibid., p. 187.

48. Robert Havemann to Jochen Steffen, in Jiri Pelikan and Manfred Wilke, eds., *Menschenrechte. Ein Jahrbuch zu Osteuropa* (Reinbeck bei Hamburg, 1977), p. 476.

49. See, for example, Weber, *Wandlung*.

50. See, for example, Hermann Weber, *Demokratischer Kommunismus?* (Hannover, 1969), p. vii.

51. See Note 28.

52. See Boris Lewytzkyj: *Die linke Opposition in der Sowjetunion* (Hamburg, 1974). See also Pelikan and Wilke, *Menschenrechte*, and Rudi Dutschke and Manfred Wilke, eds., *Die Sowjetunion, Solschenizyn und die westliche Linke* (Reinbek bei Hamburg, 1975).

53. See, for example, Thomas Rothschild, *Wolf Biermann, Liedermacher und Sozialist* (Reinbek bei Hamburg, 1977) and Jürgen Fuchs, *Gedächtnisprotokolle* (Reinbek bei Hamburg, 1977).

54. See Peter Lübbe, *Der staatlich etablierte Sozialismus. Zur Kritik des staatsmonopolistischen Sozialismus* (Hamburg, 1975).

55. See Note 35.

56. Bahro, *The Alternative*, pp. 318ff.

57. See Hermann Weber, "Zu den Entwicklungs- und Strukturbedingungen der DDR (Thesen)," *kritik*, No. 17 (Verlag Olle und Wolter, 1978), pp. 115ff.

58. See for example J. Wolfgang Görlich, *Geist und Macht in der DDR* (Olten, 1968).

59. See on this point Hermann Weber, "Demokratischer Sozialismus," Meyers *Enzyklopädisches Lexikon*, Vol. 22 (Mannheim, 1978), pp. 163ff.

60. See on this point Robert Havemann, "Bin ich Marxist?" in Havemann, *Berliner Schriften*.

61. I cannot go into detail here on Bahro's significance; see such diverse authors as Ernest Mandel, *Kritik des Eurokommunismus* (West Berlin: Verlag Olle und Wolter, 1978, pp. 94ff; and Fritz Schenk and Günther Bartsch, in *Deutschland Archiv*, 11, No. 5, May 1978, pp. 469ff.

62. Bahro, *The Alternative*, p. 311.

63. It is therefore also wrong to see Bahro only as an "ideologue of the technical intelligentsia." See *Das Argument*, no. 108, pp. 241ff.

HERBERT MARCUSE

Protosocialism and Late Capitalism: Toward a Theoretical Synthesis Based on Bahro's Analysis

Bahro's significance for an analysis of late capitalism

The following text focuses on issues in Bahro's book that have a universal significance extending beyond his analysis of the GDR. This means that concepts articulated by him, which in his framework (that of "actually existing socialism") could not be further developed, can be shown to have relevance to late capitalism as well. The second part of this essay is my contribution to an analysis of those tendencies in late capitalism which correspond to the tendencies noted by Bahro in protosocialism. His book is not merely a critique of "actually existing socialism," it is at the same time a Marxist analysis of the transition period to integral socialism. It is the most important contribution to Marxist theory and practice to appear in several decades.

Bahro's transformation of method

When one says that much of Bahro's critique applies, *mutatis mutandis*, to late capitalism and that, *mutatis mutandis*, the alternative is valid for both social systems, this does not mean that Bahro outlines some sort of convergence theory. Rather, he has demonstrated that unity between progress and destruction, productivity and repression, gratification and want, which is rooted in the structures of both of these (very different) societies. This unity, which in very different forms, is common to both societies (and whose stabilizing potential Marxism has fatally underestimated), can be broken only in a socialism that does not yet actually exist.

Does "not yet" exist: thus the concrete utopia (and its monstrous negation in existing society) becomes the guiding thread of the empirical analysis. The empirical analysis itself reveals that the transcendence [*Aufhebung*] of utopia is an already existing, real possibility—indeed a necessity. The conclusive demonstration of this possibility is the result of a revolution in method: socialism shows itself to be a real possibility, and the basis of utopia is revealed in what already exists, only when the most extreme, integral, "utopian" conception of socialism informs the analysis. For it is not the abolition of private ownership of the means of production (though this remains the indispensable precondition of socialism) which as such determines the essential difference between the two systems; it is rather the way in which the material and intellectual forces of production are used.

> . . . the entire perspective under which we have so far seen the transition to communism stands in need of correction, and in no way just with respect to the time factor. The dissolution of private property in the means of production on the one hand, and universal human emancipation on the other, are separated by an entire epoch.[1]

Bahro finally breaks with the distinction (which has long since become a repressive ideology) between socialism and communism. Socialism *is* communism from the very beginning—and vice versa. The essence and goal of a socialist society—the "total individual," the encroachment of the realm of freedom into the realm of necessity—must (and can) already here and now become the project and guideline of communist policy and strategy.

This revolution in method in fact returns Marxism from ideology to theory—and to praxis. What transpires in the course of Bahro's analysis of class relations in the GDR is the recapturing of the concrete, its liberation from ideology. The absence of all jargon, of mere rumination over Marxist concepts (or better, words) testifies to the grounding of the analysis in social reality. Instead of stubbornly hanging onto theses that have long since become historically obsolete, Bahro's analysis develops the Marxian concepts in confrontation with the changed structure of the postcapitalist society of the GDR—and of late capitalism! A decisive result is that historical materialism makes a genuine advance: the relationship between base and superstructure is redefined, the focal point of the social dynamic is shifted from the objectivity of political economy to *subjectivity*, to consciousness as a potential material force for radical change.

It [the human race—H.M.] must continue its ascent as a "journey inwards." The leap into the realm of freedom is conceivable only on the basis of a balance between the human species and its environment, with its dynamic decisively shifted toward the qualitative and subjective aspect.[2]

In this shift, Bahro sees socialism's "essentially aesthetic motivation, oriented to the totality and to the return of activities to the self."[3]

This marks the retrieval of the element of idealism originally in historical materialism: the liberation from the economy that is the aim of historical materialism. Historical materialism remains intact; it is the dynamic of the base itself, the organization of the ever-increasing productivity of labor, which makes the activity of self-emancipating subjectivity the focal point of change.

As Bahro's analysis proceeds it becomes apparent to what degree the turn toward subjectivity applies to late capitalism as well. Even more than in actually existing socialism, in the highly developed capitalist countries liberation has become contingent on the spread of a form of consciousness that is rooted in yet at the same time transcends the process of material production. Bahro calls this "surplus consciousness" [*überschüssiges Bewusstsein*]. It is "that free human [*psychische*] capacity which is no longer absorbed by the struggle for existence" which is to be translated into practice. The industrial, technological-scientific mode of production, in which intellectual labor becomes an essential factor, engenders in the producers (the "collective worker") qualities, skills, forms of imagination, and capacities for activity and enjoyment that are stifled or perverted in capitalist and repressive noncapitalist societies. These press beyond their inhuman realization toward a truly human one.

In the subjectivity of surplus consciousness, compensatory and emancipatory interests are forced together into a unity. Compensatory interests concern mainly the sphere of material goods: bigger and better consumption, careers, competition, profit, "status symbols," etc. They can (at least for the time being!) be satisfied within the framework of the existing system: they compensate for dehumanization. Thus, they contradict the emancipatory interests. Nonetheless, Bahro insists that compensatory interests cannot simply be reduced and rechanneled in the interest of emancipation; they are a form of the demand for happiness and gratification that is deeply rooted in the psyche. Through them, what exists receives its legitimation. The revolution cannot be carried through on the backs of the people; but the power of compensatory interests and their satisfaction stifles the realization of emancipatory interests. The revolution presupposes a rupture with this power—a rupture which in turn can only be the result of revolution!

This, then, is the vicious circle that recurs so often and is formulated in so many different ways in Bahro's book. It is the central historical problem of revolutionary theory in our time. Between today and tomorrow, between "unfreedom" and emancipation, lies not only the revolution but also the radical transformation of needs, the rupture with "subaltern" consciousness, the catastrophe of subjectivity. The contradiction between an overwhelming productivity and social wealth on the one hand, and its miserable and destructive uses on the other, is not propelled toward this catastrophe with the necessity of a historical law—not even when it is guided by a Marxist-Leninist strategy. The increase in productivity and the abolition of private ownership of the means of production do not have to lead to socialism: they do not necessarily break the chains of domination, the subjugation of human beings to labor. Bahro suggests that there is a tendency in Marx that implies such a continuity—the idea of ever-growing productivity and ever more efficient (and more egalitarian) production.

At the height of industrial civilization, subordination to labor is demanded by no other reason than the reason of the ruling class and the preservation of its power. In actually existing socialism, subjugation is justified by the lag in the economic, military, and technological competition with capitalism. But once a new form of domination is established, necessity is transformed into virtue: the "first stage" is prolonged into an indefinite future. The qualitative difference of a socialist society is lost, and all the more rapidly the more this socialism adopts the consumption model of the highly developed capitalist countries. Compensatory interests work against emancipation. The vicious circle exists in both societies. How can it be broken?

The economy of time, surplus consciousness,
and the role of the intelligentsia

The question takes us back to Bahro's concept of "surplus consciousness" as a transforming power. This consciousness has its material base in the scientific, technological mode of production, in its "intellectualization." At this stage, it is "embodied" (but not reflected) in the "intellectualized layers of the collective worker."[4] Beyond this, surplus consciousness exists in all strata of the dependent population, in an obstructed and inactive form. There is a dim awareness that there is no longer any need to live the way we do—that an alternative exists. This dim awareness becomes a certainty in the *catalyst* groups (the expression is my own—H.M.) of the opposition: the student movement, women's liberation, citizens' initiatives, concerned scientists, etc.

Wherever the great majority of the working class is integrated into the existing system, class relations tend toward an *elitist* structure in which the intelligentsia plays a leading role as a part of the collective worker. Bahro defends the provocative thesis that the intellectualized layers "set the tone" during the preparatory and transitional period and that they assume a leading role in the reconstruction of society.[5]

The intelligentsia plays a leading role for two reasons:

1. More than ever before, knowledge is power. Information about the scientific and technological, economic and psychological mechanisms that reproduce the developed industrial society gives the possessors of such information knowledge of the objective possibilities for change. Of course, knowledge alone is not enough to realize this potentiality. But the intelligentsia does not function in isolation. It is the process of production itself which becomes "intellectualized," and in it the intellectualized strata play an increasingly important role. In the GDR they are a part of the apparatus that controls the means of production; and among them (according to Bahro) there is a considerable opposition to the dictatorship of the political bureaucracy.

2. For the intelligentsia, the realization of their compensatory interests is no longer a matter of daily concern. They share with the party functionaries the high-level privileges in the material and intellectual culture. In capitalist countries this is the case only to a very limited degree, and then only for a small circle of more or less conformist intelligentsia. The majority of the not-so-privileged strata at least have the privilege of education, which can open the otherwise closed horizon of knowledge that transcends the existing state of things.

The creation of the space and time required for the development of emancipatory interests beyond the material sphere, which today determines all and everything, is the task of socialist education and a socialist division of labor. Even in its transitional period, socialism is basically a problem of the *economy of time*. The new distribution and organization of labor aims at reversing the proportional amount of time spent in necessary and in emancipatory labor in the interests of the "total individual." Insofar as this redistribution of time on an overall social scale also requires a radical reorganization of *necessary* labor (Bahro gives very concrete suggestions for such a reorganization), the new economy of time would amount to the emergence of the realm of freedom *within* the realm of necessity. And insofar as it would be carried out throughout all strata of the society, it would demolish the privileged position of the intelligentsia by universalizing it.

Domination, state, and antistate

Bahro rejects any conception of the transitional period that purports to be able to dispense with a communist party, a bureaucracy, and the state, as anarchism and adventurist left radicalism. He even speaks of the state as the "taskmaster of society in its technical and social modernization"[6]—modernization meaning the creation of emancipatory institutions. Such a state would be a "taskmaster" in the form of a truly universal educational system, embracing the material as well as the intellectual culture, and having as its goal the liberation of needs from their class-determined psychic base. The absence of initiative among the masses and the absorption of the working class into the prevailing system of compensatory needs rob the idea of the "withering away of the state" of its empirical historical rationale. Socialism must create its own antistate and its own system of administration. "People and functionaries—this is the unavoidable dichotomy of every protosocialist society."[7] Only the *proto*socialist? That would be a reversion to the two-stages theory.

Bahro's conception seems to imply that universality will still be institutionalized even in a fully developed socialist society: the antistate as state. The state is *anti*state insofar as it contributes to the further unfolding of emancipatory needs and gives wider play to spontaneity and individual autonomy; it is *state* inasmuch as it organizes this process in the interests of society as a whole (in setting priorities, distributing work, education, etc.), and indeed does so with a binding authority legitimated by the people. In the antistate the dialectic of the autonomy and dependency of needs repeats itself: The socialist state "makes note of" the needs of individuals in the form in which they appear within the prevailing system of needs and "transcends" them [*hebt sie auf*] in new emancipatory forms, which then in turn become the individuals' own needs.

Bahro sees the requisite rational hierarchy still needed even under integral socialism as the counter-image of the established apparatus of domination in actually existing socialism. He envisages a democratically constituted and controlled hierarchy from the base to the top. At the summit, this hierarchy becomes a dual power [*Doppelherrschaft*]: the communist party and a "league of communists." The latter would be independent of the party, recruited from those members of the intelligentsia in all strata of society whose consciousness is most advanced. This league is the brain of the whole: a democratic elite, with a decisive voice in the discussion of plans, education, the redistribution of work, etc.

The inertia and powerlessness of the masses, their dependency, manifested in the dichotomy "ruling class—people" in the capitalist countries, and the dichotomy "bureaucrat—people" in actually existing socialism, gives rise to an almost inevitable tendency for the top level to become autonomous. Bahro examines this tendency where it has already evolved into full-fledged domination: in protosocialist society. He believes that this tendency may be counteracted by the gradual building up of a kind of *council organization* (self-management, cooperatives) whose rudimentary forms already exist within the existing system. He shows convincingly that the traditional concept of social democracy is too exclusively oriented to the sphere of material production and hence remains the representative of particular interests. The situation under protosocialism (and under late capitalism—H.M.) with its expanded working class in which the intelligentsia is a decisive factor in the production process, should make it possible to broaden council democracy. A relatively small number of scientists, technicians, engineers, and indeed even media agents could, if organized, disrupt the reproduction process of the system and perhaps even bring it to a standstill. But "that's not the way things are." It is precisely their integration [*Einordnung*] into the production process, to say nothing of their privileged income, that works against the radicalization of this group. Nevertheless, the social position of these groups gives them a leading role in the revolution.

During its preparatory and transitional periods, the revolution requires a leadership that can *stand up against* the compensatory interests of the masses as well. It too must face up to the necessity of repression, repression of "subaltern consciousness," unreflected spontaneity, and bourgeois and petit bourgeois egoism.

Obviously, at this central point, Bahro's analysis falls back on a position that has been tabooed by both Marxism and liberalism: Plato's position (an educational dictatorship of the most intelligent) and Rousseau's (people must be forced to be free). In fact, the educational function of the socialist state is inconceivable without a recognized authority; for Bahro that authority is grounded in an elite of intelligence. However consistently Bahro may insist that the league as well as the party leadership must come from all social groups and remain accountable to the people at all levels, the scandal remains and must be sustained.

The question of the subject of the revolution

It is precisely here—where Bahro's interpretation of socialism is so vulnerable to defamation and ridicule—that the full radicalism of his approach, and his fidelity to Marxian theory, stand out clearly. The question of the *subject of the revolution*, which the integration of the working class has put on the agenda, finds its answer here on the level of actual historical development. The fetishism that says that the working class, by virtue of its "ontological position," is predestined by the iron logic of economic and political development to be the subject of the revolution— this stipulated unity between the logical and the historical (according to which "what appears as finished from the logical point of view must immediately be historically finished too"[8])—this fetishism is abolished not by dictum but by the course of history itself. "The fact has since become quite evident enough that the proletariat cannot be a ruling class."[9] In capitalist countries the working class is "too narrow a base for transforming society (do not specifically working class interests often even play a conservative role?)."[10] The radical turn toward emancipatory interests lies beyond the reach of subaltern consciousness; it takes place as part of a process of "internal emancipation," as a condition for external emancipation. Given the social conditions of the class (alienating "full-time" labor, exclusion from educational privilege, unemployment), only a minority can accomplish this rupture.

No particular class can be the subject of the universal emancipation which has become possible at the present historical stage. The identity between the proletariat and the universal interest has been superseded—if indeed it ever existed at all. Universal emancipation is today no longer a question of "securing the material basis of existence," although this remains the "unalterable presupposition" of emancipation. The problem is rather: what sort of existence? It is a matter of the reconciliation of human beings and nature, of nonalienated labor as creative activity, the creation of human relationships freed from the struggle for existence. It is a matter of rending asunder the beguiling coherence of aggression and destruction. It is a matter of

> the potentially comprehensive appropriation of the essential human powers objectified in other individuals, in objects, modes of behavior and relationships, their transformation into subjectivity, into a possession . . . of the intellectual and ethical individuality, which presses in its turn for more productive transformation.[11]

This is orthodox Marxism: the "universal individual" as the goal of socialism. Bahro's revolutionary method transposes the ultimate goal to the beginning. Inasmuch as he consistently conceives of the revolution as a "cultural revolution," he invests it from the outset with a meaning totally different from the Maoist sense of this concept with regard to subjectivity and its demands for happiness and the possibilities of happiness. Even the very first measures of socialist construction should free human beings from the "extensive dynamic of the economy." The fundamental measures in this direction are: universal participation in simple work; shortening of psychologically unproductive labor time within the necessary labor time; definition of needs, differentiating only with regard to age, sex, and talent.[12] Once again the libertarian idealism which announces the *telos* of historical materialism, finds expression:

> The problem is to drive forward the "overproduction" of consciousness, so as to put the whole historical past "on its head," and make the idea into the *decisive* material force, to guide things to a radical transformation that goes still deeper than the customary transition from one forma-

tion to another within one and the same civilization. What we are now facing, and what has in fact already begun, is a *cultural revolution* in the truest sense of the term: a *transformation of the entire subjective form of life of the masses. . . .*[13]

Bahro repudiates unequivocally the simplistic argument that a country having to engage in more or less hostile competition with the economically and militarily stronger capitalist countries cannot afford the construction of an integral socialism. This is said to be the situation of actually existing socialism with regard to Western capitalism. Bahro answers with a generally repressed yet nonetheless illuminating hypothesis: The situation could be just the reverse, namely, the construction of a free socialist society could exert a "transforming pressure" on Western countries.[14]

Bahro's analysis implies the provocative thesis that socialist strategy is essentially the same before and after the revolution. The cultural revolution is a total transformation, but even before the revolution, its collective subject is oriented in its consciousness and its behavior toward the final goal. This is what occurs in the praxis of *catalyst groups* in all strata of the population, albeit in forms that are more or less isolated from the society as a whole and hence are precarious and often unauthentic. The work of these groups is essentially to demystify and enlighten—in theory and practice. Here again the focus of revolution is on subjectivity. The goal of giving "*priority* to the all-round development of human beings" and "to the increase in their positive capacities for happiness"[15] already determines the elementary stages of subjective emancipation. Rather than serving as a means of escape and privatization of the political, of pottering about with and mollycoddling the ego, the "journey inwards" serves to politicize surplus consciousness and imagination:

> For much as the "journey inwards," the internalization of individual existence, involves a component of emotional abstraction from everything objective, its fundamental content naturally is and remains the same overcoming of alienation, the same metamorphosis of the civilization created by our species, that Hegel saw as the major work of the subjective spirit.[16]

Political education requires a radical "mental upswing," an "emotional uplift," which "particularly inspires the majority of young people directly at the level of the political and philosophical ideal."[17]

The revolution of subjectivity is the revolution of needs which Bahro sees as the precondition of universal emancipation. The main tendency of such a revolution of needs is clearly indicated: "away from the appropriation of the material means of subsistence and enjoyment that is characterized principally by consumption" and "towards the appropriation of culture"; in other words, the "far-reaching elimination of material incentives."[18] The domination of compensatory interests, which reproduce material incentive over and over again, must be broken: not through a policy of reducing consumption but through a "genuine equalization in the distribution of those consumer goods which determine the standard of living." In all the talk about the insatiability of human needs, Bahro sees only a "reaction to existing conditions."

The reconciliation of material and intellectual culture *within* material culture requires the *abolition* of the performance principle with regard to income distribution, and its *realization* with respect to the development of nonalienated creative work and nonalienated enjoyment. The reduction of necessary labor time and the burden of alienated labor makes possible this reversal; it also heals the rift between subjectivity and objectivity by the "opening up of a general space for freedom for self-realization and growth in personality in the realm of necessity itself,"[19] and through the incorporation of nature into this free space.

Bahro ridicules the anxiety among the New (and Old) Left over reintroducing bourgeois, or even petit bourgeois concepts such as personality, mind, and inwardness into Marxism; indeed, it is within Marxism that these concepts can be authentically transcended. He wastes no words on the reproach of idealistic deviations, etc. He uses these terms, not in order to rescue once again the humanistic young Marx, but in order to develop the transcending content of the categories of political economy. Exploitation, surplus value, profit, abstract labor, are not only categories of inhumanity that have acquired objective form under capitalism; they are also the negation of that inhumanity by that socialism which has now become an objective possibility. The realization of this socialism, which is blocked under capitalism, is the object of the cultural revolution.

The cultural revolution encompasses the ethical and aesthetic dimensions as well. Bahro makes only a suggestive allusion to the ethics of personal relations: Eros, education and marriage are, as

far as possible, to be brought "into harmony with one another."[20]
Aesthetic motivation becomes operative in

> . . . a shift of priorities away from the exploitation of nature by material
> production towards the adaptation of production to the natural cycle,
> from expanded reproduction to simple reproduction, from the raising of
> labor productivity to care for the conditions and culture of labor. . . .[21]

Production also "according to the laws of beauty" (Marx). The
precondition for this is a science and technology suited to human
beings and nature.

It is time to pose the key question: Assuming that Bahro's theory
of the foundation of socialism has been conceptually and empirically demonstrated, how can the transition from the existing order
be conceived? Revolution remains the precondition: now more than
ever before, it is true that a revolution is necessary to obtain reforms.
For the countries of actually existing socialism, where private ownership of the means of production has been abolished, the fall of
the dictatorship of the political bureaucracy would already be the
first revolution. Bahro believes that the opposition within the bureaucracy is widespread enough for such an overthrow to be a real
possibility. But what is the situation in the capitalist countries,
whose objective "ripeness' for revolution has long since been recognized? Both question and answer lie beyond the bounds of
Bahro's analysis, but it provides some important indications.

A summing up of the critique of the
Marxist-Leninist model of revolution

Today it is evident to what degree the Marxist-Leninist model for
revolution has become historically obsolete. There are two major
reasons for this:

1. In countries where the ruling class has at its disposal strong
military and paramilitary organizations equipped with the most
advanced weaponry, and on whose loyalty it can count, armed rebellions and seizure of power by the revolutionary masses are beyond the realm of real possibility. This is the case in the most highly
developed countries.

2. With its tremendous productivity, late capitalism has created
a broad material basis for the integration of diverse interests within
the dependent population. The very concept of revolutionary
masses has become questionable for these countries. This does not

mean that the (expanded) working class has "made its peace" with the system. The policy of economic cooperation and confrontation may very well become political and yet not transcend the system itself in the direction of socialism. The tendency is rather toward a new *populism*; a popular rather than class opposition, for which armed uprising is not on the horizon, to say nothing of the seizure of power.

Toward an analysis of late capitalism and a new concept of revolution

Working class, intelligentsia, the collective worker, and the people

Is it possible to develop another model of revolution on the basis of the current tendencies in class relations?

The construction of such a model requires that we revise the traditional Marxian concept of class, and proceeding from there, that we develop a concept appropriate to late capitalism. This is especially necessary for the concept of the working class. It is sufficient to briefly mention the well-known facts:

1. The nonidentity of the working class and the proletariat. Into the twentieth century, "proletariat" remained the orthodox and official Marxian term for the working class. But integral to the Marxian concept is the misery, the deprivation of rights, the negation of bourgeois society, by virtue of which the proletariat is not a class of this society. For today's working class this is no longer true.

2. According to Marx, the proletariat constitutes the majority of the population in developed capitalism. The category of workers which today most closely corresponds to the proletariat, that is, those directly engaged in the process of material production, no longer comprises the majority.[22]

3. The restriction of the concept of "working class" to "productive" workers, i.e., to those who create surplus value, is untenable. The creation and realization of surplus value are not two separate processes, but rather two phases and stages of the same overall process: the accumulation of capital.

4. In late capitalism the separation between manual and intellectual labor has been diminished by the "intellectualization" of the labor process itself, and by the growing number of intellectuals employed in that process. White-collar workers, salaried employees, even those who are "unproductive," whose incomes are often lower than those of blue-collar workers, belong to the working class insofar as they do not share decision-making power over the means of production. But even the more highly paid white-collar workers in the distribution and administrative processes belong to the working class: they are divorced from the means of production and sell their labor power to capital or its institutions. This *expanded* working class comprises the great majority of the population.

5. Class consciousness? The (expanded) working class is itself split into manifold layers, with very different, and in some cases opposing, interests. The trend is toward a dominance of compensatory interests, which seek satisfaction through active or passive participation in the system. Petit bourgeois rather than radical consciousness prevails.

In fact, late capitalism has expanded the labor necessary for its reproduction through the growth of the sector comprising the middle layers between the small class that actually rules and the industrial workers. The society reproduces itself by generating more and more unproductive work and spreading it throughout the population. The fundamental contradiction between capital and labor continues to exist in all its sharpness, but in this period it has become totalized: almost the entirety of the dependent population is "labor" in opposition to capital. This would also redeem the Marxian concept of a socialist revolution as a transformation carried through by the majority of the population.

This dichotomy characterizes late capitalist society, which is reproduced by the *"collective worker"* and controlled by a small clique. The collective worker becomes the *people*, constituted by the dependent layers of the population. Within this unity contradictions are rife. There is no people's consciousness [*Volksbewusstsein*] which would correspond to a class consciousness. The various compensatory interests extend over the full range of material and intellectual culture, from radicalism to conservatism and fascism, from the will to achieve to the desire to abolish work. Democratic integration allows for such a differentiation within the unity of dependency. Can the interest in a *universal* emancipation burst forth within it?

In all likelihood, social reproduction at the customary level of consumption will become ever more difficult: late capitalism itself gives rise to oversaturation of the market and the increasing difficulty of accumulation. The system will become more repressive and will bring the contradiction between the capitalist mode of production and the real possibilities of liberation ever more explosively into consciousness.

Class consciousness and rebellious subjectivity

Whose consciousness? Not the consciousness of a particular class (the industrial proletariat in late capitalism *is* a particular class within the all-embracing totality of "the people"), but the consciousness of individuals from all strata. Just as universal emancipation, in accordance with its *telos*, aims at the emancipation-in-solidarity [*solidarische Befreiung*] of the individual as individual, so the preparation for that emancipation is also grounded in individuals: individuals from all strata, who, despite all differences, constitute a potential unity by virtue of their common interest. They are the potential subject of an oppositional *praxis*, which is often still concentrated in and limited to unorganized groups and movements. Here, in these groups and movements, exists the *"collective intellectual."*

Bahro defines the collective intellectual primarily in terms of the otherness of a consciousness and an instinctual structure, which rebel against subjugation and press toward a renunciatory praxis. A quite unacademic definition, but one devoid of that ever popular and cheap ridicule of eggheads, armchair socialists, etc., which has always served to defame the concrete utopia and to sacrifice the idea of revolution to the existing order.

The diffuse, almost organizationless opposition of the collective intellectual has no mass base, and the charge of elitism and voluntarism is all too easy. This is the expression of a fetishism of the masses and stands in direct contradiction to the history of revolutionary movements under capitalism, which have acquired their mass base only in the process of revolution itself. The basis on which the initiative of the masses can become a determining force for socialist emancipation emerges out of an antistate politics which from the very outset implements measures that deprive the traditional mentality and its affirmation of their social foundation, in the first place (as already mentioned) through a radical reorganization of labor (abolition of its hierarchical organization) and a new "economy of time." But, if the principle of self-determination is otherwise to remain a leading principle, this means that centralization must be abolished; to be reconstituted, however, as the institution of the *plan*, which represents and serves the general interest. This centralization is the nucleus of socialist dictatorship; in it, necessary and surplus repression are forced together.

The intelligentsia can fulfill its preparatory function only if it preserves its own surplus consciousness, in which the existing order is concretely transcended. Its prerevolutionary potential and its ambivalent, often contradictory relationship to the masses is rooted in the structure of society. The privilege of education, the result of the separation between intellectual and manual labor, isolates the intelligentsia from the masses. However, this has also given it the opportunity to think freely, to learn, to understand the facts in their social context, and—to transmit this knowledge. This opportunity must be won in struggle against the institutionalized education system (and on its terrain!). Participation in the privilege of education is today a question not only of income but also of *time*, which the masses, exploited full time, do not have at their disposal. Democratization of the educational system must therefore go hand in hand with a reduction in labor time. Democratization does not require the popularization of learning and knowledge. This has always led to a leveling of the transcendent content of thought, the enervation of surplus consciousness and emancipatory interests, and has served to reproduce the existing order. Rather, the human beings who are imprisoned in their societies, must be brought to the point where they can make unmutilated knowledge and imagination their own—which in turn already presupposes the revolution.

Knowledge and the communication of knowledge have evolved within a horizon of social relations which codetermine the course of research and inquiry. Theoretical and applied science are two phases in the same process; in late capitalism the difference between the two is reduced by the growing role of intellectual labor in the process of material production. Accordingly, it has become necessary to broaden the privilege of education through "general education." Hand in hand with the democratization, however, goes a decline in the emancipatory power of knowledge. A large number of the achievements of science and technology have benefited aggression and destruction, or have served as gadgets, as toys, and sports for the compensatory interests of the dependent population and their gratification, and have reinforced subaltern consciousness.

Instinctual structure and revolution

The unity of progress and repression facilitates the management of the politico-economic contradictions within the global structure of late capitalism. The question "For how much longer?" cannot be answered rationally: theory is not prophecy. Nonetheless, it remains true (and the facts point in the general direction) that capitalism produces its own gravediggers. However, these are no longer the proletariat, but the collective worker, and the consciousness dammed up within it—rebellious subjectivity. Just as capitalist progress itself creates the objective conditions for its own abolition (structural unemployment, saturation of the market, inflation, intracapitalist conflicts, competition with communism . . .), so it creates the *subjective* conditions as well. "Surplus consciousness" is only one component of subjectivity: its emancipatory interest extends to the knowledge of what is happening now and what must happen, but the domination of compensatory interests prevents the translation of consciousness into practice. The subjective side of the revolution is not only a matter of consciousness, and of action guided by knowledge; it is also a question of the emotions, of instinctual structure, at each of the two levels of change: (a) the radical critique of things as they are; (b) the positive and concrete anticipation of freedom, i.e., the presence of the goal in the here and now of life.

The sociohistorical "ripeness" of subjective conditions includes not only political consciousness, but also the vital, existential *need* for a revolution, anchored in the instinctual structure of individuals; it includes (at least in the twentieth century), not only the will to survive and prosper, but also the cessation of the struggle for existence, of enslaving production, and the endless process of exchange; in short, the desire for a *joyous* freedom, for self-determination.

To say that something is anchored in the instinctual structure (assuming the truth of Freudian theory) is to say that in class society the revolution is "invested" with Eros' drive for emancipation from socially determined surplus repression, for gratification and intensification of the life instincts. (Primary civilizing repression, such as the incest taboo, toilet training, and certain forms of social intercourse, are no longer obstacles to emancipation.) The essential demands of the revolution—abolition of alienated labor, equal opportunities for self-determination, pacification of nature, solidarity—thus have an *erotic basis* in subjectivity (just as fascism has its roots in the destructive character structure). Society, and emancipation as a sociohistorical process, act through Eros itself—in sharp distinction to sexuality and sexual liberation, which can take place just as well within class society. The unfolding of the life instincts, Eros, requires social change, revolution; the revolution requires the instinctual foundation.

Social change is not merely a change in human nature; it is also a change in external nature. The kind of nature that is suitable to capitalism may very well turn out to be an insurmountable *limit* of the system. To be sure, it is very efficiently subordinated to the interests of capital, but there remains an unmastered residue that could become decisive for further development.

The natural limits of capitalism become visible in those protest movements in which nature becomes a potential force for the transformation of society. Nature becomes such a force as the concrete counter-image of its incorporation into the capitalist production process, and not only in the sense that the organized defense of nature threatens the profits of big industry and the interests of the military. In the rebellion against nuclear energy and the general poisoning of the environment, the struggle for nature is at the same time a struggle against the existing society, while the protection of nature is at the same time a challenge to capital.

But even apart from this, the ecology movement has psychological roots as well. Nature, experienced as the domain of happiness, fulfillment, and gratification, is the environment of Eros—the antithesis of the performance principle applied to nature. This antithesis (for the most part unarticulated, and even repressed) is also alive in the women's movement. The performance principle is the historically developed form of patriarchal domination. To be sure, socialist society will also have its performance principle—the negation of the present one. It would determine precisely that dimension of social life which is devalued or blocked under capitalism: competition in the unfolding and enjoyment of the creative faculties of individuals and the creation of preconditions for using the scientific-technical achievements of capitalism in the service of the common interest, instead of in the service of the private interests of capital. Under capitalism, the overcoming of the performance principle appears only in false garb, embodied in the contrasts and fantasies that have become stylized as "woman's nature" (receptivity, sensitivity, emotional capacity, closeness to nature, etc.). These images reveal the biopsychological dimension of the women's movement. Latent in women's struggle for true equality and equal rights, for universal emancipation in all domains of culture, is the rebellion of nature which has been made into an object.

The anti-authoritarian movement, the ecology movement, and the women's movement have intrinsic links with one another: they are the manifestation (still very unorganized and diffuse) of an instinctual structure, the ground of a transformed consciousness which is shaking the domination of the performance principle and of alienated productivity.[23] This opposition thus mobilizes the forces of revolution in a dimension which has been neglected by Marxism (and not only by Marxism), a dimension that could halt capitalist progress in the late stage of its development: rebellious human and external nature.

In reestablishing nature as a factor in political praxis these movements distinguish themselves fundamentally from the escapist movements in the New Left, where nature, elevated to absolute status, becomes the criterion of a nonalienated, authentic existence. The escapist movements invoke nature (both inner and external) against intellect, immediacy against reflection. They cultivate the very dichotomy that is supposed to be abolished in the process of emancipation. The cult of immediacy is reactionary: it is a retreat from nature as a force in the social dynamic (as subject-object), and a reversion to nature as pure subjectivity, which as such already represents the true and the good against the false and the evil in society. But in pure immediacy the false and the evil are not overcome, they are only repressed or shifted onto others.

The "theses on the alternative and escapist movements" criticize this ambivalence, which prevails throughout the movement:

> The criterion of political action has long since ceased to be correct theoretical analysis, in particular, a critical analysis of the economy; it has

been replaced by the subjective experiences of the respective individuals. Thus one wants to experience, preferably in one's own person, that for which one is supposed to act. However, what at one stage had represented an extremely important politicizing and critical factor with regard to orthodoxy and dogmatism, has today been transformed into a problematic cult of needs in many areas. No longer accessible to theoretical analysis and rejecting every irritating element of reflection, experience has been reduced to the average quantum of emotional stimuli. It has thus lost its refractory quality and to a large extent it has become amenable to integration. Thus absolutized, experience has been transformed from a medium of autonomy into a medium of integration and adaptation.[24]

The proposition that capitalist domination and exploitation of nature is *eo ipso* domination and exploitation of human beings as well, can now be put more concretely. Capitalist progress is the transformation of nature under the principle of increased productivity and profitability. Nature becomes mere objectivity: a universe of things and relations among things, whose *telos* is service in the process of production and reproduction (nature as organized re-creation). This requires the suppression of nature as resistance to the performance principle. Since inner and external nature constitute a (historical) totality, the performance principle operates *against* Eros' striving to develop itself in the life-world, against emancipation from the omnipotence of alienated labor. Hence the increasingly internalized repression imposed by society on human beings. Nature must be destroyed, it must be assimilated to the destructive society. That nature which is still whole (although not immune to the possibility of its own destruction), must not be allowed to become a countercultural life-world in which individuals find happiness and fulfillment in opposition to the well-being provided by society. But the more obvious the possibilities created by capitalism for emancipation from the performance principle become, and the more the expanded reproduction of capitalism propels the destruction of nature, the more pressing becomes the overactivation of destructive energies. The "blend" of the two primary drives becomes denser: Eros itself seems to be charged with an aggressivity that individuals often direct against their own bodies (rock and punk music, brutality in sports, drugs . . .).

The anchoring of the opposition in an emancipatory instinctual structure should make possible *qualitative* change, the totality

of the revolution. But the development of an emancipatory instinctual structure is only conceivable as a social process, and it is
precisely this process which produces and reproduces the repressive instinctual structure that internalizes capitalism. Again, the
vicious circle: How can an emancipatory instinctual structure
emerge in and against a repressive society whose rulers (unlike the
opposition) have long since learned to mobilize the psyche?

Only personal *experience* [*Erlebnis*], the experience of individuals that breaks through subaltern consciousness, leads or forces
the individual to see and feel things and people in a different way,
to think other thoughts. Bahro quotes Gorky:

> Everything unusual prevents people from living the way they would wish.
> Their aspirations, when they have such, are never for fundamental change
> in their social habits, but always simply for more of the same. The basic
> theme of all their moans and complaints is: "Don't stop us from living
> the way we're accustomed!" Vladimir Ilyich Lenin was a man who knew
> like no one before him how to stop people living their accustomed life.[25]

The development of the instinctual structure is linked throughout to that of consciousness: erotic and destructive energies are
realized within already existing social frameworks. The instinctual
structure becomes emancipatory only in union with an emancipatory *consciousness* which defines the possibilities and limits of
this realization and absorbs that which is merely instinctual into
itself.

The social process of revolution begins in those individuals for
whom emancipation has become a vital need. However, it is just
these individuals who have advanced beyond the Ego. The emancipatory instinctual structure makes *solidarity* the force of the life
instincts. Although they are "value free," the primary drives themselves already imply other human beings. This holds true for Eros
and for destructive energy alike. They contain the universal: they
are drives of the individual, but of the individual as "species being."

The foundational experience [*Erfahrung*] which roots the need
to refuse in the psyche of individuals, thus never remains at the level
of personal subjective experience [*Erlebnis*], the level of an immediate relation to the self. In the Ego the "journey inwards"
encounters others and the Other (society and nature) not as mere
limits to the Ego but as powers constitutive of it. The foundational
immediate experience, in which relevance for the concrete individ-

ual could serve as the verifying criterion, is such only as *mediated* immediacy, and the behavior that motivates this experience is that of a comprehending subjectivity that goes beyond the Ego. "Politics in the first person" is a contradiction *in adjecto*. The journey inwards is necessary, because the dynamic of Ego and Id is obscured by efficient social control and because individuality itself becomes a commodity under late capitalism.[26] If, however, the journey stops at the unmediated Ego, and the manifestations of that Ego are proclaimed as authentic, the journey falls short of its goal; it succumbs to the fetishism of the commodity world and the counterculture built up on that basis becomes part and parcel of the established culture.

In conclusion, I have emphasized the ambivalence in the turn toward subjectivity. Here too there is the danger of making a virtue of necessity. The necessity resides in the isolation of the radical emancipation movements (especially the socialist ones) from the masses and in the structural weakness of these movements in the face of the material and ideological might of the established apparatus of domination. In the light of this constellation, protest and rebellion beyond (or this side of) the political and economic class struggle appear as *retreat*. This holds even for the militant opposition within the industrial working class (local self-management, factory takeovers, wildcat strikes). Compared with the great mass actions in the history of the labor movement, these seem to be feeble trailings of a revolutionary tradition.

But the appearance is not the whole. Movements such as the worker opposition, citizens' initiatives, communes, student protests, are authentic forms of rebellion determined by the particular social situation, counter-blows against the centralization and totalization of the apparatus of domination. Not being strong enough to oppose this apparatus with an effective centralized force of its own, the rebellion concentrates itself in local and regional bases, where there is still a certain latitude and freedom of movement and room to act. And precisely this retrogression *anticipates* the objective tendencies toward disintegration in the existing society, namely the crumbling away of the system as a result of the formation of economic and social units of autonomous control. Such a development would mean that the concept of "the masses" had indeed been transcended, and hence that one aspect of liberation had already been achieved: a mode of life in which individuals feel and act in solidarity with one another.

Summary

Bahro's analysis breaks through the fetishism of Marxist pseudo-orthodoxy and the counterculture of immediacy. His dialectical analysis leads to an authentic "internal" advance of Marxist theory, informed by the comprehended reality. The radicalism of its perceptions is primarily revealed in the following key points of theory and praxis:

1) The rejection of the Marxist-Leninist model of proletarian revolution, which has long since been surpassed in advanced industrial society (seizure of power by the revolutionary masses, dictatorship of the proletariat). The elaboration of a new model corresponding to real social trends.

2) A new definition of class relations (both in actually existing socialism and in late capitalism); the expanded working class; the proletariat as a minority in it; the integration and extension of dependency; the transformation of the working class into the "people"; its conservatism.

3) The key role of the intelligentsia in the transitional period, corresponding to its position in the process of production. The fetishism of the masses.

4) The shift of the focal point of the social dynamic onto subjectivity; the "journey inwards" and its ambivalence; consciousness as a revolutionary force.

5) The new formulation (and answer?) of the question of the subject of the revolution—the consequence of point 2.

6) The demonstration that integral socialism is a real possibility if decisive measures are implemented (redistribution of work and income, gradual abolition of the performance principle, a democratic educational system, a council system expanded beyond the factory . . .). The new economy as an economy of time: progressive reduction of socially necessary labor time. The realm of freedom *within* the realm of necessity.

Translated by Michel Vale and Annemarie Feenberg
with the assistance of Andrew Feenberg.
Translation revised by Erica Sherover Marcuse.

Notes

1. Rudolf Bahro, *The Alternative in Eastern Europe* (London: New Left Books, 1978), p. 21.

2. Ibid., p. 266.

3. Ibid., p. 288.

4. Ibid., p. 329.

5. Ibid., pp. 400, 329.

6. Ibid., p. 129.

7. Ibid., p. 241.

8. Ibid., p. 44.

9. Ibid., p. 196.

10. Ibid., p. 258. An alternative rendering of this passage: "do not specific working class interests play, ever more frequently, a basically conservative role?"—E.S.M.

11. Ibid., p. 272.

12. Ibid., p. 415.

13. Ibid., p. 257. An alternative rendering of the first part of this passage: "It is a matter of forcing the 'overproduction' of consciousness so as to stand the historical process 'on its head,' and making the idea into the *decisive* material force. Things are tending toward a radical transformation from one system to another within one and the same civilization."—E.S.M.

14. Ibid., p. 431.

15. Ibid., p. 406.

16. Ibid., p. 267.

17. Ibid., p. 375. An alternative rendering of this passage: "Political education requires a radical 'psychic impetus' [*Aufschwung*], an 'emotional uplifting' [*Erhebung*], which raises the majority of the youth in particular directly onto the plane of the politico-philosophical ideal."—E.S.M.

18. Ibid., pp. 402ff.

19. Ibid., p. 406. An alternative rendering of this passage: by "opening up a general free space for the self realization and growth of personality in the realm of necessity as well."—E.S.M.

20. Ibid., p. 291.

21. Ibid., p. 407.

22. In 1972, 60% of the gainfully employed in the USA were in the services sector. The Congressional Joint Economic Committee estimates a figure of 80% for 1980 (cited in Daniel Bell, *The Coming of Post-Industrial Society*, and Al Goodman, in *In These Times*, October 18-24, 1978).

23. See my article "Marxism and Feminism," in *Zeitmessungen*, Frankfurt, Suhrkamp, 1975.

24. Wolfgang Kraushaar, in *Autonomie oder Ghetto?* (Neue Kritik Publishers, Frankfurt/M, 1978), pp. 45f.

25. Bahro, p. 100.

26. Kraushaar, pp. 37ff.

HELMUT FLEISCHER

Bahro's Contribution
to the Philosophy of Socialism

Rudolf Bahro, as we know, received his academic training in philosophy. Fortunately for his philosophical cast of mind, however, he was not received into the guild of professional GDR philosophers. Instead he successively traversed a number of domains of social praxis, where he was able to restore the concept of philosophy as "its times articulated in thought"—an encouraging contrast to the scholastic notion of philosophy, cultivated and administered by the guild, as a kind of alienated consciousness detached from the social reality around it. Bahro writes: "By philosophy here we mean of course simply the general concept for what is contained in the overall range of social sciences from the standpoint of the subject, inasmuch as this is oriented to the question of meaning and links truth to humanity's subjective practice."[1]

It is natural that the principal interest in Bahro's book should derive from his substantive descriptions of the emergence, mode of functioning, and future prospects of the "protosocialist" social formation. Indeed, for many readers the two first analytical sections will serve as but a background against which the most urgent question of the times may be posed: what's going to happen now, or rather, what should happen now? This question is dealt with by Bahro in the third, programmatic section of his book, entitled "A Strategy for a Communist Alternative." In judging his book as an attempt to arrive at a *philosophical synthesis*, I shall be approaching it from a somewhat different perspective. Above all, I shall be interested in the *theoretical conceptual framework* Bahro has used to synthesize our historical experience with socialism up to now.

His attempt has a long historical tradition behind it. The question is: what new does he contribute to theorizing on socialism, what existing limitations to theory does he surmount, and what limitations does he not surmount? I refer here to those attempts to provide a critical account of socialist movements and revolutions that have gone beyond mere rebuttal from an outsider's position (as for example, in Karl Kautsky as early as 1919) and fastened on the "inner logic" of a partisan involvement (such as we can find in the factional differences within the communist movement since the days of Rosa Luxemburg's critique of the Russian Revolution). In the postrevolutionary factional struggles within the Russian revolutionary party, this "self-criticism of communism" was soon brutally suppressed and thereafter could be undertaken only from without—as by Trotsky, for example—with no direct day-to-day contact with the vital forces of the postrevolutionary society.

In the process of internal self-criticism which resumed at the end of the Stalin era, Bahro's undertaking definitely represents a high point with respect to the vast range of topics he covers in his compendious text, as well as in the dimensions of the regained theoretical sovereignty it represents, and finally as regards his revitalized theoretical categories, i.e., the ideas he utilizes to digest this sociohistorical experience. We should not view these ideas as merely a personal preference of the author as compared to his diverse predecessors (such as Roy Medvedev in the USSR, J. Kuron and K. Modzelewski in Poland, S. Stojanović in Jugoslavia, or the Czech contributions to socialist theory), but rather as a positive consequence of the fact that Bahro had behind him an above-average amount of personal experience on which to draw (and that not only of a scientific nature), and moveover, in a social context that featured perhaps the highest degree of differentiation within the world array of protosocialist states.

I should like to direct particular attention to the following points with regard to Bahro's theory:

1) What is his relationship to the Marxist theoretical tradition? What analytic and critical evaluative use does he make of the precepts of the Marxist doctrine of socialism?

2) How does he define the epoch-making significance of the socialist movement in the modern world, specifically the sociohistorical contours and potential of this movement?

3) How does he define the sociohistorical context and future prospects and potential of the Russian Revolution?

4) What logical interpretive categories, what key concepts, what interpretive models move onto center stage in his analysis of protosocialist societies (and the socialist movement in general)?

5) How does Bahro introduce the perspective or normative values that are crucial for a progressive extension of the processes of socialism? That is, what factors define the "human emancipation" that is the purport of the "cultural revolution" he envisages?

In discussing these questions, I will have occasion to mention not a few things that I consider to constitute an important advance in our thinking on the subject of socialism. However, I shall not be able to refrain from observing a number of questionable points as well. On the whole, Bahro's is an intellectual accomplishment of which hardly any of us here in the West would have been capable. Nonetheless, from a more "contemplative" position, such as so many of us assume, a number of problems may perhaps be formulated more sharply and some counterpoint may be added to the synthesizing process going on as part of the present discussion. To put it succinctly: if one examines Bahro's text from a methodological perspective, a quite pronounced leaning toward the view that sees history as a sequence of essentially *predefined tasks* is in evidence very early in his analysis of past historical events, and even more so in his anticipatory reflections on the future—what historical task did the October Revolution have? what was the task of the working class? what are our tasks today? what "should" and "must" yet be accomplished? It would seem to me that what is needed here is to tie the content of the actions in question more closely to "materialistically" demonstrable instances of "the real life process." Bahro furnishes an explicit justification for his renaissance of the utopian; but it is probable that in this he was bound by his situation. Indeed, in situations of extreme impediment there has always been a temptation to refashion practical philosophical hypotheses into crutches to help the forward-looking mind to hobble freely onward, while the inert social mass still stagnates in inactivity.

Marxism in perspective

For decades, adherence to "Marxism" was the article of faith of those who refused to allow their conviction of the profoundly destructive nature of the capitalist social formation to be undermined by any illusions of social peace, and of those who imposed on revolutionary practice a meaning that went beyond the limits of capitalist society. That this "Marxism" became so largely an article of faith was due to a considerable extent to the overall situation of confrontation, as well as to the power relationships within which intellectuals found themselves once they had extricated themselves from the clockwork of capitalist society (or from historically older hierarchical systems) and discovered a socially more potent partner in deed, namely, factory workers who were in opposition to their life conditions at a very elementary level (or craftsmen who were against assimilation into the factories).

The real power of this workers' emancipation movement served these intellectuals as a basis for a much expanded definition of the historical potential for freedom. This practical hypothesis then crystallized into the axiom of the "historical mission of the working class"—the very term is already rife with ideological implications. In Marx's thought, this (and the concomitant hypostatization of Marxist premises into a consolidated body of thought, "Marxism") had a very frail logical justification at best, and in fact, reflected if anything a quite different line of reasoning. Indeed, Marx was not merely being ironic or smug when he once said that he was no Marxist. The emancipatory meaning of the entire undertaking, to say nothing of the key precepts concerning social forces and ideologies, is fundamentally opposed to the transformation of the theoretical achievement of Marx the *citoyen* into a confession, i.e., "Marxism." Only the proud defiance of a dissident minority, outlawed and ridiculed by the ruling clique and their retinue, could be sufficient psychological motivation for wanting to make some outward show of one's confession of faith; and particularly when turned inward, back on the socialist formation itself, the hypostatization of Marxism could indeed be only the expression of an uneliminated constitutional weakness. On the other side, manifestations of non-Marxism or anti-Marxism were in fact often enough reflections of a lack of clarity of thought in comprehending social reality, or simply evasions even to the point of "cowardice before the enemy." Thus, there was yet another reason why Marxism acquired the status of a faith.

Today we may ask whether we perhaps have now arrived, or shall soon arrive, at the historical point where an advanced socialist thought, become more sure of itself and of its difficulties, can now give up the confessionalization of Marxism and adopt a less coercive reliance on Marx as an aid in formulating ideas and directions. I think that Bahro is at least very close to this point. He finds that "it is no longer sufficient to be a Marxist in the traditional sense."[2] He thus moves, visibly free, nimbly and unconstrained, back and forth between tried and true Marxist assumptions and those that have become untenable, consigning Marx to his historical place.

What is really decisive is not the "Marxist" tone of an argument or the programs for action presumed to derive from such argument; it is rather the social aspects of action and the form of social relations that precede any theory or intellectual effort which may acquire a more or less far reaching "socialistic" or "communistic" relevance. Thus, for Bahro it was quite relevant for both discussion and intellectual consistency to call to mind the four concrete elements of Marx's communism: the assumptions and postulates of the socialization of the forces of production, the abolition of the old division of labor, the abolition of political domination, and the unification of mankind.[3] This becomes important for working out the fundamental difference between "Marx's project" and actually existing socialism, but not for the purpose of exploiting this difference to denounce actually existing socialism. For Bahro, comparison of the ideal with the reality serves a quite different function, and if his dismissal of the ideological claims of the lawyers of state socialism that the ideal has been realized takes on a polemical tone, this is only due to the hypocrisy of that apologetic window-dressing.[4] However, neither is it a question of using the programmatic doctrine inherited from Marx as a yardstick against which to measure the achievements of history.

> Historical materialism itself prohibits us from judging whether conditions in the Soviet Union, People's China, etc., realize "authentic Marxism" . . . What is authentic is not the letter of theory, but the historical process.[5]

In the introduction to his book Bahro sets a clear methodological line when he rejects any critique that attempts to compare the ideal with reality. Practice can, of course, be compared with theory, "but it should not be measured by it."[6] The deeper one penetrates theoretically and analytically into problematic relationships, the more one can renounce denunciation and invective.[7]

In taking this position, Bahro draws a distinction between himself and most Marxist critics, calling them "deformation theorists,"[8] referring thereby not only to their theoretical consistency, or lack of it, but also to the practical upshot of their criticisms.

> Most Marxist critics of our orthodoxy make things too easy for themselves by taking a merely methodological approach. They stick to the confined categories of ideal and reality, so that discussion can be easily shifted to an undecidable conflict as to whether the realization of the ideal is "inevitably still imperfect" or actually "bad." The "idealists" who speak explicitly of deformations, denounce the departure from some supposed principles, and demand the introduction or restoration of various norms, while they may have temporary demagogic success, have neither theoretically nor in practical political terms reached the ground on which their opponents stand: the deviating reality.[9]

In particular, Bahro mentions Stojanović's criticism of socialism in his book entitled *Between Ideal and Reality*. Describing the critical point he states that Stojanović, after he has shown the socioeconomic roots of the contrary types of state bureaucratism and anarcholiberalism, "in the next breath expects these same dominant conditions to produce more democratic socialist individuals," yet does not think that saying this is an abandonment of a Marxist materialistic approach.[10] Here I should like to object to Bahro by saying that one could better do justice to Stojanović and criticize him persuasively on other points as well.[11] Nonetheless, I agree with the main tenor of Bahro's criticism of the normative way of thinking in questions of socialism, and consider this an eminently important line to take for any further reflection on what socialism means.

All in all, an advanced reflection on the process of socialism could make use of its Marxist theoretical heritage in a manner that might be described alternatively as follows: Many (but by no means all) of the Marxist postulates for analyzing society are still useful for illuminating the evolution of socialist societies. However, no constitutive theoretical use, either normative or programmatic, can be made—especially of those of Marx's aphoristic sayings that express the desiderata, i.e., the "hopeful" constituents, all that is normative or programmatic in his thought.

Forces of socialist transformation

In constructing his theory of society and its historical evolution, Bahro's foremost concern was to demonstrate that the "proto-socialist" societies that have emerged as a consequence of the Russian October Revolution can only marginally be understood as having grown out of the conditions established by industrial capitalism in its most developed phase and by the forces it set free; the origins of these societies are rather to be sought in the archaic formation that has come to be called the "Asiatic mode of production" (although it can be found worldwide). Indeed, this heritage has had a far more telling effect on the real possibilities of postrevolutionary development than anything the revolutionary party carried home with it from the hopes and expectations of West European socialism. From the outset, the real problem—beyond any programs—was what was bound to be preserved of Russian society "when the capitalists were chased out together with these landed proprietors who were yesterday still semi-bureaucratic, semi-feudal . . . Junkers? What survived . . . was the peasant basis of Tsarist despotism, along with its 'petty bourgeois' periphery . . . as well as the 'countless army of officials, which swarms over Russia and plunders it and here constitutes a real social estate' (Engels)."[12]

But let's put aside for a moment the question of what the Bolsheviks nonetheless had actively been able to do with this heritage. Let me first of all merely delimit the theoretical frame of reference within which, according to Bahro, the historical experience of the entire socialist movement and its revolutions down to the present may be interpreted. Let us examine, for instance the following statements:

> The October revolution, already, was not, or was at least *far more* than, the (from our confined European perspective of waiting) "deformed" representative of the proletarian rising in the West that has not taken place. It was and is above all the first *anti-imperialist revolution* in what was still a *predominantly precapitalist country*, even though it had begun a capitalist development of its own, with a socioeconomic structure half-feudal, half "Asiatic." Its task was not yet that of socialism, no matter how resolutely the Bolsheviks believed in this, but rather the rapid industrial development of Russia on a noncapitalist road. Only now, when this task is by and large completed, is the struggle for socialism on the agenda in the Soviet Union.[13]

Now here we have a twist of thought that I think may be viewed as quite questionable: namely, the viewing of historical processes in terms of "tasks" that are "objectively" given and must be solved. The highest-order "task" is ultimately universal and total "human emancipation." At an earlier stage in the process, and perhaps even coordinated instrumentally with this highest goal, is the task of spreading the benefits of civilization worldwide; but it was just this last task which could not be solved by the noncapitalist way of industrialization, and the means used were quite unequivocally subordinated to this task. "Because of the positive task of driving the masses into an industrialization which they could not immediately desire . . . the Soviet Union had to have a single, iron, 'Petrine' leadership."[14] "In Russia, the revolution had to dispense with Soviet democracy in order to save its own life."[15]

For mankind as a whole, Bahro ascribes a positive significance to this solitary road of revolution taken by the more backward peoples, and indeed does this from a perspective that has not been customary for socialists. The socialist movement's detour through Russia had for a long time been seen as a "European accident," but the Chinese revolution gave things a quite different complexion.

> But since the People's Republic of China came into being, but still no proletarian revolution in the West, the indication is that the entire perspective under which we have so far seen the transition to communism stands in need of correction, and in no way just with respect to the time factor. The dissolution of private property in the means of production on the one hand, and universal human emancipation on the other, are separated by an entire epoch.[16]

What is significant here is the fact of the anticipatory revolutions of economically backward nations; but just as significant of course is the failure of the socialist labor movement of the advanced countries to live up to the revolutionary expectations with which Marxists had endowed them.

> History has furnished a decisive corrective to this original Marxist prognosis. While the capitalist order is already in a third phase of its internal contradictions, and *moving* in them instead of succumbing to them, as Marx had predicted for its first phase, and Lenin conclusively for its second, many peoples in the precapitalist countries have set out on their own road towards socialism. The proletarian revolution in the West did

not take place; and its appearance in the form previously anticipated has become ever more improbable.[17]

Seen on an intercontinental scale, it would indeed seem that the revolutions in Russia, China, and so on have contributed more to overall progress "than the proletarian revolutions hoped for in the West could have done."[18] Bahro reaffirms these thoughts in both aspects when he asserts: *"With the revolutions in Russia and China, with the revolutionary process in Latin America, in Africa and in India, humanity is taking the shortest route to socialism."*[19] Further, because a socialist order cannot be "based on material preconditions that are merely provincial in character," the "civilization gap" between the advanced and the backward nations must first be overcome. As regards the working class, Bahro says that it "obviously has a task in Western Europe," but the revolution intended for it at one time in Europe led not to socialism, for which Marx hoped, but to a far more "Prusso-German formation," as Bakunin had predicted.[20]

From his historical reflections and present observations of the "working class" under socialism, and out of basic theoretical considerations, Bahro decisively and uncompromisingly rejects the expectations that had been linked with the traditional labor movement and the segments of the working class sustaining it (still essentially the wage laborers, excluding the technological and administrative intelligentsia); and he insists that it is not he who on this account is a pessimist, but those who hold fast to the old hopes.[21] The historical relativization of Marxist postulates is most decisive on this point, and the concept of a working class beyond capitalism becomes a totally inapplicable concept (the entire seventh chapter deals with this point).

> Precisely under actually existing socialism, it has been shown quite clearly that the industrial proletariat as such has not attained the perspectives predicted of it. . . . That the proletariat is to be . . . the actual collective subject of universal emancipation, remained a philosophical hypothesis, in which the utopian component of Marxism was concentrated.[22]

Marx had himself noted which functional differentiations within the industrial collective worker were growing in importance, but, according to Bahro, he failed to recognize the independent significance of its class-like nature.[23] It has since then become obvious that the pivotal productive force potential rests with engineering (and related occupations)[24] and the thematic stress as regards what now can be called "socialist transformation" shifts from questions of property and political power to the problems of the division of labor and its abolition, as Bahro sketches it out under the heading "cultural revolution."

Concerning the material aspects of Bahro's class analysis, I should like to enter my plea for as open and positive a reception as possible. The difficulties come more from the diverse, almost historically binding tasks that seem to have been set down in some remote transcendent realm. An emancipation that is understood as a "task" is still quite deeply rooted in subalternity. And I find it even more unsatisfactory when from the same perspective the major historical initiatives (or failures of initiative) of our century, displayed in the forces of change being mustered on an international scale, are assessed in terms of a hierarchy and sequence of tasks, rather than simply being regarded from the standpoint of contingent "opportunities" and challenges, of the unplanned conditions and limitations of the possible. I should think that the distinction between saying "the task was otherwise" or "the forces were too weak" is not an unimportant one. We shall come back to this formal question later in our discussion of the reorganization of the basic concepts of social analysis (point 4).

The flaw in Bahro's analysis concerning the "real tasks" of a revolution such as the Russian Revolution of 1917 lies, in my opinion, in the fact that the explanations or justifications are not undertaken in terms of the interests, latitudes for action, and social power of specific circumscribed social groups, but that such particular forces are recognized *a priori* almost unquestioningly as the "attorneys" of an all-embracing social totality. The categorical distinction here is as follows: either one assesses diverse special interests (e.g., the bureaucrats) as an added factor that modifies the collective and general interest as it is objectively defined by the overall situation, or the totality itself is evaluated as the strained, conflict-ridden resultant of particular interests, whatever their number. Bahro himself makes more than clear how the particular interests of the bureaucracy are able to play such a determining role through the sway that bureaucracy holds over the society as a whole:

Finally we should give up the last residues of the illusion that the mass of political and administrative bureaucrats are in any sense communists, who are simply superficially commissarized or bureaucratized. No, the bureaucracy has long since ceased to be merely a superficial and alien form. It has become . . . the political form of existence of a major group of people with pronounced special interests . . . The general interest of society now has to find a way through these special interests . . . precisely as was the case under all previous historical relations of domination.[25]

The historical possibilities of the October Revolution

Bahro's unbending notion of how a social process is to be understood leads him to a very harsh general thesis:

The Bolshevik seizure of power in Russia could lead to no other *social structure* than that now existing, and the more one tries to think through the stations of Soviet history . . . the harder it becomes to draw a limit short of even the most fearsome excesses, and to say that what falls on the other side was absolutely unavoidable.[26]

Bahro himself notes that the critical realism of this analysis may give the appearance of an apology. He counters this objection by pointing out the doubtfulness of the opposing view: "If only people, especially those in the Bolshevik party, had willed more intensely and acted more wisely, if instead of actually existing socialism we had genuine socialism, or at least a different or better road!" And then the reply: "There is no need to be fatalistic to distrust conclusions of this kind."[27]

Nonetheless, Bahro does allow the question (albeit with reservations, it would seem):

Not wanting to leave the idea of a possible better path to complete contingency, I would suggest one point for further reflection. Can we conceive of a different procedure from that of Stalin, given that the aim was to carry through that consensus in the party that was absolutely necessary for a unique but more favorable practice of protosocialist industrialization?[28]

Bahro clearly has here in mind a general possibility, not the individually determined possibilities of 1917, 1934, and 1938—Stalin's specific possibilities. One could conceive of a somewhat different possibility had Lenin not been eliminated from the picture in 1922, to die soon thereafter. "The question of a past possibility is always speculative and inherently unanswerable."[29] Nonetheless, Bahro thinks it is still meaningful to pose the question, insofar as the question of other historical possibilities is still relevant today. Indeed, the question recurs continually, but perhaps it can be profitably reformulated to eliminate the unreal, illusory, idle speculation over unfulfilled yet genuine possibilities, and to pinpoint of what exactly the real historical possibilities consisted (and finally to explore critically whatever ideological aspects may lie implicit in assumptions concerning unrealized possibilities).

On the whole, I would firmly support Bahro's general thesis that the Russian Revolution had but one historical possibility— the one that was actually realized—however much that may seem to fly in the face of the traditions of critical history. Let me quote a passage from one of my earlier writings: "A materialist critique of history does not expect retroactively of the actors more and different things than had been in their power to do and than they had actually achieved; it does not make out of the superior knowledge of its later vantage point a belated 'We know better' that reckons up for the past its greater and for the most part unrealized possibilities. The frame of reference for a retrospective critique of history is not the unspecified margins of 'objective possibility'; rather, it is the range of variation of potential for action that had actually been drawn on. The other 'possibilities,' the actually existing ones, are the possibilities that other people actually put into practice, i.e., within the limits of their powers at the time. These are limited particular possibilities, not a surplus added to overall possibility. In the strict sense, a retrospective critique of history consists in distinguishing and earmarking the divergent social meanings entailed by particular actions, and it ends with a definition of the historical limits beyond which no individual initiative could have gone within the given constellation of conditions and forces."[30]

Accordingly, the concept of "possibility" cannot be applied in a global and general manner to a total formation in any given total situation; rather it must be "parceled out" to individual groups, persons, and types. In the proper sense it refers to their capacity to act. The possibilities of Stalin and his apparatus are different from those of Trotsky and the other members of the opposition; and the critical function of the concept of possibility consists in determining the specifics of all these possibilities for action and of contrasting them and evaluating them qualitatively and quantitatively against one another. Bahro correctly points out that "the political weakness of the opposition and thus of the hypothetical alternative it represented was itself part of the secondary phenomena of the given situation."[31]

Bahro is especially right in that he does not take "the historical task" of "realizing socialism" as the point of reference for evaluating the Soviet revolution. We might add, moreover, that in subjective terms as well, i.e., in the ideas of the key actors, the "task of socialism" was by no means so clearly articulated that it could have functioned as a "guide to action." For good reason Bahro quotes Lenin's informative reflections from his last notes, "On Our Revolution," where it is clear that for him the issue was ultimately "in some way" to accomplish for Russia a breakthrough to modern civilization and culture. Indeed, we all know the much quoted formula "communism equals Soviet power plus electrification," which was both clear enough and unclear enough at the same time. But what does it mean to say that "civilization through industrialization" appeared on the horizon as "the objective historical task" of postrevolutionary Soviet Russia? After a perusal of Bahro's text, I think it is quite urgent to arrive at a reading less conducive to broad generalizations and less open to mystifications. Indeed, the same problem is encountered in looking to the future, now that we must (and this is true to the same degree for both protosocialist and capitalist countries) think about how a continuation of the process of civilization is possible under the restrictive ecological conditions that have now become evident.

It is of course from Lenin's own terminology that Bahro is borrowing when he speaks of the "tasks" of postrevolutionary development: take for instance titles such as "The Tasks of the Proletariat in the Present Revolution" (the famous April Theses), or "The Principal Tasks of Our Day" (with the motto: "You are miserable and rich, powerful and powerless at the same time, Mother Russia"), and "The Next Tasks of Soviet Power." Thinking in terms of tasks belongs to a framework of action in which enormous energies for action come together but there is but little room for free creativity. Nonetheless, for a rational historical consciousness, there are a few things here in need of deciphering. The strongly authoritarian thrust comes into the picture on account of a presumed and hardly controllable adversary—world imperialism on the outside, and reactionary, torpid, or narrow-minded primitive social forces within. For this reason, mere survival often imposes stern imperatives and reduces a spectrum of possible actions to crude alternatives: Lenin or Kaledin? (from Rosa Luxemburg). Bahro then goes on to quote Lenin's formula that it is "our task" to spare no effort to hasten the assimilation of Western industrial civilization by "barbaric Russia," not "hesitating to use barbarous methods in fighting barbarism." Bahro then goes on to say:

> At least for the overwhelming majority of the Russian population of the time, the peasantry, this meant the prospect of decades of revolution from above, in the "interest" of an unborn third or fourth generation. It meant that they could not be spared the pains of primitive accumulation of capital. In the "second revolution" of collectivization, the peasant masses were the object of progress.[32]

Bahro describes how this collectivization came about, which in all its violence has oppressed the Russian village community with effects lasting down to this very day:

> The unprepared turn that now followed, toward collectivization of the rural economy without industry having prepared the ground, and hence also to the violently excessive rate of accumulation of the first five-year plans, was a *response* to the question of survival of the noncapitalist order raised by the kulaks at the head of the peasantry.[33]

But now we get into theoretical problems with regard to praxis:

> In view of this development, to which the Bolsheviks were driven, the criticism that is possible on purely economic grounds, i.e., that the overall process of industrialization was far from achieving its potential optimum, can only have an academic character.[34]

Bahro then leads the discussion back into the terms of his theory of historical tasks: "Without the apparatus of force that the Bolsheviks set into motion, Russia today would still be a peasant country, most probably on the capitalist road." (Or should one at once say: the colony of German fascism, ruler over a vast empire?) Bahro leaves it to the Soviet experts to determine "how far modifications might have been possible, which could have reduced both the extent of the sacrifices and losses, and the depth of the subsequent depression of the rural economy. But the collision itself was unavoidable."[35] The polemics are against Ernest Mandel, who fixes the optimal possible conditions for industrialization in Soviet Russia, under which the living standard, the effect of accumulation, and the defensive capacity of the country as well as its democratization would all have gained. This was true of course of the entire policy of the state party, i.e., the policy toward both peasants and workers. Here Bahro describes the historical situation:

> As early as the immediate post-civil war situation, when there could be no question of too high a rate of accumulation, the Bolsheviks did not have the political preconditions for a democratic discussion with the majority of workers as to the necessary extent of the sacrifice to be made.[36]

This passage is followed by a number of further historical reflections that for the most part I accept as valid.

But now to the core of the problem. Let me first say that historical reflections on fulfilled or missed optimal possibilities are by no means of mere academic interest; they also perform an important methodological and heuristic function for interregional analyses (and especially for delimiting practical perspectives). However —and here Bahro is right—they do not have any retroactive corrective informative function for any given individual historical case, but rather can only point up the forces that are operative in varying degrees of potency. Mandel's discussion is important as a necessary corrective against the apologists who celebrate what is real as that alone which is rational.

At the core of the problem with Bahro is that he has a theory that lacks a crucial term. The theory moves along an action-reaction paradigm. An impulse without produces an action in response, whose collective subject is "the Bolsheviks": here they "were forced," there "conditions slipped out of their hands." However, at such critical junctures it is surely quite important what material and social capacities for action and cooperation have been gathered together in this collective subject; indeed, these capacities extend over a broad and diversified spectrum. In these matters we have more extensive information than did Bahro, and find that a searching penetration into the alchemy of Soviet history, for the purposes of discerning, understanding, and comprehending, is of utmost importance for any advanced theoretical discussion of the subject. Indeed, Bahro himself repeatedly sets out in this direction, but what we in fact need is a more thorough theoretical integration, so that the drawing up of historical accounts comes out differently in some respects.

The missing middle term in the deductive argument concerning the necessary or unavoidable effects of violence, destructiveness, and ruthlessness, which *cannot* be derived from any higher-order tasks, is to be found in the wide variety of interests and abilities of concrete persons. In Soviet history, these "subjective forces of production" represent an antagonistic rather than an integrated totality. An important part of Russia's internal history played itself out to the tune of a kind of quite unfortunate negative dialectic such that, given the extreme scarcity of the higher forces of culture, the extra strong lower forces outmaneuvered and crushed the weak higher forces, because the former were able to draw to themselves strength from the overall social field for a longer time and to a greater degree than the latter, which lost strength increasingly as revolutionary ferment subsided. Trotsky described this process quite graphically in his chapter on Thermidor.

The "general will" that was the ultimate outcome—the will of the leadership—which steered society and in the end held exclusive sway, naturally absorbed all the handicaps of the outward conditions of existence and of the various levels of interests within the society. The bureaucracy took over general social functions but in its own way—refracted and filtered through the prism of its own special interests, including the major one in its own privileged monopolistic position. Just as the interest of socialist development had soon become wholly irrelevant (except for the resolve not to relinquish the management of production and society again to private capitalists), so too did the interest in social revolutionary progress elsewhere in the world (except to the extent that it fit into a pragmatic calculation of the interests of state and power, interests which in turn bore their own class-specific bureaucratic traits). Indeed, even the more elementary interest in the integrity and stability of the nation was probably not absolutely dominant; when special interests collided with it it could suffer severely, even catastrophically, such as occurred when the major portion of the army command was annihilated shortly before the Second World War. A phrase from Bahro describes this basic situation: "The bureaucratic universe is curved back in on itself just like the cosmic universe in relativity theory; there is no straight line leading out of it"[37]—and we might add, no line to any higher-order historical tasks either. Some congruencies are "purely accidental," externally contingent, in the best of cases imposed.

> The general interest of society now has to find a way through these special interests—precisely as was the case under all previous historical relations of domination.[38]

Nonetheless, I suggest that we should discard this last verbal vestige that has been carried along with the baggage of rhetoric about historical tasks of the protosocialistic bureaucracy. It is possible, and moreover makes for more clarity, to describe the bureaucracy's exercise of its functions without such a teleological distortion.

A conceptual framework for comprehending praxis

The scholastic social philosophy of the GDR, institutionalized as historical materialism, has developed a very astute system of concepts and propositions intended to enable every thinking contemporary to assimilate social processes in the modalities strategically controlled from the "commanding heights."[39] This historical materialism functions primarily as a kind of subordination training—autochthonous, but heteronomous. Outsiders experience it as a lifeless canon, but the life of the bureaucratic logos of this social formation is codified in its formulas and figures. The whole thing is nothing but a contrivance to systematically prevent such trains of thought as Bahro develops in his book. This book is not only a sociological contribution to an analysis of the overall situation in the GDR, but also a contribution to a reformation of philosophical thought under socialism. For good reasons, Bahro does not get lost in a scholastic criticism of the local scholastic philosophy. Nonetheless, his analysis of society contains the basic concepts of a social philosophy that could serve as a tool of thought for evolving socialism beyond its protosocialistic larva stage.

The key concepts that sum up negatively the central meaning of social formations, but also negate this negation, are subalternity and emancipation. A concern for how human life endures in a state of insurmountable subalternity brings his analysis to the reality entailed by the division of labor, which continues to exist even after the means of production have been transformed into social property. Human labor and activity in general still take place on a number of quite different *functional levels*. Bahro enumerates the different levels in a table, in which the most important indicators both of activity with things (the technology of exchange with nature) as well as of social cooperation are broken down into five stages from top to bottom:

5) analysis and synthesis of the natural and social totality— thus, activities with explicit direct bearing on the totality;

4) creative specialist work in science;

3) reproductive specialist work in science;

2) complex specialist empirical work;

1) simple and schematic compartmentalized and ancillary work.[40]

First we must establish the facts of this social inequality as clearly, as drastically, and as mercilessly as possible, even in the protosocialist formation. And this is more than merely a matter of a schematic distinction between physical and intellectual labor: for Bahro, the decisive criterion is how and where the "synthetic" functions are exercised. Participation in the social synthesis (and synthesis of the historical process) is the way to escape from a subaltern existence. This is an important problem of specialized training, as well as a problem of having an effective opportunity for, or access to, the performance of ever higher synthetic functions.[41] Between the one and the other is the interest, the desire for such an access. All in all we are still far from a harmonization. It is still generally true that creative work is scarce, that individuals must compete for access to it, and that society's educational system is geared toward rationing the acquisition of skills in accordance with the opportunities for exercising them. In addition to this are the mainstays created by the reality of bureaucratic domination, for example the establishment of privileges and bureaucratic rivalry as a major form of social relations.[42]

The broad range of functional levels is also the framework within which a network of social relations of interest and differences of interest is formed. Indeed, having access to and being a part of any functional level are in their turn to the highest degree the content of the principal social interest that motivates men.

> In this way, competition for the appropriation of activities favorable to self-development, for appropriate positions in the multidimensional system of social division of labor, becomes the specific driving force of economic life characteristic of actually existing socialism. It is not by

chance that competitive behavior between individuals in our system is so strongly focused on the phase of education, in which access and admission to favorable positions in the system of overall social labor is determined, with those strata who have already acquired education and influence holding the center of the stage.[43]

The official interpretations—which of course want to hear nothing of such fundamental conflicts of interest in their socialism, and deduce existing differences "scientifically" from the objective needs of social development—are forcefully undermined by Bahro:

> It is quite nonsensical, moreover, to assume that a society still divided into groups with essentially different interests could bring its general interests onto a *scientific* common denominator, such as would prescribe impartially to social contradictions the direction of their development.[44]

Indeed we have already seen how the particular interests of bureaucracy stand behind the pretended general and universal interests of the society.

But Bahro sees a deeper, more fundamental problem behind the reality of different interests. A qualitative analysis shows that there are indeed differences of rank between the manifestations of human needs or even interests in general, and that, moreover, there are very delicate relationships between the variously ranked kinds of needs. Bahro pragmatically avails himself of a *fundamental distinction* between two classes of needs—"compensatory" and "emancipatory":

> The *compensatory* interests . . . are the unavoidable reaction to the way that society restricts and stunts the growth, development, and confirmation of innumerable people at an early age. The corresponding needs are met with substitute satisfactions. People have to be indemnified, by possession and consumption of as many things and services as possible, with the greatest possible (exchange-) value, for the fact that they have an inadequate share in the proper human needs. . .
>
> The *emancipatory* interests, on the other hand, are oriented to the growth, differentiation, and self-realization of the personality in all dimensions of human activity. They demand above all the potentially comprehensive appropriation of the essential human powers objectified in other individuals, in objects, modes of behavior, and relationships, their transformation into subjectivity, into a possession not of the juridical person, but rather of the intellectual and ethical individuality, which presses in its turn for productive transformation.[45]

As a general anthropological premise, he allows that human be-ings "strive precisely to arrange their fields of activity to the best advantage with respect to the degree of freedom of their own be-havior."[46] However, the higher degrees of freedom are reserved to the top layers in the vertical, class-determined division of labor and function, and the greater freedom, enjoyed as a privilege, is in turn itself precarious: one is not really so free in the exercise of so-cial control.[47] Thus there arises a need for compensations for the wanting freedom, both at the top and at the bottom of the society. One such compensatory interest, which has flourished exuberantly among the upper layers, is the striving for power.[48] Among smaller people, for whom, of course, such a striving does not go far, com-pensations run in smaller coinage. They need compensations for the state of subalternity in which their lives and doings take place, and for the poverty of their communicative relations. Thus the masses must compensate for their subaltern situation through the acquisition of material comforts. They must hang their self-con-sciousness on external props and kill their leisure time "since they cannot take part in social communication as equals."[49] In summing up Bahro says: "In the process, the gratification of compensatory interests—often subaltern enough themselves—keeps human be-ings in their traditional state of subalternity." What stands out typologically here is something that is present in all human beings in varying proportions, and which in the totality of social move-ment forms a dynamic structure which Bahro attempts to eluci-date by means of a schematic diagram at one point in his book.[50]

The analysis of compensatory and emancipatory needs assumes an important function in Bahro (as it has with other authors, for example André Gorz, who takes the Czechoslovakian discussions as his reference point) when he reflects on the situation of compe-tition in protosocialism as compared with the old capitalist world, and moreover from a general ecological perspective. Since emanci-patory aspirations are stillborn under a bureaucratic domination, the key to satisfaction and pacification is also compensatory con-sumption. But under socialism the latter still lags behind what cap-italism has to offer, and unfortunately will continue to do so. The party leaders are, grotesquely enough, thus less the creators of a new civilization than "the interpreters of those impulses which 'over there' in late capitalism keep technical and economic prog-ress in full swing." The upper stratum of the bureaucracy offers the people this orientation, especially in the Soviet Union, so that the apparatus "finds itself sitting on a volcano of unsatisfied needs."[51] The protosocialistic formation, under its bureaucratic apparatus of domination, thus lives undiminished in the historical dead-end situation of "industrialism," in that "essentially quantitative progress leading into a bad infinity."[52]

The conceptual foundation of Bahro's analysis rests on the categories of active and interested subjectivity. This has a special significance in Marxist theory, especially in the shadow of the tradition of thought founded by Soviet Marxism. Characteristic for this tradition is a peculiar systems-theory approach, where it is not so much active subjects and their behavior within objective and social relations, but rather circumstances (as "objective" as possible) in their relation to other circumstances, that are the keynote. Bahro represents the return to what one might call "vital relevance." The argument centers on the characteristics of the activities, in particular the trained skills of the active subject, and the reference points of action and purposes (needs that must be satisfied) which are of interest for the subject's own personal life.

The methodological significance of this for an analysis of the process of socialism was pointed up years ago in Charles Bettelheim's brief text entitled "An Analysis of New Social Formations." This text signals another similar shift of focus, after the analysis of socialist societies in terms of structural economic perspectives derived from Marx's analysis of capitalism—commodity production, the law of value, and so on—had for a long time been common currency. Bettelheim opposes this with the resolution "that from the standpoint of socialism, the decisive factor is not the way the economy is organized, but the nature of the *class in power*. In other words, the basic question is not whether market or plan rules the economy, but what sort of class has the power in its hands."[53] (I would say that such shifts in theoretical focus are valid not in reference to some abstract and general epistemological ideal, but only in subservience to some historically determined practical interests. Who is satisfied with an objectivist system-theoretical approach, and who not? Who needs a settling of accounts based on an analysis of praxis?)

The philosophical nature of Bahro's reflections on socialism lies not so much in his movement from sociological and sociohistorical analyses of functions and stratification to the fundamental social anthropological definitions of self-determination and determination by others. What is decisive is the subjective interest that forces such a radicalization of categories—the interest in broad human emancipation. But since the materialist turn of Marx and Engels it has been an extremely delicate question as to how an active, humanistic, emancipatory engagement can find acceptance in a way that is sound methodologically, in a theory that has been tempered in the scientific spirit. Bahro is well aware of the problem, clearer than many earlier spokesmen for "socialism with a human face," who merely put in their word for a normative essence in opposition to a reality that had become alienated therefrom. He considers it a necessary step forward that the desiderata of humanism in Marx have lost their earlier "immediacy." [54] In the following we shall separately discuss the basic concepts and methodology of Bahro's new program for "human emancipation."

Thoughts on emancipation

In the third part of this book, under the title of "A Strategy for a Communist Alternative," Bahro develops a program for a cultural revolution, the sole way by which a fully socialist society can evolve from the larva stage of "protosocialism." The quintessence of his argument involves surmounting the old division of labor, social subalternity, and the entire former system of the civilization process. The venerable title for this, as we have said, is "human emancipation." Bahro is well aware of the difficulties in his project, and right at the beginning of the tenth chapter, on present-day conditions and prospects for universal emancipation, he tells the reader that this is the most difficult, the least sure, and hence the most inadequate part, and he explains:

> The programmatic dimension moreover, is something that should derive, not just on epistemological grounds but also on sociological, from collective public practice, which for us in the countries of actually existing socialism is for the time being still notoriously forbidden. [55]

I would object here and say, Indeed! On epistemological grounds as well! For an anticipation of future steps and results, in thought before practice, initiated on a mass scale, is not only materially inadequate and insufficiently concrete but also fundamentally distorted, inasmuch as it shifts the entire constitutive level from its authentic site. Bahro does his best to approach his promised land in a kind of pincers movement. From one side he puts forth a rigorous historical imperative:

> *Today it is general emancipation that is the absolute necessity*, since in the blind play of subaltern egoisms, lack of solidarity, the antagonism of atomized and alienated individuals, groups, peoples, and conglomerates of all kinds, we are hastening ever more quickly towards a point of no return.[56]

Then, from this "absolute necessity" Bahro derives a long series of "should" and "must" propositions; thus the overcoming of subalternity is a "historical task," the only possible alternative to the limitless expansion (which is also becoming impossible) of material needs.[57] Yet Bahro is enough of a political thinker to have a firm grasp of the inadequacy of a merely normative, imperative, and utopian approach, and he therefore also does his best to prepare the way for a sociohistorical prognosis from his vision and projection of the future. This is the other road to the promised land: a probing of the forces that exist even now, although they have not yet achieved their full effect, forces that, as explained in the eleventh chapter, are the potential for a new reshaping of the society.

> If I see the cultural revolution as not only necessary but also possible, as far as its most essential objective conditions are concerned, this implies a clear idea also of its active subject. . . . Only if what is necessary and possible shows itself to be a field of needs, demands, and compulsions requiring action by concrete social forces, are we faced with a genuine perspective.[58]

Within this framework, then, Bahro's analysis of compensatory and emancipatory interests has its place as well. However, this pincers movement of which I spoke apparently has not embraced any major preliminary sections: whatever real, onward-pressing opposition already exists in this entire region is for the most part not very rational, and what is rational is not yet very effective. It is a situation similar to the one in which Marx, in 1844, wrote his "Introduction to the Critique of Hegel's Philosophy of Law," where the gap between the categorical imperative of human emancipation and the "radical needs" without which no revolution is possible, was still very wide. It was a cardinal problem of the philosophically educated and politically experienced author Bahro to find a way out of this situation—not only practically but theoretically as well. Perhaps it is easier to note how what is precarious in the situation is translated into problematic theoretical constructions from a distance than it is in the midst of practical engagement. Thus he seems, unawares, to make a higher necessity out of his bitter need to write, when he attempts to justify the significance of the content of utopian thoughts by appealing to an imminent turning point in world history. Utopia, he says, acquires a new necessity, because historically the task is to replace the spontaneity of the historical process with conscious planned action.[59] And finally, when he has some second thoughts that in his speculative construction of the future he may already perhaps have gone too far, he nonetheless affirms his conviction that "communist propaganda today must demonstrate more than ever with *concrete possibilities.*"[60]

The extreme exertion of his social imagination, and the offering of its recruiting forces, acquires its own theoretical foundations in Bahro's reflection on surplus consciousness. This is the term he uses to describe that "energetic mental capacity that is no longer absorbed by the immediate necessities and dangers of human existence, and can thus orient itself to more distant problems."[61] He makes quite extensive use of this basic concept. On the other side of the coin, however, it should be pointed out that for some time the scholastic philosophers he has around him have knocked about the concept of consciousness, so that one can no longer be sure whether he is talking here of consciousness in a relatively strict sense, or whether the term has had all sorts of things stuffed into it (as has long been the case with the concept of class consciousness). One of the theorems of the scholastic system of historical materialism is the retroactive "role of consciousness," and it is in this sense that the party clerics interpret their role in shaping society.

Bahro is surely right in opposing a pseudo-Marxist interpretation in which consciousness "necessarily arises from the existing conditions."[62] He counterposes to this: "Marxism has always claimed that being can determine consciousness precisely to determine being anew."[63] Bahro then goes on to make "surplus consciousness" a keystone of his perspective. "The substance of common interest is surplus consciousness; it is this which engenders the mobilization against the politbureaucratic dictatorship." However, it becomes immediately apparent that "consciousness" here figures as a collective term for, in addition to thoughts and ideas, nothing less than the "overall mass of accumulated expertise, or subjective productive force," technical as well as social; and on the side of social qualifications, the "tendency to subaltern behavior" and its counterpart the "tendency to integral behavior."[64] Thus, Bahro is able to begin resolutely, albeit with less categorical precision, "to analyze the potential for the impending social transformation in this way, as a question of a structure of social *consciousness*" whereby "consciousness is involved here not in its function of reflection, but rather as a factor of social being, whose growing role itself possesses a 'consciousness-determining' significance, i.e., a significance that alters its *content*, something that is expressed in the spread of emancipatory needs or interests." Consciousness itself thus becomes a "completely material and economic reality."[65] But the philosophical *concept* of consciousness becomes, in my opinion, an obfuscating factor. Some may perhaps be inclined to be less severe concerning this point, but as I see it the categories Bahro uses here are unable to bring full clarity into the constitutive relationships. Much of what Bahro describes with regard to the impending cultural revolution seems to me to be shaped throughout by such initial biases concerning a process of consciousness, extending from the statement that "the *intellectual life of society* is the battlefield of the cultural revolution"[66] to his outline of a league of communists (and a number of others). This gives Bahro's concept of change all too literally the character of a "strategy"— something, moreover, toward which Bahro himself is thoroughly critical, as in the strategic form of the old labor movement (e.g., a combination of a troop command, officers corp, and infantry).[67]

As an answer to Bahro I would myself put forth a double plea: as regards basic concepts, a plea for an analysis of the forces of social movement that is less centered in traditional concepts of consciousness, and as regards social perspectives, more openness for the unprecedented—in other words, simply more indeterminacy in favor of a more specific analysis of the currents that already exist. These objections are merely a few preliminary reflections to a discussion that will only become possible when the conditions that originally constrained Bahro to utilize just these conceptual forms in expressing his thoughts have been overcome.

Such a criticism need not make any claims toward superiority. As regards the digestion of our current, present-day practical experience of socialism, Bahro is far ahead of us all. It is equally true, however, that the *historical* account of the evolution of socialism and, in particular, the assimilation of critical contributions, has a richer tradition—or in any case, a broader material basis—on our side. We should understand that contemporary socialist theory nowhere exists in some superior form, but is being worked out piecemeal just as socialism itself is, to cite one of Lenin's observations that is quoted by Bahro.

Concluding remarks

In our attempt to do justice to Rudolf Bahro's book as a worthy contribution to the philosophy of socialism, it was not our purpose to discuss the hypothesis concerning the genesis and sociohistorical locus of state socialism, nor to enter into the sociology and political science of current functional analyses, nor finally, to test the plausibility of his programmatic positions. In full accord with Bahro's concept of philosophy, I have endeavored from the standpoint of the subject to inquire into how Bahro comes to terms with the *meanings*, and their various mediations, to be found within the reality with which he deals. I found myself in agreement on a number of essential points, but also of divergent opinion on a number of not unessential issues. To conclude, I should like to make a comparative evaluation of the three lines of inquiry pursued in the three parts of Bahro's book.

In socialist doctrine, advancement must be measured not only in terms of some standard of theoretical cognitive efficiency, thematic completeness, or empirical logical coherence, and so on; it has always a directly practical index, and shows itself to be linked to gradations and ever higher degrees of ability to form social relations—in particular, the ability to relate with some degree of autonomy to oneself as well as in solidarity and cooperatively to others. The formations in which the struggle for socialism has been waged up to now have in this respect been limited, and this, more than any strategical line pursued by the leadership, has set the historical limits of these formations.

If we now ask, To what higher level of human competence, beyond the present-day power of both the anticapitalist and the socialist options, could an expanded combination of social forces lead? it is important that we understand how to pose this question on the thematic level. I should like to think that a heightened awareness in this matter is almost in itself an indication that this development toward a higher level of human competence is already in progress, however narrow the basis for this may still be. Rudolf Bahro's pinpointing of the key problem of socialism as the problem of accumulating an adequate groundwork in human competence (the subjective force of production) is in my opinion his most important contribution, and accordingly I think those parts of his book in which this categorical focal point is most clearly enunciated are the ones that are most valuable. These are mainly the sections where he lays bare the anatomy of existing socialism in terms of its real formative forces, i.e., the second section, with a few strands extending into the other sections (for example, the analysis of compensatory needs at the beginning of the third section).

In contrast, his attempt in the first section to situate the proto-socialist formation within the framework of a universal social history is unsatisfactory in two respects: first, his use of the notion of Asiatic modes of production as a key concept, and second, the teleologically distorted conception of historical necessity with which he operates. But above all, the entire project of the third section, which soars far past any analysis of the real vital forces (including their latent tensions and reserves), as it were, to "preempt the future" in thought, seems to me the most questionable portion of his entire line of thought. No *ad hoc* theory concerning a tendentially growing awareness of an imminent process of cultural revolution can sufficiently justify such an overstretching of the concrete utopian imagination; there is more necessity than virtue at play here. In my opinion, his analytical diagnosis of the "conditions of possibility" is much more valuable because it gives us more real information than his bold venture into the "realm of the possible." In the first place, we would gain more if we could go beyond his anatomy, which is still on a rather crude level, into a more subtle analysis of the functional aspects of the physiology of existing socialism. Not just one step of "real movement," but even a step further toward the *understanding* of real movement, is worth more than a "hundred programs."

Translated by Michel Vale

NOTES

1. Rudolf Bahro, *The Alternative in Eastern Europe* (London: New Left Books, 1977), p. 287.
    2. Ibid., p. 31.
    3. Ibid., pp. 29-30.
    4. Ibid., p. 37.
    5. Ibid., p. 54.
    6. Ibid., p. 13.
    7. Ibid., p. 12.
    8. Ibid., p. 13.
    9. Ibid., pp. 18-19.
   10. Ibid., p. 19.
   11. The fourth chapter of Stojanović's book [*Between Ideals and Reality: A Critique of Socialism and Its Future* (New York: Oxford University Press, 1973)], begins with the explicit methodological question of how one should approach the historical process we call socialism. Stojanović tries to get away from a mere normative approach, from operating with a purely normative definition of socialism. However, Stojanović feels that such an operation is legitimate for Marxists provided that criteria used for socialism are derived from the real historical process itself. He finds these criteria—and this is perhaps his most vulnerable point—in the intentions and declarations of intent of those participating in the process. Stojanović conceives these intentions as essential and real possibilities, and in his analysis of history he operates throughout with such alternative possibilities: "After the October Revolution there were two possibilities...." "Here we must pose yet another question: could the unachieved have been achieved had practice been different?" And there are numerous cases of positive norm-setting: "The obligation of a Marxist is solely to the truth of humanism and the humanism of truth." We might mention in passing that Bahro too proceeds in an ideal-normative manner when he charges that Stojanović is not exactly Marxist and materialist in his thinking on a questionable point. One might also ask, "materialistically," where materialism is possible and in what contexts of social praxis do ideal-normative methods acquire their own "necessity" (suggestive compulsion). That it is possible to work unimpeded in Yugoslavia, as Bahro says, has long not been the case for Stojanović. He was dismissed from his professorship many years ago. And Bahro is completely wide of the mark when he claims that Leon Trotsky too operated with the opposites of ideal and reality in his final critique of Stalinism, in *The Revolution Betrayed* (which, in an embarrassing mistake, he remembers as "Socialism Betrayed"). Bahro finds it quite understandable that Trotsky at that time had *never* asked himself the question of "whether or not his opponent had achieved his position of leadership precisely because he possessed the historically necessary passion to create the apparatus of power for the terroristic transformation from above. . . ." The problem here is probably that Trotsky's writings are still inaccessible in the GDR. However, Bahro carries his reasoning even further and attributes to Stalin the qualities that Russia at that time needed. Of course, Trotsky never went that far for well-weighed reasons, and rather understood the specific historical necessity of the triumph of the Stalinist bureaucracy more causally and less fatalistically and teleologically.
   12. Bahro, pp. 88-89, quoting from Friedrich Engels, "On Social Relations

in Russia," in Marx and Engels, *Selected Works*, vol. II (Moscow, 1969) p. 390.

13. Bahro, p. 50.
14. Ibid., p. 116.
15. Ibid., p. 38.
16. Ibid., p. 21.
17. Ibid., p. 53.
18. Ibid.
19. Ibid., p. 61.
20. Ibid.
21. Ibid., p. 53.
22. Ibid., p. 198.
23. Ibid.
24. Ibid., p. 174.
25. Ibid., p. 240.
26. Ibid., p. 90.
27. Ibid., p. 139.
28. Ibid., pp. 117-18.
29. Ibid., p. 118.
30. Helmut Fleischer, "Parteilichkeit und Objektivität im Geschichtsdenken nach Marx," in *Theorie der Geschichte* 1, DTV, WR 4281, pp. 359-60.
31. Bahro, p. 101.
32. Ibid., p. 100.
33. Ibid., p. 101.
34. Ibid.
35. Ibid., pp. 101-02.
36. Ibid., p. 104.
37. Ibid., p. 214.
38. Ibid., p. 240.
39. See the essay "Philosophie als Führungswissenschaft: Aspekte des Marxismus in der DDR," in Helmut Fleischer, *Sozialphilosophische Studien* (Berlin: Olle und Wolter, 1973).
40. Bahro, p. 164.
41. Ibid., p. 146.
42. Ibid., p. 212-13.
43. Ibid.
44. Ibid., p. 245.
45. Ibid., p. 272.
46. Ibid., p. 220.
47. Ibid., p. 199.
48. Ibid., p. 272.
49. Ibid., pp. 281-82.
50. Ibid., p. 315.
51. Ibid., pp. 237-38.
52. Ibid., p. 262.
53. Charles Bettelheim, "Zur Analyse neuer Gesellschaftsformationen," *Kursbuch* 23, p. 4.

54. Bahro, p. 24.
55. Ibid., p. 253.
56. Ibid., p. 254.
57. Ibid., p. 271.
58. Ibid., p. 304.
59. Ibid., p. 253.
60. Ibid., p. 452.
61. Ibid., p. 257.
62. Ibid., p. 256.
63. Ibid.
64. Ibid., pp. 313-14.
65. Ibid., p. 316.
66. Ibid., p. 317.
67. Ibid., p. 378.

HASSAN GIVSAN

A Critique of Bahro's
Alternative Writing of History

Who dares the child's true name in public mention?
The few, who thereof something really learned,
Unwisely frank, with hearts that spurned concealing,
And to the mob laid bare each thought and feeling,
Have evermore been crucified and burned.

Goethe's "Faust"

The opponents of freedom—freedom of thought as well as of word—have always been blind to the dialectic whereby the crucifixion indeed becomes a monument to the heretic. By forbidding Bahro the word, the "dialecticians" in the East (who have managed to reduce the dialectic to no more than an "Our Father") have only confirmed the justice of his critique. And if these self-appointed heirs of Marx have a perverted relationship to criticism, this only testifies to their perverted relationship to Marx. Marx, of course, regarded his philosophy as a critique; it is no accident that his major works use this term in their titles. In one sense, "critique" means explaining the historical origins of present relations and how they function. This was just what Bahro hoped to do in his book *The Alternative*, subtitled "A Contribution to the Critique of Actually Existing Socialism."[1]

I should say that the best way to assess the merits of an author's work is by approaching it critically. And Bahro deserves a critical assessment in a spirit of solidarity, if for no other reason than that he has revived the best and most fundamental in Marxist thought in just those areas where it seemed to have been dead, having given way to an official scholasticized version. Bahro's book is perhaps the most important work on contemporary history that has been

written in the GDR, and in saying this one ought not to overlook
the communicative situation in which he wrote his book: in isolation. Does this also mean that he was isolated from the influence
of his environment? By no means. He is the product of his surroundings. To be sure, he rejects those surroundings; at the level of
theory—and Bahro is after all a theoretician—he shows to what
extent he has freed himself from its habits of thought. Nevertheless, Bahro remains to a large extent entrapped in his environment
on a number of points, as we shall try to show in the following
pages.

In the analytical-theoretical first part of his book, Bahro attempts to write an alternative history, not only as a rejoinder to
the official orthodoxy but indeed against the Marxist tradition in
general. The object of his inquiry is actually existing socialism. His
key category is oriental despotism, or the Asiatic mode of production. As a methodological-theoretical justification for his alternative, Bahro invokes the unsuitability of Marxian categories for the
formative aspects of history. I would like to examine the substance
of this fundamental methodological point of Bahro's, i.e., to examine whether Bahro really does offer an alternative in analysis of
the genesis of socialist societies. In doing so, we shall not be com-
paring Bahro's analysis with those of other authors, but shall be
examining to what extent Bahro has made the category of the
Asiatic mode of production into a fruitful tool for his inquiry and
to what extent it can be made fruitful at all; in other words, to
what extent this mode of production has been of historical significance as a social formation in its own right *alongside* capitalism.
Indeed, it is only to the extent that this mode of production has
served as a positive autonomous force in determining history, and
not merely by virtue of its backwardness, that Bahro's reproach
that Marx "overestimated" capitalism and the capitalist world
market will prove to be relevant.

Let me state emphatically that I am not concerned with salvaging Marx's authority, but only with analyzing the methodological
aspects of Bahro's argument against Marx. His alternative is, after
all, ultimately directed against Marx. Thus, at issue is Bahro's
method, and of course the issue also includes how he apprehends
Marx. Thus, our purpose is not to affirm our own argument against
Bahro's alternative, but rather to examine Bahro's argument in its

methodological aspects and its implicit theory of history. I presume that it is methodologically legitimate to concentrate mainly on quoting Bahro against himself.

First, let's let Bahro speak for himself; later, on the basis of these passages, I shall develop my criticism. (I beg the reader's indulgence for these extensive quotations.)

Programmatically, Bahro insists that actually existing socialism must "be explained in terms of its own laws"; its origins, he continues, are in the noncapitalist road of Russia's development "from agricultural to industrial despotism."[2]

> It is not sufficient simply to make clear the inapplicability of the categories of communism to our present conditions, necessary as this negative activity is. The point is rather to understand the new field of struggle on which we find ourselves on the basis of its own becoming, its own laws. If actually existing socialism is not the abolition of capitalist private property—what then is its inner nature? We must bear in mind, however, that in investigating this epochal problem we cannot begin with countries like the GDR and Czechoslovakia, which are untypical precisely because they already had capitalist industry. The key lies in Asia, partly in a past that is far behind our own European past. And then, naturally enough, in the specific past of Russia and in the Soviet present.[3]

This is all the more urgent because history

> has furnished a decisive corrective to [the] original Marxist prognosis. While the capitalist order is already in a third phase of its internal contradictions, and *moving* in them instead of succumbing to them, as Marx had predicted for its first phase, and Lenin conclusively for its second, many peoples in the precapitalist countries have set out on their own road towards socialism.[4]

At the turn of the century the issue was decided, and

> since 1945 it has become apparent ... that the progress of humanity in the twentieth century is following different paths than Marx and Engels managed to foresee. They had analyzed those social formations which the *European* section of mankind (including North America) had attained on its specific path through ancient slavery and Germanic feudalism, and drawn the conclusion that the *internal* antagonisms of capitalism they had discovered would *directly* lead to its being burst asunder by a proletarian revolution.[5]

Lenin was the first to recognize the "movement of the revolutionary storm center to the 'East.'"[6] What is meant here is non-

European civilizations based on the Asiatic mode of production, where private ownership of the means of production has never played such a formative role for society as in Europe.

> The ultimate issue is the fact that progress in our epoch proceeds less directly from the *internal* contradictions of imperialism, but more from the *external* contradictions that are the result of these.[7]

> The shifting of the main line of battle from the internal to the external contradictions of imperialism . . . is of the greatest importance for a definition of all other positions in revolutionary programs today. We must realize that this was not expected by the classical Marxist tradition. It has theoretical as well as practical implications for the Marxist conception of history.[8]

Of what exactly did Marx's methodological mistake consist, i.e., what prevented him from seeing all this? Bahro answers:

> The Hegelian tradition, and a Europocentrism that was scarcely avoidable, may have been responsible for the way that Marx focused his attention too one-sidedly on capitalist private property and saw the entire past and future historical process passing through this nodal point.[9]

An element of the Hegelian tradition which plays such an essential role in Marx is

> the methodological hypothesis of the unity of the logical and the historical; although Marx certainly adopted it in a critical manner, in many respects it still had its effects even in spite of this general distancing. It comes to the fore in the way that Marx often dispenses very cavalierly with the historical tendencies he has so genially grasped, since what appears finished from the logical point of view must immediately be historically finished too. . . . A still more consequential step, related to the methodological principle of the unity of the logical and the historical, is the *overvaluation or even absolutizing* of the role of private property.[10]

And finally: "Besides the maturity of the European productive forces, Marx also overestimated the extensive spread and the intensive operation of the capitalist world market."[11]

But now we must determine Bahro's particular theoretical achievements. From his declared programmatic intent, and given the breadth of Bahro's concern with the complex set of factors of the Asiatic mode of production (which is dealt with extensively not only in the first part of the book but elsewhere as well), we expect some theoretical results from Bahro that will shed some light on the formative historical connection between the Asiatic mode of production and the protosocialist societies. That is, we expect that it will tell us something about what historically determining role this mode of production played in the starting potential of these societies, or what significance this mode of production had in the initial situations of these countries alongside of and against capitalism; i.e., we expect results that are not to be found in any other analyses of these societies nor in classical Marxism.

However, the conclusion of Bahro's analysis as far as real history-shaping potential is concerned is all but too well known, namely, the industrial backwardness of Russia. This backwardness gave rise to a central problem for a postrevolutionary Russia (external circumstances, of course, contributed their share as well), i.e., bureaucracy. Bureaucracy is more than an ossified form of getting things done within the administration. It is also a form of dominance: class domination despite the absence of private ownership of means of production. This form of domination has its origins in the old economic despotism. In both cases the key lies in the vertical division of labor.

When I use the word "conclusion," I do not mean that this constitutes the conclusion of Bahro's analysis of the Asiatic mode of production. Actually, he starts out from the historical fact of Russia's industrial backwardness and arrives at the notion of Asiatic despotism only in the course of explaining the phenomena of postrevolutionary Russia. That is, methodologically the Asiatic mode of production appears first and foremost in his explanation of the phenomenon of protosocialist society, rather than serving as a historical premise. However, other authors also start out from this fact and arrive at results more or less similar to Bahro's as far as the present-day reality of these societies is concerned; they too see phenomena such as bureaucracy, etc., as economically necessary consequences of the historical starting point. They get along without the category of Asiatic mode of production. But then, Bahro does not make this category into a fruitful starting point.

Bahro's historical theory is not sufficient for a better understanding of actually existing socialism. It seems that his original contribution is to have shown that class domination is possible even without private ownership of the means of production. He generalizes this point as follows: Just as the fundamental elements in the social division of labor and the state had existed for an entire epoch before the historical appearance of private ownership of the means of production, the elimination of private property on the one hand and the supersession of the division of labor and the state on the other hand can also take place an entire epoch after capitalism.[12]

Let me just say a few words on this point. This fundamentally speculative extrapolation is superfluous, since classical Marxism had already stipulated two stages in its theoretical calculations for the epoch beyond capitalism, starting out from the actually existing situation. In the first stage both the state, i.e., the dictatorship of the proletariat, and the division of labor will continue to exist; what should the performance principle [of reward according to work] otherwise mean? As these are gradually eliminated, the second stage begins. Here is the only place where Bahro's theoretical intention of showing that Marx had overestimated capitalist private property, and hence of undertaking a correction of Marx's conception of history, is stated explicitly. Bahro writes:

> The first ruling exploiter class in history grew directly from the needs of the production and reproduction process itself, in the shape of the priestly caste, this process being mediated not by commodity production and private property, but rather by large-scale cooperation and its direction.[13]

Its "power of disposal grew out of the priestly magic as a task of consciousness that, while privileged, was expressly *necessary* for the progress of the community."[14] In general the old despotism was "a ruling class organized as an ideological and administrative state apparatus."[15] From what has been said, Bahro concludes that at variance with Marx, he must underscore the roots of alienation in the division of labor itself, since it cannot be attributed exclusively to commodity fetishism.[16]

Let me just say that if Bahro's purpose was to present history as the crown witness for his thesis, there would be nothing to object to; but since he sees himself constrained to correct the Marxist conception of history, it is not inappropriate to remind him that Marx and Engels themselves had already accomplished this correction and thus have deprived Bahro of his originality. Even in the Paris Manuscripts Marx refers to private property as the product of alienated labor, i.e., says that alienated labor was the cause of private property, not that private property was the cause of alienation. For him the division of labor is the economic expression of the social nature of labor within alienation. Indeed, in *The German Ideology* he even speaks of the division of labor and private property as identical expressions.[17] In this same passage, Marx and Engels begin the division of labor much earlier than Bahro; they speak of the division of labor within the family—the man rules over wife and children. Finally, in the same manuscript they say that the division of labor first became real, i.e., historically efficacious, with the division into material and intellectual labor (a marginal note by Marx mentions the priest).[18]

To sum up: Marx and Engels knew very well that the division of labor was the constitutive precondition for the evolution of class domination, even where no private ownership of the means of production yet existed, and that the first historically significant form of domination emerged with the division of labor into intellectual and physical labor. That is, they saw very well not only the possibility but also the factual reality of the domination of intellectual over physical labor.

Nonetheless, the independent domination of intellectual labor persisted only as long as it tied together ideological labor with administratively necessary productive labor under its own control. But in most of the old civilizations a division set in very early— typically from the moment when religion shed its primitive form of magic and philosophers replaced magicians—so that the intellectual laborers in the end were able to gain their existence as ideologues and/or officials within the administrative ruling apparatus. Their existence as functionaries was indisputably linked with privileges, but they were never sure of these privileges; their existence depended on the grace of those at the top of the hierarchy, and in this they are distinguished from direct owners. The identity of the division of labor and private property is total here: those who performed a social but general labor of domination and control—the Asiatic despots performed such labors with their irrigation tasks— also disposed over the social surplus product or property; with their labor they reprivatized property. Actually, the European Middle Ages provide a better example of the domination of intellectual labor. The Catholic Church was never brought under the direct control of secular power: the dispute over investiture was in the end resolved in favor of the Church in that it established its autonomy alongside of the secular power. The foundation of this autonomy was (and is) that the Church became a sacred as well as a secular power; it was (and is) not only the generator of ideology, but also at the same time a lord of production, disposing over vast landed estates and other sources of production (quite apart from income through taxes).

Marx and Engels were also aware that the division of labor derives solely from the needs of the production process; for them the distribution process is only a function of production. Marx was quite clear that commodity production presupposed the division of labor. Further, he also knew that alienation was historically much older than commodity fetishism. It would appear to be a theoretical misconception when Bahro, after giving us an account of the domination of intellectual labor in the old economic despotisms, goes on directly to remind us of Marx's controversy with Bakunin, and writes that Marx rejected the possibility that intellectual labor could assume "a position of independent significance, at least for the epoch beyond capitalism."[19] I will return to Bahro's methodological mistake concerning this controversy later. For now let me only point out that for Marx, communism (and his controversy with Bakunin does concern drafting an outline for the communist system) was distinguished by the abolition of the division of labor. In *The German Ideology* we read that in contrast to all previous revolutions, which left the mode of activity intact, the communist revolution is directed against the previous *mode* of activity.[20] In his later draft Marx sees a transitional stage between capitalism and communist society.

Finally, with regard to the problem of bureaucracy as a form of domination without private ownership of the means of production (i.e., not only as a mere mentality or cast of mind), we can say that it is not specific to Asiatic despotism alone. European absolutism with its court aristocracy (especially the French, and we will say nothing of Rome) leaves the Asiatic despotism in the shadows in this regard. In the second stage of capitalism, theoreticians such as Weber not only perceived the bureaucracy but in fact even regarded it as necessary. Indeed, especially now in its late phase, capitalism shows the phenomenon of bureaucracy in its full breadth, with all the attributes Bahro described for the protosocialist system—and this in both the state and the industrial sectors. This industrial bureaucracy has misled many sociologists to speak of the rule of managers, which was supposed to have replaced the rule of the owners of capital.

Thus far, I have been concerned with determining to what extent Bahro has made the category "Asiatic mode of production" a fruitful one for our understanding of actually existing socialist societies. In the process I have pointed out a number of key flaws in his argument. Now let us see what historical validity this mode of production has in our epoch. As we have already said, its impact cannot merely lie in its static and sluggish backwardness; rather it must exert whatever impact it has in its positive, autonomous, disruptive dynamic in opposition to capitalism. The answer to this question will also decide whether the second aspect of Bahro's reproach of Marx—namely, that he had overestimated capitalism and the capitalist world market—is correct.

Indeed, in his introductory comment Bahro himself asserts that the main line of battle has shifted from the internal to the external contradictions of imperialism. Although Bahro's historical realism is evident here, for the reader it is somewhat of a disappointment: one had expected a historical dynamic derived from the initial categories, not a dynamic of imperialism. Moreover, it doesn't change things much when Bahro speaks of the external contradictions of imperialism, since according to Bahro himself these contradictions derive from its internal contradiction—i.e., "the East" is no more than a field in which the contradictions of imperialism are being played out. It is not the internal contradictions of "the East" itself which have shifted the revolutionary center, but rather, this shift is a product of imperialist dynamics.

Bahro is correct to point out that Lenin was the first to have recognized this shift. But while Bahro shows that Lenin, in contrast to Marx and Engels, had no general theoretical concept of the Asiatic mode of production as an economic social formation,[21] he forgets to mention that Lenin's insight here was a product of his theory of imperialism (we should remember that Lenin called imperialism the highest stage of capitalism); that is, Lenin recognized the uniqueness of our epoch, but not as derived from the Asiatic mode of production. Lenin's notion of the weakest link in the chain was developed in the light of his view of imperialism as the open world domination of capitalism, and the sharpening of uneven development that was its consequence. This means that Lenin, standing squarely in the mainstream of the Marxian tradition, correctly points out that in the present epoch it is capitalism which determines the dynamics of history, even where capitalism comes under attack. To be sure, Bahro does speak of the October Revolution as the first anti-imperialist revolution,[22] but fails to draw the necessary theoretical consequences from this assertion. It seems that he uses the expression anti-imperialist more to stress the precapitalist, Asiatic structure. Consistent with this view, he recognizes the connection between the October Revolution and the imperialist war.[23] This does not mean that the imperialist war is seen merely as an external spur, and the revolution as merely a reaction to it, but rather that the effect of the war made itself felt on Russia's internal structure. Just a few days before the revolution Lenin wrote:

> The dialectic of history is such that the war, by extraordinarily expediting the transformation of monopoly capitalism into state-monopoly capitalism, has *thereby* extraordinarily advanced mankind towards socialism.
>
> Imperialist war is the eve of socialist revolution. And this not only because the horrors of the war give rise to proletarian revolt . . . but because state-monopoly capitalism is a complete *material* preparation for socialism, the *threshold* of socialism. . . .[24]

The objection that capitalism was not at all developed in Russia would not affect Lenin's statement, since the process of concentration, whether in monopolistic or in state-monopolistic form, is possible even without a highly developed capitalism. Monopoly is found everywhere in the Eastern countries as well. Bahro should also have noted that following the October Revolution, the Chinese Revolution and indeed all revolutionary upheavals in the countries of the East have been closely linked either with an imperialist war or with a crisis brought about by imperialism. To be brief, in all these movements the determining role of capitalism is patently evident. Bahro cannot avoid acknowledging this role, although he avoids drawing from it the theoretical implications, on that basis to rethink his initial categories. His first correct observation is that the social structure of the countries of the East did not of itself engender any disintegrating dynamics[25]; that means that such an effect had to be derived from without—also from imperialism. Bahro's second important observation is as follows:

> The industrial civilization that has changed European life beyond recognition in the last two centuries *leaves other nations no alternative*; whether they had already reached the threshold of capitalism and industrialization in their own evolution, or whether it encountered them epochs removed from it—they must go through this crucible.[26]

And the high point is reached with the following:

> In its very negativity it [the term "noncapitalist" is meant here—H.G.] expresses the fact that it is still European and American *capitalist* industrialism, now joined also by the Japanese, that sets the rest of the world its problems, even if the balance of forces is gradually tilting against it.[27]

Does all this mean anything else than that old social formations are irrelevant to the dynamics of history in the epoch of the capitalist world market? Bahro might have recognized this, since he himself adumbrates the point; had he done so he would have ascribed another theoretical historical importance to the Asiatic mode of production. But we do not mean to dispute that in their (revolutionary) development these countries will not have their own tradition-determined specific features, and so forth, just as the countries of the capitalist sphere are not homogeneous. The important point here is to stress, in the face of Bahro's insistence on Asiatic despotism, that where a revolution takes place is less important than the dynamics it sets into motion and how it determines the further process of development. Bahro himself asserts that the internal development of the Soviet Union took place (and is still taking place) under the influence of world capitalism.[28] This experience makes clear the practical importance of Marx's assumption that communism is empirically possible only on a world scale. From what has been said it follows that Marx, in conceding a central place to capitalism in his theoretical analyses and reflections on history, has been borne out by the real course of historical events, and that he did not at all overestimate capitalism and the capitalist world market. This then is the key point with which we shall be dealing below: the reproach of exaggeration.

The term "exaggeration" is too imprecise and unusable for an analysis of history. History cannot be measured. But however much that may be, we must come to terms with the objection. Bahro bases his position on an analysis of the fact that the proletarian revolution did not take place in the capitalist countries: therefore, Marx overestimated the maturity of productive forces (and therefore also the capitalist world market). Further, in the light of this one-sided exaggeration of capitalist private property, Marx also evolved a narrow, one-sided conception of world history. Bahro's intention was—at least so it appears to the reader—to correct this one-sidedness with the category of Asiatic despotism. In the foregoing I attempted to determine whether in his theory of history he provides us with any methodological or factual basis for modifying this purported one-sidedness. Since the question of the maturity of the productive forces is related to the question of social revolution, and since Bahro reproaches Marx for exaggerating the former on the grounds that the latter failed to occur in the capitalist countries, we must determine what constitutive role the productive forces play in Marx's conception of revolution (indeed, Bahro should have posed and examined this question himself).

This connection is stressed in Marx's preface to *A Contribution to the Critique of Political Economy*. Owing to the length of the text, I shall quote only a few extracts.

> At a certain stage of their development, the material productive forces of society come into conflict with the existing relations of production.... Then begins a period of social revolution.

Here a distinction is made between the material upheaval and the ideological forms through which men become aware of this conflict. Marx speaks of the consciousness of such a revolutionary epoch, which must be explained "from the contradictions of material life, from the existing conflict between the social productive forces and the relations of production," and also of the decline of a social formation, which assumes the full development of its productive forces.

How this text should be interpreted has remained a much disputed question; most disputed is the category of productive forces. Without wishing to diminish the importance of the objectified productive forces, there are sufficient reasons for placing the productive force "man" in the center. First, it is men who make history. Second, it is men who carry out revolutions. Third, it is men who objectify themselves in the technical instrumental productive forces. Fourth, it is men who produce and represent the material mediation between productive forces and relations of production, and this in a double meaning of the term: for the first, because without men the instrumental forces of production do not function, nor would there be any relations of production, and second, because in the union of their person, men are both productive force and the bearers of relations of production. Fifth, since it is only men who dictate, it is only men who can contradict, and articulate the contradiction. Sixth and finally, since the decision of when this "certain stage" is present is a practical question, and since praxis is the mode of men's existence, men articulate and indicate when the stage has arrived through their contradictions.

The passage on consciousness is usually interpreted as if consciousness were of no importance, or at least no decisive importance. In my opinion, Marx in this passage is referring to consciousness as a yardstick of the contradiction. If consciousness is in contradiction with relations, this means that the existing forces of production come into contradiction with existing relations of production. This is the meaning of the passage in *The German Ideology* where it is stated that when theory, philosophy, and so on come into contradiction with existing relations, this can happen only by the existing social relationships' coming into contradiction with the existing forces of production. Finally, when Marx speaks about the decline of a social formation, we must distinguish between the possibility of social conflict in a country and the necessity of universal negation of this formation. The former does not necessarily presume developed industrial forces of production. In *The German Ideology* it is stated:

> . . . to lead to collisions in a country, this contradiction need not necessarily have reached its extreme limit in this particular country. The competition with industrially more advanced countries, brought about by the expansion of international intercourse, is sufficient to produce a similar contradiction in countries with a backward industry (e.g., the latent proletariat in Germany brought into view by the competition of English industry).[29]

Against this theoretical background, the October Revolution represents no exception to the rule, inasmuch as it occurred in a country which on a scale of gross industrial production occupied fifth place behind the United States, Germany, Great Britain, and France, and which was roughly comparable with France in terms of the level of industrial forces of production; i.e., in a country where the proletariat, especially in heavy industry, languished under the rule of European and especially French capital.[30] It is wholly and completely conceivable within the framework of the Marxian theory of revolution, especially when one considers the imperialist war as the obvious expression of competition within European capitalism, which affected the Russian proletariat quite strongly. To make Marx's theoretical position on revolution more comprehensible, an example is in order.

In the 1840s, when Germany was still in a state of national fragmentation and capitalism was weakly developed—in brief, when the existing situation was not exactly rosy in economic terms—

Marx saw the germs of the first proletarian revolution in Germany and not, for example, in the capitalistically developed England. What are the philosophical and theoretical implications and the real premises of Marx's assumption? What was first and foremost necessary was the overcoming of the Middle Ages, both politically and economically. The weaver rebellions were already some years in the past, and only a few years remained before the revolution (even if it was not exactly the revolution which Marx had in mind); i.e., Germany was in a state of revolutionary ferment. The bourgeois French Revolution was more than a half century old: its fruits were accessible to all. One now knew what slogans such as freedom, equality, and fraternity meant in a postrevolutionary bourgeois society. In a word: the living reality itself gave witness that the actual demand for freedom meant bourgeois freedom. Although Marx was sufficiently ironic to vindicate this role for the German political authorities, he wrote urgently against it:

> As soon as criticism concerns itself with modern social and political reality, and thus arrives at genuine human problems, it must either go outside the German *status quo* or approach its object directly.[31]

This critique found a double means of expression in Germany: in philosophy (namely, in the Marxist philosophy) and in the high political and theoretical consciousness of the proletariat. That this consciousness had come into conflict with existing relations—for that a developed domestic industry was not necessary—was "through the appearance of the contradiction, not within the national orbit, but between this national consciousness and the practice of other nations, i.e., between the national and the general consciousness of a nation."[32]

The French and the English provided the living praxis; likewise, neither would the Russian Revolution be an infraction of the rule. Marx's fundamental conception of the subjective side of history (namely, that it is men who make history) became especially clear in his polemic against Arnold Ruge, the "Prussian." He argues that Ruge's reasoning led to trivialities,

> such as that *industry* in Germany is not so developed as in England. . . . On the other hand, suppose the "Prussian" were to adopt the correct standpoint. He will find that *not one* of the French and English workers' uprisings had such a *theoretical* and *conscious* character as the uprising of

the Silesian weavers. . . . The Silesian uprising *begins* precisely with what the French and English workers' uprisings *end*, with consciousness of the nature of the proletariat. . . . Not only machines, these rivals of the workers, are destroyed, but also the *ledgers*, the titles to property. And while all other movements were aimed primarily only against the *owner of the industrial enterprise*, the visible enemy, this movement is at the same time directed against the banker, the hidden enemy. . . . As for the educational level or capacity of the German workers in general, I call to mind *Weitling's* brilliant writings, which as regards theory are often superior even to those of *Proudhon*.[33]

It would be interesting to draw up a similar balance for the October Revolution. But for the present, let one comment suffice: Had the October Revolution been a change in power in the tradition of the Asiatic mode of production, then nothing need have changed in the social structure (at least nothing essential), since that was what was specific to this formation. I think that it has become clear what aspects of the Marxist theory of revolution play the constitutive role.

Now to the second aspect of the revolution. The dialectic of the world historical effect of capitalism and its world market is such that, although it makes possible regional collisions despite underdevelopment of the productive forces, capitalism can only be negated as a social formation on a world scale; i.e., communism, as this negation, is possible only with the abolition of the world market.[34] So much for our theoretical considerations.

But a proletarian revolution did not take place in Germany, nor in any of the other developed capitalist countries. The facts of the case are sufficient for Bahro to reproach Marx for having overestimated the maturity of the forces of production (as a consequence of the Hegelian tradition) and to allow him to utter the all too familiar phrase that history corrected Marx's prognosis. Although Bahro himself claims that the historically schooled productive force —man—is the sole decisive factor,[35] and that the maturity of the forces of production cannot be judged alone in terms of technical criteria since social movements also play a role,[36] he never once poses the question of why such a movement did not take place in, for example, Germany. The question is not merely an academic one. It is of practical significance as well.

Was it the immaturity of the forces of production which prevented a revolution from occurring, or was it rather their maturity which enabled capital to corrupt the upper layers of the proletariat and its organization? Was it not imperialism, with its open plundering of the peoples of other regions, which then provided capital with the conditions for granting the proletariat at home a quasi-bourgeois standard of living (Lenin recognized this early enough), and so on? Was it not these factors which induced the Social Democratic Party to lay aside its revolutionary goals and programs and proclaim its adherence to evolutionism? Bahro does not ask these questions (the same Bahro who so vehemently and zealously tries to justify a defense of Stalinism), nor would they fit into his notion of history. In this part of his book he makes history into an autonomous (i.e., metaphysical) subject standing over human beings, which poses its tasks according to its plan, assumes them, resolves them, imposes the next task, etc.; that is, a subject that makes men into its tool as it wishes, that makes the working class, the Bolsheviks, the Russian Revolution, the socialist revolution, the Asiatic revolutions, etc. into the executive organs of its tasks, and finally charges Stalin with a world historical mission—all this in accordance with the task of history.[37] Even in his introduction Bahro writes:

> We must try and do justice to the historical character of the Stalinist structure of domination. The political history of the Soviet Union is not one of abandonment of the "subjective factor," but rather of its transformation by the task that it had to undertake of industrializing Russia. It is the new tasks of today that demonstrate the anachronistic character of the old-style party and not just certain principles of political morality.[38]

It is this task-fetishism and the metaphysical-objectivist conception of history that have induced Bahro to step in in defense of Stalinism wherever the opposition tries to impute even a bit of relevance to subjectivity; and indeed it cannot be otherwise, for Stalin fulfilled a world historical mission. Bahro's cutting attack on Trotsky and Trotskyists is in the service of this metaphysics and apologetics, although Bahro performs this service without any mission. How otherwise can we understand it when he writes that the Yugoslavian praxis in no way demonstrated

> that socialist democracy "in and of itself" is economically more effective in the Mandel sense [of the term]. For the Soviet Union in the 1920s and 1930s, the opposite would unfortunately seem to have been true.[39]

The basis for the purported overestimates is provided by Bahro with an ingenious and barren inspiration. It rests in the Hegelian methodological hypothesis of the unity of the logical and the historical, in which Marx remained largely entrapped. In this way, for Bahro the question is resolved; he then proceeds to undertake a complete revision of the Marxian conception of history. I shall only touch on this very briefly here. Since Bahro does not tell us what the term "unity" is supposed to mean, let me recall that in Hegel, unity means the same as identity. But Bahro's assertion is wrong from the fact alone that, had Marx been entrapped by this hypothesis, he would have had to proceed differently in his central analysis—i.e., in his analysis of capital—in such a way that he would have referred to money capital, which had existed historically for thousands of years, as capital as such (i.e., conceptually, as a concept in itself, or in Hegelian terms, logically). In short, Bahro's assertion does not apply to Marx's central categorical analysis.

The extent to which Marx happens to be Hegelian cannot be discussed here. The theoretical and real historical issues relevant to Marx's position have been discussed above. But after so much fuss, Bahro nonetheless tries to modify his reproach: "We are only maintaining, of course, that this conception has its *formal* basis in the Hegelian tradition. . . ."[40] But in Hegel, "formal" and "methodological" are identical expressions, or, more precisely, the method is the form in which the essence moves, and the formal, i.e., what pretends to the form, is essential to the object. So does Bahro mean that Marx is Hegelian only in method? That is just what was supposed to have been modified. Bahro would have done well to leave Hegel to himself, and turn to questions that illuminate the real historical background of Marx's assumption.

To conclude, I would like to say a few words on another one of Bahro's methodological mistakes. This consists in that Bahro reproaches Marx (I have in mind his repeated invocation of Marx's controversy with Bakunin[41]) precisely where Bahro himself made Marx unassailable. It was Bahro himself who asserted that his object of inquiry was different from the one that Marx had foreseen. In short, Bahro is in the end investigating a system that in his own opinion must be explained with categories other than those of the communist perspective. But in this controversy, it is the description of such a system that is at issue. Thus it is not permissible— Bahro himself says so—to invoke Marx to explain phenomena of

industrial despotism. (Despite numerous protestations that in analyzing this sytem one must proceed without Marx, etc., etc., Bahro
loads his book with innumerable quotations from Marx and Engels
without it ever being clear to the reader what Bahro is trying to
say thereby, so that his argument resembles more a collage than a
consistent explication of his own categorical premises.) Bahro's reproach against Marx comes to a head in the following statement:

> It was probably necessary to be both an anarchist *and* a Russian, to per-
> ceive behind the authority of Marx and his doctrine, in the year 1873,
> the shadow of Stalin. Marx did not see this shadow, he could not and
> would not see it.[42]

Bahro is not the first who espied Stalin behind Marx and Marxism. It is not Bakunin who made this statement; he would have
had to have lived another three years to experience even the bio-
logical birth of Stalin. Kolakowski, Raddatz, the New Philosophers
in France, and so on, have seen it for some years now. They have
been praised and celebrated by the press and other media, especially
when they make this revelation as insiders, and their books become best-sellers. When Garaudy called these New Philosophers
the "Playboys of Philosophy" he must have meant to say something about the general consciousness of the Western public as well.
Since it is likely that Bahro does not know about all this, I mention it merely to point it out.

Translated by Michel Vale

NOTES

1. Rudolf Bahro, *The Alternative in Eastern Europe* (London: New Left
Books, 1978).
2. Ibid., p. 13.
3. Ibid., pp. 47-48.
4. Ibid., p. 53.
5. Ibid., p. 49.
6. Ibid.
7. Ibid.
8. Ibid., p. 50.
9. Ibid., p. 43.
10. Ibid., p. 44.
11. Ibid., p. 46.

12. Ibid., p. 47.

13. Ibid., p. 70.

14. Ibid., p. 144.

15. Ibid., p. 81.

16. Ibid., p. 142.

17. Karl Marx and Friedrich Engels, *The German Ideology*, in Robert C. Tucker, ed., *The Marx-Engels Reader*, 2nd ed. (New York: W. W. Norton, 1978), pp. 159-60.

19. Bahro, p. 82.

20. *German Ideology*, p. 193.

21. Bahro, p. 86.

22. Ibid., p. 50.

23. See Lenin's "The Military Program of the Proletarian Revolution."

24. "The Impending Catastrophe and How to Combat It," in V. I. Lenin, *Collected Works*, vol. 25 (Moscow: Progress Publishers, 1964), p. 359.

25. Bahro, p. 66.

26. Bahro, p. 127 [My emphasis—H.G.].

27. Ibid.

28. Ibid., pp. 60, 131 ff.

29. *German Ideology*, p. 197.

30. See Richard Lorenz, *Sozialgeschichte der Sowjetunion*, 1 (Frankfurt/M, 1976), pp. 27, 34.

31. "Contribution to the Critique of Hegel's *Philosophy of Right*: Introduction," in Tucker, ed., p. 56.

32. *German Ideology*, p. 159.

33. Karl Marx, "Critical Marginal Notes on the Article 'The King of Prussia and Social Reform,'" in Tucker, ed., pp. 128-29. The Mensheviks also argued like Ruge before the Revolution. Lenin's reply was roughly: "So let's make the revolution in order to create such conditions."

34. In *The German Ideology* it is stated that "empirically, communism is only possible as the act of the dominant peoples" (p. 162).

35. Bahro, p. 92. Despite this insight, Bahro misunderstands Lenin's call for the creation of a new civilization and culture. Bahro reduces this to labor discipline and habits.

36. Ibid., p. 125.

37. The term "tasks" occurs in the following sentences: ". . . that the Russian socialist movement at the turn of the century found another task to fulfill than that to which they had believed themselves called"; ". . . that history had then to assume a new task than the one formulated by Marx"; "Their task was not that of socialism, however honestly the Bolsheviks believed so, but rather than of Russia's rapid industrial development. Only now, when this task has been largely resolved, does the struggle [the task] for socialism stand on the order of the day"; "The principal world historical task is the preparation of socialism"; "When the Bolsheviks seized power they were clear . . . that they had assumed the task . . ."; "The world historical mission of Stalin"; "The actual task of these revolutions" (those of the East); "The

industrially developed civilizations of the present are faced with the tremendous task. . . ." The list can be continued.

38. Ibid., p. 13.
39. Ibid., p. 104.
40. Ibid., p. 46.
41. Ibid., pp. 40 ff., and elsewhere.
42. Ibid., pp. 41-42.

LAWRENCE KRADER

The Asiatic Mode of Production

These lines are offered in the way of contribution to the dialogue that Rudolf Bahro has instituted in his discussion of the Asiatic mode of production. The point is not to enter into polemics but to extend our knowledge and to deepen our analysis of the nature of class society, the history of civil society, and the theory of value.

A mode of production is defined as an economic formation of society.[1] As such it is a twofold classification device; first, it is a means whereby the social whole is related to its economic basis, and therewith, the superstructure to the basis; second, it is the means for the periodization of history. In relating the social whole to the economic basis of the society, one element of the basis is selected out over all the others; this element is the process of social production; the elements of the economy that are set aside for these purposes are the relations of exchange, distribution, and consumption. The reason for the choice of the process of social production as the significant device for relating the whole, the basis and the superstructure, is to be found in the historical dynamics of economic and social development; this has been formulated in connection with the question of periodization.

Periodization of history is a device of classification whereby acts and events are grouped together for a purpose, whether stated or unstated, conscious or unconscious. In the theory of the modes of production, the index of the transformation of one historical period into another is given by the changes in the relations of social production in a given epoch; these relations characterize the economic formation of the society as a whole. The mode of production itself is constituted as the system of the forces of production; the forces of social production are the relations of the producers, expressed as living labor, both immediate and mediate, to the means of production in their particular forms; the forms of production that are of relevance in this case are property or ownership of the means of production; the means of production are dead, past, crystallized and objectified labor activated and applied in the process of social production by living, present labor, or social labor which is at once abstract and concrete, both objective and self-objectifying labor.

The Asiatic mode of production is not the earliest mode of production in human history; it is, however, the earliest social mode of production. Prior to the historical appearance of the Asiatic mode of production, the economic formation of society was communally organized; labor was communally and collectively combined and divided; production, distribution, and consumption were collectively organized; the principal means of production was shared and distributed; it was communal or collective; it was not individually owned; such means of production were hunting grounds, fishing banks, arable land, and the like. This communal or collective organization of production is expressed as the communal or collective mode of production; it had little to do with commodities, exchange relations, or the expression thereof as exchange value. The capability of reckoning up the amount of labor time expended in production, whether communal, private, or social, was poorly developed under this condition; hence the law of value, which is the expression of the amount of labor time thus expended, was poorly developed, if it was developed at all. The market was scarcely developed, and circulation, with expressions in money terms or prices, even less so. Exchange was practiced, but to a large extent it was ritual exchange, undertaken in conjunction with ceremonials, the offering of gifts and counter-gifts, together with forms of mutual hospitality and veneration practices.

With the development of exchange, exchange value is introduced, together with commodity transactions, the market, and some kinds of money and the circulation thereof. The unit of consumption is no longer the same as the unit of production, and specializations in production are developed. Labor comes to be combined and divided, by the effect of the mutual reinforcement of the factors of exchange, and by the separation of the unit of production from the unit of consumption, in conjunction with the increasing specialization of function in production; the combination and dividing of labor does not appear for the first time in history, but the forms of its combination and division are now utterly different from the forms in the communal or collective condition of social life in the archaic and primitive bands, clans, village communities, and tribes of prehistoric times. The communal organization of production is now replaced by the social organization thereof; the relations of labor are socialized, and therewith, production is socialized, distribution is socialized, being no longer simple sharing, or sharing out. Exchange is now socialized, being now opposed to ritual and ceremonial exchange; exchange is freed of its mystery.

The social organization of labor, of production, and of the economy as a whole is first brought out in history in the Asiatic mode of production; in this condition, production is socialized, but only in a partial and defective way. The relations of production are determined on the one hand by relations of social exchange, as opposed to ritual exchange, hence of commodity transactions, and their expression in the law of exchange value is to be observed, together with the laws of use value and of value. In its form, however, the unit of production is still the archaic clan, village community, gens, sib, or tribe. At this stage of development, a social surplus is produced and is alienated from its immediate producers by a group in society that is opposed to those who have produced it; this social surplus is expressed by the law of surplus value. The order in which the laws of exchange value, value, and surplus value are introduced into the system is not of significance, for this is not the way or the order in which they make their historical appearance; these laws do not stand in a causal relation to one another; none is a cause of the other. Yet each is a condition of the other. The relations of social exchange, of social production, and of production of the social surplus together constitute the social substance; this substance, in the Asiatic mode of production, is opposed to the form, which is still communal. The contradiction between the communal form and the social substance is the characteristic of the Asiatic mode of production that distinguishes it from all the other social modes of production, for, in the Asiatic mode of production, the village community, clan community, etc., continue to display and set forth the formal condition of their existence, whereas the substance of their economic and social relations has been transformed.

By the effect of the relations in the economy that are summed up in the law of exchange value, the relations of production and the relations of labor have been socialized, whereby society in the modern sense of the word has been formed, and the archaic and primitive condition of social life has been overcome. By exchange, commodity and market practices, the producing unities organized in villages, clans, gentes, sibs, bands, and tribes have been formed into a society, a people, a nation. The autonomy and autarky of the unit of production has been thereby overcome. At the same time, the archaic communal forms have survived, and indeed they survive down to the most recent times, even into the nineteenth and twentieth centuries, standing in contradiction to the social substance, as we have seen. By the effect of the economic and social relations that are summed up in the law of surplus value, the society has been divided into two opposed social classes, the class of those who have produced the necessaries for their maintenance, and an excess over the necessary amount, the excess being alienated by a social class that has not produced it, that excess being applied to the maintenance of the latter. This excess is unearned, for it is not exchanged with those who have produced it, and thus destroys the relation of equal reciprocation which is expressed in the law of exchange value. The law of surplus value thus gives expression to an antisocial relation.

The social substance of the Asiatic mode of production and of all subsequent modes of production of bourgeois and civil society[2] is constituted of these social relations of equal exchange and of the antisocial relations of alienation of the surplus. The contradiction between the social substance and the communal form in the Asiatic mode of production is obliterated in the latter stages of the Asiatic mode of production and in the later stages of the ancient-slave, and the feudal-serf modes of production; the contradiction between this form and substance has little significance in the modern capitalist mode of production. Labor in the Asiatic mode of production is unfree, being bound in the ancient village-communities, clan communities, and so forth. The Asiatic mode of production was so named by Marx because it was first detected in reference to the traditional history of India, China, Persia, Indonesia, and other Asian empires. At the same time, he found evidence of it in ancient Egypt, Inca Peru, and Aztec Mexico; perhaps therefore the term "Asiatic" should be dropped from the discussion of this mode of production, and the characterization "communal-social" mode of production should be substituted, for the reason that production and labor in this mode of production are *pro forma* communal, whereas they are social in their substance, as we have seen.

The Asiatic mode of production has been sometimes identified as early class society; this is an error, however, because a mode of production is not the same as a society; the mode of production is, as we have seen, the economic formation of the society. The mode of production, furthermore, is not the whole of the economic formation of the society, but is the sensitive indicator of the relations of the economy and the society, and their economic and historical dynamics, in relation to the opposition between the social classes, and in relation to the opposition between the combination and division of social labor on the one hand, and the forms of production on the other. The Asiatic mode of production designates the conditions under which the early class society has been formed. This society has been formed into a unity in the modern sense of the word by the action of the divisions and oppositions between the social form and communal substance, between the social classes, and by other divisions and oppositions as we shall see. The unity of society is constituted not by symbolic action, nor yet by force, but by the social relations of exchange and by the antisocial relations of exploitation. The worldwide presence and development of this mode of production has made sure that this mode of production is not homogeneous in its constitution, but is developed by a host of local, regional, and continental variations in the social conditions under which it is introduced and extended. Thus although there has been a general uniformity in the communal forms, yet these differ considerably among themselves: clans, villages, kin groups, lineages, sibs, and gentes are found in various forms and combinations in the different parts of the world, being constituted in different ways in Africa from the way they are in Asia, Europe, or the New World.

In respect of the Asiatic mode of production, these differences are formal and not substantial differences. In its substance, the society that is constituted on the basis of this mode of production is divided into the opposed social classes. The class that is constituted of those who are opposed to the immediate producers in society has a privileged place therein, and asserts its privilege by the declaration of interest in the alienation, allocation, redistribution, and latterly sequestration of the social surplus produced in the form of surplus labor and surplus product; the social class maintained by the social surplus by declaring its privilege asserts its interest in the alienation of the social surplus, which it both defends and prosecutes by transforming itself into the ruling class in society. The interest is neither subject alone, nor object alone, but is at once subjective and objective. The ruling class is not formed into a ruling class by the psychological motives of greed or lust; these motives may or may not reinforce the objective and subjective factors of class interest; the same may be said of personal factors of respect or sense of justice. A class interest is a social phenomenon, which is other than, and may not be reduced to, a psychological factor or an individual and personal one. The means whereby the social class maintained by the social surplus transforms itself into the ruling class is by the separation of the total power of control, force and coercion in the society into a concentrated part and a diffuse part.

The potential ruling class does not initiate this separation, but participates in it, contributes to it, and manipulates it in its own interest; the members of the potential ruling class, being conscious of the possibility of manipulating this separation and the profitability of concentrating this power, thereupon seize hold of it. The concentration of the force and power of coercion does not initiate the said process of formation of the ruling class in society; that class reinforces the process, manipulates it, and profits from it. The power must be first divided into a diffuse and a concentrated part. The diffuse part is the power of the people as a whole; the concentrated part is the central authority; the separation results from and is determined by relations of labor, exchange, and production, including the production of the social surplus, and the relations of the social whole, comprising the formal-communal and the substantial-social relations of the given historical period. The central authority monopolizes the socially concentrated power in the interest of the privileged social class, holding the official and governmental means of coercion or the threat of such coercion by the military and police arms, thereby bringing under its control the totality of the society in general, and the relations between the social classes in particular. The state in one sense is the abstract expression of this concentration of the explicit social control in society.

In this social stage of development, the chief means of production is the cultivated land; like the other means of production, it is owned, the juridical expression of the arable being the community. The ruling class is personified in the monarchy, and has no other juridical form whereby property in the means of production may be expressed than the community; the monarchy concretely, and the state abstractly, make their historical appearance in this stage as the overarching community which is the chief landowner. In theory therefore, the state is the landowner as the community magnified; the local community owns the land in practice; the members of the community, the local peasantry, appear as what they have been before, the holders of the land in possession, and not as tenants of a superior lord. Thus the relation of the peasants, as the immediate producers in the Asiatic or communal-social mode of production, differs fundamentally from the relations of the immediate producers in the classical-antique and in the feudal modes of production, to the means of production; the relations of the immediate producers to the means of production differ in these, the precapitalist modes of production: differ not only among themselves but also from those of the capitalist mode of production. The main difference between the form of the state in the communal-social mode of production and the form of the state in all subsequent historical epochs of the economic formation of society, and of the formation of society generally, lies in the nondifferentiation of the ruling class into a public and a private sphere. This nondifferentiation of the ruling class is determined by the nondifferentiation of this stage of society as a whole into a public versus a private sphere; this differentiation comes about only at a later stage of the development of this mode of production, of society, of the ruling class and the state, as can be shown in view of the following considerations:

It is sometimes held that in the Asiatic mode of production, or in its caricature, the Oriental despotism, there is no private property in land nor private landowners. This assertion is inaccurate, however. Neither private property in land nor public property in land is weakly developed in this stage of development, nor are they strongly developed, for they are not differentiated from one another. It would be anachronistic to take the developments of a later social stage as the measure of those of an earlier one. *De facto*, the public sphere exists as the means of concentration of the official powers of government; *de jure*, neither the public nor the private sphere has been brought forth at this stage, nor have they been given official, legal expression; yet the category of public property and that of private property alike are juridical expressions and hence the juridical and not the factual side of the matter is relevant. The social surplus that is alienated from its immediate producers still living in the archaic communities is given neither the form of public tax nor that of private rent in this stage of social development, but is indifferently rent-tax or tax-rent. It has the expression of surplus value, but its juridical form is neither public nor private, just as the land and labor that have produced it are neither public nor private, but communal *pro forma*, the state being the community magnified, as we have said.

Travelers from Italy, France, England, and Germany came to the realms of the Shah of Persia and of the Great Mogul in India, where they observed the great power and pomp of the monarchy. In particular, these travelers held that the rulers in the Orient were despots, and that under this condition the land was converted into an infertile desert. This news from the Orient was welcome to the advocates of mercantilist policy and of laissez-faire capitalism, personified by Colbert, Controller-General of Finances under Louis XIV. It was in the interest of the policy that he formulated to publish the finding that the strengthening of the institutions of the central regime and the weakening of the private ownership of the means of production led to the ruin of nations and the downfall of empires. The acceptance of the doctrine of the Oriental despotism and its deleterious effects on industry in Europe during the seventeenth century does not heighten the veracity of the travelers' reports of that time; it merely explains, at least in part, how this tale came to be embedded in European political and historical thought then, and came to be promulgated by the doctrine of free enterprise during the eighteenth, nineteenth, and twentieth centuries, until it achieved the fixity of a popular prejudice. Nevertheless, the doctrine of the Oriental despotism, with its hatred of state ownership of the land and of the means of production generally, remains today what it was three centuries ago—an interested expression.

The Asiatic mode of production comprises the twofold oppositions within itself: that between the communal form and the social substance, and that between the social classes. These contradictions have continued to exist for thousands of years, even if latterly in a travestied form, from the time of their earliest introduction in Ancient Egypt, Crete, Mesopotamia, India, and China, down to the nineteenth and twentieth centuries. In the later development of this, the communal-social mode of production, certain oppositions that were not present at its commencement made their historical appearance. Thus, the opposition between rural and urban production, and between the interest of the town and that of the countryside, appeared late rather than early in the history of this mode of production; the opposition between head and hand labor, just as that between the mediate and the immediate producers, did not come forward at the beginning but only later, after the initial stage of development; and the opposition between the public sphere and its interest, and the private sphere and its interest, was a development of a later and not the earlier stage of development of the mode of production in question.

The historical course of the development of these oppositions was a slow process, the time periods during which they were introduced being measured in centuries or even in millennia; they therefore give the superficial impression of stagnation. This is not the case, for changes were inherently developed therein over the course of time, albeit at a slower rate than the rate of change of the modes of production in the history of Europe, which underwent the transformation of the ancient Asiatic mode of production, as exemplified in the history of Crete during the second millennium before the present era, on the mainland of Greece at about the same time, and on the Italian peninsula some time later. Out of this transformation the classical-antique mode of production arose in Greece and Italy during the first millennium before the present era, in which slavery played an important role in social production; the classical-slave period was replaced and transformed into the feudal-serf mode of production in the history of Europe; the feudal period was replaced and transformed by the development of the capitalist and bourgeois mode of production. Of these various modes of production, the communal-social mode alone is worldwide by inherent development; the slave and servile modes are inherent, but localized in European history; the capitalist is worldwide by the force of having been externally imposed on the non-European parts of the world.

In the precapitalist modes of production here enumerated, labor was unfree both in its form and in its substance: in the communal-social mode of production, labor was bound to the village by tradition and custom; it was bound by the contradiction between communal form and social substance; and it was latterly bound by debts, rent and tax obligations. The slaves and clients of ancient Greece and Rome were bound to the persons of the owners and masters; the feudal serf was bound to the soil which was ruled over by the feudal lord, but not to his person. In the capitalist mode of production, the working class is free, the members being able to contract for the sale of labor power with this capitalist or that; in its substance the working class in capitalist society is unfree, being bound by the wage system.

The communal-social mode of production and colonialism

The history of modern bourgeois society and the capitalist mode of production begins effectively in the fifteenth and sixteenth centuries, at which time it was developed in Northern Italy, Spain, and Portugal, on either side of the North Sea and Channel, in England, the Low Countries, and the Rhine lands, where both internal and external factors made possible this development. The internal factor was the exploitation of the working class at home, this class having been torn loose from the rural communities in which it had lived and worked, seeking employment in the urban centers, only to be thrust back to the land, and then to the cities again. The external factor in the early development of capitalism was the trade with and conquest of the West Coast of Africa, India, Indonesia, Ceylon, Burma, Mexico, Peru, and the neighboring lands in Africa, Asia, and the New World. Here were predominantly lands of the communal-social mode of production, in either an early or a later stage of the development of that mode; the colonialist exploitation of these peoples contributed to the flow of wealth to Italy, Spain, Portugal, England, Holland, and France, during the eralier and later history of capitalism. The relation between capitalism and the so-called Asiatic mode of production, the communal-social mode of production generally, is expressed in, and in turn determines, the history of colonialism and the theory of colonialism. The communal-social mode of production was not present in North America; here colonization was practiced, in a different form than in colonialism, and the European colonial system was overthrown in the eighteenth century. There is no trace of the "Oriental society" in the history of America north of Mexico. The English, Dutch, French, Spanish, and Portuguese empires continued down to the nineteenth and even the twentieth centuries in North Africa, Africa south of the Sahara, South Asia, and the neighboring lands, where the communal-social mode of production had been conquered and exploited without cease.

The discussion of the Asiatic mode of production in tsarist Russia

The period of the Tartar yoke in Russia during the thirteenth, fourteenth, and fifteenth centuries led many historians, including some Marxist historians, to the conclusion that the history of Russia is a part of Asian, not of European history. This interpretation was reinforced by the consideration that the economy of Russia was predominantly rural, illiteracy was widespread in the countryside, and industry was backward in comparison with that of central and western Europe down to the time of the Russian Revolution. Thus the Russian poet Alexander Blok sang in his poem entitled "Scythians," "*Da—aziaty, my,*" (Yes—Asians, we). The early leaders of Russian Marxism, among them G. Plekhanov, brought out the thesis that the land reforms of the 1860s, whereby the serfs were liberated, together with accompanying changes in landownership, the strengthening in parts of Russia of the rural commune (*mir*) system and of communal government among the peasantry, the general backwardness of the rural economy, and the great social distance between the rulers of Russia and the peasants, created conditions for the Asian misery of Russia—*Aziatchina*. During the debates with Lenin at the beginning of the twentieth century Plekhanov argued for division of the land in the rural economy into municipal units, so-called municipalization of the land, and against nationalization thereof, holding that such nationalization would lead to an Asiatic restoration. Lenin argued for nationalization, holding that the restoration of a Muscovite Rus, that is, "a restoration of the Asiatic mode of production," would be the purest absurdity; he held that the capitalist mode of production was predominant in Russia in 1906, and out of this mode, an Asiatic restoration cannot follow.

In the course of his debate with Lenin, Plekhanov made a number of untenable assumptions: he identified nationalization of the land in the rural economy as a practice of the Asiatic mode of production; but this, as we have seen, is a superficial historical judgment in which a part is mistaken for the whole, making a nondeterminant part into a historical determinant, and misrepresenting nationalization as an "Asiatic" practice. It was nothing of the sort, for the nation did not own the land in the Asiatic mode of production; the ownership of the land was of a communal form—both in the village in practice, and in the agencies of the state in theory—in the so-called Asiatic mode of production. Here ownership of the land was differentiated from possession of it; but public versus private ownership was not differentiated in theory, whereas this latter differentiation was brought out in the reference to the policy of nationalization in the twentieth century meaning of the term. Moreover, Plekhanov implied that history could roll back in time and recreate past conditions; but such roll-backs are fantasies, in the form of agreeable wish-dreams or of nightmares. (Restoration is a well-known term in the history of Europe, Plekhanov's reference to it aside. Take the examples of the restoration of the monarchy in England after the Civil War of the seventeenth century, or the restoration of the Bourbons in France after the defeat of Napoleon; in either case the so-called restoration resembled its predecessor as mere externality, a show of form and theater. De Maistre and de Bonald were expressing their dreams and desires, they were not making historical analyses in advocacy of restoration of the monarchy, with all the disastrous consequences that come when the wish and the reality do not conform to one another.) The equation made between Muscovite Rus and the Asiatic mode of production is at best a thesis resting merely on a superficial resemblance between the economy of Russia in the middle ages and the then contemporary economy of parts of Asia; nationalization of the land was the means for attaining neither to the one nor the other, from the standpoint of the class struggles in the twentieth century, which was the common ground of Plekhanov and Lenin.

The organization of Russian agriculture during the latter part of the nineteenth century was the expression of a policy that took seriously the constitution of the Russian peasantry in the system of the *mir*. The argument in favor of the *mir* organization had a sound point of fact to make, but this factual soundness was lost by many at that time in the face of a wholly anachronistic conception. The sound point, brought out in one way or another by Ewers, Haxthausen, Chicherin, Leontovich, Sergeevich, Kliuchevskii, Kovalevskii, Platonov, Grekov, and Druzhinin, was that the *mir* as an institution of the peasant collectively existed in the nineteenth century; but the related point advanced by many was that the *mir* was continuous in history with the ancient Russian rural commune, the *obshchina*. Yet between the ancient *obshchina* and the modern *mir* a host of intervening historical developments obtruded, including the formation of class society, civil society, and the state; the development of public, state, official, and church forms, policies and interests in landownership; and the opposition between the public and private interests in this regard. The Russian peasants were emancipated during the course of the reforms of the 1860s in different ways and at different times in respect of the different types of landownership—accordingly, as they lay in private, state, church, and crown hands.

The historical and systematic discontinuity between the Russian commune of antiquity and the nineteenth century Russian peasant community was pointed out a century ago by Chicherin and others; the debate between Plekhanov and Lenin began not only from a false premise of Asiatic restoration, it began from a distortion of the history of the commune in Russian history. The danger to socialism, both in theory and in practice, of concentrating power over the means of production in the hands of the concrete agencies of the state by the nationalization of the land (which was Plekhanov's implicit point) has justification, but the introduction of issues that are irrelevant to this point reduced Plekhanov's credibility as a Marxist historian, and likewise as a politician.

The Leninist thesis of the predominance of capitalism in Russia, although far more tenable than Plekhanov's argument, is not transparent, and is in need of qualification, for the prospects of revolutionary victory lay not in the presence of capitalism in Russia but in its weakness. Both the proletarian movement and capitalism were weakly developed there, hence the Leninist vanguard was able to place itself at the head of the former, and insert itself in the revolutionary struggle. Capitalism was weakly developed in Russia, both absolutely, in relation to the forces of change and of conservatism in the Russian empire, and relatively, in its relation to capitalism in Great Britain and Germany at that time. The capitalists as a class in Russia did little to direct or improve their condition, and were almost helpless to do so. The Bolshevik-Leninists were able to assert themselves in view of the weakness of their enemy and of the movement that they led. It was not the vestiges of the Asiatic mode of production that made capitalism in Russia weak; rather it was the forces and relations in the history of Russian society, in the relation between the social classes, in the relations of production, and the forms therof. In its external relations the capitalist class in Russia was subordinate to and dependent on British, French, and other foreign capital of that time. These external enemies and so-called friends drained off the profits from Russian mining, transport, and other branches of industry. No one found an interest in common with Russian capital that helped to shore it up in the period 1900-1917; all the world's capitalists enriched themselves at the expense of Russian capital.

This situation was reversed after the First World War, when world capital, faced with the problems of German capital, broke up into groups, some working with the German capitalists against others, thus preserving it in the face of internal revolutionary threats. German capital was in any case stronger than the Russian, despite the losses in the War of 1914-1918. Thus Lenin's judgment that capitalism in Russia was predominant must be qualified, and the strategy of Lenin's party is to be evaluated in view of these qualifications. The revolution of 1917 in Russia was victorious for the Bolsheviks because of the weakness both of Russian capitalism and of the proletarian movement, at the head of which the Bolsheviks set themselves as the Leninist party has declared. The nature of imperialism and of the imperialist powers since World War II has changed in view of the lessons learned from the victory and defeat of the revolution in the various parts of Europe during the twentieth century.

The agricultural policy of Stalin, which concentrated the ownership and control over the means of production, was continuous with the policy advocated by Lenin in the debate with Plekhanov over the Asiatic restoration. Nationalization of the land proceeded on two levels: the right to the land, according to Stalin's doctrine and plan, lay with the collective farms, which asserted that right by working the land; the ultimate right over the land, both in the collective farms and in the state farms, and over both in theory and in practice, lay and lies in the concrete agencies of the state in the Soviet Union. The questions of ownership, which, just as those of the Oriental despotism, lie not in the basis of society but in the superstructure of society, were converted into counters in the Cold War between the Soviet Union and the West during the 1940s and 1950s; these counters are a credit to none who then applied them.

The Asiatic mode of production was propounded as a theory during the period 1925-1931, in reference to the Chinese revolution, its causes, consequences of the defeat, and to its aftermath, by Soviet and Hungarian theoreticians. Their theory distinguished between the history of Russia and the Orient; they did not apply the category of the Asiatic mode of production to the history of Russia; at that time, L. Madyar, E. Varga, M. Kokin, G. Papayan, and others applied the theory of the Asiatic mode of production to Chinese history, both ancient and modern, i.e., twentieth century Chinese history. It has been said that they also applied the category of the Asiatic mode of production in practice, but this is an error. Varga called for a program which if developed would then have been applied to the Chinese revolution, but such a program was not developed. The others did not go as far as Varga in this direction, but developed the category only in history, and where possible in theory. It was little developed in either case, for it was developed not critically but merely as an exposition. Yet these Marxist historians and theoreticians were aware, as Plekhanov was not, that the institutions of ancient China, such as the *ching-t'ien* (well-field) system which bears the elements within itself of the archaic communal unity of the villages, were discontinuous with the village system of modern China. They started out with the presupposition that the ancient Chinese village system was opposed to the archaic one from which it sprang, while the ancient system was continuous with the modern, which was its historical development, and that the village system at the time of the collapse of the Chinese empire in 1911 carried forward the antecedent system in a destitute condition, being exploited by both local and foreign agents of world capitalism.

The theory of the mode of production

The theory of the mode of production as the economic formation of society as a whole is a powerful weapon for the analysis of the periodization of human history, for it is the means to bring out that history as the history we make, in opposition to natural history, or evolution, which is the history we do not make. The strength of this theory, as it has been developed hitherto, has rested in its usefulness as a classification device in history, which is a static conception of both the theory and human history. In the foregoing pages, a contribution has been made to dynamic side of the theory, in reference to the contradiction between the communal form and the social substance of one of the modes of production, which has been known hitherto as the Asiatic.

Two further directions for the development of the historical dynamics of this theory relate on the one hand to the opposition between the forms and forces of production, and on the other to the relations of labor. The relations of labor in society are either free or they are unfree; if they are free, they are either free in their form or in their substance. We have seen that in the Asiatic mode of production, village labor, which was the preponderant and determinant labor in that mode of production, was unfree, being bound by custom and tradition, in this sense by customary law, by tax-rent obligation, and by debt, to the village community. In the servile modes of production in European history, during the slave period of classical antiquity, and during the serf period of medieval feudalism, social labor was unfree. During all these precapitalist modes of production, labor in society was unfree both in form and in substance. During the capitalist mode of production, social labor has gained its freedom, but only *pro forma*, being free and equal as a party to the contract for sale and purchase of its labor power against a wage; in its substance wage labor throughout the history of civil society is unfree. This relation and status of social labor has not been changed in the condition of modern civil-socialism, in which the contract for the sale of living labor, as labor power, against a wage is the predominant form of labor; labor in this condition is formally free, substantially unfree. Labor time of free social labor throughout the history of civil society, whether in its civil-bourgeois form or in its civil-socialist form, is a commodity, and is sold and bought as such, being subject to contract for its labor power. Thus the periodization of human history by application of the theory of the modes of production and the same periodization by application of the theory of the modes of social labor undergird each other, proceeding *pari passu*. The theory of the mode of social labor is in a reciprocally supportive relation to the theory of the mode of social production.

There is a superficial weakness in the theory of the modes of production; thus, many students of African society and history are loathe to apply the term "Asiatic" to the peoples whom they study. This is merely a terminological question, and may be readily dispensed with. The term "African" may be applied if it is understood that in the case of the ancient Asante, Mali, Ghana, Oyo, Benin, and other kingdoms of precolonial Africa, the same conditions of formation of social classes, civil society, and the state were in force, together with the relations gathered under the expression of the laws of value, exchange value, and surplus value; then there should be no apparent difficulty in calling the one "African" and the other "Asiatic," each with reference to regional variants of the same mode of production. Alternatively, these variants in the New World, among the pre-Conquest Peruvians, Ecuadorians, Bolivians, and Mexicans.

There is a more profound difficulty with regard to these modes of production as a scheme of classification of world history, however. Thus, the mode of production which some have called African, some Asian, etc., might be referred to by the analytic term "communal-social," which is the proposal here set forth; yet this mode of production is not comparable to the classical-antique and the feudal-serf. The Afro-Asian, communal-social mode of production is a development of world history, being the expression of the conditions of early formation of the social class, civil society, and the state; these conditions make their historical appearance among the peoples of the several continents, and at different times. Whether they are a single phenomenon or a series of independent occurrences, whether they are separately "invented" or diffused from one center, is an irrelevant question. They appear as the set of related conditions where economic exchange, trade, commodities, and commerce are developed, and where the social surplus that is produced is alienated from those who have produced it. In its first historical appearance, these relations of production and exchange and alienation of the social surplus are social in their substance; these laws hold for production in the conditions of traditional Africa, both North and South of the Sahara, in traditional Eurasia, in the Mediterranean world, and in parts of the New World, as we have seen. These historical phenomena are not regional but worldwide, and are in this sense *general* in the conditions to which they relate; they are not *particular* to a particular or to a closely related group of peoples. The mode of production of slavery in classical antiquity and of serfdom in medieval feudalism are different from the foregoing, being localized; they are the particular phenomena of European history.

The capitalist mode of production, like slavery and serfdom, is a particular development of European history; at the same time the capitalist mode of production is a worldwide phenomenon, which has freed itself from its particular and regional base. Unlike the communal-social mode of production, however, the capitalist is not an intrinsic, still less an inherent worldwide phenomenon, but has been externally imposed upon parts of Asia, Africa, and elsewhere by means of mercantile, military, diplomatic, and financial practices. Capitalism is an extrinsic development of world history. In the period of colonialism the lands of the communal-primitive and communal-social modes of production were brought under capitalist control by commercial and military means and by guile, integrated with the political, economic, and religious systems of European history, and therewith into the world history of capitalism. The Soviet system in Central and Eastern Europe is in this sense no less an extrinsic historical development.

A distorted theory of the Asiatic mode of production has been given currency, in which undue prominence is attributed to water control in the establishment of the Oriental society (despotism, so called). According to this version of the general theory, the lands of the Asiatic mode of production have either too little or too much water, or the one or the other at the wrong time of the year, so that the amount of water necessary for agriculture and for cultivation generally must be stored up, dammed, released, reconducted, diverted, channeled, sluiced, dispersed, raised up, lowered, and preserved from evaporation. All this has been accomplished historically by human effort that has been organized communally or centrally; by labor forced, voluntary, paid, and unpaid; combined in vast projects or divided in small-scale undertakings; by human labor that integrates head and hand or divides the one from the other. Water control is necessary for cultivation in the valleys of the Nile, Tigris, Euphrates, Punjab, Ganges, Huang-Ho, and Yang-Tze, in the chinampas of ancient Mexico and the qanats of Persia and Central Asia. It is a required means of production, but it is not the sole means of production under these circumstances, nor is it the chief means of production. It is necessary for the given form of cultivation under historical conditions in which the arable land is the chief means of cultivation and is fertilized by manure, watered, ploughed, seeded, and harvested. Seed, the plough, hoe, mattock, scythe, and sickle are part of the totality of the means of production, together with the earth and water; animals for ploughing, harvesting and for transportation are part of that totality.

Water has no mystery about it; it was used for irrigation by the villages before it was brought under the central control of the state through its concrete agencies. The particularity of water control is that it has been applied in history in direct conjunction with control over the people, by the central state apparatus. The theory of the Oriental despotism has been developed in conjunction with seizure upon water control not in order to explain the functioning of the Asiatic mode of production, nor the organization of the Oriental society, nor yet to account for the technology of agriculture under these circumstances, but to aggrandize the role of the concrete agencies of the state in the process of production in the traditional Oriental society. This role is historically attested, but it is one-sided history. The agencies of the state also used the monopolies over salt, iron, and other commodities in order to undergird their monopoly over the armed might in the society. Moreover, water control is only a part of the historical picture in another sense: As history it begins not at the beginning but in the middle; and as the system of history of the Asiatic mode of production, water control begins not with the primary factor and moment, but with the secondary. The village communities had undertaken irrigation practices before they were centralized by the agencies of the state in the civilization of the Nile, Tigris, Ganges, Huang-Ho, etc., as we have said.

The emphasis on water control is the means to bring out the technological factor in history. This factor is not to be ignored, but it is not the factor with which we begin as the primary one in history. The concrete agencies of the state, which control the water by means of technics they did not develop, are themselves the result of the historical development of the relations between the social classes and of civil society, of the combination and division of social labor, and the organization of the social whole. The agencies of the state are not the cause but the auxiliaries of causes whose moments lie elsewhere. The agencies are the abettors; they are neither the initiators nor the initiatives of history as such, but are engaged in the historical movements by other factors. The theory of water control in the Asiatic mode of production, in conjunction with the doctrine of the Oriental despotism, has a connection to the managerial theory of the state, according to which the state plays an independent and necessary role in production, to wit, the management of water resources in the ancient Asiatic mode of production, and the management of industry in the modern period. Thus the history of Soviet Russia and the history of the modern Chinese People's Republic are made into variants of the history of the Asiatic mode of production, following Plekhanov's line by other means. Thus Plekhanov's doctrine of the Asiatic restoration is wedded to the theory of technocracy, which likewise assigns to management an independent and necessary role in production, in order to bring out the managerial theory of the state.

The indirect relation of the Asiatic mode of production to modern history

The revolutions in Russia and China during the twentieth century took place in lands where capitalism was developed but weakly in comparison with its development in Central and Western Europe and in North America. The Russian and Chinese working classes were then preponderantly peasant, engaged in agriculture by traditional means. As a result of internal weakness and of blows suffered by foreign capitalist interests both in peacetime and during the First World War, the capitalist class in Russia could not withstand the attacks made against it by the Bolsheviks. The theory of the Asiatic mode of production is utterly irrelevant to these considerations.

There are, to be sure, certain parallels between the society in Russia in 1917 and the society of the Asiatic mode of production, as there are between society in China in 1949 and the traditional society of Chinese history. In addition to the predominantly rural and agricultural situation of the working class, and the high degree of illiteracy and of traditional relations of production, science was applied in industry in traditional ways, save in localized industrial enclaves. Between the peasantry and the central power there was a vast social distance; between the peasantry and the highest authority, communication was almost entirely ruled out. The history of the rulers and the history of the peasantry appeared to run independently of one another both in the society of the traditional Asiatic mode of production on the one hand, and in Russia and in China on the eve of the respective revolutions in these countries on the other. The peasants were exploited by the local landowners, rich peasants, usurers, and merchants, as well as by the agencies of the state and by the great controllers of the capitalist markets for the peasant product and labor. The peasant rural institutions were traditionally the family unities, the village unities, and voluntary associations for production and marketing, mutual aid, protection, and control. The villages were highly if incompletely self-sustaining and autarkic; intrusions into these village republics were made by the money-lenders, market representatives, and collectors of taxes and rents.

The parallels between the Asiatic mode of production and the peasant mode of production under capitalism during the early part of the twentieth century in Russia and China are effective, but only up to a point. The Asiatic mode of production was already reduced to a ruined form in the nineteenth century in Asia as a whole. Its vestiges were already in the process of elimination in China at this time, and the capitalist mode of production was already ascendant throughout the world, under the control of European and American powers. The local merchants and money-lenders were transformed thereby into local capitalists. The relations of the Asiatic mode of production in particular, the communal-social mode of production in general, are those of commodity exchange and production, the production and alienation of the social surplus; but the product is consumed in the main within the community that produced it, and thus commodities have small importance in the reproduction of the communal economy. There is little circulation of money under these conditions. The peasant sectors of the economies of Russia and China at the beginning of the twentieth century were little changed, quantitatively, from these relations. The principal difference between the conditions of the Asiatic mode of production and those of prerevolutionary Russia and China lay in the development of capitalism throughout the world in the twentieth century and in the opposition between town and countryside under this condition, in contrast to the absence of these conditions in the Asiatic mode of production. Capital is produced in the Asiatic mode of production, but on a microcosmic scale; the transformation of commodity into capital was not invented out of nothing under modern capitalism. The production of capital is expanded under modern capitalism, as is commodity exchange and the circulation of money; yet these are present in a small degree in the communal-social mode of production, and in a smaller degree in its antecedent, the communal-primitive mode of production.

Property

Property is the formal expression of the juridical right over a thing. As such, it is the external, officially recognized and public formality of a relation between a person and a thing; it is not the relation itself. Some property is a commodity, but if the property has no exchange value—it if cannot be sold, if it is subject to restrictive covenant, or entailed—then it is not a commodity. Property comprises the expression of rights not only over things, but over persons who are in whole or in part transformed into things; reification is the transformation of a human being in whole or in part to a thing. Unfree social labor is thus reified, the living labor time of wage labor, sold as a commodity is reified. Property is thus either directly thingly, or indirectly so if it is reified. Property, whether directly or indirectly thingly, is opposed to possession, which is likewise an expression of human relations to things, proceeding by three forms: 1) by physically laying hands on a thing; 2) by shaping or forming it; 3) by demarcating it. Possession is not a right, for it is not the expression of a social relation between the human world and the world of things. It is in this sense an expression of a direct relation; hence it is not formal or official.

Property is the expression of the social relation, given official, formal, and public acknowledgment, of the relation between the human world and the world of things. It is in this sense an expression of a mediate relation, whereby a right over a thing, or a bundle of such rights, is recognized by others and is publicly acknowledged as such. These rights vary considerably between peoples, and from one juridical system to the next. In one juridical system subsoil rights, surface, and supersoil rights go together in purchase and sale, unless otherwise specified; in another system they are separate rights that must be contracted for one by one. The rights being socially mediated are socially variable.

Property right in the history of civil society is either public or private. At the beginning of the history of civil society, in the communal-social mode of production, this opposition is scarcely developed, whereas in the later stages of the history of civil society, from the later period of the Oriental society, classical, feudal, and modern capitalist to modern civil-socialist, it is more fully developed, whereby the internal contradiction between property that is communal in form and social in substance is overcome. The land at the beginning of the history of the communal-social mode of production is held in possession as individual parcels by the members of the village community. The land is the property of the village community as a whole, and is distributed according to custom among the members who have a common right in the whole. The land in whole or in part can only be alienated with the consent of the village as a juridical body, the alienation of land being therefore the subject of a restrictive covenant, and the tenure thereof likewise. This early conception of property in the history of civil society is in practice the expression of the principle that the land is the property of the community, and only of the community, there being no other landowning body. From this it follows that the state as landowner is the overarching community, the community of communities; the monarch owns the land as the personification of the state. The local community owns the land practically and concretely; the state is the ultimate landowner abstractly, and concretely through its agencies, in the first place the monarchy. The opposition between public and private landownership under these circumstances is excluded. As we have seen, the social surplus that is alienated by the concrete agencies of the state in this stage of development has neither the public form of tax nor the private form of rent, but the undifferentiated form of tax-rent.

In the subsequent history of civil society, the private sphere is differentiated from the public sphere, the private interest is opposed to the public interest, and ground rent is opposed to ground tax, the tax in general being thus opposed to rent on the one hand, and to private profit on the other. The policy brought out by Adam Smith, whereby the public interest of the state is opposed to the private interest of capital, gives expression to an inherent development in the history of civil society between the public sphere and the private sphere. This development comes forth historically out of the opposition between the communal form and the social substance at the beginning of civil society. The opposition between the public and private spheres is the basis of civil society, as it was summed up by Hegel. This opposition was taken over and elaborated by Marx in connection with his theory of civil society, which has its basis in the opposition between the social classes. The two oppositions, between the social classes and between the public and private spheres, are not two different theories of civil society, but the theory of one and the same society at different stages of its development.

Public property is opposed to private property, both being developed out of communal property, which at the beginning of civil society is communal only in form. There is a widespread notion that the public property alone emerges out of the communal property; this however is a confusion of terms. The ancient form of public property fell under the *res publica*, the public thing or interest in Roman history. But this public matter or thing presupposed that the division between public and private had already taken place. The public and private lands are differentiated from the common land, which is neither public nor private; vestiges of the communal past may still be found in the category of the village common, where the sheep of every member of the village may graze. The members of the ruling class of ancient Rome identified that which is common with that which is public in their own private interests; this confusion is therefore an interested confusion. It is carried forward today in the practice according to which "the Commonwealth" is another name for the state, as though that which is common is the same as that which is public. In the theory of the state, however, that which is common ceases to be common, having been alienated by the ruling class through the public sphere, which is embodied in the concrete agencies of the state. The public affair, matter, or thing is first diffuse, then concentrated by and in the state in both its abstract and concrete historical manifestations, whereby the ruling class exerts its control over the opposed social class and over the whole of society.

Property is not the same as private property, nor is it the same as public property. Property in its public or private expression is a form that is opposed by the prevailing relations of production, and is determined by them. It is sometimes said that there is an economic and a juridical meaning of property, corresponding to a supposed opposition between an economic and a juridical form of property. This is a confusion of the theory of property, encountered not only among certain Soviet theoreticians but elsewhere as well. According to this theory, property is the term for private property, economic property the term for public property; property of the state is the same as public property. In this schema, private property and juridical are the same. This is a kind of wordplay, for property in all its social forms is the expression of a privative relation. Thus a thing, by being acknowledged to be property, is made the subject of restrictions in the use or enjoyment of it. Restriction is enjoined both in respect of public and of private property, and is in either case privative. Private and public property alike are expressions of juridical as well as economic relations, in opposition to the archaic-communal practices in primitive societies, in which all was held in common. In this case *communal* and *property* are contradictory to one another. In the civil condition of society, communal property, or common property, is communal in form only. Common is in this case opposed to private, and is usually and normally associated with public property, being subject to ownership in the public sphere and to control by the agencies of the state.

The ruling class in society has as its agency the public sphere, which is, in its formal and abstract expression, the state, the state being able to act concretely and practically through its various historical manifestations, personifications and agencies, which are the governments, republics, sovereignties. The concentration of authority in the public sphere of society is a privative act, whereby the right of the social whole is diminished, a part of society being excluded from the supreme power. The private sphere of civil society, within the ruling class, has access to the centralized authority indirectly, through the public sphere. The public sphere has the power over the social whole directly through the agencies of the state. The right of each sphere, public and private, is the power of redistribution of the social surplus; the two spheres, public and private, have opposed interests in this redistribution. The power over the alienated social surplus is not called into question by this opposition; moreover, the opposition between the necessary and the surplus part of the whole social product is not eliminated by this opposition between the public and private spheres. The opposition between the necessary and the surplus parts of the total social product is the primary conflict in the history of civil society, and is the initial factor in its formation; the conflict between the public and private spheres follows thereafter. Both conflicts are present in civil society today.

A juridical right is associated with an obligation on the one side, and with a duty on the other. A right is a part of a reciprocative system, whereby it is socialized, and is opposed to the right of the first, of might. A fully socialized system of right is fully reciprocative. In civil society in all its historical manifestations, a part of the social product is returned to its producers, a part is not. The part that is not returned is the social surplus, and the right to it which its producers have is not recognized by the State. It is not a reciprocated relation, the alienation of the surplus being the antisocial act whereby civil society is founded. The right is not a force in itself, both the right to the product and the alienation of the unearned part being aspects of the totality of forces and controls exerted in the society, on the one hand by the whole, on the other by the ruling class. The state is founded not by force but as the abstract expression of the two sets of forces, the reciprocated and the nonreciprocated, in society; the forces correspond to the reciprocated and the nonreciprocated relations of society and of social production. In the subsequent development of civil society the public and private spheres come into opposition to one another over the redistribution of the social surplus, and its allocation to this interest or to that, to this sphere or to that. The interest of Colbert and Adam Smith was evidently in the redistribution of the social surplus, in the form of rent and profit, to the private sphere of capital, as opposed to the public sphere. The modern civil-socialist mode of production is opposed to the modern capitalist mode by bringing out the public sphere and interest as opposed to the private; in the former case the means of production are transformed into public property right, in the latter case into private property right.

The world is ruled by capital. The relations of wage labor, commodity exchange, and surplus value dominate the economic and social relations; and under these circumstances, the history of property, public and private, has not come to an end. The internal opposition between public and private property will be eliminated when the opposition between the interest of the part, whether public or private, versus the interest of the social whole is overcome. The unity of civil society is abstractly expressed by the state, which arches over the opposition between the social classes, and between the public and private spheres; the state arches over the entire history of civil society. Civil society is not the same as class society, for the social classes came into existence and into opposition to one another before civil society and the state made their appearance. Civil society is a form of class society in which the social power is centralized, in which the public and private spheres are formed, and in which the state is given both abstract and concrete expression, in order to bring together that which has been sundered. While the state is an abstraction, it is not a fiction. It is thus more narrow than civil society, which has brought it forth, for civil society is at once abstract and concrete, real, actual, and fictional. The existing state is the proof, if any proof be needed, that the opposition between the social classes and between the public and private spheres has not come to an end, either in history or in theory. Civil society and the state were brought into being historically by the oppositive forces in the communal-social mode of production in general, in the Asiatic mode of production in particular, in the servile modes of production of European history, in the modern capitalist and the modern civil-socialist modes of production. Civil society and the state arch abstractly over the totality of these modes of social production, and are manifested concretely in each of them.

The difference between modern capitalism and modern civil socialism lies not in relations expressed by the laws of exchange value, use value, and surplus value, nor yet in the commodity relations of labor and its product; the difference between them lies in the opposition between private and public property and in the changed nature of social welfare. By the class struggles, social labor has gained its freedom *pro forma*, but has not gained the substance thereof; this is the case of urban labor in the modern civil-socialist mode of production as it was in medieval feudalism. The right to gain a wage by labor is a substantive right in the Soviet Union, the contribution to the social welfare being assured to each and from each thereby. The doctrine "from each according to his abilities, to each according to his work" accompanies the doctrine of the right to work at a gainful job. This body of doctrine is closely related to the utopian socialist doctrine, particularly that of the Saint-Simonians, "To each according to his capacity," "reward according to works." Thus, the welfare of the society is the contribution of each working individual, who derives from it in the measure of his contribution. The practice in the Soviet Union is the individual contribution of his work, and the derivation of his welfare thereby; the welfare of the whole is the sum of the individual derivations of welfare, in theory. The practice in this case does not diverge from the theory, save by factors that fall outside design in general, plan in particular. Under capitalism, the social welfare is likewise a matter of individual undertakings; but in this case it is a residual category, for there is no right to work that is recognized in this mode of production. The right to contract for the sale and purchase of labor power is an equal right of social labor and of the representatives of capital; thereby the individual welfare is assured; the social welfare is not. The social welfare is the right under capitalism of the sustenance of the unemployed, the industrial army of the reserve, likewise of the indigent and of the lumpenproletariat. It is the negative category of welfare that is filled when the positive labor power of these unemployed is unfulfilled, by being uncontracted for. This is a matter of partly controlled, partly uncontrolled social and economic conditions. The right of sale of labor power is therefore only a voluntary, private, and individual right; it is not a public right, into which it has been transformed in the juridical system of the Soviet Union.

The doctrine of the universal right to work was advanced during the nineteenth century not only by the Saint-Simonians, but by the Fourierists as well. The doctrine of the right whereby each contributes according to his capacities was conceived as being mediated by the communes according to the utopian socialist theory in certain of its redactions. This doctrine has been transformed according to the Soviet juridical system, whereby the public sphere, through the concrete agencies of the state, mediates between the individual contribution, the social welfare, and the individual return from his or her contribution; it is the conception of individualism, comprised within the doctrine of universal public right. It has a general relation to the theory of socialism, in the same sense that the doctrine of the utopian socialists has such a general relation. At the same time it is directly derived from the theory and practice of civil society. There is no overt contradiction here, for the theory of socialism likewise has a general derivation from the history and theory of civil society, class society, and the state. The public relation of welfare under the Soviet juridical system, and the private relation of welfare under the capitalist, are both dominated by the relations of commodity exchange, of living labor as a commodity, the alienation of surplus value, and of production and valorization of capital.

Property is a passive form that does not determine the historical movements, but is the expression of these movements, which are in the first place the opposition between the social classes, between the central power and the diffused power of society as a whole, and between the public and private interests. Property is not therefore a means, nor a thing, but is the indirect expression of the rights over things, rights that must be socially recognized as such and thereby socially mediated. Property at the beginning of the history of civil society was not yet differentiated into the public and private spheres, and was only later opposed in this way, within the same economic formation of society. At the present time, property has been developed in the capitalist mode of production in a form that is predominantly private in its juridical expressions. In fact, the participation of the public sector in capital production has become increasingly predominant under capitalism in recent times, for the reason that under the conditions of contemporary industry and finance, the formation of capital goes far beyond the capacities of most private firms and even of small nations, rich and poor alike, so that they must concentrate and combine, even as did capital in the hands of private capitalists in the history of the industrially advanced countries of Europe and North America.

Public organization and control of the process of capital production is thoroughgoing in the Soviet Union and China; for that reason, capital in the Soviet Union has assumed a favorable competitive position in certain branches of industry, albeit at the expense of others, and of agriculture. These selective prospects may be predicted in reference to China, and for the analogous reason. Thus, economies of scale in capital formation, rational disposition of labor skills, unity of the market, planning in terms of an organized whole, and the overcoming of regional and ethnic differences have supported the development of capital production in the USSR, within the limits mentioned, as they have in Western capitalism in the past; the European Common Market likewise seeks solutions in this direction. The thesis that Western capitalism and Soviet capital are in competition, and behave in conformable ways to these exigencies of competition, is an attractive notion. Superficially there may even be some justification for it. Yet, however attractive the parallels between the two systems may be, they lie primarily in the superstructure of the society. Profound differences between the two systems have already been alluded to, and remain to be further explored.

NOTES

1. The evidence for the theses here set forth, the critique thereof, together with the bibliographic documentation, is brought out in a number of works. See: Lawrence Krader, *The Ethnological Notebooks of Karl Marx* (Assen: Van Gorcum, 2nd ed., 1974); idem. *The Asiatic Mode of Production* (Assen: Van Gorcum, 1975); idem., *Dialectic of Civil Society* (Assen: Van Gorcum, 1976); idem., *Treatise of Social Labor* (in press, at the same publishers); *Die Ethnologischen Exzerpthefte von Karl Marx* (Frankfurt: Suhrkamp, 1976); *Ethnologie und Anthropologie bei Marx* (Berlin: Ullstein, 1977). They have been the subject of my seminars given at the Free University of Berlin, and are in no small measure the result of discussions with my students there. They are moreover the working out of ideas which were discussed with my late friend, Karl Korsch.

2. For a discussion of the concept "civil society," see chapter 1 of *Dialectic of Civil Society*.

LUCIO LOMBARDO RADICE

State Socialism

To Rudolf Bahro, and to all the German comrades who struggle for the communist alternative

When one wishes to understand the nature of the economic-political-ideological system that people tend more and more to call "real socialism" or "actually existing socialism" (precisely due to the difficulty of reaching an agreement on its definition), it is necessary to account for several complexes of facts *simultaneously*. A definition of "real socialism"—particularly of its typical expression, the "Soviet model"—that does not satisfy all the "boundary conditions" imposed by those complexes of facts, by those evident phenomena, cannot be accepted. First of all, let us try to list, not necessarily in order of importance, the facts for which a theory of real socialism must account.

Thirteen boundary conditions

First. We have to deal with a rigorously centralized, tendentially totalizing economic-political-social structure. Everything is the property of the state; all political and cultural activities are controlled by the authorities.

Second. The state and the Communist Party (the only one, or one proclaimed the leading party in perpetuity over all other legal parties, by constitutional decree) are intertwined and substantively fused into a single power apparatus. At the summit of the state *cum* party is the secretary-general of the party; he is the supreme and unassailable authority, with truly monarchical powers.

Third. Structures of this type—very similar, if not identical, among themselves—were constructed in countries very different from one another, starting out from quite diverse initial conditions: in countries with backward agricultural economies, without a democratic-bourgeois tradition (Russia, China), as well as in countries in which a higher level of industrial development and a high level of political-cultural pluralism existed before the revolution (Czechoslovakia, and to a lesser extent, East Germany, Hungary, Poland).

Fourth. In regimes of real socialism there has been a tremendous development (in some cases even an historic take-off) of the productive, civil, and cultural structures. The less developed nationalities—in Central Asia, the Caucasus, Siberia, central China—have been brought into contact with modern history, culture, scientific rationality, formal schooling, and a common alphabet through the profound transformations effected by the revolution in the postrevolutionary period (in all its diverse and contrasting phases —see point six).

Fifth. Industrialization (more generally, the headlong development of science and technology) has been the hallmark of the "Soviet model," whose point of departure was a quite underdeveloped agrarian society. But a great leap forward in industry, technology, and science has occurred even in countries (most remarkably in the GDR) that applied the Soviet model on the basis of an already notable capitalistic industrial development (and this despite the sometimes rather heavy-handed forms of Soviet stipulations and interventions).

Sixth. If one excludes some very recent and anomalous cases of countries proclaiming themselves socialist (Cambodia, Ethiopia) and finding credit with this or that great socialist power, the authoritarian, centralized phase of the regime of real socialism has generally been preceded by a democratic phase of intense mass participation, with the masses "emerging" for the first time in history into the political struggle and the new postcapitalist power. (This brings to mind the 1920s in the Soviet Union, the political weight of the soviets and the internal debates of the Bolshevik Communist Party; the years 1945-48 in the countries of Eastern Europe, and the experiences of the people's democracies before February in Prague.)

Seventh. Marxist-Leninist doctrine has become a true "religion of the state" in the authoritarian, centralized phase of the regime of real socialism. In the preceding phases, however, and particularly in the USSR, Marxism was fermented by a veritable political, cultural, philosophical, and pedagogical *Sturm und Drang*; all ideas and all institutions were brought into play and transformed.

Eighth, and very important. Within the monolithic, centralized, authoritarian system we have become accustomed to calling "real socialism," the forces that gave birth to a period of liberalization (the Twentieth Party Congress, Khrushchev), of democratization (Spring and Autumn in Prague, January 1968 through April 1969, the first and second Dubček periods), and of debureaucratization (the Chinese Cultural Revolution of 1966) managed to affirm themselves even after many years of apparently stable rule. These efforts at relatively deep-going *renewal* of the typical "real socialist" regime have had as their protagonists the leaders of the "system" itself and have come *from within*, not as a result of an overthrow from the outside. Moreover, among the more active elements in the *socialist renewal* (the revolution, and the abolition of private ownership of the means of production are not brought into question) there are men who had been hit hard by the terrible repressions of the regime of the preceding period and who have nevertheless remained communists.

Ninth. The efforts of these men have so far had, if not an ephemeral, at least a relatively brief life. Despite the failure of these attempts at "enlightened socialism," at socialism "in freedom" or "with a human face," and at antibureaucratic socialism with direct participation of the masses in politics and power, a leftist opposition nonetheless continues to be produced, one may well say, within all the "Soviet system" countries. This opposition is if anything becoming broader and more aware, and is beginning to create politicians, historians, and theoreticians who attempt to delineate the prospects and the forces of a *communist alternative* to actually existing socialism.

Tenth. Outwardly seen, the totalizing political-ideological regime of real socialism appears to be bound to a fusion of party and state, and to generalized state ownership. In fact, the socialist regimes that have moved away (in a relatively anti-authoritarian direction) from the Soviet model are the Yugoslav (decentralization, auto-gestion, significant elements of cultural freedom) and the Cuban (organization in communities, in collectives; the political will of a leader who is in direct rapport with the masses, to avoid institutional ossification).

Eleventh. Another characteristic period common to the systems of real socialism is the unanimous and often spontaneous resistance of the great popular masses to imperialist attacks aimed at the destruction of the socialist foundation of the regime (in the USSR, the civil war of 1919-21, and the Patriotic War, 1941-45; the long popular mass resistance in China and Vietnam against the Japanese and against the European and American colonialists). In sum, one must also explain the fact that, contrary to what happened in fascist Italy, not defeatism but full solidarity with the regime has reigned during the gravest wartime crises (in Italy, defeatism was a mass phenomenon during the fascist war).

Twelfth. Real socialism—typically the Soviet system, albeit not it alone—has to date gone through *two* periods with different characteristics. *First period*: Brutal liquidation, with bloody and extremely severe repression (trials, the gulag) of the first postrevolutionary democratic phase (in the sense clarified above). *Second period*: A trend toward a relatively moderate and tolerant regime (in the USSR, after Khrushchev's liberalizing turn), if with fluctuations depending on the magnitude of danger posed by the opposition, some of whom were able, for periods of varying length, to dissent openly without being arrested or exiled. Control becomes the dominant element, in place of direct repression—i.e., *control* over public officials, the unions, the soviets, the schools, the means of mass communication, the internal mobility of citizens, foreign passports, etc. It must be stressed, however, that hand in hand with the tendency toward relative tolerance and a relatively peaceful divestment of the critics went an increasing *loss of drive*, a *tendency toward stagnation*, a *loss of consensus* and of *credibility*. The period of the establishment of the absolute power of the party-state was, on the contrary, *dynamic* and *constructive*, and based on broad mass *consensus* and the *enthusiasm* of the volunteers for the construction of socialism.

Thirteenth. The Soviet Union (and here we shall limit ourselves to it) has without a doubt played the role and pursued the policies of a great power, and it would not be difficult to list a number of cases in which Soviet foreign policy has followed the classical canons of the defense and affirmation of state interests in the traditional sense. Nonetheless, one must stress that (1) the rapid breakdown, and hence failure of the German-Soviet nonaggression pact of August 1939, demonstrates that beyond all tactics and every strategy of neutrality, the *very nature* of Stalin's Soviet Union on the one hand made Hitler's aggression inevitable, and on the other hand placed the Soviet Union in the center of the antifascist camp; (2) on the whole, the victory of the Chinese Revolution and the end of colonialism in general are unthinkable without Soviet presence, even though in the end the outcome has often been hostility to the Soviet Union; (3) the one great power that has systematically opposed (and still does) antiworker and antipopular dictatorships throughout the world is the Soviet Union; (4) alongside the manifestations of genuine exploitation, the dependence of the "people's democracies" of Eastern Europe upon the Soviet Union has led, as we said above, to some notable progress in many areas—which by contrast, absolutely has not taken place in countries that have remained in the camp of imperialism (one need only think of the contrast between Soviet Armenia and Turkey). We shall leave aside for the moment the question of Chinese foreign policy, insofar as China, in a seemingly knee-jerk action, takes the side of whoever is against the Soviet Union.

The inadequacy of degeneration and deformation theories

Let us examine, first of all, whether or to what extent all of the phenomena listed under our thirteen boundary conditions bear out the theory (or theories) according to which the authoritarian, centralized Soviet regime—in particular, the Stalinist regime—is the product of a deformation or degeneration of the socialism (without a qualifying adjective) constructed after the revolution in the USSR.

The first communist who applied the term "degeneration" of socialism to the Stalin era was Palmiro Togliatti, in his deservedly famous 1956 interview in *Nuovi Argomenti*. Togliatti spoke of the "degeneration" of the socialist system in polemical contrast to the explanation officially put forward at the CPSU's Twentieth Party Congress, now usually summed up as the "cult of personality." This formula (Mikoyan's) and Khrushchev's "secret speech" blamed Stalin's despotic personality for the trials, purges, and deportations, and set as their objective the restoration of socialist legality and collective leadership, leaving the underlying structures of Soviet society untouched.

Togliatti was fully correct when he stated that the "personality cult" theory diverted attention from the search for the deeper causes that had steered development away from democratic norms and legality, to "degeneration." And his stand on the matter was "earth-shaking" at the time, in the words of Franz Marek.[1] For the first time since the founding of the Third International, a major Party leader opened up a Bolshevik thesis to debate, rejected the principle of the "leader state" and "leader party," and advanced the new theory of polycentrism.

Togliatti nonetheless remained steadfast in his conviction that the socialism that had been realized in the USSR under Stalin's leadership was Socialism with a capital *S*, in need of no adjectival qualifications, but that it had suffered deformations that could be corrected without changes of the system as a whole. Togliatti pursued the question further, and in the doctrine of the exacerbation of class struggle *after* the victory of the revolution discerned the theoretical core of the degeneration of Stalinist despotism.

Why do we reject the degeneration theories? After all, they are compatible with one of the most important of the phenomena we listed—the fact that the despotic regime was preceded by a democratic-revolutionary phase. But such theories draw no basic distinction between the two phases, using the same term for both of them: "socialism," without qualifications. Rather, the central question would seem to be: *which* socialism?

No embodiment of the kind of socialism sketched out by the founders, Marx and Engels, is to be seen in the Soviet model. In the words of Rudolf Bahro:

> Our actually existing socialism is a fundamentally different social organization from that outlined in Marx's socialist theory. This practice may be compared with that theory, but it should not be measured by it. It must be explained in terms of its own laws. All theories of deformation, however, from Khrushchev to Garaudy, lead away from this task.[2]

The impossibility of separating structure and superstructure

Actually existing socialism—first and foremost the Soviet model—is a system fundamentally different in essence from that delineated in Marx's socialist theory, for one basic reason. In the Soviet model, the state, a separate body, not only does not die out but in fact swells to enormous dimensions, with a tendency to control everything and to become omnipotent:

> There is no more striking antithesis between Marx's communism and the actually existing socialism of the Soviet bloc, even from the theoretical standpoint, than in the character of the state.[3]

Without going into the (difficult) topic of Marx's conception of socialism, one point is certain: what Marx very clearly had in mind was that a new political structure based on direct democracy, which we shall call the commune, was to be rapidly substituted for the state as a power apparatus with its own separate existence.

Now the present Soviet system, though I am absolutely convinced it is a postcapitalist system (we shall discuss this later on), still has, nonetheless, as its *essential* characteristic, the omnipotence and omnipresence of the state. The state in the USSR, and in the other countries that have adopted it as a model, is the supporting structure of production and the economy (general state ownership, management of the economy through ministries, centralized planning, internal and external markets regulated by state organs, and so forth).

This hierarchically organized state, owner of everything, could indeed be compatible with different political forms (consider the tyranny of Stalin, Khrushchev's enlightened rule, and the moderate bureaucratic government of Brezhnev), but it is not compatible with *all* possible political superstructures. State socialism—that is, a postcapitalistic regime in which the state is all (or strives to be all)—is certainly not compatible with democracy, understood as the emancipation of a nation's toiling citizens, and their full and free participation in the government of public order. Moreover, an analogous situation also exists in a capitalist economy. Capitalism is compatible with quite different political structures and institutions (from fascism to constitutional monarchy to parliamentary republic). It is *not* compatible with a political superstructure in which power is in the hands of a network of worker councils, nor is it compatible with the transformation of the opposition class into a class that exercises power *within* democratic parliamentary institutions. (Consider developments in Chile in 1970-73: the distinguishing feature of bourgeois democracy is that it allows freedom to workers only in opposition.)

The *two periods* thesis thus appears to be utopian: "The Soviet Union must carry out a political revolution of the bourgeois type after having destroyed private ownership," says the Soviet Marxist critic Leonid Pliusch quite explicitly.[4] The fact of the matter is, however, that either a strategy in which political institutions (despotism) and economic institutions (state ownership) are changed together must be mapped out and carried through, or efforts at liberalization and/or democratization are doomed to failure, as the fundamental historical experience of the Twentieth Congress has shown.

The same criticism regarding the separation between structure and superstructure can and must be applied, in my opinion, to the definition of the Soviet system as a "socialism with illiberal features," often heard from the leaders of the Italian Communist Party. This slogan seems in fact to imply the possibility of abolishing the "illiberal features" so as to get at (or recover) the "good" socialism beneath, although—we repeat—illiberal features are part of the very nature of pan-statism. This is not to say that the battle for democratic freedoms and civil rights, even elementary ones (e.g., freedom of information) cannot—nay, even must not—be the starting point and the spark for a transformation of the whole. It is a necessary but not a sufficient condition. The events in Czechoslovakia of 1968-69 cannot serve as an absolute standard for judging, because the "new course" was halted by an armed force from without. However, it can perhaps be said that one element of weakness of the "new course," perhaps the principal one, was the fact that the regaining of basic freedoms was "out of phase" with the reform of the basis of the power system. I say "out of phase" because the 1968 Spring was marked by an emerging freedom of information, of assembly, of the press, of public debate, while it was only the "Autumn" (September 1968-April 1969) which saw the quite broad and rapid development of a council network—"soviets" in the original sense of the term. And one must examine closely the reason for the "second occupation," the one of April 1969, which brought about the final fall of Dubček and the beginning of the Husak regime. In fact, it is quite likely that, in allowing the leaders of the "new course" to return to their leadership positions after the forced talks in Moscow, the Soviet leaders envisioned a Hungarian-style development (a "Kadarization"), that is, a moderately liberal regime, compatible, as we have already said, with state socialism. In the Autumn the factory councils movement developed, and that was incompatible with state socialism; the underlying reason for the second intervention and for the total "normalization" was probably the base movement for reform of power, not the four stone-throwing incidents at Aeroflot's windows.

The dominant thesis in the Spanish Communist Party also seems to me to suffer from the same defect of separating structure and superstructure. (I say "dominant," not "official," because in the Spanish Communist Party, as in the Italian Communist Party, an absolutely free debate has opened up on the nature of real socialism.) In the formulations of the top-level Spanish Communist leaders[5] this separation appears as a clear distinction between "society" and "state." It is in fact said that the Soviet *state* is not a socialist state, while Soviet *society* must be considered socialist—although perhaps "primitive," "medieval," or "in a larval stage." Thus the criticism expanded upon above holds: Society cannot be separated from the state here; both must be reformed together. (I add, but in parentheses, that a *state*, as such, can never be socialist.)

Postcapitalist society: a tentative choice of terms?
Transitional society: from what to what?

In the language of the Italian left the expressions "postcapitalist society" and "postrevolutionary society" have been enjoying increasing currency as equivalents for the "Soviet system," or, more generally, for "actually existing socialism." Note, for example, the title of the *Il Manifesto* meeting in Venice—"Power and Opposition in Postrevolutionary Societies"—which gathered together representatives of all the factions of the European left.[6]

The expression seems acceptable to me as a tentative descriptive term; moreover, it is politically clearer than "real socialism." The expression in fact permits a first, tentative identification of the two antithetical camps, putting together all those who hold fast to the historical assessment of October and its consequences as a revolutionary break that led *beyond* capitalism. Whoever does not accept calling the "real socialist" countries *postcapitalist* societies, denies them *any* socialist or at any rate revolutionary feature. The fact remains, however, that the term "postrevolutionary society" is not a definition but only a label for a postwar camp.

"Postcapitalist" is a *negative definition*; it in fact means that in the system defined by that adjective, private ownership of the means of production has been abolished, and along with it, capitalist profit and land revenues. In the rest of this article, I shall use the term *socialism* with the same, identical, purely negative meaning—a synonym, in sum, for *postcapitalism*. With this as a premise, once we affirm the socialist (postcapitalist) character of the "Soviet system" we must next ask, *what* socialism?

In the Italian left and in the Italian Communist Party as well, there are those who tend to define "real socialism" as a *postcapitalist society in transition to socialism*, thus attributing a positive meaning (democracy-emancipation) to the term "socialism." Even this definition, or hypothesis, is contradicted by the persistence and continued development in "real socialism" of the state, of a state that ever more completely controls the life of the country from above. If by "transition" one means what is customarily meant as a *natural* and peaceful *passage*, an *evolution*, it is impossible to see how such a state, with such a tendency to continued inordinate expansion, hierarchy, and bureaucraticization, could evolve toward a socialist democracy (whatever the form, which for our present purposes is neither here nor there). Such a state is in itself opposed to any process of democratization, inasmuch as such a process *must* also be (we repeat) one of a dismantling of the state. A break and a reversal of the tendency seem, therefore, inevitable if a change is to take place in which we firmly believe (we shall explain how and why later on); it could take place in the form of a *crisis*, but not in the form of a *transition*.

At this point, however, we must take a step backward to consider a thesis quite prevalent on the left, according to which the "Soviet system" is not socialism (not even only in the negative meaning explained above) but is, on the contrary, capitalism—state capitalism, with a new state bourgeoisie.

State capitalism? New bourgeoisie?

That there exists in the Soviet system, and in those modeled on it, a vast, numerous, *separate* body of bureaucrats, who govern the party-state from above, is a *fact* beyond any doubt. Moreover, the "separation" of the bureaucrats from the citizens has been abundantly documented even by the official Soviet satirical magazine; from *Krokodil* one can compile an ample anthology of cartoons and jokes poking fun at the chasm between the bureaucrats and the people. This, however, is an observation of fact, and is hence of but provisional character.

Who are these party-state functionaries, whom for brevity's sake we shall call bureaucrats? Do they constitute a specific category by virtue of their function? a social stratum? or indeed, a class? The notion that the Soviet bureaucracy constitutes a *new class* is certainly not new: one need only recall that *The New Class* is the title Milovan Djilas gave to the book that signaled his transition from the communist tradition to social democracy. We should like to discuss this notion, taking as basis the argument that seems to us the most solid and the most consistent, namely, Charles Bettelheim's, which refers to a "state bourgeoisie" that "disposes over state power," "through whose mediation it disposes over the means of production."[7] But let's examine Bettelheim's argument more closely.

Bettelheim denies the validity of the principle that "identifies the abolition of capitalism with . . . the abolition of private ownership of the means of production in the USSR" (as Stalin affirmed in his speech on November 25, 1936, when he presented the draft for the new Soviet Constitution).

> Reality has itself repudiated this falsely optimistic conception. Since then, other analyses have led to a more dialectical conception. Such is the case with Mao Zedong's texts on the continuation of the class struggle under the dictatorship of the proletariat, texts published beginning in 1956, in particular his analysis of the contradictions among the people, and above all, his speeches during the cultural revolution. From these speeches emerges the basic thesis regarding both the existence of a bourgeoisie within the Party and the risk of the transformation of the leading Communist Party into its exact opposite, a fascist party, as has happened in the Soviet Union.

The identification of the abolition of private ownership with the abolition of capitalism, continues Bettelheim, is a "postulate" that "portrays *state ownership* as a form of *social appropriation* that has abolished the proletariat." On the contrary, says Bettelheim, this is not true: in the USSR there exist wage laborers and a state bourgeoisie; "the social relations that characterize the USSR are fundamentally the same as those that characterize the capitalistic mode of production." In sum, in the USSR there is "a capitalist state" of a particular type, "state capitalism" with an exploiting state bourgeoisie and an exploited proletariat.

> But what is this bureaucratic class really? For its existence to be confirmed by facts, the "surplus value" would have to be transmitted from father to son. Yet this is absolutely not the case. In the USSR, posts in the Party, in the administration, in the management of industry, in the unions, etc., are not transmitted from generation to generation. They are nontransmittable functions. It is true that in many cases a position offers certain advantages, certain privileges. Often Party functionaries, the *apparatchiki*, are better paid than highly skilled workers. Many of them have a car or the right to purchase from special stores.

The first argument brought by Jean Elleinstein[8] against Bettelheim's thesis is a good place to begin my criticism. Let us continue. Does it make sense to speak of a state bourgeoisie in a society in which a capitalist sector does not exist, a *non*state bourgeoisie? Where state ownership and private capitalistic ownership of the means of production coexist, a process of symbiosis and intermingling is set in motion which Luciano Barca has called a "singular mechanism," thanks to which private capitalists become managers of nationalized sectors and, vice versa, the leaders of state-shareholding enterprises are transformed into private capitalists or come to have a share in capitalist profit. But how can there be capitalism and a state bourgeoisie, where state ownership is total and universal?

I would say that Bettelheim's position, like that of so many others, is based on a series of linguistic abuses that make it propagandistically rather effective, but scientifically inconsistent. Privilege becomes "profit," state functionaries who direct a wholly state economy become the "bourgeoisie," state socialism becomes state "capitalism." But let us examine seriously what happens to the *surplus*, the surplus product over and above wages in the Soviet system. It is distributed and utilized according to a public plan (however good or bad it may be, it is *public*, the work of labor collectives), not according to the logic of the (nonexistent) private *profit* of the bureaucrats. "It may be presumed" (to quote Elleinstein once again) "that a minimal portion of the product of labor not distributed to wage laborers (in the form of wages) and taken back by the state is appropriated by the party and state functionaries in abnormal proportions. This is a logical consequence of the bureaucratic phenomenon: but to go on from this to speak of *surplus* value, or of a bureaucratic class is a long step to take!"

There is also a great difference, we add, between *privileges* in daily life, in *consumption*, and the *profit* deriving from capitalistic exploitation! To confuse well-being, comfort, or even waste of consumer goods with profit, to confuse a privileged stratum with the bourgeoisie, seems to us,, frankly, to reduce the discussion to a very low level. Criticism of Soviet reality falls still lower when the label "fascistic" is used indiscriminately for *every form* of despotism and when "totalitarian state," Soviet state socialism, and a counterrevolutionary fascist dictatorship instituted to save and defend capitalism are united under a single formula. No matter that these arguments have been put forth by such outstanding personages as Mao Zedong or Benedetto Croce. They are what they are: *ideologies* instrumental *for waging a struggle* against the Soviet Union, *not theories for understanding* it as a historical reality. We settled accounts with this type of ideology forty years ago when we had to drive it from the consciousness of the antifascist cadres and masses to achieve the unity necessary to defeat fascism; rather than waste much more time on it, let us go on to more serious investigations and theses.

State socialism and the Asiatic mode of production; the theory of backwardness

One of the more illuminating contributions to the "critique of actually existing socialism" that Rudolf Bahro made with his book is the structural parallel he draws between today's modern state socialism and the ancient "Asiatic" mode of production. It is worthwhile, I believe, to give a quotation that roundly illustrates Bahro's point of view.

> ... in its classically high form as economic despotism in ancient Egypt, Mesopotamia, India, China, and Peru, the Asiatic mode of production, the formation of transition to early class society, exhibits an instructive

structural affinity to our own epoch of decline of class society. In 1881 Marx finally expressed the view once again that the road to communism can be understood as a dialectical process of return to relations equivalent, but at a higher level, to archaic ones.

The transition stage between communism and developed class society, which was initially crossed "forwards," and is now to be crossed "backwards," is characterized in both cases by a specific function of the state which arises directly from the social division of labor and cooperation. Productive forces which belong to the state, which are either no longer social or are not yet so, are what provide the specific characteristic of both epochs. We will understand better the real contradictions that lay in wait for us beyond capitalism, if we take a somewhat closer look at the old "Asiatic mode of production," the old economic despotism.[9]

In this, the despot, owner of all the land, "is in fact only the representative and administrative summit of a ruling class [perhaps it would be better to say "caste" or "corporation"—L.L.R.], which stretches down through the church and state bureaucracy to the tax collectors and village elders as well as to the heads of official corporations of merchants and craftsmen."[10]

Without a doubt, Bahro brings out some quite notable structural analogies between ancient preslavery despotism and state socialism. In the first place, the surplus—that is, in the Asiatic mode of production, the excess agricultural output levied by the tax collector —is used, for the most part, on the large public works necessary to the entire collective (first and foremost irrigation, regulation of waterways in the case of ancient despotism); it is not transformed into the private incomes—or profit—of the ruling bureaucracy. In either case, i.e., at the beginning and the end of the history of class society, this bureaucracy is an open nonhereditary corporation that can co-opt the more active elements of the people into its ranks. Moreover, an analogy may also be drawn between the "theological" character of the state and the sacral character of the orthodoxy watched over by the bureaucrats.

At this point, however, a problem arises. In harking back to the ancient Asiatic mode of production, is the intention merely to prove that an omnipotent sacerdotal-bureaucratic caste can exist without, however, being *an exploitive class* (neither of the slavery, nor the feudal, nor the capitalist type), or is it *also* implied that a certain direct historical link does indeed exist between the ancient and modern state ownership?

What meaning does the term "semi-Asiatic" have as far as the

Soviet Union is concerned? Is it true, as Rudi Dutschke asserts even in the title of his book,[11] that to "set Lenin on his feet" he must be put into the historical context of Russian "semi-Asiatic" backwardness? Is it correct to contrast a "semi-Asiatic way" and a "European way" to socialism, or rather does the opposition between state socialism and emancipatory socialism consist in something else?

It is useful to divide this problem into two parts. *First question*: Was tsarism a regime with "Asiatic" traits, and thus "semi-Asiatic," or, on the contrary, a semifeudal regime advancing to capitalism? *Second question*: Accepting the "semi-Asiatic" nature of tsarism, what sort of connection exists between the bureaucracy of the Soviet party-state and the tsarist bureaucracy; is it a continuation by inertia of the latter or is it not?

Bahro replies to the first question affirmatively, in disagreement with Lenin:

> . . . Lenin could not have known the detailed drafts Marx made for his ultimately very short letter to Vera Zasulich of 1881, where Marx saw the fundamental character of the traditional Russian mode of production as analogous to the Indian, and stressed the typical complementary relationship between the fragmented patriarchal peasantry, still redistributing the land in their village communities, i.e. possessing it collectively, and the central despotism. In Lenin's first major text against the Narodniks, he went so far as to reduce the ramified system of Tsarist bureaucratic despotism simply to the agency, if not already of the bourgeoisie, then at least of the compromise between landlords and capitalists, as if this despotism was simply a case of Western European absolutism.
>
> The Tsarist state machine had always been *more* in precapitalist times than the executive organ of the nobility, *more* than a "serf state." And beside its modern function, which Lenin of course did see correctly, it maintained till the end of its days an *independent socio-economic relationship* to its historic peasant base, this persisting *alongside* the serf relationship (which presupposed the Tsars). This was precisely the sense in which Marx and Engels called the old Russia "semi-Asiatic."[12]

I am not at all competent to judge if, or to what extent, Bahro's criticism of Lenin, and his assessment of tsarism in its final phase are correct. I shall, nonetheless, hazard an hypothesis: it is probably a *question of emphasis*. Perhaps Bahro is right to stress the "Asiatic" residue of tsarism; Lenin, however, was right to place the emphasis on the aspect of modern, feudal-capitalistic despotism evident in the tsarist apparatus. It must be said—in passing, because it does not bear on the rest of our argument—that *questions of emphasis are as important* in historical theory as in political struggle. Putting the emphasis on the (relative) continuity between the tsarist bureaucratic structure and the postrevolutionary state apparatus is very risky politically, because it does facilitate in some measure the *purely ideological* efforts of the *practical* adversaries of socialism in any form, who distort and dilute the insight, retaining only the point of stress. Serious discussion is thereby abandoned in favor of common propaganda: "In Russia there is a new tsarism, exactly like and perhaps worse than the former."

This brings us already halfway toward an answer to the second question, which, however, rather than serving the ends of political propaganda, should—within the present writer's competence in this regard—serve as a historical refutation of any link of continuity between the "semi-Asiatic" prerevolutionary bureaucratic machinery and the postrevolutionary party-state apparatus.

State socialism followed a historical democratic-revolutionary break

In the first place, when it is said, as Leonid Pliushch said in good faith and without any anti-Soviet sentiment, that "the arbitrary power of the tsar was succeeded by the arbitrary power of the Communist Party," quoting a statement made by Korolenko in the twenties, but presenting it as the dominant opinion today among Marxist critics, then clearly, it would seem, a position is being upheld which is not compatible with one of the congeries of historical facts that we listed in the beginning of this paper, which constitute the "boundary conditions" that any acceptable theory of the Soviet system must meet.

It is not permissible to *backdate* the state socialism that Stalin established with ruthless severity in the thirties, to the twenties, the first postrevolutionary decade. Here too the problem is one of emphasis (although of crucial significance). Enrico Berlinguer was right when he commented in an interview in *Repubblica*, August 2, 1978, that "It is true that internal dissent was beginning to suffer restrictions toward the end of Lenin's life, that is, before Stalin's appearance on the scene, and this fact we do not hesitate to reprove and criticize." He is even *more correct* (I stress once again that the question is one of emphasis) when he adds:

But it should not be forgotten that it was Lenin who brought persons who had previously opposed his line and even the insurrection of the Soviets in October 1917, like Zinoviev and Kamenev, into the ranks of the Party leadership and Soviet power. . . . The deformations of "organic centralism" and of "bureaucratic centralism" . . . have nothing to do with the democratic centralism that Lenin conceived and put into effect: i.e., not a unanimity *ex ante* but a method to ensure, *in the end*, an indispensable unity in the Party's orientation and concrete work. That is, *after* the possible diverse positions have been stated freely and democratically, the majority position would rightfully become the position of the *entire* Party.

I think we may profitably consider the internal democracy of the Communist Party (Bolshevik) in Lenin's years after the Revolution and Stalin's first years. This was, indeed, the decisive element in what we call, by common consent, *soviet democracy* of the twenties. It is on the other hand true that in the Congress of the Soviets which immediately preceded the October Revolution and which, with its Bolshevik (and left Social Revolutionary) majority, constituted the precondition of the revolution, a political battle took place among the various parties. It is also true that the opposition parties did not immediately disappear with October, as the elections for the Constituent Assembly showed, and that the left Social Revolutionaries were in the first governments of the People's Commissars. But it is also true that the fundamental precondition for democratic debate within the soviets was free debate among Bolsheviks.[13]

The crucial comparison is not between state socialism and tsarism, not between the post-October period, considered as a whole, and the democratic-bourgeois February-October periods, but rather between *state socialism* and *soviet democracy*: between two postrevolutionary phases, between *two conceptions of socialism*. The great slogan of October was "All power to the soviets!" i.e., direct democracy by the councils, quite like, if not identical with, postrevolutionary community democracy—a first historic example of which Marx saw in the Paris Commune. In the course of, let us say, about fifteen years, the prospects of soviet democracy faded and finally died; the soviets remained such in name only, in reality being transformed into organs of the omnipotent and centralized state built up in the thirties. Thus the Party passed from "democratic centralism" to "bureaucratic centralism," transformed (degenerated) into the executive organ of a "vertical" state apparatus.

When I say "soviet democracy of the twenties," I do not mean to oppose a mythical model of emancipatory socialism to later state socialism. Quite the opposite: My purpose is but to underscore the fact that soviet democracy was not capable of constructing *that other* socialism which, however, is contained potentially —although confusedly—within it. But beyond this, let me leave thorough critico-historical examination of Russia in the twenties —which would be impossible (both objectively and subjectively) here anyway—to others, and to limit myself merely to pointing out that there was a revolutionary rupture in all areas. A new leading class, new protagonists, burst forth onto the historical scene, traditions and "common sense" were knocked down and overturned; in cultural life, revolutionary poets, film-makers, and revolutionary directors developed apace and influenced not the aristocracy but the great masses.

As directly regards the central problem we have raised—the transformation of soviet democracy into state socialism—let me be clear at once that the supporting structure of the future omnipotent state was to be the workers and revolutionary cadres formed during the democratic-revolutionary phase. Note well that the bourgeois specialists, or even the old bureaucrats who were used or re-used, were placed under the control of functionaries whose class origin and/or politics provided a full guarantee of their fidelity to socialism. Indeed the case of Dzerzhinskii, the first and leading organizer of the new political police, which became, in the thirties and forties, the terrible state within the state, uncontrolled and secret, of the Abakumovs and Berias, is quite symbolic. Dzerzhinskii is the sublime figure of the idealist revolutionary; Makarenko, the champion and patron of reeducation of the *bezprizorniki* [street children] dedicated his second "colony" to him (the first was dedicated to his literary and moral teacher, Maxim Gorky, a central figure of soviet democracy of the twenties).

I am speaking of the twenties, because even the Moscow of 1930 where Woland was to organize his Sabba, in *The Master and Margarita*, was a Moscow in which the bureaucrats and critics of the regime were quite powerful, but far from being absolute monarchs.

The clear, definitive (insofar as the use of such an adjective has historical meaning) transition to state socialism occurred with the forced collectivization in the countryside and forced industrialization (five-year plans). The backwardness of this vast country, or better, of this multifaceted continent made it necessary to force the primitive accumulation which in the West had taken place over the course of the preceding centuries. Stalin's way of forced movement and rigorous regulation from above prevailed over Bukharin's gradualist, and hence democratic perspective.

From "people's democracy" to the "soviet model"

We should like yet to make a brief, unequivocal comment about the Sovietization of Eastern Europe after 1948, a process that constituted a rupture and defeat of any other way toward socialism, a way summed up in the motto "people's democracy" or "progressive democracy."

The people's democracies of 1945-48 were not merely a tactic that Stalin came up with; he had already had in mind the successive imposition of the Soviet model on Bulgaria, Hungary, Poland, Czechoslovakia, and Rumania. They constituted a new historical reality with deep popular and national roots in the antifascist United Front, in the general understanding (during these years) of the necessity for a democracy that was open to socialism in order to extirpate (as was said at the time) fascism at its roots. We shall limit ourselves to a few quotations from Adriano Guerra's book,[14] which we recommend for a more thorough study of that period and the subsequent historical crisis hallmarked by the 1948 Czechoslovak *coup d'état* and the condemnation of Tito's Yugoslavia.

I share Guerra's statement that "the Cominform's condemnation of the Yugoslavian Communist Party in 1948 was in reality the condemnation of the very principle of a 'national way' to socialism." But let's see how such a principle was enunciated in the years 1945-48 by some of the leading exponents of "popular democracy."

Dimitrov 1946: "Bulgaria will not be a soviet republic but a popular republic in which the leadership function will be performed by the vast majority of the people, workers, peasants, artisans, and intellectuals with ties to the people . . . there will be no dictatorship, but the fundamental and decisive factor will be represented by the working majority of the nation."

Gomulka 1946: ". . . The Soviet Union had to pass through the stage of dictatorship of the proletariat, whereas in our country we do not have this stage and know that it can be avoided . . ."

Gottwald 1946: "The experience and teachings of Marxism-Leninism show that the dictatorship of the proletariat and the construction of a soviet regime are not the only road to socialism. Under certain conditions socialism can be reached by other routes. The defeat of fascism and the sufferings of the people have, for example, revealed in many countries the true face of the ruling class and together have strengthened the self-confidence of the people. At such moments of history new ways and new possibilities are opened . . ."

During those years, the years between the end of the Second World War and the beginning of the Cold War, Stalin considered, I believe, this other way to be possible (and even others: according to authoritative testimonies, he told a labor delegation that at least two different ways to socialism existed—a Russian one and a British one). It was the Cold War, I believe, which pushed Stalin to impose by force (and what force!) the Soviet model on the people's democracies, pushed by the obsession (not just his, but that of the system created by him) of keeping everything under control. After 1948, "people's democracy" was still spoken of, but only as a national variant of "dictatorship of the proletariat." It is time, however, to bring our discussion to a close.

State socialism meets all the conditions posed at the outset

"To conclude . . . In the USSR the ownership of the means of production is administered by the state . . . What type of state, what is its relation to society? It is still a centralized and bureaucratic state, relatively separated from society. The administration of the economy is not socialized; politics is not socialized. Without socialization of politics there can be no democracy and without democracy there is no socialism . . . socialism as Lenin conceived it . . ." Thus says Luciano Gruppi.[15]

Agreed. It follows from this, as a logical corollary, that "real socialism" (the "Soviet model") is a new, original, unique economic-social-political formation; a socialism different from the one Marx outlined and from which Lenin had begun to build. The most effective term to apply to this new formation seems to me to be *state socialism.* Without trying to verify this laboriously, point-by-point, it nevertheless seems to me, in the light of all the preceding arguments, that the "boundary conditions" spelled out at the outset are satisfied by this definition of "actually existing socialism." And this includes the last condition (if we may mention it in passing), namely, the state's acquisition of a personality and logic of its own as a separate being; at least in part, this logic is the logic of every state, the logic of power. The fact that one is dealing with a state *socialism,* however, seems to us to be borne out by the overall progressive character of the Soviet state's foreign policy (see our last point).

We have already said that an element of despotism is inherent in state socialism as such. The word despotism, however, is rather ambiguous and polyvalent: it must be qualified with the right adjective, lest we fall back into such terms as "totalitarian state," used to describe both revolutions and counter-revolutions alike.

We find Paolo Cristofolini's essay on "Western despotism" to be of great help in delineating the specific characteristics of the kind of despotism inherent in state socialism.

> With regard to . . . Stalinism and the history of the USSR, the static features ascribed to Asiatic despotism are not easily reconciled with the cruel and harsh forced accumulation nor with the creation in a few decades of an industrial apparatus of the dimensions of the Soviet one . . . It may be asked how much sense there can be to talk of despotism with regard to the USSR, when the presence, in the crucial phase of its construction, of elements so far removed from the Asiatic model, is ignored. The answer can even be extended so as not to exclude the presence of elements of despotism in the construction of the USSR, but one may only, in this case, consider elements of that evolutive "Western despotism" linked to the increase of labor's productivity, which liberal apologists are less inclined to discover in the socialist state.[16]

The contradictions of state socialism

We think we can take Paolo Cristofolini's analysis a step further and suggest the term *"socialist despotism"* for the specific kind of despotism inherent in state socialism.

This should bring to light the first contradiction in real socialism. By virtue of their postcapitalistic and postrevolutionary nature, societies currently organized in the form of state socialism are extremely dynamic. In them the same despotism that enabled them to become dynamic, industrial, scientific, modern, will serve as a Procrustean bed or an *"eiserne Jüngfrau,"* an "iron maiden," to use one of Rudolf Bahro's images, for their further development.

> What the Czechoslovak transformations brought to light was simply the real structure of the society emerging from the East European revolutions and ultimately from the October revolution. And the pace of he transformations, above all the rapid restructuring of the Communist Party itself, showed how pressingly this new structure is waiting, at least in the industrially developed countries, to throw off the armour that protected it in its larval stage, but now threatens to choke it. Only with violence was the social potential released in 1968 forced back into the straitjacket it had outgrown. The potential still remains, and it will rebel again —first of all with passive resistence to the inadequate superstructure— until one day this system will be fully rejected by history, even in the Soviet Union itself.[17]

We should like to conclude with these words of Rudolf Bahro, strong words expressing an unshaken faith in the capacities of socialism, even "state socialism." A word of concern, if not distrust, should be in order. The longer the breakdown of the system is artificially delayed by the powerful conservative element, the more serious the crisis of transition will be. The party-state, born of revolutionary cadres, cannot go on *ad infinitum* reproducing from within itself revolutionary cadres to drive the needed renewal forward. Prague 1978 is no longer Prague 1968, nor can it be. There has been a regression and qualitative change in the ruling apparatus. The condemnation of Rudolf Bahro, a communist critic who, from within real socialism, sought to transform it into emancipatory socialism, is another negative sign, which must be cause for concern to us socialists and revolutionaries.[18]

Translated from the Italian by
Richard Gardner with Michel Vale.

NOTES

1. Franz Marek, in R. Medvedev, R. Havemann, J. Steffen, et al., *Entstalinisierung—Der XX. Parteitag der KPdSU und seine Folgen* (Frankfurt am Main: Suhrkamp, 1977), p. 177.

2. Rudolf Bahro, *The Alternative in Eastern Europe* (London: New Left Books, 1978), p. 13.

3. Ibid., p. 31.

4. Il Manifesto, *Potere e opposizione nelle societa postrivoluzionarie*, Alfani editore, January 1978 (Atti del Convegno di Venezia, November 11, 12, 13, 1977), p. 56.

5. See Santiago Carillo, *Eurocommunism and the State* (Westport, Conn.: Lawrence Hill, 1978).

6. See note 4.

7. *Potere e opposizione*, pp. 93-96.

8. Jean Elleinstein, *The Stalin Phenomenon* (Atlantic Highlands, N.J.: Humanities Press, 1976).

9. Bahro, p. 67.

10. Ibid., p. 81.

11. Rudi Dutschke, *Versuch, Lenin auf die Füsse zu stellen. Über den halbasiatischen und den westeuropaischen Weg zum Sozialismus. Lenin, Lukacs und die dritte Internationale* (Berlin: Wagenbach, 1974).

12. Bahro, pp. 86-87.

13. On relations between the soviets and the Party see Giuliano Procacci, *Il partito nell'Unione Sovietica, 1917-1945* (Bari: Laterza, 1974).

14. Adriano Guerra, *Gli anni del Cominform* (Milan: Gabriele Mazzotta Editore, 1977).

15. *Momenti e problemi della storia dell'Urss*, Istituto Gramsci (Rome: Editori Riuniti, 1978), p. 188.

16. Paolo Cristofolini, "Il dispotismo occidentale," in *Critica marxista*, no. 3, 1978, pp. 71-90.

17. Bahro, p. 10.

18. See my article on Bahro and Communist opposition in the GDR in Lucio Lombardo Radice, *La Germania che amiamo* (Rome: Editori Riuniti, 1977); and the multi-authored volume edited by Hannes Schwenger, *Solidarität mit Rudolph Bahro—Briefe in die DDR* (Hamburg: Rowohlt, Reinbeck, 1978), in which part of the article mentioned above was translated.

Was "Actually Existing Socialism" Historically Necessary?

The authorities of the GDR would have us believe that the sentencing of Rudolf Bahro to eight years at hard labor had nothing to do with his book (whose publication is not authorized in that state) but with espionage. The book, which certainly required much time to be thought out and written, would appear to be nothing but a diversionary action, a novel device for concealing the real work of a spy——a "cover" that entailed the devotion of long hours and great efforts of thought in the areas of sociology, history, economics, and politics.

What Bahro's heavy sentence actually attests is how much the GDR authorities fear the accusation which *The Alternative* represents and, above all, the program it calls for——a "cultural revolution" against "actually existing socialism," that is, against the privileged ones of this supposed socialism. For, in our opinion, the most essential part of this book is that which concerns the program and the steps to be taken in order to pass from actually existing socialism to the construction of a truly socialist society.

Bahro's description and analysis of the societies of actually existing socialism are generally deeper and more precise than those found in other authors, who for the most part have focused on injustices and police brutality, or on the false rhetoric, etc. Still, in this area we learn little from Bahro that we did not already know. However, taking this analysis as a starting point, Bahro goes on to develop a program——one that does not renounce Marx and socialism, but, on the contrary, links up with that which is most basic and most profound in Marx. His program——and this must be particularly emphasized——is in no way a program of reforms that would be acceptable to the most "progressive" or most enlightened

currents in the bureaucracy. And there continues to be such political differentiation in the bureaucracy, even at its highest levels.
There is scarcely an old communist from an Eastern European
country who, though no longer a party member but still a communist, has not said to me in substance: "In every Central Committee, including in the Soviet Union, there exist potential Dubceks,
because these countries can no longer be governed as they have
been up to now; many see this, but they dare not confront their
own thoughts or do not know what to do. The change did not succeed in Czechoslovakia; but it will start up again, and one day,
somewhere, it will succeed. That is the time when all the real problems will be posed and a variety of programs will be born."

At that time some will be content with a few reforms that enable the machinery of state to turn a little better or a little less
poorly; others will want to go further, much further, in the
direction of socialism. The program Bahro describes was conceived
with this in mind. We do not intend to examine its details; it will
surely require corrections, adjustments, and additions that experience will bring. We must not forget that Bahro's book is the work
of a single man, whose source materials were certainly limited
because of the conditions in the GDR. It is probable that Bahro
had discussions with his friends and fellow workers and, in this
sense, his book gives a good picture of the feelings and general
climate throughout the GDR; but, to avoid arrest before com-
pleting his book, Bahro had to have proceeded alone to his generalizations and theoretical statements, which show his power as a
political thinker.

Bahro is not satisfied with such proposals as denial of the privileges or the many advantages that are given to bureaucrats and
their families, especially the privileges their children are guaranteed
for the future. He does not only question the absence of democratic rights, or propose the abolition of piecework, which the
labor movement has spent decades fighting for under capitalism. He states that, although in the enterprises there are no more
bosses or capitalists, there remains a hierarchical relationship of superior to subordinate that is no different from that in capitalist
enterprises. The worker is tied to his work post and he may not
and cannot control his activity: he is just a part of the machinery.
And, he says, it is at this point that we must start our fight to go
beyond "actually existing socialism." To achieve this, he advances

a number of clearly defined demands. He stresses the need for a sharp reduction in the work week and for making higher education available to all, citing *inter alia* the following statements of the world-renowned Soviet physicist Kapitza:

> Economists are of the opinion that, given the present level of labor productivity, only a third or even a quarter of the labor-power in a country is needed in order to provide the population with sufficient means of subsistence of all kinds—food, clothing, housing, means of transport, etc. . . . Today there are no economic reasons (*sic*) to prevent an economically developed country from giving its entire youth not only a complete high school education up to age sixteen or eighteen, but also a university-level education up to age twenty-one or twenty-three. *The state will probably have to offer the entire population the opportunity to pursue higher education, quite irrespective of whether this is necessary for the practice of their profession or not.*[1]

Bahro explains his position on the matter as follows:

> In no case can the conditions for freedom be measured in dollars or rubles per head. What people in the developed countries need is not the extension of their present needs, but rather the opportunity for self-enjoyment in their own individualized activity: enjoyment in doing, enjoyment in personal relations, concrete life in the broadest sense. . . . A working week of five six-hour days, for example, would no longer place a quantitative barrier on individuals.[2]

Concerning work in the enterprises, he states: "Without a reserve of labor-power in relation to the plan, democracy within the factory is well-nigh impossible for the production workers," and he calls for "several individuals for each job, several jobs for each individual."[3]

The general orientation of his program notably recalls the ideas Marx expressed in the *Grundrisse,* but it is not a matter of simple repetition: it is a kind of bringing up to date, a rendering of accounts for the time that has gone by since Marx and for the lessons to be drawn from "actually existing socialism." Such a program is essential knowledge for the revolutionary Marxists of the Fourth International as a means of enriching their program of struggle with respect to bureaucraticized worker states, and also their transitional program in advanced capitalist countries. There it is necessary to combat not only capitalist ownership but also, as has been clearly shown, a whole series of social relationships (family, education, environment, etc.)—questions that for a long time were treated only in an abstract way, as pertaining to an undefined future.

This is all we will say on the subject of the program, adding only that it is rare to find a book written under such difficult conditions that is as rich in ideas as this one is. But this book also contains viewpoints we consider wrong and which we want to discuss. We will skip over certain differences that are mainly terminological or that rest on substantive divergences of opinion, to the extent that they are important. For example, Bahro is opposed to the term "transitional society" and does not use the term "degenerate worker state" to designate those societies in which capitalism has been eliminated and in which bureaucracy holds a despotic reign. This difference seems relatively minor to us. Bahro is in fact far from the theories of "state capitalism" and a "new class" when he writes: "Despite occasional experiments, there has never been any question in the countries of actually existing socialism of production for any kind of *profit* on the state's part."[4]

This is not production of *surplus value* but of *surplus product* with regard to the requirements of the producers themselves. It is not a question of theoretic subtleties, for this state of affairs has major implications at the enterprise level. Bahro has this to say about it:

> Our state—and despite its draconian and martial forms of law, the same applies also to the Soviet—is essentially, i.e. from the standpoint of its place in history, in no position to *enforce* the same intensity of labor as capitalism can. It forms part of the assumptions of its existence, the elementary conditions of its constitution in the play of both domestic and international forces, that the contradiction between it and the immediate producers does not become too marked. From the standpoint of political economy, under actually existing socialism the workers have a far greater opportunity to blackmail the "entire society" than do the trade unions under capitalism, and they do actually use this, against all surface appearance, even if they can do so only in an unfruitful way, i.e. by holding back on their output.[5]

Thus, in spite of the despotic nature of power and in the absence of organized unions independent of the state, in actually existing socialism the workers carry more weight in society than unions in the most democratic of capitalist societies as far as work pace is concerned. This is not a gratuitous statement on Bahro's part; many union militants in the FRG have been able to find this out for themselves during trips to the GDR. We see how different bureaucratic omnipotence is in nature from the implacability of the law of value in a capitalist society.

Bahro's internationalism stands out clearly in several passages of his book, in particular when he proposes *"doing away with the law of value in trade with the less developed countries . . . the solution must consist rather in exchange according to equal expenditure of labor-time."* [6]

But his views on international relations and their development in the twentieth century are, in our opinion, deeply flawed, and they lead him to conclusions that are equally flawed. Here is what he says:

> The Soviet tragedy must be grasped for what it is. Its basis is that the Russian socialist movement at the beginning of the century found a different objective task to fulfill than that to which it believed itself called. So long as there was simply the Soviet Union (with or without a Western periphery) it was possible to consider the harsh "detour" of the socialist idea via Russia simply as a higher-order accident of European history. But since the People's Republic of China came into being, but still no proletarian revolution in the West, the indication is that the entire perspective under which we have so far seen the transition to communism stands in need of correction, and in no way just with respect to the time factor. The dissolution of private property in the means of production on the one hand, and universal human emancipation on the other, are separated by an entire epoch. [7]

> The proletarian revolution in the West did not take place; and its appearance in the form previously anticipated has become ever more improbable. [The Russian revolution was of a completely different type.] The nature and character of a revolution are only determined up to a certain point by the programme and the heroism of its vanguard, who can only achieve the first steps. The Soviets of 1905 and 1917 continued the Paris Commune, but after them this continuity was broken. Today, adherence to the hope of a classical socialist overthrow in the West must lead to a pessimism that is actually groundless. The revolutions in Russia and China, in the Balkans and in Cuba, have probably contributed not less but rather more to the overall progress than the proleterian revolutions hoped for in the West could have done. [8]

> *With the revolutions in Russia and China, with the revolutionary process in Latin America, in Africa and in India, humanity is taking the shortest route to socialism. . . .* The role of the working class, who gave the decisive impulse to the Russian revolution and who obviously have a

task in Europe, must be seen afresh in this context.[9]

The Bolshevik seizure of power in Russia could lead to no other *social structure* than that now existing, and the more one tries to think through the stations of Soviet history, which would lead us too far afield for our present purpose, the harder it becomes to draw a limit short of even the most fearsome excesses, and to say that what falls on the other side was absolutely avoidable.[10]

In the West, private property is abolished in the regulative state monopoly structure in such a way that the second wave of the organized labor movement is already setting out on a "long march through the institutions" and meeting up in this way with the first wave. It seems to be becoming ever more impossible simply to smash the state machine, and not because of its armed strength. In the countries of actually existing socialism, furthermore, the state machine played a predominantly creative role for a whole and decisive period. The Stalin apparatus *did* perform a task of "economic organization," and also one of "cultural education," both of these on the greatest of scales.[11]

In other words, there have been no socialist revolutions in the West, nor could there have been any, and there can be none now; there, the "way to socialism through institutions" is proposed. Backward industrial countries have not been able to emerge from their backwardness without going through revolutions such as in China. The leaders of the Russian revolution thought their revolution was of the type Marxists considered classic, whereas they actually had made another kind of revolution, which later came to be regarded as valid for backward countries. To industrialize these countries was possible essentially only on the basis of their own resources. The masses had to be forced to work, and since work is not natural to man, a bureaucracy disposing over despotic means to compel them was necessary. "Actually existing socialism" was thus a necessary, inevitable historic phase on the way to socialism such as Marx conceived it, and which for Bahro retains its full validity. According to him, Marx and Lenin were not mistaken about the future of humanity, but about the real possibilities in their respective periods:

It would appear that Lenin overestimated the *degree* of capitalist development in Russia at the beginning of the twentieth century in a way similar to that in which Marx and Engels did for Western Europe in the mid-nineteenth century.[12]

Without underestimating the political importance of agreement with Bahro on the present problems and tasks in countries of actually existing socialism, we should not dismiss our differences with regard to the interpretation of the past, for they imply serious theoretic differences. The first point that occurs to us after reading Bahro's book is: nothing is proposed for the transition of capitalist countries to socialism except his undefined "march through existing institutions," which is more or less that of Eurocommunist parties and socialist parties today, a march that by all appearances is at a standstill for socialist parties and which for the Eurocommunist parties will lead nowhere. Another point: Bahro takes as a fixed point of departure, as an almost immutable fact, the present division of the world between developed capitalist countries and countries that have followed or will follow the path of "actually existing socialism." We are literally astonished that he does not mention in his book the problem of the unification of Germany, a problem that has been put in cold storage for more than 20 years, but which exists all the same and which will inevitably come up again one day.

It cannot be said that there have been no revolutions in the West. There have been, in particular in Germany and in Spain, not to mention Hungary and other revolutionary crises. What we have not had are victorious revolutions, even though a revolution basically succeeded with its own resources in Yugoslavia, a country intermediate between the West and the East, a little more Western than tsarist Russia. The fact that there have been no victorious revolutions in the West does not mean that this need necessarily have been so. In several countries, the working class has started great struggles in which capitalist power has been objectively called into question. The fact that these struggles have not always been carried far enough or that they were put down was not historically inevitable. The failures or betrayal of the bureaucraticized and reformist leaderships have played an important role, as have the counter-revolutionary steps taken by the Soviet leadership (the Yalta, Teheran, and Potsdam agreements). The working class's path toward consciousness of its historic goals is not a straight one. How many failures and defeats were necessary before recognition was given to its unions and parties, to democratic rights and universal suffrage! How much more tortuous the road leading it to the conquest of power has proven to be![13]

It is dangerous and wrong to think that all that has happened in

history was historically inevitable: the way from historical deter-
minism to fatalism would then be easy. Should we think that
Hitler and Franco were also inevitable and thus absolve Stalin
from his "third period" politics and his Popular Front politics?
The role of the workers' leadership (socialist parties and communist parties) has been considerable and, in many cases, decisive in
determining the outcome of working class struggles.

Indeed, Bahro believes that the bureaucracy has been an indispensable factor and even, for a certain period, a positive one. As
for the Eastern European countries, bureaucratization arose from
the fact that these countries were socially transformed due to the
presence of the Soviet Army. While its intervention in Czechoslovakia in August 1968 shows that this bureaucraticization can only
be maintained by force, the Yugoslav example shows that, where
the working masses have been the main element in the social liberation of the country, and where the Soviet Union could not intervene, the leadership, in spite of the enormous political confusion
in which it found itself with regard to the Kremlin, was compelled
to seek recourse in workers' democracy, albeit in diluted and
bastardized forms. There can be no doubt that if a working class
came to power in Western Europe, it would go extremely far on
the path to socialism—as we saw in May 1968, which Bahro warm-
ly embraces.

The Stalinist type of bureaucraticization originated in the Soviet
Union, as Bahro points out in the first pages of his book:

> The "world socialist system" and the world communist movement are
> torn apart by fundamental internal contradictions, which have their main
> roots in the unmastered history of the Soviet Union itself, or must at
> least be grasped from this starting-point.[14]

Hence, the question: was bureaucratic power an inevitable historical necessity? Some of Bahro's evaluations on what has happened
in the Soviet Union since the revolution contain viewpoints that
are at variance with such a conclusion. For example, he sees that if
they had followed the proposals of the Left Opposition, they would
not have wasted five years, a delay that later was dearly paid for
materially and politically. He also states that leaders like Trotsky,
Zinoviev, Bukharin, et al. could not be assimilated into the bureaucratic regime. Need we add that, even after the horrible and
extreme collectivization, the Party, by that time domesticated by

Stalin, still showed signs of assuagement and liberalization? To carry out his bloody purges, Stalin had to rely on the basest and most backward elements of society. All this was not inevitable; it was the outcome of struggles that lasted nearly ten years. The factors that were decisive for the outcome were, first, the sequence of failures of revolutions throughout the world, as well as the underestimation of the bureaucratic danger by the majority of the Bolshevik Party, including the majority of its leadership. The development of the Soviet Union, in the absence of victorious revolutions in Europe, could certainly not have come about without great economic difficulties. But the difficulties had been as great during the first years of the revolution, and this did not stop the Bolshevik leaders from doing their best in this period to unite the masses for the necessary tasks and sacrifices; they did not impose a regime in which all liberties and rights were suppressed, even the right of a poet or painter to express himself as he wished.

We agree with Bahro that economically backward countries can liberate themselves only through revolutions of the type we saw in China, in Cuba, etc.; in other words, they will not follow the path of advanced countries and will not have a period of flourishing of capitalism and, as in Cuba, of a relative expansion of bourgeois democracy. They will take the path Trotsky calls "permanent revolution," that is, a revolution led by the working class, starting with the accomplishment of bourgeois democratic tasks that the native bourgeoisies are unable to carry through, and then moving on without interruption to the tasks proper to the socialist revolution itself. We will not take up the whole history of the problem of the Russian revolution, from Marx, who in 1881 envisaged that tsarist Russia might not have to go through a capitalist stage if a socialist revolution were victorious in Europe, down to Lenin and Trotsky after the revolution of 1905 who, despite the differences between them, both understood that the future Russian revolution would not lead to a bourgeois regime of the classic European type. No one—and certainly not Bahro—will blame them for not having foreseen the bureaucracy, or, more precisely, the form it has taken since Stalin. Even after 1917, Trotsky did not extend his theory of permanent revolution to other colonial or semicolonial countries until July 1927, during the second Chinese revolution. He generalized it at that time because the October revolution had put an end to the era of bourgeois revolutions by depriving the capitalist system of its domination of one-sixth of the globe. But did the Russian revolution necessarily have to lead to Stalin's actually existing socialism?

Before we take up the problem of bureaucracy, we must examine Bahro's position on the concept of the "party." He advocates a communist party different from the East German Socialist Unity Party, and which he calls a *League of Communists*. But his concept of a workers' party, including those of capitalist states, is not the one currently used by Marxists. According to him, there is no party that can rightly be called a workers' party: "Right from the beginning, the socialist parties had a double face, and by no means just in Russia: both parties *of* the proletariat, and parties *for* the proletariat." He justifies this as follows: "The workers—individual exceptions apart—were never Marxist in the strict sense. Marxism is a theory based on the *existence* of the working class, but it is not the theory *of* the working class."[15]

Marxism would thus seem to be merely a view of things that intellectuals formulated about the progress of mankind, taking the working class as history's instrument for making this (correct) theory a reality. But the working class, aside from individual exceptions, has not been able to go beyond defense of its immediate interests in capitalist society. Socialism then must come to it from without, and hence workers' parties invoking Marxism would be parties *for* the proletariat rather than parties *of* the proletariat. In *What Is To Be Done?* Lenin does indeed say that socialism is brought from the outside to the working class, which itself cannot go beyond trade unionism, but he did not go as far as Bahro: a few years later he acknowledged this as an incorrect polemical excess on his part. Marxism was not born *ex nihilo* in any intellectual's head, not even in Marx's. He showed that industrial capitalism, still underdeveloped, would spread throughout the world, and that the aspiration to socialism was not an illusion but would be the result of proletarian struggles at the time still in embryo, or at any rate limited to a few cities or scattered areas of Europe. Marx did not have to look for an object or instrument for his theory; it was the workers' struggles themselves that led Marx to Marxism. True, the workers' movement almost everywhere started with intellectuals and highly intellectualized workers, but it could not have been otherwise. How could the great majority of workers, having neither the necessary education nor free time, have understood the workings of the society that exploited them? The great majority of workers arrive at that understanding through the class struggle; the mass workers' parties were not formed through the accession of individuals who had understood the analyses of *Capital*, but as a result of class struggles of all kinds. We should also add that there are now hundreds of thousands, perhaps even millions of worker militants in the world who have a quite good knowledge of Marxism and who are at the forefront of the struggles of their class, not merely to improve working and living conditions in capitalist societies, but to overthrow them.

There is another point in Bahro's book concerning party and class which we must examine. He writes: "Beyond capitalism, the concept of the working class not only loses its operative sense. . . . The proletariat loses its specific socioeconomic identity together with the bourgeoisie."[16]

From this Bahro arrives at the "single unified party," although organizations for the defense of immediate interests of various sorts have their *raison d'être* as well. Bahro defends the view that minorities can exist in the "one and only party," defend their positions in it, and even keep them after having been beaten in a congress. But are we sure that, even in such conditions, coexistence in the same party of two widely divergent positions would be possible? And, if not, what is left of the one and only party? Let us leave this question and return to what Bahro says about the working class in actually existing socialism. In the period of transition to socialism, he is sure that the working class itself will be transformed and will give way to an association of free and equal producers. We do not have Bahro's knowledge of actually existing socialism, but from reading *The Alternative* and what it tells us about relationships in enterprises, we cannot see that any real tendencies toward such a transformation exist at present among the working class. Social differences between workers and the state and party apparatus are enormous. These differences are great enough to justify not only the existence of unions independent of these apparatuses to defend the immediate interests of workers, but also of a political party of these workers to struggle to bring an end to this actually existing socialism and to implement the program of cultural revolution that Bahro calls for.[17]

Before proceeding further on this point, let us return to the relations between the workers' parties and the working class they came from, and for whose interests they are or should be the political voice. These relations are neither simple nor are they permanently fixed. History shows that twice (first with the socialist parties prior to 1914, and then with the communist parties), parties that were created as parties of the socialist revolution have been bureaucraticized and transformed into reformist parties. How and why? These parties were created by minorities in the working class in struggles often quite bitter. They had to train a group of permanent officials to function systematically, thus creating "specialists" for particular jobs—in other words, an apparatus. Because of the conditions in a capitalist society, this apparatus tended to place itself above the party and, consequently, above the class, thus becoming more vulnerable to the pressures from capitalist society. Where the party did fulfill its functions in leading the revolutionary struggle and overthrew capitalism, that is, in Russia, it was rent asunder as a workers' party by the new state it had created, and inundated by the tens of thousands of specialists who tended to place themselves above society.[18] The cultural development of the working class does not proceed at the same pace as its political development; the program of cultural revolution that Bahro sets forth is in fact aimed at reducing this gap and giving workers the necessary time and education to eliminate specialists who otherwise tend to dominate all of society.

There is no doubt that objective conditions giving rise to bureaucratic deformations in a society where capitalism has only just been overthrown exist, and that these conditions are more compelling in hitherto backward societies where illiteracy is still widespread, where the number of specialists, varying in their abilities, is minimal, and where the problems of industrialization and, more generally, of economic development, occupy a large place. But must we draw the conclusion from this, as Bahro did, as to the historic necessity of a social stratum playing a progressive role, that of constraining the masses for work, and, accordingly, the historic necessity of actually existing socialism? We certainly cannot go along with Bahro on this point. First of all, let us mention our doubts as to man's natural hostility to work: We believe that this hostility exists only to forced, imposed work, whereas the pleasure of puttering about for oneself is extremely common. Furthermore, even in societies of actually existing socialism, the masses have often accomplished prodigious feats of labor when convinced that they were working for themselves—whether this happened to be true or false. This happened, for example, during the first years of the Russian revolution and even during the first five-year plan, as well as in a number of countries after wars of liberation. Forced labor, on the other hand, has never been particularly productive.

The real problem of society is not that of eliminating specialists, so long as they are necessary, but of controlling them, of keeping check on the quality of their work, of reducing the advantages they may reap from their being so few in number, and of curbing potential abuses on their part. Marx brought up this problem in this way in his 1871 address "The Civil War in France," in the aftermath of the defeat of the Paris Commune:

> Instead of deciding once in three or six years which member of the ruling class was to misrepresent the people in Parliament, universal suffrage was to serve the people, constituted in the Communes, as individual suffrage serves every other employer in the search for the workmen and managers in his business. And it is well known that companies, like individuals in matters of real business generally know how to put the right man in the right place, and, if they for once make a mistake, to redress it promptly.[19]

Was Marx wrong on this point? Must there be a higher directorate in order to control and choose the "specialists" needed by a society that has abolished capitalism? No, a thousand times no! Even if one accepts for the moment Bahro's view that the working class cannot go beyond the defense of its immediate interests and proceed to the general problems of society, we cannot from this conclude that it is incapable of selecting, of watching over and, if necessary, of bringing bureaucracy back into line. At a time when the working class had much less knowledge and fewer qualifications than it generally has today, it proved itself capable of confronting the ambitions of capitalists and their managements head on and cutting them down to size as far as the organization of labor in an enterprise was concerned, and of obtaining guarantees in this domain. Why should it then be incapable of acting in the same way and of knowing how to judge bureaucrats in a society where there are no more capitalists? The oppressed have always been able to evaluate rulers in their capacity to rule. Why then should this not be likewise the case when there is no more ruling class, and when there is but one hierarchy that still exists, a legacy from mankind's past, condemned to disappear in time? Both the selection and supervision of "specialists" are within the capacity of the workers, even in economically backward countries, and there is no objective fact that makes actually existing socialism historically inevitable. It can be explained by a confluence of circumstances that we have known about for a long time. It is a historical accident— obviously a prolonged one—but it is not an inevitable necessity.

Who will make the cultural revolution? Bahro is quite skeptical of the revolutionary potential of the working class, yet he does not give us a clear answer to the question. The example of what happened in Czechoslovakia in 1968 and of what he sees in the GDR certainly have had a great impact on his thinking. Clearly, one cannot reckon with a mass workers' movement from the very outset; it is the peripheral social layers that are the first to take action. But that is not peculiar to actually existing socialism; we see the same phenomenon in capitalist countries. There, too, peripheral layers (students, etc.) are the first to move because they are the first to sense the growing instability of society; they also have greater freeedom to act, and they are also often the most vocal. But, in the final analysis, such movements cannot become revolutionary movements unless they ultimately come together with mass actions on the part of the working class. In France, May 1968 was not first and foremost a student revolt, but essentially a general strike of ten million workers—probably the greatest movement of the working class in its history. In Czechoslovakia, the Prague Spring did not begin with the working class, but was the result of a crisis within the bureaucracy. The Kremlin took fright when, going beyond the reforms initially intended by the leadership, a powerful showing by the working class brought the Dubček team to yield to, rather than to repress it. The Kremlin understood where real danger lay for it, not only in Czechoslovakia, but ultimately—Bahro also sees this—outside the country's borders as well, including in the Soviet Union. Bahro also recognizes the fear workers inspire in bureaucrats when he points out that in the GDR the bureaucracy no longer defines [the working class] in a manner permitting it to be distinguished as an entity in statistics. The fact is that as soon as the working class takes action in actually existing socialism, bureaucracy becomes powerless, but in a way that differs from the impotence of capitalists in their society. On this point, the Polish example, or rather examples are noteworthy, and the Kremlin did not hesitate to aid Gierek economically to appease the workers' demands. Despite the persistence of "actually existing socialism," it has never been anything more than a crisis regime. Bureaucratic repression was not at all the product of "historic necessity," but the result of the considerable internal instability of a political regime whose life is in danger whenever a rift appears within the ranks of those in power, a rift that is visible to all and into which the hostility of the masses can flow. This is why the leaders of these bureaucraticized worker states are incapable of solving their problems in public debates and are obliged to settle things secretly before bringing the matter in their deceitful way before the public. The leaders of these countries are the last to think that the working class does not constitute for them the greatest revolutionary danger.

We shall conclude now with but a few more brief words. In thinking that workers' parties are not actually workers' parties, that the working class is not capable of achieving a comprehension of the general problems of society, that Marxism is the product of intellectuals, it is not merely, as we have stated, a grave mistake about the relationship between Marxism and class that Bahro is making; he also unwittingly errs with regard to himself. It is not just Bahro, the intellectual, who is making this forceful analysis of actually existing socialism and defining a program to build a true socialist society. Whatever he may think, he is a product of the German working class and its rich revolutionary theoretical and political traditions. We mentioned earlier the problem of the re-unification of Germany. Must we be reminded that a united Germany was part of the revolutionary programs from the very beginning of that country's workers' movement? There are not two traditions of the German workers' movement, one in the West and one in the East; there is only one. This is also why a great number of worker militants in the Federal Republic have identified with Bahro's *Alternative*, where they see not only aspirations of the workers in the GDR but also their own, that is, their aspirations for a unified socialist Germany. Now that industrial development has spread throughout the world, the German working class today is no longer the center of the world workers' movement that it had been for over half a century; still, it has a huge contribution to make toward the building of a socialist society on a global scale.

From this perspective, Bahro's struggle for liberation is not just one man's struggle for liberation; it is also a struggle to hasten the liberation of the entire German working class, artificially divided, and for this reason considerably paralyzed by the deliberate wills of the United States and of the Soviet Union, now in concord, and now opposed; it is the struggle for the German socialist revolution in both West and East.

Translated from the French by
Mark Rosenzweig with Michel Vale.

NOTES

1. Rudolf Bahro, *The Alternative in Eastern Europe* (London: New Left Books, 1978) pp. 284-85. (The source for Kapitza is given as *Wissenschaftliche Welt*, vol. 15, 1971, no. 1.)

2. Bahro, pp. 406, 413.

3. Ibid., pp. 421, 425.

4. Ibid., p. 114.

5. Ibid., p. 207.

6. Ibid., p. 432.

7. Ibid., p. 21.

8. Ibid., p. 53.

9. Ibid., p. 61.

10. Ibid., p. 90.

11. Ibid., p. 39.

12. Ibid., p. 85.

13. Bahro in fact believes that the masses in backward countries will not be able to achieve socialism without a revolution, of necessity a bloody one, while workers in developed capitalist countries will be able to do this "through the institutions," that is, at little cost. This is a grave mistake: how can we explain Nazism if not as the will of a great bourgeoisie to stop the birth of a socialist society at any price? A direct copy of fascism is not within the current capacities of capitalism, but it can find other brutal ways to defend its power, and it will.

14. Bahro, p. 8.

15. Ibid., pp. 194 and 197.

16. Ibid., pp. 184-85.

17. It is understood that this party will include not only workers as such, but also members of other social categories adopting communist positions. But this party must have its principal base in the working class.

18. See especially Christian Rakovsky's letter to Valentinov, known under the title "The Professional Dangers of Power."

19. Robert C. Tucker, ed., *The Marx-Engels Reader* (New York: W. W. Norton, 1978), p. 633.

JIRI PELIKAN

Bahro's Ideas on Changes in Eastern Europe

Rudolf Bahro's *The Alternative* is without a doubt one of the most significant, stimulating contributions of the last decade to the discussion on the nature of the system in Eastern European countries and on the potential prospects for development of what is called "real socialism." If this book is indeed used as a basis for discussion between the Marxist opposition in those countries and the Western left, and if it serves as a point of departure for further studies of this sort, then without exaggeration we can speak of a new stage in the struggle for a socialist alternative and for changes in Eastern Europe. This stage is hallmarked by an objective and scientific analysis of the Soviet model of socialism, and not just by an emotional publicist approach as heretofore. This analysis should yield political conclusions concerning the strategy and tactics in the struggle for change of the present situation.

However, since changes in Eastern Europe cannot remain without an effect on developments in Western Europe (and to a considerable degree the situation in Western Europe reciprocally influences developments in the East), this debate is also having a direct effect on all political currents in the West striving for change in the present political situation. Rudolf Bahro's book is a suitable basis for such a general international discussion, especially as it is not restricted to an analysis of the situation and perspectives of the GDR but embraces the entire region in which the Soviet model of socialism has been instituted, and moreover, considers developments in the rest of the world as well. For Bahro, the first step out of the current crisis of both systems lies in a process of emancipation that must occur throughout the world, although in different forms and in different intensities.

For me the principal advantage of Bahro's study is that it starts out on the basis of a deep and personal knowledge of his society, yet at the same time is able to go beyond personal experience to a broader knowledge. Further, Bahro not only gives us a testimony, as several others have done before, but is also capable of providing a scientific analysis that generalizes from his immediate experience. With his book Bahro shows that he—in contrast to the majority of the ideologues of the countries of real socialism—has actually studied Marx, Engels, and Lenin, and has mastered the method of historical materialism as an instrument for analyzing new phenomena. His book helps us to salvage the deformed and discredited theory of Marxism, even though we must immediately add that his Marxist terminology will probably discourage from study of his work many of those who today are striving for changes in the Eastern European countries, yet reject all the official clichés and terminology misused by official propaganda to gloss over the actual state of affairs.

In this essay I would like to limit myself to two questions on which my views partly agree and partly disagree with Bahro's: first, the analysis of the changes brought about in the Eastern European countries by the Soviet intervention in August 1968, and second, the forms and content of the struggle for an alternative.

What was changed by the 1968 intervention?

I am in agreement with the basic theses of Bahro's published analysis of the present-day regime in Eastern European countries. Our views begin to diverge in the evaluation of the consequences of the Soviet intervention in Czechoslovakia in August 1968. It seems that Bahro underestimates the negative consequences of this intervention, not only in Czechoslovakia ("The moral authority of the reform policy remains unbroken"[1]) but also in the other countries taken as a whole ("Even though the trauma of 1968 still has its psychological effects, the other countries under Soviet domination today have a greater room for maneuver in domestic policy"[2]).

The military intervention in 1968 was followed by purges of the party and state apparatuses in all the countries of Eastern Europe; thousands of active communists were expelled from the party and from public life on the suspicion of having sympathized with the Prague Spring, or simply because they were regarded as potential revisionists. At the same time, dogmatic and Stalinist elements were revived in all areas of politics and ideology, and the role of the security agencies was expanded. In Czechoslovakia a fundamental change in the situation took place after the intervention: the Communist Party of Czechoslovakia was transformed into an obedient instrument of Soviet policy by the expulsion of 500,000 communists; thereafter it had no more ties with the broad masses of the population. Now there is no longer that segment of the party which in earlier times was ready to take up a dialogue and to implement changes, and which in the 1960s constituted the source of personnel for the process of democratization.

Aside from the fact that the reform communists were completely expelled from political life and became the object of an extended repression, the prestige of socialism was also seriously undermined by the fact that the party leadership under Dubček—under pressure, of course—signed the capitulation in the form of the so-called Moscow Protocol and hence opened up the pathway to "normalization," which negatively affected the majority of the population. This without a doubt weakened the prestige of the reform policy of 1968. Bahro correctly criticizes the attitude of the Czech Communist Party leadership at the time when he states: "The group around Alexander Dubček did not have the ultimate resoluteness; this had especially to do with their illusions about the Soviet Union and about the social nature and the interests of the Moscow leadership." (Bahro refers to the attitude of Tito as a counterexample.) The Dubček leadership in the Czech Communist Party of course stressed that "Czechoslovakia did not wish to become a second Yugoslavia," and then delivered up the destiny of the Prague Spring to the Soviet leadership, in complete contradiction to the feelings —both political and national—of the majority of Czechs and Slovaks, including party members. After such an attitude, and especially after all that followed this capitulation, how could the moral authority of the reform policy of 1968 remain unimpaired?

In other Eastern European countries the negative consequences of the military intervention were less dramatic in terms of repression. Nonetheless, they were just as profound as far as their effect on the population's frame of mind was concerned. The military intervention demonstrated that any attempt at a democratization in a single country of the Soviet bloc was doomed to provoke a hostile attitude in the Soviet leadership, and that it would be suppressed in just as decisive a way as the Prague Spring of 1968. The inevitable consequence of this is a certain sense of powerlessness and passivity, and among communists, a deepening of the pragmatism and cynicism that Bahro describes so well in discussing the party apparatus, its leading members, and its rank and file.

In Poland the explosion of dissatisfaction in 1970 necessitated a change in the party leadership. It was forced to give some free play to public opinion and it learned how to exploit the various oppositional currents quite skillfully and flexibly. But Poland today is the only country in Eastern Europe in which a political and cultural life actually thrives parallel to the official life, and almost on a legal foundation; moreover, it is a country in which the ruling party exhibits a differentiation similar to that observable in the Czech Communist Party before 1968. If, however, this situation should remain an isolated phenomenon, the question arises how long it can withstand the combined pressure of the Moscow bureaucrats and the national bureaucrats, who demand the restoration of order and discipline and the end of anarchy.

This situation is leading many former communists to the conclusion that the defeat of the Prague Spring ended the stage of reform communism or revisionism for all of Europe (Leszek Kolakowski). Such views are also found today in the oppositional movement in Czechoslovakia and especially in Poland, to say nothing of the Soviet Union itself, where the majority of the dissidents, with the exception of Roy Medvedev and other individuals, identify socialism with Stalinism (they have of course no other experience) and therefore reject socialism as a system, even if it were to be reformed or reorganized in every conceivable way.

I personally am not in agreement with these views, though I can understand them quite well as an emotional and moral reaction to the present situation. An objective analysis of the situation in Eastern Europe and of the power relationships in the world as a whole leads me to agree with Bahro's view that the future of these countries rests in a socialist alternative, on the basis of gradual but fundamental reform of the present system until an actual emancipation of the entire society is achieved in consonance with the original ideal of socialism. This does nothing to alter the fact that if truly secret and free elections were possible today in the Eastern European countries, the majority of the population would probably vote for some form of parliamentary democracy of the Western type but would be content with the public sector of the economy and various social achievements of the present system. In other words, they would probably choose social democracy.

The consequences of the military intervention in Czechoslovakia, however, consist mainly in the fact that after 1968 the potential source of change shifted to *outside* the party and the official establishment, whereas up to 1968 there were possibilities that pressure from below would find response *within* the ruling party. Indeed, at that time in the party there was a current that was accessible to dialogue and which understood the necessity of economic and political reforms; the combination of the pressure of these two wings offered a possibility for gradual reforms without violence and without dramatic conflicts. Thus there is now a movement of protest, of opposition, of general dissatisfaction or simple dissidence. It can exercise pressure on the group in power and force them to yield concessions, or it finds its articulation in spontaneous explosions. The opposition movement can only attain a real influence on the ruling power if it is sufficiently strong and is able to appeal to the principal bearers of change, namely, the working class, the youth, and the engaged intelligentsia.

If this pressure is sufficiently strong and lasting, it can set off a process of differentiation within the ruling party, again giving rise to a tendency positively disposed to reforms. However, this time there will be no repetition of the process "from above" that was so characteristic of the situation in Czechoslovakia before 1968 (and partly for Poland in 1956, and for the Soviet Union during the Khrushchev era), when the incentives for reforms and change came from above, from among the inner ranks of the ruling party (though this represented only part of the party). To be sure, these incentives also set off a process of democratization from below, from the base. The ruling parties and their apparatuses are now, as Bahro correctly shows, "the enemies of change of any kind, because they would unavoidably suffer from it. . . . And they . . . stand constantly in need of military intervention in their support, as the guarantee of their own safety."[3] The movements from below have thus become a crucial element in further developments. On this point I am in complete agreement with Bahro. However, we have differences in the evaluation of the tasks that are before communists and Marxists in this movement, as well as with regard to the question of the content and goal of this movement—"the cultural revolution"—which is supposed to lead to a real communism, as Bahro sees it, or to a pluralistic democratic socialism, which as I see it, is the only possible alternative of today's situation.

On the role of communists and intellectuals
and the problem of political plurality

Since for Rudolf Bahro the goal of real communism is the emancipation of human society, it is only logical that as the bearers of change he sees communists (not, however, those within the party apparatus or associated with it). For him, the best instrument for the struggle against the dictatorship of the political bureaucracy is a new party that will call itself the League of Communists. It is my feeling that such a perspective and the means proposed are quite remote from reality and from the feelings of a considerable portion of the forces striving for democratizing change in the countries of Eastern Europe.

First, one must consider the fact that the word "communism" has already been discredited in the eyes of the people of Eastern Europe because it coincides with the idea of the rule of a single party, i.e., the dictatorship of the party apparatus, supported by the hegemony of Russia. However, resistance to communism cannot be equated with resistance to socialism—if by that we mean a social system based on the collective ownership of the means of production. Even the majority of those in Eastern Europe who today consider themselves anticommunists and do not believe in socialism as an ideology, by no means think it feasible that the large factories and plants should be returned to the control of private persons after the dictatorship of the Communist Party apparatus has been eliminated, or that the agricultural collective should be dissolved into individual family farming operations. Certain measures have become an integral component of life, and intelligent people understand that one cannot turn back everything, even if the present forms have their flaws. People simply want the nationalized plants to be managed by qualified specialists and to produce commodities that meet the needs of the population, rather than products prescribed by the bureaucratic apparatus in accordance with Moscow's needs; they want workers and technicians to receive salaries corresponding to their training and their function, and to be able to buy with their wages what they need. At the same time they want the economy to be controlled by the public, statistics on the state of the economy to be published, and workers to be able to participate in management and in the proceeds of the economy. These demands are of course accompanied by demands for the formation of independent trade unions capable of defending workers' interests, even against the state as employer, as well as for a political life that would make possible a control over the economy and the executive branch and which would express the most varied and even the most contradictory interests of various social layers.

In the people's minds, the principal obstacle to the realization of these goals is presented by the communist parties and their monopoly over power, justified in a Marxist terminology and presented as a dictatorship of the proletariat that is allegedly necessary for society's transition to communism as an end goal. At one time many of the ruling communist parties actually did have the support of the broad masses, because they promised to build up socialism as a society in which the majority of workers would be given more freedom, more justice, and a broader participation in the government as a system of parliamentary democracy (for example, in Czechoslovakia). However, these goals were not realized by the communist parties; they began gradually to move away from the masses and to rule with administrative coercive measures, which reached their peak in the political trials and repression during Stalin's time.

After the Twentieth Party Congress of the Communist Party of Soviet Union, there were hopes that one could return to the original ideals and that the gigantic tragedies had only been temporary deformations. However, these hopes were thoroughly dashed by the bloody intervention in the Hungarian Revolution in 1956, by Gomulka's normalization of the Polish October, and by such absurd measures as the Berlin Wall. The Prague Spring revived these hopes—and not only in Czechoslovakia. Its crushing by military intervention only confirms the reactionary character of communist parties in power, and hence their overall ideology, among the majority of the population. Today people even see the communists as the cause of this catastrophic situation and accept as allies in their struggle only those former communists who have clearly dissociated themselves from the past and present policy of the Communist Party, have distanced themselves from it, and are ready to impose the rules of democratic relations and absolute equality among all parties. For the people of Eastern Europe, communism is too closely linked with Stalinism and the hegemony of the Soviet Union for it again to be positively received in any form, even after a renaissance.

An additional factor in this situation is that the goals of communism as taught in the schools (but also as described by Rudolf Bahro) seem to today's citizens in the "real socialist" countries to be completely unrealistic, and even dangerous inasmuch as through their idealized notions they veil the most repressive regimes and even justify their existence.

It may be objected that this is only a question of terminology, that it would be sufficient to rehabilitate communism if it were purged of non-Marxist voluntarism and its practice changed. However, I am afraid that this is not possible, since the contradiction between what the masses in the countries of real socialism demand and that which Rudolf Bahro takes as his point of departure is also a contradiction of content.

This shows up first and foremost in Bahro's attitude toward the demand for political pluralism. As he described it in his book: "the conception of party pluralism seems to me to be an anachronistic piece of thoughtlessness, which completely misconstrues the concrete historical material in our countries."[4] For Bahro, political parties are the expression of different class interests, just as the official ideology of the ruling communist parties continually assures us—in this way justifying its monopoly of power. The works of innumerable Czech and other Marxist sociologists and philosophers even before 1968 had demonstrated that there were different class and group interests even in socialist society, and that consequently it is completely justified that they should be able to find expression through political structures. Of course, this need not take place in the form of political parties: the labor unions, the workers' councils, mass organizations of all kinds, but of course also political parties with different conceptions of socialism, could fulfill this role.

Political pluralism under the conditions of socialist society does not reside *only* in the existence of a few political parties, including the opposition; indeed, a developed society *could not exist without* this form of political alternative. This is how the communists conceive of the process of further development of socialist society and the process of democratization in Czechoslovakia, even if they see its realization to be a gradual development, in certain stages, contingent on the internal and international situation. The masses of workers must, however, have guarantees that this is actually the goal toward which one is moving and that no new kind of dictatorship of a party or party apparatus is concealed behind these temporary measures.

Bahro premises his argument on some sort of mystical mission that invests communists, and only communists, with the task of leading the process of human emancipation, and, in the particular case of Eastern Europe, the process of transforming the totalitarian dictatorship of the apparatus into a state of democratic socialism. This of course had its rational origins: since in these countries the Communist Party is the only political institution and platform through which one may act on society and live a political life, it should of course be primarily communists who begin this process and lead it. However, all the events we have described here, events that cannot be eradicated from the consciousness of human beings, have in the eyes of the majority of the citizens cost the communists the moral right to lead such a process (and this includes also the reform communists, the revisionist communists, or any other such communist factions). It would therefore be necessary for these communists to re-earn this right and then enter into loyal collaboration with other citizens, without any claims on hegemony or any other exclusive position, just as those Czechoslovakian communists who were expelled from the Czech CP are trying to do in the Charter 77 Movement for civil rights.

Bahro himself understands that his notion of the leading role of the communists will not be shared by the renaissance movement, for he writes:

> It is even to a certain extent probable, unfortunately, that the minimal program of a democratic revolution against the politbureaucracy becomes historically autonomous, and demands a stage of its own.[5]

Unfortunately (!) he sees democratic demands as necessary aspects of the impending changes, but he regards them as "the self-restriction of the movement to the specific interests of the intellectuals."[6] This is also linked with the remarkably traditional notion, taken root in the communist movement, that such demands as freedom of speech, freedom of assembly, access to information, freedom of research and artistic creativity (but first and foremost, freedom of speech) are on the one hand only components of a bourgeois restoration or the bourgeois system without any class content, and that on the other hand they express the specific needs of intellectuals endeavoring to expand their own privileges.

In this context, a short polemic against Bahro's view on the role of Czech intellectuals in the preparation and implementation of the Prague Spring is in order. He mentions a few times that these intellectuals were primarily concerned with their own "glorious revolution" which did not have much in common with the overall process of democratization to which the popular masses aspired. This shows that Bahro has not understood the role of the Czech intellectuals, which seems all the more odd since Bahro correctly demonstrates how the apparatus tries to exploit the backwardness of one part of the population to provoke envy and opposition of the popular masses toward the intellectuals, who, because of their analytic competence, are capable of touching the most sensitive points of the ruling regime. During the years 1963-67 Czech intellectuals demanded no new privileges for themselves; rather, they used their moral prestige and their privileges as a means to express themselves in public, to travel, to learn new things, and to formulate their thoughts in artistic or journalistic form in such a way that they expressed the views, feelings, and needs of the majority— for this majority had no possibility of advancing its interest by means of political or trade-union structures and organizations. The Czech intellectuals acquired this privilege and this tradition under the historical conditions of dependency of the Czech and Slovak people, and hence they were able to assume the role of initiator of a process of democratization before and during the spring of 1968. (A few excesses and exhibitionistic elements of a small minority of intellectuals could alter nothing in this positive appraisal; in any event, these excesses and so on were often caused by the resistance of dogmatic forces and by distrust of the permanence of the immanent changes.)

Basically, one can say the same about the role of the intellectuals in the other countries of Eastern Europe, including the Soviet Union—pointing out, naturally, that there is also a high degree of differentiation within this population group and that some of them have become integral parts of the ruling machine. It is this part which belongs to the most dogmatic elements, and it is these people who are the initiators of campaigns against intellectuals and in certain situations even organize repression against intellectuals. Bahro also sees this correctly:

> The propaganda against intellectuals, in the broadest sense, which is in part overt and in part subliminal, comes from a corporation which *is itself made up of intellectuals who have become reactionary and bureaucratized*, who have usurped all social power for themselves.[7]

I attach great importance to Bahro's observation that the struggle for change and the conflicts between the new forces and state power cannot be understood in the categories of traditional class contradictions, and that the "subject of the emancipatory movement is to be found in the energetic and creative elements of all strata and spheres of society."[8] Bahro often sounds almost non-Marxist and heretical; but in these cases it is obviously his own experience which is speaking, an experience of life in a country where an anonymous bureaucracy rules, needing obedient servants with no views and no initiative of their own. Bahro's conception of these creative elements embraces the intellectuals (scientists, engineers, physicians, artists, etc.) as well as the youth and the workers, about which he has a correct, nonorthodox view without any of the illusions of many Western Marxists, who are used to evaluating everything from the standpoint of the interests of the working class. In a friendly polemic with Volker Braun, Bahro states:

> Up till now there have been no signs, not even in Poland, that "the workers" under our conditions could be a "class for itself," and that their "objective interests" could effect the next step toward general emancipation.[9]

Undoubtedly, the long years of depoliticization by the Stalinist system are partly responsible for this. Bahro therefore concedes that progressive intellectuals in this structure must play the role of initiators of these changes:

> As soon as the politbureaucracy is "off its guard" (as it sees it), as soon as it has a weak moment, then the *de facto* hegemony of the intellectual elements immediately comes into play over the entire social bloc that feels itself spoken for by them in its surplus consciousness. . . . And that is why any serious opposition on the part of the intellectuals, when it attains any real scope, so quickly touches the nerves of the power apparatus.[10]

However, it should be pointed out that not only must the workers consider how indispensable an alliance with intellectuals is for them; the ruling groups too must draw a lesson from the events in Czechoslovakia, Hungary, and Poland, and do everything possible (maintain censorship, ideological control, selection of cadres, repression and corruption, and splits within the intellectual front) to see that the intellectuals are unable to fulfill their role in a crisis situation.

The importance and the means of the struggle for civil rights

Our knowledge of the realities in the East European countries tells us that the principal demands of the majority of the working people are concerned with democratization and not communism, though there need not be any fundamental contradiction between these immediate goals and the final objective in the conception of Bahro and the antibureaucratic Marxists. For either of these two processes to be set into motion, the power of the apparatus must be weakened and the power monopoly of the only existing party must be broken. Bahro is correct when he says that the political condition of the overall process of emancipation must be the following:

> The politbureaucracy must be disarmed, the *domination* of the apparatus over society removed, the relationship between society and state newly arranged, and the communist movement newly constituted. . . .[11]

He thinks, however, that the demand for democratization and civil rights is some sort of a detour, whereas at this stage the broad masses see just this demand as the most immediate and important in all of Eastern Europe.

This struggle for civil rights did not emerge in the aftermath of the initiatives of the Carter administration (Charter 77, for example, emerged even before Carter proclaimed these principles to be an integral component of the policies of his administration). Rather, they were the result of the hard experience of the most qualified portion of the population of Eastern Europe, including their experience from the defeat of the emancipatory movements in Hungary, Poland, and Czechoslovakia in years past. However, a league of communists, or any reorganized Communist Party, is hardly the best means for unfolding this struggle; something completely new in both form and content, something that might be called a movement for democratic socialism, must be created. Under the conditions of a totalitarian dictatorship it is not realistic to form a new party or an organized operative base such as the League of Communists is meant to be, because the ruling power would declare it immediately to be an illegal organization, arrest the organizers and those working with it, and then convict them in the courts as enemies of socialism and as conspirators. However, even beyond this, the foundation of a new or another Communist Party would elicit the wrong feelings in a considerable portion of the citizens. This feeling would be intentionally fortified by the opponents of socialism, who would say that it was only a matter of some internal struggle among the communists in which those who are in power are on one side, and those who have been excluded from participation in power and now want to be in power are on the other side. Thus the struggle within the power elite does not interest the workers and employees at all; indeed, it even provokes their mistrust and indifference.

On the other hand, a movement for citizens' rights or for democratic socialism has the advantage that by its very character it shows clearly that it is something new and different from the organizations and institutions of the establishment: such a movement could indeed only exist without a rigid organization under the conditions of totalitarian dictatorship or the domination of the apparatus. It needs no chosen leadership, only spokesmen; it needs no organizational structure which would enable the police to infiltrate it and disrupt the whole organization through the exposure of a member; and above all, it makes possible the practical application of political pluralism, which today is so typical of the socialist opposition in Eastern European countries.

The principal way that this movement could exert its influence might be through periodicals of the *samizdat* type, in which the most varied and even contradictory views of all those who proclaim themselves to this movement could be published, as could the declarations of the movement's spokesmen—these being restricted only to those standpoints which expressed the common views of all, and through which the movement could take a clear position with regard to individual problems in the country. Practical examples of such a movement are Charter 77 in Czechoslovakia and the Workers' Defense Committee in Poland. This basis has made it possible for former communists, socialists, Christians, Trotskyists, and liberals to work together, not on the basis of a common ideological platform, but on the basis of respect for the law and civil rights which are not observed by the ruling apparatus, and indeed cannot be observed without the apparatus itself being swept away.

One could object that such movements entail the risk that political groups with their own programs would be dissolved in them and that, in the light of its lack of a common political program, the movement would be restricted to putting through day-to-day demands without any political perspectives. Indeed, there would be such a danger if this joint movement were to mean the liquidation of all currents of thought and all differences. However, coming together into such a movement in no way means that individual components of the opposition should cease to exist or give up their views. Joint solidarity, discipline, and tolerance do not rule out the continuation of discussion and the development of a parallel political life outside the movement, i.e., in individual groups or currents. One of these groups would definitely be a reform communist movement, which—given its members' experiences, their real program, and their numerous contacts with the ruling party— can play a very important active role in the process of democratization and the creation of conditions for a socialist alternative. Enjoying equal status alongside this group, however, there would also be other groups and currents, including a revolutionary socialist and a liberal and a Christian current. Only their mutual cooperation and their respect for one another can achieve the creation of such a parallel political life, which could show to the mistrustful that changes are possible and that another socialism, different from the current "real socialism," is possible.

A concrete and immediate goal of the struggle may be the formation of a situation of dual power, i.e., a division of social power and the institution of a progressive dialectic between the state and social forces, as Bahro describes it.[12] In practical terms this means the formation of parallel structures alongside the official institutions—for example, book publishing houses and periodicals, universities, autonomous trade unions, workers' committees, petitions to official agencies, committees to defend the persecuted, etc. However, above all it means that the movement must raise not only the sorts of demands suited to it alone, demands that are concerned only with the active minority daring to take the risk and which remain alien to broad working strata. Workers and employees should indeed be able to recognize that the new movement is better able to defend its interests in the official organization, and that the official powers can be pressured by this movement to make concessions to the advantage of working people.

The danger of nationalism
and the new internationalism

Even if such a movement were so strong that it could achieve not only individual concessions but also a change in the situation and an opening up of the way toward a new renaissance process of the Prague Spring type, it could not count on a lasting success if it remained within the confines of a single country. The vanquished or suppressed conservative forces would not shy away from salvaging their positions through a new Soviet military intervention. The experiences of Hungary and Poland in 1956 and Czechoslovakia in 1968 only confirm this. The prime precondition for future success of the process of democratization will be its extension into other countries of the Soviet bloc—for example, to Poland, Czechoslovakia, the GDR, and Hungary. To be sure, this does not rule out the possibility of military intervention, but it would be somewhat more difficult. For example, if the Soviet leadership were faced with the alternative of either a simultaneous military intervention into several countries, with the risk of popular resistance and a bloody struggle with all its international and domestic consequences, or of granting political concessions and entering into compromises that would make it possible for the authentic leaders of the peoples of each country to implement political and economic forms in the direction of a democratization, there could be an exchange for guarantees to respect the military-strategic and economic interests of the Soviet Union in Eastern Europe. It cannot be ruled out that the Soviet leaders if faced with such an alternative would choose the second way. Jacek Kuron, one of the leading representatives of the Polish opposition, described this alternative as "the Finlandization of Eastern Europe," which, in contrast to a Finlandization of Western Europe, would represent a historical step forward for the people of that part of the Continent on the way toward emancipation and democratization.

So one must agree with Rudolf Bahro's critical observation that the "sore point of oppositional conceptions is in their nationalistic narrowness." Bahro sees that "nationalism has an objectively necessary role to play in the destruction of the holy alliance of party apparatuses," but at the same time he sees the necessity of overcoming this situation:

> The opposition will learn to take not just its own national conditions but the entire East European stage as its battleground, and to steer clear of any kind of nationalist prejudices and stereotypes. . . . What are decisive here are not the national differences and animosities, but rather the fundamental contradiction between social interests of *all* peoples of Eastern Europe and the interests of their political bureaucracies.[13]

The solidarity with Charter 77 in other countries of the Soviet bloc, or conversely, the solidarity of Charter 77 with the Soviet dissidents, with the Polish Workers' Defense Committee, or with Rudolf Bahro, are concrete signs of this new solidarity and consciousness of a common goal and of the necessity for a common struggle. To spread this solidarity among the broadest layers of the population is one of the most important tasks of all democratic oppositional currents, and especially the Marxist current.

Correctly enough, Bahro sees the tremendous significance of the development of nondogmatic socialist and communist forces in the developed countries of Western Europe; this for him is one of the preconditions for the process of democratization in Eastern Europe. However, it seems to me that he overestimates somewhat the degree of evolution of the so-called Eurocommunism. At present it is only a potential tendency within the international communist movement; so far, it has not yet been able to develop its own ideological platform and organizational alternative, and many of its representatives even reject such objectives. Bahro feels quite correctly that the "nonintervention mentality" is the principal obstacle to solidarity of Eurocommunist parties and other groups in the left with the opposition in Eastern Europe; at present this mentality is characteristic of the majority of Western communist parties. In this sense, Bahro also overestimates the possibility of "effective solidarity of Western European communists with a serious and responsible opposition in the countries of actually existing socialism," as well as the possibility that these parties would open up their periodicals and book publishing houses as a speakers' tribunal for the socialist opposition in the East. These communist parties have official relations with the leadership of the apparatuses in the Eastern European countries, and it is very difficult for them —they often see it as impossible—to decide between solidarity with the oppressed or with the oppressors. This explains the attitude of West European communist parties to the conviction of Rudolf Bahro and to the regime that brought Bahro to trial. The concrete steps Bahro proposes for internationalizing the struggle of the socialist opposition in the East would sooner be realized by the noncommunist left, which is not bound by the rules in force within the international communist movement and especially as regards the relationship to the Soviet Union.

But the decisive step—one which the Eurocommunist parties of Western Europe must accomplish in their own interests as well if they wish to gain the credibility necessary for their own election, and which at the same time would also be a great help to the left opposition in Eastern Europe—is for these Eurocommunist parties to promote "the other socialism," that is, democratic socialism with freedom of speech and a legal opposition, with independent unions and local control, and with political pluralism, not only for their countries (the developed countries of Western Europe) but also for the peoples of Eastern Europe, who are also ripe for democratic socialism. When the representatives of Western communist parties stand on the speakers' tribunal at a party congress of the CPSU in Moscow and call for the application of such fundamental principles of socialism in the Soviet Union as well, and when they speak out there against the one-party system, the monopoly over the trade unions, and censorship both in the Soviet Union and in the Eastern countries, only then can one expect that the broad masses in Eastern Europe will regain their trust of communists, and that the current minority groups of the opposition, which are Marxist and reform communist, will get the chance to play the noble role Bahro wishes for them in the process of change in the system.

For those who experienced the Prague Spring in 1968, Bahro's book is an extremely valuable encouragement in showing that our efforts served as a laboratory for testing new lines of thought, and that the ideals of the Prague Spring, despite temporary defeat, still live on in the consciousness of an ever larger number of people. The example of the personal courage of the communist Rudolf

Bahro gives these new lines of thought an even greater persuasive force.

Trandlated from the German
by Michel Vale.

NOTES

1. Rudolf Bahro, *The Alternative in Eastern Europe* (London: New Left Books, 1978), p. 342.
2. Ibid., p. 332.
3. Ibid., p. 318.
4. Ibid., p. 350.
5. Ibid., p. 308.
6. Ibid., p. 309.
7. Ibid., p. 329.
8. Ibid., p. 326.
9. Ibid., p. 327.
10. Ibid., p. 330.
11. Ibid., pp. 311-12.
12. Ibid., p. 361.
13. Ibid., p. 334.

RUDI DUTSCHKE

Against the Popes: How Hard It Is to Discuss Bahro's Book

By way of an introduction:
An open letter to a former Spanish Civil War fighter
who became lord over the life of the communist Bahro.

To Stasi-Chief Paul Verner—

Don't look so surprised, Herr Verner. Why shouldn't a European socialist and communist, for whom "Europe" does not end at the Elbe, venture to address you in public? You are a representative of the state security agency of the GDR, that fragment of a nation, which I was compelled to leave, soon thereafter to become better acquainted with the other fragment—the FRG and West Berlin.

So you're not a complete stranger to me, Herr Verner. Back then, your colleagues made sure that the nascently independent thought of a young Christian socialist came to the realization, quickly and first hand, that subordination of the political and social thought of other men is an essential condition of your institution's right to existence. You can perhaps imagine that I am a little closer to your prisoners—Rudolf Bahro, Nico Hübner, and above all Robert Havemann—than to you.

Your path and mine, Herr Verner, parted completely long ago. It was shortly before the Chinese wall was built in Berlin by the Party and Big Brother. But I was not alone . . .

In 1973, despite the concluded détente agreements, you personally saw to it that for the first time I was not allowed to go over the border to East Berlin. I suppose I was not worthy of permission to be a spectator at the World Youth Festival games. But you had to beat a quick retreat when West European youth organizations threatened to demonstrate in East Berlin. Wolf Biermann and I, along with our friends, were then duly chaperoned by your well-paid lackeys and treated to many pseudo-discussions. Your party-state security agency (ultimately even Stasi-Chief Mielke is answerable to it) tried time and again to build Potemkin villages, but you were not always successful with your game. Any state security agency will be made a little thinner and little more worried by a mass front and potentially independent, autonomous activity.

In 1976 I once again passed a few hours in your capital city — of course after first having been searched from top to bottom on the border. Nonetheless, in the home of a friend I was handed two bulky typewritten texts on which, after a superficial examination, I thought I detected your fingerprints. Much of it seemed familiar to me, but I had never heard any of the East Berliner oppositionists take such a theoretical position in an analysis of Russia. The author of the typewritten text was of course not named—which was understandable, although it made us uncertain and mistrustful. Perhaps, from the opposite standpoint, something similar happened to you when you were handed the texts of Bahro's book, long before its publication in the Federal Republic.

By various ways you can well imagine, the first two parts of the manuscript were soon delivered to me in Denmark. After a closer perusal, I became quite certain about one thing: whoever had written it was indeed closer to me than to you—though you should not forget, Herr Verner, that in the early 1940s you too were not unfamiliar with the political and moral premises necessary for an authentic reevaluation of the question of Russia. Just as did I and others after the occupation of Czechoslovakia in 1968, Bahro took up anew the study of Russian and Soviet history in order to be able to trace political phenomena back to the social structures behind them, not only to celebrate them or lament them. And, just as your present prisoner, condemned without any public or real justification, had been shocked by the occupation of Czechoslovakia, you too were once shocked—in 1940, by the Soviet Union's attack on Finland.

It was not in vain that you then said to the comrades and companions in struggle with whom you fled Spain and were interned or imprisoned in Sweden, "We must once and for all put an end to this hurrah patriotism." Herbert Warnke must have been surprised by your latent political-moral internal turnabout, and would soon have suppressed it. And like him, you too soon suppressed your impulses toward change. Historically it is no surprise, after all, that German fascism's attack on the Soviet Union followed soon thereafter. If the Spanish commissar Panzenbeck, from Austria, should still be alive however, he will remember your statement of that time just as exactly as Günter Berkhahn, your former Münzenberg coworker, once a KPD member and Spanish Civil War fighter, who told me about it.

How the pathways of the Spanish Civil War fighters diverged in the next decade! El Campesino, one of the most famous generals of the Spanish Civil War and a member of the Communist Party, had almost a decade in Russian labor camps behind him when he succeeded in fleeing through Persia in 1949, while you, Herr Verner, were firmly ensconced in some party-state position in that same Soviet Russian regime. It has never been easy to see through history in all of its contradictions, absurdity, and repetitiveness. Surely it is some sort of macabre tragicomedy when those same Spanish communists who, from Moscow or Paris, denounced El Campesino in 1949 after his documented analysis of Russia, have today gone the furthest of all the communist parties of Western Europe in their criticism of Russian conditions—while you, Herr Verner, within your party and elsewhere, denounce Eurocommunists for their anti-Sovietism and even blame them for anticommunism. Your projections are as patently obvious as your historical suppressions. Intellectual poverty and a wealth of repression are still with us indeed.

There is one question I have asked myself several times: Might this Paul Verner not have rediscovered himself, even for a moment, when he came into possession of Rudolf Bahro's text? Did he feel —in a covert way, of course—a certain pride in once again having a *communist's* critical materialist analysis in his hands? Probably not. One should expect merely uncertainty and aggression from Paul Verner, the "professional idiot" (Marx's term) in the party-state security service with its hierarchical division of labor (Bahro). You thrive—or more precisely, reign—from a lack of history, just as do the others who rule and dispose freely over the means of production and means of authority. But as prisoner of the Central Committee and the State Security Service Rudolf Bahro says, "the cynics are increasing steadily in number in our country." And those who really turn against this cynicism are punished especially severely.

The mistrust nourished by the ruling administrators for writers, intellectuals, workers, students, and others—even down to their own bureaucrats—is unsurpassed. For you, Herr Verner, and for the other good sirs, every individual initiative becomes an unmanaged burden and a hazard. And when personal initiative takes on political dimensions, and challenges your right to wield power and to maintain your anarchic rule, all your roles of authority and the very structure of certain relations of production and authority are endangered. The "cosmonaut show" suited you just as well as your colleagues in Czechoslovakia and elsewhere, especially those in the Soviet Union, where no soviet has control of the state. "Surplus consciousness" (to use an expression coined by your prisoner Rudolf Bahro) can always be compensated and siderailed for a while at least. But don't suppose that you can abolish objective contradictions in that way. And furthermore, don't think that only we in West Germany are discussing Rudolf Bahro and you. The fetishism of day-in, day-out work in the GDR is enough in itself to make consideration of an alternative indispensable, and over the long term the West German television and the West German credits will be of no help to you for maintaining your unpolitical antipolitical "order and tranquility."

For you, your institutions, and the existing conditions, it was and is not at all a mistake to arrest Rudolf Bahro or others, because for you the *intervention of a despotic state* with no social control, belongs to the very essence of class domination. But all this notwithstanding, I must ask you the absurd but necessary question: Would you, Herr Verner, have the courage to accept an invitation from the Bahro Congress and visit us in West Berlin, to answer questions from socialists, communists, and democrats in the European tradition? Your *inability to enter into public discussion* is an accurate reflection of the determining production relations in which you conduct the offices of your security agency: your answer, or more precisely, your silence is clear.

One of your historical colleagues in the Soviet Union, Felix Dzerzhinsky, said in 1923-24: "Only saints or scoundrels can serve in the GPU [State Political Directorate], but now the saints are all abandoning me and leaving me alone with the scoundrels." There's little to be gotten from saints, and organized villainy was, is, and will always be the negation of progress, regardless of where it is. And you can organize as much as you want and invest in your giant apparatus, but then ideas and human credibility, books even, suddenly break through, from Robert Havemann to Wolf Biermann, from Rudolf Bahro to Jürgen Fuchs and many others. At any moment your bankruptcy, and the surplus product that the working people have created, and you and your institutions have wasted, are evident. Who knows what else you have in mind for Robert Havemann?

In his as yet unpublished book on fascism's hunting down of a young socialist, your former colleague-in-arms, Günter Berkhahn, formulates that older communist's thoughts as to why he did not go into the Eastern Zone, into the GDR, at the end of World War II:

> Over there there's no communism and even no socialism, for they haven't handed over the factories to the workers. The industrial plants, the banks, and the land are held firmly in the hands of the bureaucrats with their state apparatus. And this bureaucratic class, which does not live at all badly on the surplus value created by the nation, wants to pretend that this is socialism. But on this point I have understood Marx and his analysis of the universal state slavery by the bureaucratic class too well for Ulbricht and his consorts to be able to fill my ears with their palaver and sell me this as socialism.

So you see, Her Verner, the difference is not a small one, it is fundamental. Günter Berkhahn's book on German fascism and the life history of this young socialist found no publisher in the West. Those who do not toe the *status quo* line find themselves thoroughly rejected by the ruling classes.

How fundamentally different the former Spanish Civil War fighters have become! Just after Rudolf Bahro's appearance on television, Günter Berkhahn wrote to me in Aarhus: "A serious, educated man, an economist, an SED member, and a convinced communist." However, he added critically: "He demands social enlightenment in the Marxist sense—all that the Soviet bureaucracy and the GDR bureaucracy must prevent unless they intend to resign voluntarily. No ruling class, and above all, no bureaucrat, resigns voluntarily."

You, Herr Verner, with your arrest of the communist Bahro, confirm the analytic thesis of this *true* Spanish Civil War fighter, who did not suppress Moscow's intervention against the revolutionary forces in the Spanish Civil War but forced himself to come to terms with it, however bitter. But you, Herr Verner, like the former Spanish Civil War fighter Hoffmann, have had to liquidate your history time and again, and so have fashioned for yourself a secure, "actually existing" antidemocratic, antisocialist, and anticommunist class standpoint. A systematized deception cannot very easily express a concrete truth. And let's not forget: it was you and no other who saw to it even back in the fifties that your superior, Stasi-Chief Mielke, interrogated and expelled the Spanish Civil War fighter General Gomez (Zaiser) and Walter Janka. That SED member Dahlem, formerly of the KPD, was able to leave Zaiser out of his memoirs, which were tailored and pruned to the dictates of the Central Committee, is understandable. Günter Berkhahn cannot and will not forget his mentor in Spain, just as little as he will forget the other Spanish Civil War fighters who were murdered and eliminated in Eastern Europe and Russia after the struggle in Spain.

The arrest and conviction of Bahro, which you can now add to your record, the arrests and convictions of your "colleagues" in Czechoslovakia, the Soviet Union, and so on, the entire structure of the prevailing conditions which you and the others have molded and to which you are all subject—all this is a direct negation of socialism. *For you, Herr Verner, everything is real and existing— except for socialism.* Günter Berkhahn's objection to Rudolf Bahro is that he was not completely clear of this: His naïveté must be criticized, because socialism is the alternative to bureaucracy. Instead of speaking as Bahro does, of "actually existing socialism," we speak of *actually existing universal state slavery.* And indeed isn't the state-security service an exemplary instance of this?

In the capitalist mode of production—universal wage slavery; and on the other side—universal state slavery. Is that an alternative? For you, Herr Verner, undoubtedly. But one doesn't give up his privileges voluntarily, whether in the East or in the West. Without a political class struggle, without the struggle for democracy and socialism, there will be no changes—neither here nor there.

But what does your prisoner say, Herr Verner? His judgment is clear: "The ruling party apparatus has as much to do with communism as did the Grand Inquisitor with Jesus."

—Rudi Dutschke

Europe begins a new self-appraisal from the ground up

The gap between the specific historical experiences of the generation that experienced, survived, and repressed or revised the Spanish Civil War, and those of our generation in the 1960s, must be tremendous or at least large. Just look at the difference between those who assimilated their core experience in the sixties, and those of the generation of the seventies whose first political, or depoliticizing, socialization experiences have taken place under altered social conditions. Marx had the following to say on the matter:

> History is nothing other than the succession of one generation after the other, each of which exploits the material, capital, and production forces it inherits from all preceding generations, and thus on the one hand continues the traditional activity under completely altered conditions, and on the other, modifies the old conditions with completely altered activity.

However, to be aware of the "old" and the "new" conditions always requires creating anew the gaps in the continuity of historical experience.

When do the suppressed, the exploited, and the injured begin to be aware of the gaps in their history, to codify their defeats and their brief victories in order then to reenter the struggle more conscious of history, with new incentives and under new conditions? Without a deeper reconstruction of the historical process, and real changes in the conditions of class struggle with the added dimension of new experiences of life and struggle, continuity in political and theoretical experience is not possible. Just look at the Spanish Civil War fighters. What breadth, depth, tragedy, and tragicomedy in this genuine "lost generation."

In the preface to his book, Rudolf Bahro pointedly raises the question of the relationship between Kronstadt 1921 and the riots in the Polish coastal cities in 1970, between the defeat of the German revolution in 1918 and the French defeat in May 1968. In Bahro's typewritten manuscript of 1976, however, he is more immediate and more euphoric about the sixties than he would be later, in the book:

> 1967 and 1968 were the years of tense hope for our countries. From the reports about China from various opponents, the idea of a new movement beckoned, an idea on which Mao Zedong based himself and his attempt to save his country from the defeats of bureaucratic Stalinism. In Czechoslovakia, a wound, still not healed, was inflicted on the same enemy, the Stalinist bureaucracy, which was attempting to block any socialist progress in our part of the world. The students and the young workers of Paris had the upper hand over the conservative party

administrators for a few weeks, and threw themselves into battle against state monopoly until the first fumblings of an alternative revolutionary rule began to be felt. The Vietnamese people inflicted a strategic defeat on U.S. imperialism with their brilliant Tet offensive. In these events, such fundamental contradictions of the present were expressed, that we could rely on their future dynamic.[1]

Didn't we, especially in the immediacy of the times, have the same thoughts—with all their ingenuousness and limitations? A certain difference, deriving from the different social situations and hence different theoretical approaches, is there, however. We shall come back to that later.

Peculiarly, the Spanish Civil War does not play such a prominent role in Bahro's references to the central issues of the class struggle in the twentieth century. Was that not one of the last great battles of the class struggle in Europe? Was it not the first front of German and Russian barbarism, the first front of the Second World War and the last attempt to prevent it? Is it really possible to separate the defeats of the sixties historically from those forces of events which shaped the *status quo* of the relationship between the capitalist imperialism of the United States and the Asiatic imperialism of Russia? The defeat of German fascism was a basic achievement of these great powers. But can that hinder the socialists and communists in Europe from going their own way? Can the Parisian May really be separated from the Prague Spring? Or to put the question more pointedly: could the armies of the Warsaw Pact ever have occupied Czechoslovakia if we had had a West European May rather than just a Parisian May lasting but a few weeks?

The objective and political-organizational, theoretical, etc. arguments are clear; nonetheless the question is still not resolved. Let's just recall the discussion between Engels and Kautsky in 1885 about Russia. Engels' fundamental assessment was: in the Russian revolutionary process, it will be *the democrats and liberals who will first take the lead, not the socialists*. Democratization was the focal point. Only after the impact of this revolution had made itself felt on Western Europe, and a socialist revolution had been consummated there, would there exist in Russia the possibility of achieving socialism.

Given a country lacking a true national market, with an extremely low commodity production, a country ruled for centuries by Asiatic despotism with universal state slavery and based on small-scale industrial production and a large-scale agrarian structure, it was only natural that in 1917 the question would be whether the "Russian 1789" (Marx) would prevail *or* the old line of domination under a new ideological banner, this time industrial and no longer agrarian, and whether the *Marxist-Leninist opium* would replace the tsars' opium administered through the churches.

My *thesis* is: February 1917 inaugurated the Russian 1789, and October marked its end for whatever reasons. This is why the Russian October could fascinate the European working class for a few brief moments and demonstrate the timeliness of the world-historical tasks of the socialist upheaval, but after that it was condemned to fall back in the negation of socialism, where it played a role that hindered rather than spurred the European working class. Rosa Luxemburg captured the essence of the matter quite clearly in her German prison cell:

> With the throttling of political life throughout the country, the life within the soviets must also become increasingly paralyzed. Without general elections, unrestricted freedom of the press and freedom of association, and the free battle of opinions, the life in every public institution dies, to become a spurious life in which the bureaucracy is the only active element.

It is not surprising that the victors of the proletarian October Revolution, which was real in appearance but soon showed itself in essence to be a Bolshevik seizure of power, never really replied to Luxemburg's criticism. What other reasons Bahro has for not taking up the question will be seen later.

Engels' strategical pattern has proven itself correct, and my *second thesis* is: Every thwarting of democratic initiative in Russia, and later in Eastern Europe, fortifies the capitalist social structure in Western Europe.

The *third thesis* is: The democratic initiatives of the Prague Spring were one of the roots of the Parisian May, the first new socialist thrust in Western Europe after the Second World War.

But what does Engels' model have to do with Czechoslovakia? First, that this country falls under the sway of the Russian brand of Asiatic despotic imperialism, which is weak in production, weak in class struggle, weak in culture, but strong in domination. Further, that democratic initiatives took place in Czechoslovakia, until they finally affected all of Europe.

The internal dynamic of the Prague Spring can just as little be separated from the economic and political misery of the Novotny government as it can be separated from the dependence of all CMEA countries on the capitalist world market and on the new situation emerging in the sixties after the completion of the capitalist period of postwar reconstruction. The wave of rationalization in the West had to affect the East if the latter was not to fall further behind—although not in the same way. For historical reasons, there were different currents in each of the ruling parties and leaderships.

Czechoslovakia had its Masaryk case, the Slansky case, but there was still room for thinking that diverged from the ruling thoughts, because until 1968 the Czechs had had no occupiers and no Russian army to control the Party more closely—the Russian Soviet conquest had not yet been fully consummated. The *political-economic and technological backwardness and the antidemocratic production relations*, which constitute the essence of the permanent crisis in Eastern Europe, were shaken up in the Prague Spring. In my view this condition was ultimately what set the stage for the Kafka discussion of 1963 within the framework of Czech history, and made the reform movement of January 1968 both objectively possible and necessary. No other country in Eastern Europe had such room to maneuver within the party.

Recapitalization was just as little on the order of the day as the introduction of *true* socialism. After decades of systematic mystification about socialism in accordance with the Moscow main line, there could be no more than just a *democratic turn* in the economy and in ideology. "Socialism in one country" was and is a deception.

H. J. Krahl gets the point, if only to a limited extent, when he writes: "The idealizing liberalism of the intellectuals and students, and the economic reformism of the democratic reform group at the top levels of party and state, complemented one another." Owing to his acceptance of the category of the "socialist camp," Krahl did not give adequate regard to the *radical* progress that democracy and liberalism meant in a situation of universal state and party slavery, whereas in fact, Engels stressed especially these points in reflecting on the repercussions on Western Europe.

The proletarian state and party slaves were mistrustful, perplexed, and full of hope with regard to their reform movement in its first moments, but decades of experience gave them something to think about. However, the major resistance coalitions among labor unions and student organizations and so forth show the extent to which they were in agreement with the reform movement. Thus, just as the democratic turn within Czechoslovakia shifted class and power relationships, it was this very turn that had the greatest internal, historical, and lasting influence on Western Europe! It was the defeat in Western Europe and the failure of the Paris May to spread that enabled, or at least made it easier for, the Moscow occupiers to strike out toward the end of Europe's first small new summer, to prevent the first stage of political emancipation from developing into a general emancipation.

The common interest of capitalist imperialism under American leadership, and of Asiatic imperialism under Russian and Soviet leadership, converged here on the central issue: the *status quo* had to be maintained under any circumstances, with NATO and the Warsaw Pact acting in consonance to ensure the impossibility of the road to socialism. But to this military view of things must be added: were not Yalta and Teheran the first unmistakable signs that the corresponding modes of production would be instituted in the respective zones after their conquest? Should Bahro's question—"Whence could groups opposing a Soviet Dubček still come?"[2]—be interpreted in this sense, in a sense quite different from the usual?

For example, Bahro calls for the creation of a unified front of progressive forces in both blocs, to create, by means of political pressure, the *preconditions* for an escalation of mutual disarmament.[3] Without any clarification of the new political and economic ties between the two blocs, their commitments to one another via the capitalistically determined world market, and especially of the situation of the opposition in Eastern Europe and Russia, this unified front unfortunately seems to me to be an illusion. In Moscow six people demonstrated on account of the occupation. In East Berlin there were no more. All learned what prisons, psychiatric institutions, or expulsion meant. Brezhnev said: Every country has six madmen, so for our mammoth country this is a mere trifle. Herr Honecker could hardly think otherwise.

A glance at the many decades of unrest in Eastern Europe and silence in Western Europe should make clear the difficulties of this new beginning. There have been bitter defeats. The uprising of 17

June 1953 in the GDR against the tighter norms and repression quickly became known to the camp internees at Vorkuta (where there were also many Germans) and led to the first strike in decades in that cold Siberian region. But the workers in West Germany and Western Europe made no move: they had other problems. And then the leftist intellectuals in Western Europe and West Germany concurred in maintaining the deception that a "counter-revolution" had taken place. Let me quote from the book by El Campesino: "I feel more shame than indignation over the blandishments directed toward the Russian leadership. They are intellectuals and thus must not be ignorant and stupid. Does corruption explain their behavior? A mixture of intellectual and material corruption? I'd like to see them in Vorkuta. The intellectuals and the artists in the USSR are the greatest lackeys of them all."

El Campesino experienced and described the physical and political-economic terror of the camp. He did not then have to experience a psychiatric institution. The CPSU's Twentieth Party Congress in 1956 marked the transition from the crudest form of state slavery on a scale of millions, to the combination of a subtle form of domination where this was possible, with a crude form of domination where necessary.

The leftist intellectuals in Western Europe received the uprising of the Hungarian people in 1956 just as coldly as they had others before. The debate between Camus and Sartre, however, marked the first sign of a new perspective. The concerns and problems of the West European working class did not yet extend beyond their immediate interests in this respect. The Continental and international situation did not change until the end of the sixties, the end of the sustained capitalist boom after the Second World War, and after the new attempts at accommodation and to exploit the crisis of the capitalist world market as a "tool" (Marx) to make up for the backwardness of the East. Differences in the experience of the class struggle did not disappear, but after the crushing of the Prague Spring one thing became clear: *Every tendency toward democratization in Eastern Europe made the question of socialization in Western Europe more acute.* Prague and Paris, Eastern Europe and Western Europe, have set out on a new course since this breakthrough in the total lack of contemporaneousness in the 1968 experience of history and struggle. It seems to me that an understanding of the defeat as the first factor for reestablishing the relevance of the struggle for emancipation and a new sense of relevance among the rulers on both sides, is grossly in error.

But *is* the situation of the reformers and the opposition the same? No, just as little as the systems are identical. They determine one another, but *for that reason* any hopes the East European opposition might place on Carter amount to a fundamentally mistaken judgment. In my opinion, how questionable it is when Bahro says: "Human rights, political democracy—certainly! But what is lacking in Eastern Europe and in the Soviet Union itself for that matter, is an *organized long-term struggle for a different overall policy*."[4]

Communists of the Leninist stamp in the best sense of the term feel most compatible with such an understanding of party and politics, just as Lenin did with his own intelligentsia. He was not sure of the genius of the people or of the various class sectors, and fundamentally overestimated the possibility of an "autonomous anticapitalist way" for Eastern Europe and Russia. Thus he underestimated the real significance of the struggle for democracy and human rights in the quite specific relations of production obtaining in Russia and Eastern Europe. We will come back to this point later.

But the ruling groups in Eastern Europe know quite well what they are doing when they combat opposition in the most varied of ways. What seems to me important here is the following: After the defeat of 1968 the opposition in both fronts began a process of rethinking, and a change set in on the basis of the new economic and political conditions. The Western European radical opposition, in the still quite brief tradition of the New Left, began to reexamine their political stance toward and analysis of Eastern Europe and Russia. Conversely, the socialist and democratic opposition in Eastern Europe began to follow more closely the new thinking in Western Europe. Naturally, this did not go unnoticed by the ruling groups.

It's sufficient to note that in 1973 the Hungarian ruling party set up an investigating committee against Agnes Heller. Intellectually impoverished lies, falsifications, and banalities are understandable in such commissions for control and self-justification: they conform to their nature. Nonetheless it is interesting to see close-up the anxieties of the Hungarian monopolistic bureaucracy. Why should they not be fundamentally the same in the other Eastern European countries? The issue was Heller's relationship with the New Left:

> The meaning of all this is that the Marxist conception of revolution is not being fulfilled in the socialist countries; that the "radical needs" which aim at changing the very structure of needs are not being met in the working class or in the working movement, whereas they have been fulfilled in hippie communes—which are of only short-term significance and of often doubtful value in the social struggles of the highly developed capitalist countries; they withdraw from society, and believe that they can realize their naive ideas on islands beyond society. In the place of the revolutionary program of the workers' movement, in the place of the revolution by the working class, we have the counter-culture movement and revolution through the commune. That is the "revolutionary" program, the program of Agnes Heller's New Left.

A systematized poverty of mind is part of the very nature of the ideologues, the administrators of authority, the lords over the means of production. Given such circumstances, it was quite inevitable that Agnes Heller's book *The Theory of Needs* should have to be published in Milan rather than in Budapest.

Bahro makes the following bitter observation with regard to such types within the ruling class of the bureaucracy:

> If one wished to abandon one's belief in a really socialist and communist future, one could of course accept the empirically current term "socialism," and simply and cynically give it a new interpretation—the actual description and analysis of our situation. And one who really set about doing this in an open way would be of some use; the cynics are becoming increasingly more numerous among us, but they are cowardly and privileged.[5]

Unfortunately Bahro does not go into any further detail in this fundamentally important clarification of terms, the categories of justification under the conditions of the Soviet Union and Eastern Europe. The rulers know quite well what this question of concepts and substantial contents is all about.

Fernando Claudin, in reflecting on the possibilities and limitations of the Eurocommunist and Eurosocialist labor parties and the present-day situation of the class struggle (he is not analyzing the politically and organizationally defeated New Left), says unequivocally in his *Eurocommunism and Socialism*:

Among the points of agreement that exist between Washington and Moscow, alongside all the contradictions and tensions, there is one that carries a special weight. It is, that no socialist—i.e., *socialist*, not social-democratic—democracy is to be allowed in Western Europe. Each of the two superpowers has its own motives for this, and tries in its own way and with its own means to outdo the other in its attacks on the European left, which represents a democratic-socialist alternative to the crisis of capitalism.

However, let me put forth my own critical thesis against this position: Every West European socialist initiative is condemned to barbaric defeat by both imperialist powers if there exists no advanced front, no security, and ultimately, no direct link-up for it in Eastern Europe. Jacek Kuron, a Pole, speaks of the "Finlandization of Eastern Europe," not of Western Europe. This other kind of democratization may be *the* central question. But this helps us to channel our efforts into a new initiative of democratization and socialization and to prevent us from inexorably becoming the targets of a "search and destroy" action on the part of the great powers.

In his last essay Lukács describes the problem as follows:

The same example time and again: trade unions—Lenin versus Trotsky (indifference or wildcat strikes, Poland as a symbolic danger for all people's democracies). Thus a universal problem: transition to real socialist democracy (democracy in everyday life) or permanent crisis.

Specific points follow: "Today nothing is decided (the Soviet Union is the decisive factor)." Then we have the question: What is the nature and trend of Russian Soviet history? Socialist democracy represents "the world's future prospects because under capitalism there are emerging signs of crisis."[6]

But how does it look for the Russian Soviet semi-Asiatic mode of production and mode of domination during the crisis period of the capitalist mode of production and domination? Second, should we forget what Bahro sarcastically affirms: "From the Elbe to the Amur, the ruling classes daily feed on the masses' longing for a restoration of some earlier state, now that the democratic initiative of Czechoslovakia has been defeated"?

Marx's methods against the Marxists, the anti-Marxists, and the Marxist-Leninists on the example of Russia

It is a recurrent joke to see how Marxist intellectuals attempt to accuse Marx of ahistorical logical essentialism, or how anti-Marxist intellectuals attempt to ridicule him for propagating a dangerous theory of universality. Both have a profoundly wrong or ignorant approach to Marxist method. Did Marx not rigorously oppose the Russian sociologist Mikhailovskii, who wanted to make a general theory of the philosophy of history out of Marx's *Critique of Political Economy* (*Capital*), which was an outline of West European history? Marx upbraids Mikhailovskii as follows: "He would have to transform my historical sketch of the emergence of capitalism in Western Europe into a historical-philosophical theory of the general development prescribed for all peoples . . . I must beg your pardon. (That would be too much of an honor and too much of an insult at the same time.)" Marx opposes emphatically all the specious "universal keys to a philosophy of history, whose greatest merit is that they are above history." In his last manuscript, the "marginal notes," he says: "According to Herr Wagner, Marx's theory of value is the 'keystone of his political system.'" Since I have never outlined a socialist system [which would have totally contradicted his method and his critique of the political economy of bourgeois society—R.D.] this is a fantasy of Wagner, Schaffler, *e tutti quanti*." Actually one can hardly count how many "*e tutti quanti*'s" we have today. The "new science" (Marx) generalizes, but it is no system. And in fact, with its revolutionary line of thought it completely destroyed the philosophical and economic "systems," revealed the internal patterns of the bourgeois system, and made them visible to all.

What is striking about these great thinkers, with their claim to irreconcilability and their "impartial" boasting about their thought holding the "universal key," is their inability to distinguish among different modes of production. Marx says of the bourgeois economists that they provide the *key* for laying bare all other formations; then he adds unambiguously: "but by no means in the manner of economists who wish to efface all historical differences and to perceive bourgeois society in all other social formations." After all historical differences have thus been blurred, a new distinction emerges and we hear about feudal society, purportedly the predecessor of bourgeois society.

What *mode of production* dominated in Russian history, what modes of production came into conflict with one another in Russian history? No one who makes the least claim to be scientific and that Bahro's work should be taken seriously, can get around this question. We're no longer in the Comintern and Cominform times, when the bishops and cardinals below the supreme pope in Moscow had better opportunities for putting in an appearance.

February (Lenin proclaimed this as early as in April 1917) made Russia into the freest country in the world. But *what took place after the October rebellion of the Leninist groups under his leadership*?

Those great times were so brilliant that Lukács, Korsch, et al. saw no problem in the way things went in Russia. Only after he had been thrown out of the German Communist Party did Korsch notice the tremendous hunger for commodities in Russia, but he did not thereafter discover Russian history and its *internal static dead end of universal state slavery*. The West European theoreticians in communist parties erased Russian history—the Comintern saw to that. But didn't this dusky line go further? Aren't Comintern and Cominform lines still to be found among many left-oriented theoreticians of the most varied persuasions? The "New Philosophers" in France with their 1920s regressive cultural pessimism, and others with their cult of October, can trace such a lineage.

And what else are they doing—these bishops, cardinals and popes, all the Party theoreticians of the Eurocommunist parties of Western Europe—than glossing over the specificities of this particular social formation? Their criticism of the Russian situation has intensified at the political surface of things, and that is very welcome. But without probing into the history of Russian production and domination, there is no way to see through the veils of self-justification around actually existing socialism and exercise a genuine and honest critique.

Given the obscurity that still surrounds the question of mode of production in Russian history, it is not surprising that such political opponents of the ruling bureaucracy in Eastern Europe as Ernest Mandel speak the same basic language when dealing with the question of the October Revolution. The only discernible differences are those having to do with personal leadership. Do Elmar Altvater and German Communist Party (DKP) Chairman Mies differ on this point? Is the situation different for the theoreticians of the October myth in the Italian Communist Party and the French Communist Party? Santiago Carrillo of the Spanish Communist Party is politically the most trenchant in his critique, but he gives just as little attention as others to the specific question of the Asiatic mode of production and universal state slavery in Russian history, attempting theoretically to evade the question via the old "primitive accumulation" error. In the 1920s Preobrazhensky put forth the thesis of primitive socialist accumulation, another veil of self-justification, and a few years later was liquidated alomg with many other comrades, millions of peasants, workers, and Christians.

Did not Marx protest against Mikhailovskii? The continuity of "the Mongol devastations," of which Marx writes in his "Introduction to the Critique of Political Economy," never occurred to them. Ernest Mandel begins his review of the book by Comrade Bahro, now sitting in jail, as follows: "Rudolf Bahro's *The Alternative* is the most important theoretical work to come out of the countries that have abolished capitalism since Leon Trotsky's *The Revolution Betrayed*." He should have added that the *theoretical* premises are fundamentally different; the profound political points that are shared in the antibureaucratic struggle of Bahro, Mandel, and myself, for example, should not deceive us on this point. It is no accident that in his review of my book *An Attempt to Put Lenin Back on His Feet*, Ernest Mandel acknowledged much, but fundamentally rejected the reconstruction of Russian and Soviet history through the categories of the Asiatic mode of production and universal state slavery. Bahro and I completely agree in our *general* theoretical appraisal of the formation and in the precise differentiation of social formations; however, we are not at all in agreement on the *positive* view of the anticapitalist order, as I presented it in 1974. Bahro is not one of those erasers of history who try to gloss over the specific feature of different formations:

> Was the old Russian empire, which was to become the Soviet Union, a capitalist country at all, albeit an undeveloped one? In 1881 Marx and Engels did not even think that Russia was feudal. They saw it as a semi-Asiatic country, and that was not a geographic but a detailed political-economic feature. The abolition of capitalist private property had no major positive significance for Russia, simply because there was very little capitalist private property there and because economic life was affected by it only at specific points.[7]

We agree here, though it was not until after 1974 that I posed the question of whether we would not be more consistent to speak of the liquidation of the embryonic forms of private property in Russian history rather than of their supersession, which then in turn brings up the problem of social formations and their dead ends and the transitional periods between them.

In the future discussions no one will any longer be able to avoid this key point of modes of production. Without this the history of realities of relations of production and social relations in general cannot be understood, nor can the specific processes of development and stagnation of the productive forces be explained. The leader of the German Communist Party for many years, murdered in a German concentration camp, was right when he said: "The testing stone for every communist is his attitude toward the Soviet Union." Tragically and realistically, however, after the events of German and Russian concentration camps, it is more necessary than ever to not lose sight of this tie to the system.

Every lack of theoretical clarity on the question of Russia has had portentous consequences for socialists, communists, democrats, and other progressive forces in their struggle against the wage slavery of capitalism. The entire history of the Western European working class is testimony to this. It is no coincidence that Rosa Luxemburg was firmly against entering into the Communist International, the first cover organization of the Bolsheviks. Further, it was no coincidence that Luxemburg wrote her evaluation and radical critique of the Bolsheviks in prison. It was not for nothing that the representative of the young German Communist Party (KPD) was sent to Moscow to speak out strongly against the Comintern's founding and to abstain in the voting. The KPD representatives were brought around with all the typically "Asiatic tricks" (Marx), by none other than Zinoviev, to giving their affirmative votes to the Communist International just after Rosa Luxemburg was murdered. With the Communist International the Bolsheviks had in their hands the crucial lever for the next decade in Central and Western Europe and used it to advance their foreign policy, above and beyond any control by the communist workers' parties outside of Russia.

Rosa Luxemburg knew the inner essence of Asiatic despotism like no one else. One can imagine the debate between the Bolsheviks and the Western European communists under the leadership and in the spirit of Rosa Luxemburg. History is a bitter, real, factional process of class and interest: it is not a "could have been" or "should have been" process. Nonetheless, in the present and perhaps in the future we must face the past as clearly as possible. The crucial question is simply the difficulty or ease with which modes of production are broken up—in this case, the Asiatic form in Russia.

Anyone who does not take seriously Luxemburg's studies on Asiatic despotism or her criticism of the Bolsheviks can of course come to no other conclusion than the formula of "insufficient de-Stalinization." But this nonsense about insufficiency completely transfigures the problem of political analysis which still remains. Bahro seemingly says something similar:

> Yet there is no meaningful and conscious solution to the Soviet problem, which concerns socialists the world over, without a deep understanding for the new Russia's process of development, for the courage and will-power of Lenin's Bolshevism, for its positive and creative achievements.[8]

But then he adds a comment on the necessity of "at least a minimal acquaintance with Russian history." It is just this very minimum that is lacked by those who prattle on about the "production relations of a new type" in Russia and Eastern Europe. But the security they derive from their lack of a sense of history leads into rough seas. Thus Bahro's "minimum" seems to touch only inadequately upon a central point. By that I mean the problem of Russia's historical formation within the central question of *social labor* in general, and "public labor" in particular. This is essential if one is to discover how the Asiatic mode of production can be broken up. Bahro is quick to observe that in a precapitalist country the transition to industrialization must take place either via wage labor or noneconomic coercion. He does *not* clarify the noneconomic coercion, the Asiatic whip of universal state slavery, in terms of the Russian formation's relationship to labor in general and in particular. No doubt the fact that Bahro does not accept Marx on this point has something to do with his special position on the China question and his idealization of the "autonomous," anticapitalist way, where he is completely ignorant of the capitalist world market and its specific role. We hold with Marx's definition of the formation: "No social order ever perishes before all the productive forces for which there is room in it have developed; and new, higher relations of production never appear before the material conditions of their existence have matured in the womb of the old society itself." The question may be posed clearly as follows: Under what conditions or premises did the constitution, establishment, and consolidation of the mode of production take place which has been dominant in Russia since the Mongol conquests, the Moscovite autocracy, and the Bolshevik autocracy, in the most varied developmental variations? In his "Introduction to the Critique of Political Economy" [*Grundrisse*] Marx says: "This abstraction of labor as such is not merely the mental product of a concrete totality of labors. Indifference towards specific labors corresponds to a form of society in which individuals can with ease transfer from one labor to another, and where the specific kind is a matter of chance for them, hence of indifference." This process is brought to its "most modern form . . . in the United States," but, Marx continues, among the Russians there is "a spontaneous inclination," an "indifference towards particular kinds of labor," which corresponds to their "being embedded by tradition within a very specific kind of labor, from which only external influences can jar them loose."[9] Wrested from the old mode of production, the semi-Asiatic dead end, only through the capitalist world market!

How great then, in reality was the influence from outside before 1917? Did it affect only a few cities, had it already deeply undermined the old mode of production and domination? Not in the least: the production of use values prevails, and exchange value is purely a superficial phenomenon. In agrarian communities, Marx says, there is "appropriation, not through labor, but presumed as labor, of the natural condition of labor, of the earth as the original instrument of labor—at once workshop, and container of the raw material . . . preconditions that appear to be natural or divine preconditions." And he draws the following conclusions: "At this stage of development, the economic and ideological relation of individuals to the world is not the goal of personal activity or individual appropriation, but is mediated through the firmly entrenched relations of these individuals to their community."

Indeed, this gets to the core of the matter: Do *labor* and *appropriation* become dissociated in a context different from that of *primitive accumulation*? The approximately 2 million proletarian state slaves and superficial wage laborers are indeed not enough to deceive us with regard to the approximately 150 million peasant state slaves, and the roughly 2 million members of the tsarist bureaucracy for universal state slavery. The low level of commodity production follows as a matter of course.

Ernst Bloch, reviewing Lukács's book *History and Class Consciousness* in 1924, called attention to an elementary Russian reality—the dead end. Although he greeted the Bolsheviks jubilantly, as a philosopher there was something he could not blind himself to: "Those Russians who act philosophically will sense a fall. Infinitely different from the revisionists, they are products of almost the same philosophical legacy, and many of them will say that Marx did not place Hegel on his feet only to have Lukács put Marx back on his head."[10]

Neither a renaissance nor a breakthrough for *humanism* was ever a real possibility in Russia's dead end. For instance, let us not forget the deep antihumanist wave in Russian literature between 1917 and 1920, a tendency that directly reflected the inner nature of the October uprising. Bukharin lamented this in 1937 in a conversation with Nikolaevskii in Paris, shortly before meeting his doom in the Moscow liquidation, and underscored the importance of proletarian humanism. The old Moscovite ways lead to a new universal state and party slavery in the most brutal form. The CPSU systematically vitiated a world-historical task for all the oppressed, exploited, and injured—namely, the task of socialism and democracy. We socialists, communists, democrats, and Christians suffered a blow from which we have not yet recovered.

The Asiatic mode of production and structure of domination has assumed several guises through the course of history, but its essence remains the same even today. To be sure, the capitalist world market crisis forced upon the ruling group the transformation from an agrarian bureaucracy into an industrial bureaucracy, and indeed, was what made such a transformation possible. However, did this transformation do away with the production relations corresponding to this mode of production? The path led from the natural agrarian umbilical cord of tsarism, which was still dominant in 1917, to a new, imposed umbilical cord of collectivization and Asiatic industrialization. The dead end of stagnation, a formation dependent on the development of the capitalist world market, could certainly not be broken through in this way.

On the question of Leninism, Bahro and I are of contrary opinions. He tries to impute a "humanistic perspective" to Leninism which the Stalin period had deprived it of. However, this can hardly be inferred from Lenin's failure to understand the categories of "freedom" and "democracy," both fundamental ingredients of socialist consciousness, to say nothing of his prohibition of factions. Once again, it is a romanticization of the "anticapitalist way" and of the specious "autonomy" of this way that lies concealed behind this view.

The *lack, and indeed, rejection, of humanism* by the Bolsheviks and by other Russian currents has a further objective basis. In Marx, real humanism had one crucial precondition: "the universality of needs, abilities, pleasures, and productive forces of the individual, as is engendered through universal exchange." Any study of the history of commodities tells us that individuality first comes into its own through exchange value, as social individuality, with all the distortions and mystifications down to individualism itself, but this individuality is far more developed in world-historical terms than that which is still tied to the umbilical cord.

The absence of law, the "semi-Asiatic lack of culture" (Lenin), the absence of direction, and the absence of the market constitute the foundation for universal state slavery in its most varied forms. The way to socialism cannot be developed out of this. The proletarian state slave is variable capital, but counted as constant capital. The "Asiatic derision of the personality" (Lenin) excludes humanism, democracy, and socialism together.

Bahro's views on the relationship between Russia and China are interesting, if quite questionable. I shall be referring to [Bahro's] typed manuscript of 1976, since in the book these passages have been largely or completely edited out. The issue once again is those countries having a socioeconomic formation in which capitalism was not able to set in motion the development of the productive forces. Bahro's thesis is: "The content of epoch-making competition, now a permanent part of world history," consists in the fact that the "disciplined and industrious people of China" are quite competitive compared to the Russians. Then follows the moot statement: "Mao Zedong availed himself of the historical chance of *being able* to oppose the Great Proletarian Cultural Revolution to the horrible Stalinist collectivization of the people's communes and Stalinist camps."

Against the background of the processes taking place in China over the last few years I can say: the generations of the 1960s in Western Europe did not want to be disciplined, we rebelled. In

China at the same time the main task was to take the first new step to get out of the internal dead end; help had to come *from without*. Mao Zedong's Great Proletarian Cultural Revolution was the last deathbed attempt of a permanent rebel to remain in the dead end of autonomy. It was of no help to him at all that the Russian threat demanded that elements of the Asiatic and semi-Asiatic mode of production should be eliminated. When *universal needs* of social individuality will come to exist in this area cannot yet be foreseen.

Bahro then falls into the illusion that Maoism is the negation of Stalin's miserable rule: "The alternative is not Stalin or the soviets, but Stalin or Mao Zedong." He is obviously vacillating here. Morally he rejects Stalin's forced collectivization, but theoretically he suggests that the kulak danger can be materialistically approached without taking up the problem of private property in the world history of social formations; the revolutionary aspect is ignored.

For Marx the Asiatic mode of production is one of the progressive formations in world history, but also one that must remain stagnant if no help comes *from without* to pull it out of its dead end. A decisive factor in this stagnation is the internal inability of this social formation to enable private property to get a foothold. Thus further progress is impossible. It is a universal stage of development that has come to a stop, and for this reason it should not be confused with a precapitalist stage. "Precapitalist mode of production" implies, suggests even, a natural pathway to capitalism, but it is just this which is not the case for societies with an Asiatic mode of production.

The failure to understand this leads Habermas, for instance, to pose the false question of whether the Asiatic mode of production might not represent a "special line of development of class society unto itself, alongside the path of ancient production" or even a "mixed form of ancient and feudal modes of production." This return to a theoretical dead end is historically all too well known from the Leningrad discussions of 1929 on the Marxist theory of social formations. Riazanov, Madjar, Bukharin, Wittfogel, Varga— none of the revolutionary experts on the question were allowed to be present. For Stalin and his Comintern ideologues the objective was to eliminate the independent status of the Asiatic mode of production from the critical theory of historical materialism. The links of despotism and bureaucracy to the ruling class of the Asiatic mode of production in general, and the Mongolian heritage and continuity of Russia in particular, were to be liquidated by every means. The Plekhanov-Lenin debate on the *Asiatic restoration* after the revolution of 1905, and Lenin's latter-day concern about the return of the old plague of the bureaucratic machinery of the state and party apparatus, might have cast renewed doubt on the victory that had already been achieved.

It is very important not to lose sight of the fundamental difference between private slavery in the ancient mode of production and universal state slavery in the Asiatic mode of production. Marx recognized the positive side of private property in the Philosophical Manuscripts, but there was and is not one single positive side to universal state slavery.

When the good sirs of the Institute for Social Sciences or, more precisely, the official theoreticians of the state and party bureaucracy of the old line, speak of a "relatively independent formation," as they have done since the times of Ulbricht, I must agree. This real formation undoubtedly does possess, despite all its dependence on the capitalist world market, a relative autonomy of such a nature as to eliminate internal opposition through the use of political and economic weapons, and to maintain itself steadily at a high level militarily. To this must be added technological backwardness. The leadership of the party must continually force the masses into public labor—"voluntary" is the official term. That's the nature of relative autonomy, the antidemocratic and antidynamic features of this formation. In this mode of production and domination, socialism is not up for discussion. The state and party controllers of the means of production have a profoundly asocial character and reflect the ways of a ruling class. But then, what *is* left for discussion? *Democratic initiative* is on the order of the day, but the bureaucracy opposes it with all the means at its disposal. On the other hand, the prevailing proponents of capitalist democracy have no objection. The path proposed by Bahro, namely to take charge of things through a better communist program, is in my view completely unrealistic, because the real relations of production and the possibilities and limitations they offer for struggle remain unaffected.

Indeed I think that the possibility for such a socialist class struggle in Western Europe is doomed to failure without democratic initiative in Russia and Eastern Europe.

Bahro asks correctly, and with dismay: If socialism is not a stage on the road to communism, how can the working class have any direct interest in it? But he will not draw the necessary conclusions at the level of his theoretical reconstruction. The few radical passages in the book are ignored, and his reviewers pluck out of it what they wish. The cardinals and popes of the left take his term "real socialism" and leave his substantive definition of the Asiatic mode of production out. Being an expert in the theory of social formations, he gives us continual glimpses of something that is absolutely hostile to his real socialism: "emancipation from the modern slavery to things and to the state" must be achieved through struggle. For many of the popes of critical solidarity, or more precisely, solidarity with the CPSU and the SED at any price, Bahro's arrest was a socialist action. However, anyone who takes a deeper look at the universal party and state slavery in Russia, instead of allowing elements of true democracy to develop, is a fundamental enemy of socialism.

Of course there are any number of points in Bahro's book that can be criticized and evaluated. However, what is decisive is that the socialists, democrats, and communists in the European and international tradition learn how to discuss together—and not merely before and during congresses, on special occasions. What would have happened with the book had its author not been sent to prison? Probably it would have drifted into obscurity, known only to the so-called specialists. Let us take advantage of the new opportunity now offered: let us finally discuss the problem of the relationship between socialists, communists, democrats, and Christians in the GDR and the FRG, in Western and Eastern Europe, in order to define more precisely the frame of reference for political class struggle—and perhaps even to define it for the first time. Otherwise the two systems and the relations of production and domination that underlie them will continue to play their game with us as they always have.

> Abridged and translated by Michel Vale,
> with the cooperation of Rudi Dutschke.

NOTES

1. Rudolf Bahro, quoted from the typewritten manuscript of 1976, p. 6.
2. Ibid.

3. Ibid.

4. Ibid., p. 13.

5. Ibid., p. 16.

6. Georg Lukács, *Gelebtes Leben—Skizze*, p. 58.

7. Rudolf Bahro, *Eine Dokumentation* (Cologne/Frankfurt, 1977), p. 71.

8. Rudolf Bahro, *The Alternative in Eastern Europe* (London: New Left Books, 1978), p. 84.

9. Karl Marx, "Introduction to the Critique of Political Economy," in *Grundrisse*, trans. Martin Nicolaus (New York: Vintage, 1973), pp. 104-05.

10. E. Bloch, "Actualität und Utopie. Zu Lukács Philosophie des Marxismus," in *Der neue Merkur*, October 1923-March 1924, p. 459.

RUDI STEINKE, WALTER SÜSS, AND ULF WOLTER

His Refrain is Heard Around the World:
An Initial Assessment of the Bahro Congress

Preparing for the Congress

The "International Congress on and for Rudolf Bahro," held in Berlin November 16-19, 1978, was the greatest and most successful expression of solidarity for the imprisoned theoretician to date. Both the quality of the discussions and the numbers of people who participated confuted all attempts of the East German authorities to portray Bahro as either an isolated idiot or the agent of some foreign power. The Congress showed Bahro to be the "agent" he really is—an agent of the international communist and socialist movement. The attempts of the government of the German Democratic Republic to "immunize" the left against Bahro's thought have in fact resulted in even more support for him, at the same time revealing to broad segments of the public the scandalous nature of GDR chicanery.

For the left in the Western countries the Congress was a success in that it brought together the diverse elements of the divided leftist spectrum into a working consensus. In spite of the differences that remained, the participants were nevertheless able to enter into a discussion concerning the central questions of modern socialist strategy and tactics. It was a truly internationalist congress, both in that the various participants learned to see their local problems and goals within the perspective of an international strategy and in that it gave a vital impulse to the internationalization of the campaign to free Bahro. In addition, we came a small step further along the way toward formulating a socialist concept based on our own experiences and not merely derived from a negative self-withdrawal from the conditions that presently exist in the GDR and the Soviet

Union. We also succeeded in avoiding the trap of being lumped together with "actually existing socialism" by bourgeois propaganda ("If you like it there so much, why don't you go over?"—a popular rallying cry of the reactionaries, especially in West Berlin—just didn't hold up in this case). An important contribution to this process was made by the comrades from the East European countries. With their attitude of support "in spite of everything," they have clearly demonstrated that the left in the capitalist countries can count on the support and solidarity of the leftists struggling in the East European countries. Even if we should have differing tasks and at times choose different paths, we will still be able to profit from one another's experiences, secure in the knowledge that their struggle is our struggle.

Thus the general goals of the Congress were achieved. However, the purpose of this essay is not just to intone a song of well-deserved praise for the Congress, its organizers, supporters, and participants. Rather, the task is much more one of profiting from our experiences, analyzing our mistakes (we were by no means perfect in our work), and evaluating the chances for future success in order to be better prepared for the tasks that lie ahead.

We realized at the outset that Bahro the person cannot be separated from his work. Hence, Bahro's *Alternative* offered us the chance to couple an expression of solidarity with the organization of discussion around burning questions confronting the socialist movement. The purpose of this was not to turn Bahro into an instrument; rather we considered this to be the most effective way of achieving a maximum expression of solidarity. Thus we were able to give a positive aspect to our protest. The Bahro committee was in itself a very modest undertaking of about a dozen or so people, most of whom, though identified with a left-socialist tendency, had had no long-term experience in political work and were not supported by any powerful organization. This small group set out to create an "international congress" that would bring together the most relevant tendencies of the left and the working-class movements, everyone from Eurocommunists to social democrats and trade unionists, from East European emigres to the New Left. The committee was too weak to be anything more than a catalyst; and our catalytic function did not mean that we would attempt to control events once we had set them in motion. There were some very sensitive areas with which we would have to deal. We often had to be able to transform our weaknesses into strengths—removing the fears of some that they would be dominated or used by us, and also being prepared to accept the limits imposed upon us by the participating groups.

An evaluation of the groupings represented at the Congress

The only thing held in common by the various tendencies represented at the Congress was the shared inability to provide a model that would bring about the conditions conducive to communist-socialist politics. This long-evident fact has finally begun to sink into the heads of even the most incorrigible ignoramuses. Gone are the days of one-faction ideological domination. In itself, this rejection of abstract principles whose untenability has been proved by the practical historical process and which have degenerated into ideologies of domination, served to unify all the tendencies. The most powerful groupings, namely the communist parties as well as socialists and social democrats, are being forced under heavy fire to retreat into positions they formerly regarded as heretical. Such a situation offers many opportunities for discussion and action. But this apparent willingness unfortunately found little if any expression in actual discussion. Perhaps this was due to the form of the Congress as well as to the obvious fact that such assemblies are very unusual and their participants need time to get to know one another. Nevertheless, this should not be allowed to stand in the way of open, candid discussion in which the participants still react to one another in a positive manner. The following is an attempt to elucidate the positions of the individual groups represented at the Congress.

The Social Democratic Party: the silent colossus

The most hotly debated question within the committee during the period of preparation for the Congress was the extent to which members of the Social Democracy or its party organizations should be involved. The concept of an inclusive conference, with broad representation of diverse political tendencies, had to be pushed through in face of a complete lack of understanding by a great portion of the committee; there would be no use in denying this.

It would seem at first that the Social Democratic Party (SPD) should have no interest in something so disruptive to its stated interest in achieving détente. Already in July, shortly before Bahro was sentenced, Peter von Oertzen wrote in the *Frankfurter Rundschau*: "The SPD as a whole is remaining silent, and even the Young Socialists are only now beginning to gradually awaken." Concerning détente he states further:

> Don't tell me such activities [such as taking a clear position in actively supporting the left opposition] in any way endanger détente. The opposite is true. It's the other side that has set the tone: a policy of détente on the international diplomatic level, but "increased ideological struggle on the political level."

Did the wind suddenly start blowing the other way? Did Peter von Oertzen succeed in awakening the SPD into a complete policy reversal? Had it succeeded in getting itself into a position where it could tie the hands of the left, as several leftist papers would have us believe? (One leaflet distributed during the Congress read, "Congress on and for tying the hands of the left by the Social Democracy," and went on to explain its version of the "willing cooperation of the SPD here in West Berlin" in the preparation and execution of the Congress.) Whoever wants to reduce the discussion to this near-sighted level would have to ask, just who tied whose hands? One thing became perfectly clear, and the West German and West Berlin SPDs, as well as members of the Italian, Spanish, and French socialist parties know it: they had come to and participated in a Congress that was conceived, prepared, and directed by a handful of leftist radicals. Who's right then? The author of the leaflet, or Peter von Oertzen?

Who initiated *Berufsverbot* [the "professional ban," or political screening of West German [public employees] and the Radicals Decree? The SPD. And now they want to do something about a persecuted communist, a communist who for them is more dangerous than our own advocates of "socialism as it actually exists" (who are able to glean no more than 0.1% of the popular vote in an election)? The SPD is not naive. They know perfectly well what problems his book can cause. To this we must add the power of the ruling SPD party and government bureaucracies, as well as the many connections that exist between here and there, the mutual business deals and other such arrangements.

Now, is there any real danger of the left being hemmed in by the SPD? Abstractly considered, this danger can seem very real: the SPD is a party of a million members and currently holds power on the federal level as well as in many of the state governments. The power relations appear to be clearly on their side, since in the final analysis the power to constrain is a question involving considerations of political power relations. Certainly there exists a wide range of positions, interviews, warnings, and demands made upon the party, emanating from either the party's left or its technocratic wing. Certainly attempts are being made to develop an activist, reform-oriented tendency within the Social Democracy, one that would be willing and able to take up the political and social struggle in various social arenas (trade unions, schools, youth counseling, women's movement, citizens' initiatives, etc.) and to tie them politically to the Social Democracy. It must be kept in mind that this faction plays no really significant role in SPD politics, and is even forced to kowtow to the political leadership which sometimes uses it like a puppet.

At this point the advantages the SPD has won from its role as governing party are turned against it. When it comes to questions of government, and these seem to be the only questions usually considered, then liberalism gets thrown out the window and everything assumes a clean, right-oriented order. Where does the SPD welcome its radical socialists with open arms? What does this party, a party that seems to be constantly moving in reverse, have to offer them? The assumption of power has caused the SPD to "bolshevize," to repress even that pitiably small opposition to its official positions within its own ranks. The result has been a dearth of meaningful theoretical and political debate. And even if a "Bernstein debate" should come about, still nothing will happen to alter the basic problem.

What remains then? First, corruption, the promise of a career in the party or at the university. But there's nothing unusual in that; that exists everywhere. Politically the SPD is bankrupt and has nothing to offer here. Then there remains the promise of attaining power. But, as we have seen, in the SPD the only ones who can practice any kind of "*Realpolitik*" are those who follow the accepted line. A colossus can do nothing to change this. In evaluating statements made by this colossus one should try to remember that, as was foreseen, Social Democrats too have become victims of *Berufsverbot*. This fact should give the most strident defender of the Constitution reason to pause. Even Willy Brandt officially admitted a while back that he had made a terrible mistake in signing the *Berufsverbot* bill into law. There is just nothing tactically new to be found here at all. As long as the SPD is responsible for ruling a capitalist West Germany, the socialist left will hardly be in danger of being coopted by it. Whoever lets himself be taken in has only himself to blame. Such a cooptation would only serve to indicate that such persons had no clear conception of an alternative in the first place.

To be sure, the SPD keeps its eyes open and tries to subsume all movements going on around it. It can also be expected that the SPD will attempt to include demands of such groups in its next watered-down party platform. Would it improve the political situation one bit were it not to do these things? Would it help matters at all if the SPD should suddenly decide to completely stop trying to spruce up its campaign promises a bit? Of course the SPD does these things just to win votes, but such a statement only indicates a recognition of the validity of the impulses coming into the party. It also serves to reveal the inability of the left to transform political thought into concrete action. The SPD will continue to play the role of transmitter for as long as the present objective conditions remain unaltered. We must reckon with this. That's the very reason why we have to talk to the social democrats. When some SPD people begin to realize that, were the left no longer to vote for the lesser evil, they could thus lose their majority, and when they begin to open channels of communication to us, that's no time for us to draw back simply out of fears of being coopted. We have to take up such opportunities to formulate immediately and offensively our positions concerning *Berufsverbot*, solidarity with Rudolf Bahro, and solidarity with the oppressed peoples in countries like Chile and South Africa. And we should also be prepared to discuss the fact that our oppositional standpoint could possibly make things a little easier for the Christian Democratic Union (CDU).

But we have still another question. Should we rejoice over the present desolate state of the SPD and its inability to find room for the left in its programs? Isn't the problem of the leftists in the SPD also our own problem? The danger of being coopted in a real political process hasn't existed for years. Let's not forget that in the period immediately following the anti-authoritarian student revolts it was the Young Socialists who enjoyed an enormous growth period, putting pressure on the party leadership and to an extent taking over its functions. In spite of whatever one has to say about their individual or group positions, it was the SPD left that forced the SPD into a progressive direction. At that time (1968-72) the SPD was able to rely on the movement, which was not incorporated in the SPD, for its support. A close look at this process will reveal that no cooptation took place here, and that the platforms of the left were put through in a forceful but practical way. The same is true for the other side: although the SPD profited enormously from the support it got from the left, it was in no way taken over by it.

The present situation is a little different. In recent years we've entered into a new phase, coupled with a decline in the left both inside and outside the SPD. Both groups are confronted with the problem of redefining their political perspectives. To a certain extent the decline of the left inside the SPD has been more precipitous than that of the non-SPD left. The new left has been able to maintain several small organizational political rallying points, whereas the SPD left has practically ceased to exist as an organized and politically effective force. The Frankfurt Circle, which had played an important role in the formation and development of a left tendency in the SPD, no longer exists. To be sure, there are many left-oriented individuals in some very important positions, but these people have no support either from within or from without, and are constrained by the limits of their bureaucratic functions in party or government. SPD leftists do not cooperate with one another. They do not discuss things with one another, pursue no unified policies, and have no general picture of things. At the Bahro Congress, the party leftists did not agitate in any way. They showed no inclination to set the tone for the proceedings, either alone or with others. The links to individual social democrats did not take place through them, but through us. We made the contacts, and created a certain political atmosphere in that we succeeded in inducing two parties of the Second International to take part officially in the conference. The German Social Democracy found itself obliged to take a position as well at the official level only under the pressure of these facts. However, in contrast to earlier occasions, it was not capable of building up a front at all. The

Berlin SPD even invited members of the Italian Communist Party and the Socialist Workers' Party of Spain to an official reception, thereby giving the Congress even greater status.

In this respect the Bahro Congress marked a considerable step forward. Not only did numerous SPD members attend the Congress and work with it, but for the first time in a long while leading social democrats sat down together with the representatives of the radical left to discuss far-ranging questions of strategy and to work together in solidarity. At the same time the official party leadership was forced to take a positive attitude, or at least to mark time. Moreover, we were able to get three important organizations of the Social Democracy to support the conference: the Federal Association of Young Socialists, the Socialist Youth of Germany, the Falken and the Democratic Socialist Action Group in the institutions of higher learning. Willy Brandt's personal letter to Tomas Kosta, director of EVA [Europäische Verlaganstalt, publishers of *Die Alternative*], in which he expressly took a position on Bahro's work and made clear that he considered it the task of all the parties of the Second International to show solidarity with Rudolf Bahro, cannot be valued highly enough. Like the concluding resolution, it provided the members of the Social Democracy and their organizations a legitimate assurance for participating in further discussions and actions.

The SPD was also surprised and overcome by the conception and the dynamics of the Bahro Congress. What attitude should one take to the initiative of people who did not stress points of division or seek to draw lines of demarcation, but instead appealed to the party's sense of responsibility and were open to dialogue? And this, moreover, was not a devious maneuver but a clear political goal. It could not be evaded; so a working attitude was taken. Nor can the Social Democracy today ignore the radical left. It must adjust itself to radical left policies. This was demonstrated clearly enough by the Russell Tribunal and the Bahro Congress. On the one hand they gave in to the efforts to sit down all together at one table, as a comment by Ernst Elitz in *Vorwärts* shows clearly, and on the other hand they were intimidated by the dynamics of the situation as it evolved. Thus we read (November 30):

> It was some novelty to see Peter von Oertzen, member of the SPD Executive Committee, together with the Trotskyist Ernest Mandel and repre-

sentatives of the Italian Socialist Party and Communist Party. Bahro, who wrote his book for the GDR, unwittingly raised the theoretical discussions in the West to a new level.

But then comes the official warning finger:

> Each side will continue to consider clear demarcations to be indispensable, and coalitions between reform socialists and advocates of the dictatorship of the proletariat will not take place, despite Bahro. The advantage of the present debate is a clarification of the front lines, not fraternization.

Thus demarcation, not critical cooperation, is to be the keynote. They are afraid of political fraternization, and that a discussion might be set off which could bring the party rank-and-file closer to a new concept and a new content of socialist policy and would lead to a rejection of sectarianism, whether social-democratic or radical, in favor of unified action, notwithstanding the continued existence of many political differences.

There is yet another aspect to the problem of the Social Democracy: why did two to two-and-a-half socialist parties participate officially in this conference? Here one must recognize a significant difference between the German SPD and Eurosocialism. The attitude of the latter toward the East European countries and their left opposition is more radical and more consistent. The fact that in particular the socialist parties of Italy and Spain supported this conference is of course also attributable to the internal political situation in these parties and their special relationship to the Eurocommunist parties. Covatta and Besostri, of the Italian Socialist Party, made this clear in an interview in the *Berliner Stimme*. There they say concerning the Eurocommunists:

> Are they ready to support this movement (of the East European left) politically and not only on a humanitarian basis? No, they are not ready. At best they are ready under certain conditions to defend the rights of individual dissidents in the Soviet Union, a far-off land that in its way is more or less stable. However, they are not prepared to defend the politically organized people and their rights in Czechoslovakia, the GDR, Hungary, or Poland ... For example, in the case of the Prague Charter 77, Eurocommunists have said that they do not have the right to upset détente.

Further we read:

> We are convinced that Eurosocialism and not Eurocommunism is the
> force that will fulfill the expectations of those who are in opposition in
> the countries of real socialism.

One might say, why not? Competition stimulates business. However, we should not be so simple. We must reflect more carefully on the implications of this position (which indeed has been assumed now by some of the left within the SPD: see Peter von Oertzen's article, quoted earlier). But in any case we should seek a discussion with the forces of Eurosocialism and use it in solidarity work. The upcoming European elections could also be a step in this direction, since they coincide almost exactly with the first anniversary of Bahro's conviction.

Trade unions: still the blind power

The question as to what extent the rupture between the new left and the trade unions can be overcome is of crucial importance for the further development of the left in the Federal Republic. It is at least a credible objection that no socialist policy can be pursued today with the Deutsche Gewerkschaftsbund (DGB) unions. But one cannot do so without them either. That is the central political dilemma. The struggles of an intelligentsia isolated from their labor movement do not bear within them the seeds for a shift to a socialist policy, i.e., one directed at changing the society, because in our opinion—and discussion of Herbert Marcuse's article in this book should also begin with this point—an intelligentsia left to its own resources cannot be the bearer of social change; at most it can provide the impulse and motive for it.

For this reason the Bahro committee attached special importance to the participation of trade-union circles, if only with moderate success. Although Bahro's *Alternative* was published by a trade-union publishing house, the EVA is not the DGB, and in a certain respect enjoyed the freedom of the court jester, for the books it has published—under conditions made steadily more difficult by the trade-union leadership—are of almost no importance for trade-union practice. This is also true of Bahro's book, although it is obvious that on many points Bahro takes up problems that today are practical problems of trade-union work, for example, questions bearing on the organization of labor in the plants, questions concerning coparticipation in decisions concerning objectives and the operation of production, etc.

Jakob Moneta, editor-in-chief of the metalworkers union news-paper *Metall* for many years and one of the sponsors of the Congress, pointed out in an article written for the occasion that Bahro's *Alternative* was also important for the West, that the trade unions should not just rest content with filing a note of protest, but should actively organize solidarity. This did not happen. The DGB trade unions did not adopt a position on the Congress unlike certain Italian trade unions (CGIL, CISL, and UIL), for example, which sent telegrams to the Congress demanding the immediate release of Bahro and the implementation of human rights and freedom of opinion and speech. Aside from the positive position taken by the DGB youth, only the two Berlin GEW unions publicly supported the Congress.

To be sure, Werner Vitt, vice-chairman at IG Chemie, spoke at the opening ceremonies of the Congress (on the necessity of closing the break between the trade unions and the new left), and the EVA, Jakob Moneta, and Heinz Brandt, were among the sponsors of the Congress, while Johannes Konrad, a colleague from Volkswagen Wolfsburg, took part in the discussions of the Congress, and a number of trade-union groups attended the Congress. But these were no world-shaking events, and one should guard against overestimating their importance. However, it would be just as wrong to ignore them. The signs have recently been increasing that some of the trade unions have taken cognizance of the learning process that some parts of the new left, growing steadily stronger, have gone through in recent years, and which has led to an abandonment of the often sectarian notions of the past.

On the other hand, of course, the rigid German trade unions have been undergoing a process of transformation. The traditional trade-union policy, for years oriented to increases in real wages, promised on the basis of a prospering economy, has itself entered a crisis under the new conditions of the persisting economic crisis. These seemingly new but actually quite old problems require other answers than mere percentage figures. Questions of labor organization, safety in the workplace (in the light of the double pressure of the economic crisis and technological rationalization), humanization of work, etc., have become central issues. The demand coming out of the factories for a 35-hour week should also be regarded in this context. The last wage discussions of the longshoremen, in the printing industry, and in metal, also show new tendencies in the relationship between capital and labor. The opposition lists have had sensational success in the factory council elections, reflecting the obvious dissatisfaction of a significant number of workers with the way the unions have represented their interests. A change in the power relationships within the unions is emerging.

One must also take into account the two-sided process of change which can serve as a foundation for an improved relationship between trade unions and parts of the new left. From our standpoint a precondition for this is, of course, that we overcome elitist sectarianism and arrive at a more realistic evaluation of the trade unions and their various factions. Although the trade unions did not come out in support of their author Bahro, the Congress was still proof that on certain points there is a possibility of cooperation with individual labor-union members, even from the nonintellectual sphere.

However, it must be also observed that the trade unions as an apparatus have their resolutions on irreconcilability, i.e., they too persecute the politically unpleasant among their ranks with bureaucratic repression. Here too the principle applies, and Bahro's sympathizers could come under this resolution; i.e., solidarity with Bahro cannot be practiced on the basis of the irreconcilability resolutions. This dimension of criticism must always be articulated in all efforts undertaken alongside the trade unions, just as we made our critique of capitalism and of the *Berufsverbot* a fundamental precondition for collaboration with the SPD and the other socialist parties. With regard to the trade unions as well, there is no room for tactical maneuvers when principles of socialist policy are at stake, and freedom of opinion stands at the very top of the list of priorities. Conversely, we should undertake every attempt possible to bring the critical reflection that has started up within the SPD on the *Berufsverbot* into the trade unions, in order to get the retrograde irreconcilability resolutions out of the way as soon as possible.

Only the politically blind or malicious could levy the accusation that the Congress represented an unprincipled alliance. Quite to the contrary, we attempted to create a propagandistic unity of action, within which no element of criticism of the ruling group and the prevailing situation in East and West would be left out for opportunistic reasons. On the other hand, we also did not wish to make the chronic mistake of all sectarians (in its literal sense the category of sectarianism is not a quantitative one; the history of the labor movement has been guilty of this mistake as no other), of looking for the differences of the various factions participating in a joint discussion and making these the main point of the debate, thus predisposing the situation to a break.

On this point concerning the relationship to the trade unions, as on all other points, the Bahro Congress did not effectively produce too much. But in our situation, the mere fact that reluctance to cooperate further was reduced rather than fortified was an achievement. We are sure that the Congress did not end on November 19 as far as the trade unions are concerned, and that the future will still bring quite a number of discussions and debates. We already know of various trade-union study courses and seminars that intend to continue the discussion of the topics touched upon at the Congress and often treated superficially there.

The same point holds for the trade unions as for the Social Democracy. Anyone who looks at this emaciated apparatus only from the standpoint of the policy of the leadership and a betrayal of working-class interests is neither capable of understanding the processes that are concretely taking place, nor is he able to intervene in these processes in any way. The example of the "life action group," an opposition group within the trade unions that has since become national, shows that the retreat of a large part of the left into a subculture is anachronistic and has little to do with concrete reality. There are quite simply more points on which socialist work within the trade unions can be begun than these people would like to believe. Of course here it is a premise that a nonsectarian idea of socialist policy must be developed, one that is linked to the existing structures of consciousness without fetishizing them. The new left is guilty of its most serious negligence in just this area, namely trade-union policy, because they have abandoned the field for the most part to the Marxist-Leninist professional sectarians or the sycophants of the DKP/SEW (German Communist Party/Socialist Unity Party-West). Rather, the task is to work out points that represent positive examples of socialist trade-union policy, for example the poster group in the Daimler Benz factory, or the workers' newspaper group at Solex.

On the whole, we can say with regard to the trade unions (as well as with regard to the Social Democracy) that there should be more discussion about the trade unions, and even more importantly, more with the trade unionists.

The Eurocommunists: two steps
forward, one step back

The Eurocommunists make a deep impression, of course, when it is a question of simple things. They have opened up a process of discussion among their ranks that is still in its beginnings. For some time now, issues that for decades were taboo have been being discussed. In many respects Bahro reformulated these points as others had done also before him. But the process of discussion in the Eurocommunist parties has not come so far that any unambiguous positions could be expected. This is one explanation why, of all the Eurocommunists, only the Italian Communist Party sent a representative, although both the Belgian Communist Party and the Finnish People's Party sent statements of solidarity. (Of course one of the factors responsible here, though a secondary one, was the fact that *The Alternative* has only appeared in Italian; publications in other languages are still to come.) In addition, there is the fact that the Congress showed solidarity with an oppositional GDR citizen, while in the eyes of many Eurocommunists the GDR still enjoys the special status of an antifascist state and a bulwark against imperialism. This view evidently caused special difficulties for the Spanish and French CPs, but it also served these parties as an alibi for their irresoluteness.

Despite several invitations to individual representatives of the different European communist parties, despite official letters to party leaderships, in the end only the Italian Communist Party was prepared to send a representative, Angelo Bolaffi, the cultural editor of the CP newspaper *Rinascita*. The only reaction we felt was that members invited directly by us revoked their acceptance; evidently there had been a *ukaz* from the top level not to participate. But these positions remained internal. To be sure, some representatives of Eurocommunist parties, such as Elleinstein and Althusser of the French CP, Carrillo from the Spanish CP, and Lucio Lombardo Radice, central committee member of the Italian CP, had come out on the side of Bahro earlier or had discussed the content of his theses; but evidently this tendency was unable to prevail. There seems to be some factional fighting going on in the Eurocommunist parties. In France it broke out into the open a short time ago, but then submerged again. Some members of the French Communist Party distinguished themselves, in relation to their own party leadership, as the leadership with regard to the Soviet Union. The occasion was a sectarian fight with Marchais, which started up in the left-wing union shortly before the elections in France and led to a completely avoidable and demoralizing defeat.

Representatives of the Italian Communist Party signed the Bahro Congress's concluding resolution, and hence have put their own party and the other Eurocommunist parties in a corner, provided they are successful in spreading this resolution internationally (especially as *The Alternative* is to be published in France, Spain, and Great Britain). They can say "no," they can say "not like this and not now," they can sign, but they must do something. Thus the resolution is especially important, since it is a catalyst for the discussion. The thorny question, boiled down to one simple point, is the seriousness of the Eurocommunists' proclamation of another notion of socialism than that which they themselves have represented for decades. The Bahro Congress made clear that there exists a definitely socialist and Marxist opposition in Eastern countries. It has made clear that a distinct demarcation must be made between the anticommunists' and the socialists' critiques of real socialism. It has shown that it is possible to speak out for the release of Rudolf Bahro before a large public without getting into alien waters. It is no longer possible to take refuge behind the agent theory when one is not willing to debate political differences.

The Congress thus reduced to tangible terms the general half-heartedness of the Eurocommunists. It made clear that Eurocommunism was only the diluted expression of a criticism that Bahro articulated much more clearly and which has been exercised in other quarters for decades now. Yet these were the same Eurocommunist parties which either actively (like the Spanish) or with more support (like the others) participated in the suppression, persecution, and even murder of critics of official communism who had said nothing more than that which these parties are today saying in emasculated form. Whoever says yes to Bahro must also say yes to Trotsky, Bukharin, Nin, and hundreds of thousands of other oppositionists murdered by the Stalinists. Just as solidarity with the victims of imperialism in Chile, South Africa, Iran, and elsewhere is inseparable from solidarity with the Eastern countries, so is solidarity with today's left opposition inseparable from solidarity with the old left opposition. If a new idea of socialism is in the offing, then let us have it without any distortions, omissions, or half-truths. The campaign for the rehabilitation of Bukharin must be expanded to include Trotsky and the other oppositionists, and this demand must be placed on the communist parties together with the demand for total solidarity with Rudolf Bahro, for his release in the GDR, and for the possibility of discussing his views there in public.

However, not only the Eurocommunists must learn this lesson; various factions of the new left must do so as well. How often have we as a committee been subjected to denunciation by the Trotskyists, still serving the same defamatory functions as in Dzhugashvili's [Stalin's] times. The rewriting of the history of the labor movement is still to be done, just as a reassessment of the production and class relations in the countries of actually existing socialism must yet be undertaken.

The Eurocommunists have just begun this debate. The results are still modest. For this reason they are unable to take a clear and unequivocal position even in questions where there are no ifs and buts, as in Bahro's case. As long as they maintain their ties to the ruling group in the state socialist countries (Lombardo Radice), they cannot show solidarity with those persons who are the victims of repression in these countries, or, if they do so, then it is at the very best only verbally, without any practical consequences. The Eurocommunists want to be neither fish nor fowl, although they are now in the process of a change designed to give them democratic credibility as communists. They must then decide whether they want to unite with those who are today sitting in the prisons and concentration camps of the GDR, Czechoslovakia, and the Soviet Union, for positions similar to those taken by today's Eurocommunist parties, or whether they want to align themselves with those who are engaged in the political fight against Eurocommunism and suppress it in their own countries with force. If they are really serious about their avowal of being in favor of the integration of basic human rights into their notions of communism, they must take clear positions on the points on which these rights are abused in the Eastern European countries. The Marxist

Bahro is a testing stone, just like the Workers' Defense Committee in Poland or the Charter 77 in Czechoslovakia. If the Eurocommunists wish to count on the votes of the new left in the upcoming European elections, then the question of total solidarity with Bahro must be made a precondition. The representatives of the Italian, French, and Spanish communist parties, after all, know only too well that nothing is to be achieved with the Communist Party in the Federal Republic.

The emigres

A further dimension of the Congress was the attempt to establish a political link between the Eastern and Western lefts. Bahro was the starting point, Charter 77 was a mediator, and the *Il Manifesto* Congress in Venice ["On Power and Opposition in Postrevolutionary Societies"] was a precursor.

The Bahro Congress was attended by representatives of the Prague Spring (Pelikan, Hejzlar), a member of the Hegedus group (Vajda), a spokesman for Charter 77 (Kavin), various exiles from the GDR and Czechoslovakia, and Boris Weil, who spent thirteen years in Soviet prisons and camps, but also various representatives of the exiled Eastern European radical left. For example, the Socialist East European Committee helped considerably in realizing the Congress. Among the emigres from the Eastern left there was thus a broad political spectrum represented, but it was not so much the differences that stood in the forefront of the debate as the realization that, at the present stage of the struggle, there are for the time being enough points in common among all these factions that a basic consensus for unified action can be achieved and energy can be generated for a process of discussion. In pragmatic terms, perhaps, the Congress was the most important for this group, since in exile it is in the difficult situation of finding its critique of the real situation under socialism intermingled with attempts from anticommunist quarters to reap political profits from this critique. By far the best way these emigres can avoid this dilemma is by placing themselves on the side of the strong socialist movement in the West that links its critique of real socialism with a critique of capitalism and is also capable of transmitting this position to a broad public: this is the only way to reach the relevant ears in the Eastern countries. In this context, of course, Bahro has a preeminent function, since he is a radical Marxist and has a num-

ber of points in common with the Western new left—which, on
the whole, is not the case with some factions of the exiles. He has
forcefully pointed out that opposition from a radical Marxist
standpoint is possible. One can only agree with Jiri Pelikan's critique of Bahro's position on the Prague Spring, on the role of
the reform communists, and on Charter 77 in a number of points.
But at the same time, while the special significance of a statement
of purely democratic demands under the concrete conditions of a
total absence of democratic rights, such as exists in the countries
of actually existing socialism, must be stressed, in our opinion
the converse—i.e., that the same position is also tenable in the
capitalist West—is far from admissible.

Balance and perspectives

It is difficult to draw up a balance sheet on the Congress inasmuch
as it took place on a number of levels and had a variety of goals,
and in each case the results varied considerably.

Solidarity with Bahro

This point is the easiest to assess. We are sure that the Congress
went the way Bahro would have wanted; indeed, he wished for
nothing more than to have his theses discussed on a broad basis.
For this he was prepared to go to prison. It was our feeling—
although some expressed the contrary opinion—that anything
that contributed to a change in the prevailing conditions in East
and West, to a consolidation of socialist positions, and to a broad-
ening of alliances for struggle, would also improve Bahro's situation. In this area, in any event, the Congress could chalk up a number of pluses. Recent times have rarely seen as much public interest generated for such questions as has been generated by the Congress. The creation of a broad basis for discussion of *The Alternative* seems to have succeeded; various groups will continue working with and discussing the text. The Congress was definitely not
the high point, but only the first step in an international campaign for the release of Rudolf Bahro in which both social and political forces will participate, and which the GDR will have to heed
in one way or other. The waves are already mounting too high
for the GDR to be able to kill solidarity with Bahro through silence. If, in addition, it proves to be possible to induce the other

Eurocommunist parties to sign the Congress's resolution, the pressure will be even greater. Moreover, these parties have a special function for the Eastern left, because it of course has easier access to the communist parties than to any left-wing groups or personages in the West. The East Berlin conference in 1976 showed as much, and Bahro stressed the point in his letter from prison. A letter to the Congress from a group of GDR oppositionists says: "There is no way to determine exactly who could induce the GDR rulers to allow Bahro to live freely in the GDR, but one thing is sure, and that is that silence from Western comrades as well will reduce the prospects to nil."

The expansion of a unit of political action

The Congress also scored high on this point, provided one proceeds from a realistic assessment of the present situation. For much that one would think normal and commonplace is not so self-evident among the left. That communist party members and Trotskyists sat down together at the same table is a political event in itself, and the same may be said when a member of the Federal Executive Committee of the SPD discusses socialism with manifest "sympathizers." Further, the fact that socialists and communists signed a joint resolution bearing on questions that previously had been a source of splits is not so usual, at least in West Germany. There is also something significant in the fact that trade unionists came to a Congress organized by the left. It would be presumptuous to claim that progress was made in the discussions. That was less the case, but there were a number of reasons for this, one of which was the behavior of those attending, which often took on the features of a revivalist meeting. But the mere fact that the various splinter groups mentioned were able to come together, and that a resolution was put together that was not a sleazy compromise but went as far as circumstances permitted—all this was in itself a political event. If this first step is to be followed by others, there is much that must be changed. It would have to be shown that the Congress's way-paving function (and this was its actual function) had actually been transformed into real debate. Nonetheless, it was shown that straightforwardness becomes more and more attractive; at least, back-biting seems to be a thing of the past (with the exception of the eternal caterwaulers of the DKP-SEW). The new concept of socialism is acquiring a political hegemony wholly in accord with the real power relations. Our task is to drive this process on further, to introduce increasingly more precision and acuity into the debates concerning a genuine and honest concept of social progress, to zero in on all half-baked notions, to permit no more lies in the name of socialism, and to resist the tendency to use such lies to conceal real crimes. We have learned that the end does not justify all means, that rather, there is indeed a close relationship between the means used and the end achieved thereby. The Congress showed that by assuming such a position a broad alliance can in fact be created.

The discussion of a new concept of socialism

As regards this point, it must be conceded that the conference did not achieve the results hoped for, at least not in the panel discussions. There was hardly any real discussion, and the individual positions were left hanging as such, without any attempt to build bridges between them. In the discussion of a very vital question, namely the relationship between socialism and democracy, the only consensus reached was that there did indeed exist such a relationship. Hardly any grouping dared to deny that the bourgeois freedoms, as they are called—i.e., freedom of opinion, speech, association, etc.—must not disappear under socialism or communism, but on the contrary, would then acquire for the first time a real material basis, in that political democracy would be complemented by social democracy. On the other hand, the way that this might come about —through the retention of parliamentary representation, in the form of council democracy, via the detour of an educative dictatorship, the acquisition of hegemony, etc.—is a question that was left out of the discussion. This vital question, which also has something to do with the conquest of power, since the means-end dialectic is also universally acknowledged, was not discussed. We must work on this question, as well as on the analysis of the production and class relations in the countries of "real socialism."

The situation in the individual work groups was somewhat different: in some, very lively and thorough discussions took place, occasionally, of course, with the usual battles over the correct line (mostly in the groups dealing with the topically sensitive questions, as was to be expected). On the whole, it may be said that although the level of discussion was not exactly earth-shaking, the fact that about 1,500 persons participated in the work groups on the various aspects of Bahro's *Alternative* and its implications was in itself an achievement. On this point as well, when drawing up a balance sheet it must be taken into account that the German left has traditionally found it difficult to carry on coherent, relevant discussions in which all sides are considered. This is the product of the authoritarian traditions of the German intelligentsia and of the sectarianism of the last few years.

In part, the level of the discussions in the work groups was so deep because for a change it proved possible to bring together at the same table groupings that really had fundamental differences; the common denominator of the various factions of the new left is, after all, rather small. We therefore decided to prepare the work groups in such a way that the participants would themselves be able to determine the direction of the discussion, the result being a real exchange of opinions rather than a debate among experts. We hope, however, that the Congress participants will carry the discussion further into their everyday lives, at home and on the job. The fact that many more than 1,000 of the 4,000 persons present daily at the Congress had come from outside of Berlin permits us to hope at least that the discussions of the Bahro Congress will yet be spread far and wide. There were at any rate enough incentives to do so, although in concrete terms not much has been done so far. The mere impulse to take up such questions cannot be valued highly enough in our times, however.

The Congress is over. Solidarity with Bahro as part of a general debate on the question of socialism continues.

Translated by Michel Vale.

NOTES

1. On this point, practice proved us right: despite the broad agitation, and despite the general attention aroused for this "case," not even 1,000 people showed up for the declaration made after his conviction in early July 1978, which focused entirely on Bahro as a person.

2. We should mention here that Rolf Berger's engagement on behalf of Bahro has cost him his post as university president. An odd coalition of offended laymen, opponents of Berger's democratic engagement (*inter alia*, against the *Berufsverbot*), and the traditionalist Moscow line of the SEW— who had heretofore supported him, yet were this time extremely annoyed about the Bahro Congress at the Technical University—managed to get him voted down as president at the University Council meeting on December 7, 1978.

About the Contributors

RUDI DUTSCHKE (1940-1979) lived in the GDR until 1961. In West Berlin, where he studied philosophy and sociology, he came to prominence as an activist in the student movement. He published *Versuch, Lenin vom Kopf auf die Füsse zu stellen* [An Attempt to Put Lenin Back on His Feet] in 1974. Until his death, Dutschke was a member of the editorial advisory board of the journal *kritik*.

HELMUT FLEISCHER (1927-   ) was a prisoner of war in the Soviet Union during World War II. Trained in philosophy, he has taught at a number of universities and is now professor in the Institute for Philosophy at the Technische Hochschule Darmstadt. Professor Fleischer is the author of *Marxismus und Geschichte* [Marxism and History], *Marx und Engels*, and *Sozialphilosophische Studien* [Studies in Social Philosophy].

PIERRE FRANK (1905-   ), trained in physics and chemistry, has been a lifelong activist in the revolutionary movement. Once secretary to Leon Trotsky, often arrested and long imprisoned, he was the editor of *Quatrième Internationale* [Fourth International] from 1946 to 1971. In 1978 he published a history of the Fourth International.

HASSAN GIVSAN was born in Teheran in 1945, and has lived in the Federal Republic since 1967. Trained in philosophy, he is an associate scholar [Wissenshaftlicher Mitarbeiter] at the Hochschule in Darmstadt.

LAWRENCE KRADER (1919-   ) was born in New York and

educated at the City College and at Harvard. For many years he worked with Karl Korsch. Professor Krader, who has taught at numerous colleges and universities in Europe and in the Americas, is presently professor of ethnology at the Free University, Berlin. Among other works, he has published *The Dialectic of Civil Society* and *The Asiatic Mode of Production*, and edited *The Ethnological Notebooks of Karl Marx*.

HERBERT MARCUSE (1898-1979) was born in Berlin and educated at the universities of Berlin and Freiburg. He came to the United States in 1934, joining the Institute for Social Research at Columbia, and later was on the faculties of Brandeis University (1954-65) and the University of California at San Diego (1965-70). Marcuse was the author of many books, including *Eros and Civilization*, *One-Dimensional Man*, *An Essay on Liberation*, and in 1978, *The Aesthetic Dimension*.

JIRI PELIKAN (1923-   ) was until 1968 the general director of Czech television, a delegate to the Czech parliament, and member of the Central Committee of the Communist Party of Czechoslovakia. Now residing in Rome, he has published a number of books about the postwar political history of Czechoslovakia and the Soviet intervention of 1968.

LUCIO LOMBARDO RADICE has been a member of the Italian Communist Party since 1938, and is now on the central committee of that party. A professor at the Mathematical Institute of the University of Rome, Lombardo Radice is the author of *Socialismo e liberta*.

HERMANN WEBER (1928-   ) became a member of the KPD after the war and held a number of party posts until his expulsion in 1954. Currently a professor of political science and contemporary history at the University of Mannheim, he has published numerous studies of the German communist movement, including *Von Rosa Luxemburg zu Walter Ulbricht, Die Wandlung des Deutschen Kommunismus* [The Transformation of German Communism], and *DDR: Grundriss der Geschichte 1945-1976* [The GDR: An Historical Outline].

ULF WOLTER, a director of Verlag Olle & Wolter and editor of the journal *kritik*, was born in East Berlin in 1950 and studied politics at the Free University. Wolter, RUDI STEINKE and WALTER SÜSS were all members of the Bahro Committee and helped to organize the "Congress on and for Rudolf Bahro."